Running Wide Open

Lisa Nowak

Published by Webfoot Publishing
Milwaukie, Oregon

Publishing

Running Wide Open

The text of this book is set in 11-point Georgia.

Book design by Lisa Nowak

Cover design by Robin Ludwig

ISBN-13: 978-1-937167-00-4

First Edition

Dedication

This book is dedicated to the memory of Eugene Speedway: the drivers who raced there, the crews who helped them, and the fans who cheered them on. In particular I would like to honor Tom Mace, Mary Haddock, and the rest of the folks from the now defunct Auto Marine, as well as the Ashleys, all of whom taught me that family is everything to racers, and if you lack one, somebody will take you into theirs.

Acknowledgments

My heartfelt thanks go out to the members of my critique groups, Chrysalis and Wow, and to my numerous beta readers, including Joel Schmitz, Eddy Kilgore, Barb Froman, Beth Miles, Paula Manley, Karen Champ, Roxie Matthews, Jenny Landis-Steward, Marian Meyer, Kayla Meyer Matsuura, Bob Douglas, Sylvia Potter, Bill and Ruth George, Bobby Shaw, Lois Lane, Gene Bradshaw, June Fezler, Josh Skinner, Mitch Hutchinson, Bill Graham, Susan Landis-Steward, Renee LaChance, Rachele Alpine, Casey McCormick, and my mom, Dorothy Hooker. I'd also like to demonstrate my appreciation to my blogging and email buddy, Christine Fletcher, and my goal-setting partner, Laura Marshal. A special thanks goes to Alice Lynn, writing compatriot extraordinaire, with whom I exchange chapters, bemoan disappointments, and celebrate victories.

Additional shout-outs go to my high school best friend Damon Atherly, who patiently plodded through my early attempts at writing; my buddies James Reagh, Kris Harper, and the late Thomas Rubick, who were there when Race and Cody first let me know they had a story to tell; my sister, Angela Moist, who added a mother's perspective; my dad, Matt Nowak, for his medical expertise: and my awesome husband Bob Earls, who puts up with my obsessive behavior and lets my cats nap on his head.

Last but not least, an extra special thanks to indie author Amy Rose Davis, who lured me over to the Dark Side.

Before

April 1989

The hiss of a paint can sounded like a roar, even over the rumble of traffic on Sunset Boulevard. Tim's drunk-assed laugh snagged my attention. His fingers shook as he used a can of Krylon royal blue to put the finishing touches on an anatomically correct and obviously proud elephant.

"Dude," I said, "his shlong is longer than his trunk."

"Why do you think he's smiling?" Tim busted into another giggle fit, doubling over and clutching his gut.

"C'mon, Cody, you're supposed to be *drawing*," prodded Mike. "That's not a picture." He was kind of an ass, but it's hard to blow off a guy you've hung out with since third grade.

"Pardon me for being able to communicate with words."

"Is that a giraffe?" Tim said. He was sprawled on the concrete now, staring up at Mike's neon pink animal as it brayed a string of four-letter words across the zoo wall.

"No, moron," Mike said, "it's a zebra. Can't you see the stripes?"

"Looks like a giraffe."

"It's a frickin' zebra!"

Mike planted the toe of his Adidas in Tim's ribs, and Tim tried to nail him in the balls with his rattle can. Then they were both rolling on the sidewalk, thrashing each other.

Why couldn't they shut the hell up? Beer buzzed through my skull, making everything go sideways. The words spilling out of my spray can had a crazy tilt to them.

Whooooop! A siren shrieked. I jerked back and dropped my paint.

1

"Cops!" Mike was up in a second, bolting down the sidewalk for the woods. Tim wasn't so fast. He'd messed up his knee last fall when he totaled his stepdad's Jeep in the Terwilliger Curves.

"C'mon," I said, grabbing his arm. Red and blue lights flashed around us as I dragged him down the sidewalk—no easy feat, considering he had five inches and fifty pounds on me.

The siren got louder. I risked a peek over my shoulder. They were close, but if I ditched Tim I could make it.

He stumbled, wrenching my arm.

"Move it!" I said, yanking him up.

Behind us, the car screeched to a stop. Doors slammed, and footsteps pounded the asphalt.

We reached the end of the zoo wall, but I knew we couldn't make it through the trees in the dark and stay ahead of the cops.

"Shit, Cody. I can't get busted again!" Tim panted.

I remembered the last time—how his face had looked when his stepdad got done with him.

"Then get the hell out of here," I said, shoving him into the bushes.

As he disappeared I turned to face the cops.

"Good evening, officers!" I called. "I don't suppose you'd be willing to discuss this like gentlemen over a dozen donuts?"

Chapter 1

I glanced around the crowded bus terminal and wondered if I'd made a mistake. After the thing with the cops, Dad had given me two choices: military school or living with my mother's black sheep brother—the only one in the family willing to take me in. I figured it was a no-brainer, but what if the guy turned out to be just like Mom?

The thought of her ticked me off, so I drop-kicked it to the back of my mind where it bounced off the other parental offenses, including this Greyhound business. A mere hundred miles between Portland and Eugene, and Dad couldn't be bothered to make the drive. Not that his lack of fatherly commitment had been any shocker. Until Mom had bailed on us a month ago, he'd looked the other way every time she went postal on me for hanging a towel up crooked or talking during her favorite TV show.

At least I didn't have that to deal with anymore. No, all I had to worry about now was living with a total stranger. The stink of diesel fumes hung in the air as my eyes swept the bus station: vending machines straight out of the '60s, back-to-back rows of orange plastic chairs holding people so bored it was a wonder they hadn't slit their own throats. No sign of my uncle.

I hadn't seen him since I was five and I didn't remember many details. Just that he was ten years younger than Mom and they didn't get along. When she'd called from Phoenix to finalize the arrangements she was too pissed to talk to me, so I'd had to rely on Dad for information. He didn't know much more than I did: my uncle was an artist, he was into stock car racing, his name was Race.

Anxiety rippled through my gut. What if he didn't show up? Our family wasn't known for reliability, and no one in the terminal seemed remotely like the person I was looking for. But then I wasn't sure what to expect. A redneck in a John Deere hat? A moody artiste wearing paint-spattered clothes? *Chill*, I told myself. At least he wasn't standing there holding some stupid sign that had *Cody Everett* scrawled across it.

A flash of sunlight glinted off the door. I turned and knew instantly that the person standing in the entrance was my uncle. He was in his mid-twenties and had a casual way of holding himself, along with the sort of build that made a guy look fit even if he didn't work out. Shaggy brown hair hung in his eyes as if he'd let an open car window do his styling for him. His jeans and Valvoline T-shirt were streaked with grease, but in spite of his slacker appearance, he looked like a younger, male version of Mom. Or maybe an older, taller version of me. I'd been fortunate enough to inherit the Morgan good looks but had gotten stuck with Dad's short, wiry build.

Race grinned across the room at me, and there the resemblance to my mother ended. Mom hardly ever smiled, except at her friends and the guys she flirted with. Race beamed like a little kid who'd asked for a stuffed toy but had gotten a real puppy. My apprehension flickered for only a second before blazing back up. Even if the guy turned out to be decent, he was sure to send me packing before the week was out. I should've opted for military school and saved myself the hassle of a second bus trip.

In a few long, loping strides Race made it across the terminal. "Cody," he said, with the grin coming through in his voice. I noticed that he had the same eyes as Mom, dark and full of feeling. They could sell you on anything, even if it cost your last penny, but I'd gotten pretty good at resisting that particular voodoo. Those eyes scanned me now, taking in my *Everyone's entitled to my opinion* T-shirt. He chuckled. "Good one."

I managed a nod. Part of me wanted to give in to his friend-liness, but I couldn't work my lips into a smile. It had been a long bus trip. A long two weeks since I'd gotten busted. There wasn't much to smile about.

"I'm sure coming to stay with me probably wasn't at the top of your agenda," Race said, "but I think we can make it work. I'm pretty easy to get along with."

If he was that optimistic, Mom obviously hadn't filled him in on what an ungrateful little smartass I was.

"And I know my sister's probably told you all kinds of hor-ror stories about me," Race continued, "but I'm really not the villain she makes me out to be."

The comment sent a twitch through my paralyzed lips. So he knew how she was.

"You ready to go?" Race asked.

"I guess."

"C'mon, let's get the rest of your stuff." He reached out to clasp my shoulder, and instinctively I ducked. Other than the smacks Mom gave me for smarting off, nobody touched me much.

Race's grin dimmed by a good sixty watts. For a second his hand hung in the air, then he pulled it back. Well, what did he expect? He should know better than to get all touchy-feely with someone he'd just met.

I followed him over to the package claim counter where we piled my boxes onto a couple of hand trucks.

"Whoa," Race said. "Whaddaya got in this one, rocks?"

No—books, but I'd be damned if I'd fess up to it. It was bad enough having Mom give me crap all the time for reading, demanding to know whether I planned on becoming a com-plete geek, like Dad. I lifted the box out of Race's hands and dumped it on top of the others on my dolley.

"Well," he said as he searched for clues in my expression. "I guess we better go."

I trailed him out the door into the blazing May sun, my conscience nagging as I wrestled the hand truck over the rough asphalt lot. Maybe I should give the guy a chance. Maybe it would be different this time.

Race stopped behind a van that might've been green sometime before I was born. Paint chipped off in big flakes, and splotches of primer marred every panel. One of the back tires was low. Okay, so he wasn't rich like my grandparents, who Mom was always hitting up for cash.

"Nice wheels, dude."

"It gets me where I'm going."

Race unlocked the rear doors of the van to reveal a rolling scrap yard. Tires, toolboxes, and an assortment of car parts littered the inside. Most of it was housed in milk crates that had no doubt been pilfered from behind some grocery store.

Race slid his stuff around to make room for mine, then, while I piled my boxes on the floorboards, he squeezed between the side of the van and a VW Bug to unlock the passenger door. The parking space wasn't nearly big enough for a vehicle the size of his beater, and you'd think the "Compacts Only" sign would have been his first clue. But I didn't figure I'd win him over by blurting out a remark about his ability to read.

I wedged myself through the door of the van, settled into the torn bucket seat, and pulled out my pack of Camel filters as Race slithered his way behind the wheel.

"If you're gonna smoke in here," he said, "open your window."

I waited for him to go on, telling me how cigarettes were a lousy habit, and they'd kill me before I graduated from high school, but that was all he had to say.

I rolled down the window. It was too hot to be riding around with it up, anyway.

Slouching back, I put my feet on the dash and rested my black Converse high tops in a pile of junk food wrappers that looked like they'd been there since Race bought the van. He didn't seem to notice that my shoes were flaking dried mud all over his accumulation of rodent bait. He just turned the key, nearly blasting me out of the seat when the stereo powered up with Jimmy Buffett's *Margaritaville*.

"Sorry," Race said, lowering the volume. He glanced across the cab at me before unthreading the van from its narrow parking spot. "So I hear you took the rap for your friend."

I snorted and turned to look out the window. "Yeah, I'm a real hero."

If my uncle thought he could buddy up to me with a few sympathetic comments, he was in for a letdown. I'd gotten enough of that phony bullshit from teachers, and school counselors, and all the other people who considered it their job to meddle in the lives of "at risk" kids. They suckered you in, got you to trust them, and always let you down in the end.

But the comment made me think of Tim. I knew I wouldn't hear from him as long as I was in Eugene. He wasn't the letter-writing type, and his stepdad would kill him if he found long distance charges on the phone bill.

At least Tim had gotten away. The cops hadn't bothered trailing him into the woods once they had me. Later he'd called me and offered to give himself up on my behalf, but I told him not to be a dumbass.

In less than a minute we were out of the downtown area. If you could even call it a downtown. I saw more trees than buildings, and I felt like I was stuck in a tiny green bowl, surrounded on all sides by low hills covered in Douglas firs. Welcome to Hicksville, USA.

The van rounded a corner with a swoop that made me clutch the door handle. A long-haired guy dressed in bell-bottoms, a tie-dyed Grateful Dead shirt, and Birkenstocks stepped off the sidewalk in front of us. Race dodged him, swinging into the other lane.

"Somebody needs to tell that dude it's 1989, not 1969," I muttered as the man grinned and waved, oblivious to the fact that he'd just missed taking the Big Trip.

Race laughed. "Eugene does have its hippie element. It's interesting because damn near the entire population of this town is made up of college students, environmentalists, and loggers, but they manage to get along without killing each other."

I grunted and went back to looking out the window. We were headed east now, passing a college. A few girls sunbathed on the lawn in front of one of the dorms. *Hmmm, not bad.*

"That's the University of Oregon," my uncle said. "Off to the left is Autzen Stadium, where the Ducks have their games, but you can't really see it from here."

Ducks, now there was a real fighting name. It was even more pitiful than what they called their rivals, the OSU Beavers. At least Beavers had teeth.

We crossed under the freeway and drove along a narrow river. "That the Willamette?" I asked, allowing curiosity to overpower my cool.

"Yup. It runs right behind the trailer park where I live."

I checked out the river. In Portland the Willamette was a monster that supported drawbridges and big ships. Here, it looked puny enough to walk across. There were even rocks sticking up out of it.

The river disappeared behind some trees, and after that the scenery went south. Rundown buildings and used car lots replaced the hotels and restaurants I'd seen near the University. Jimmy Buffett began crooning *Changes In Attitudes, Changes In Latitudes.*

"So what kinda stuff do you like to do?" Race asked.

I shrugged. Did he really think I'd spill my guts? For all I knew, he'd report everything I said to my dad. Things were messed up enough with him. He thought I'd gotten off too

8

easily—that a week or two in juvie might have done me some good. I had no idea why the zoo had dropped charges against me, but the fact that they did proved it wasn't any big deal, right?

Race tried again. "You into heavy metal?"

I answered with another shrug. Years ago I'd learned that this simple gesture was a good supplement to any vocabulary. People got fed up with it pretty quick then they tended to leave you alone.

"I'm not gonna get on your case about anything like that, if you're worried," Race said. He made a right turn just before a bridge that, according to a sign, crossed the river into the city of Springfield.

"I figure a kid your age needs space. There's a couple things I'm gonna draw the line at, like messing with drugs or getting in trouble with the cops, but I won't nag you on matters of taste."

I took a final drag off my cigarette and threw it out the window. "Whatever," I said, calling up my next-best tool for putting an end to a conversation.

Race nodded like he didn't give a rip that I'd brushed off his attempt to be a good guy, but a twinge of disappointment flickered in his eyes. That figured. He was nice, but he was just like my dad. Weak.

Race's trailer looked old enough to be the first place Noah rented when he got off the Ark, and I was pretty sure I recognized the mobile home park from a recent episode of *Cops*. About fifty feet to the north, a railroad trestle rose up out of the brush.

My uncle literally lived on the wrong side of the tracks.

I glanced across the van at him, hoping he'd made a wrong turn and taken me to the landfill by mistake.

"This is it, kid."

That military school was looking better all the time.

I hopped down from the van and swung wide of the carport, which leaned dangerously to one side. It looked like the rusty car parts stacked around it were the only things holding it up. The trailer's wooden steps, lined with a waist-deep pile of yellowing newspapers, felt spongy from dry rot as I climbed them.

Inside, the living room, kitchen, and dining area were one open space. Dishes overflowed the sink, dirty clothes peeked out from under the coffee table, and the whole place smelled like a Jiffy Lube.

"Damn," I said. "This looks worse than my room back home."

Race glanced around like he was seeing the mess for the first time. "I'm not much on housework."

No kidding.

"Well, look, kid. This trailer's kinda small, but you can have the back room. I mostly just use it for storage, anyway."

"Don't you sleep?"

"Sure, but I crash on the couch. Go ahead and put your stuff in the bedroom. I'll be back in a minute to box up my junk, then we can take it down to my shop."

A snort almost escaped me as I sidestepped Race's drafting table, which filled damn near the entire kitchen. It was a neat-freak oasis in a desert of disarray, organized into tidy stacks of papers and art supplies. Clearly, my uncle was nuts. But there was no denying his talent. The sketches of cars and people tacked to the walls above his workstation looked totally realistic.

I slipped down the hallway that led between a closet and the tiniest bathroom I'd ever seen. At the back of the trailer, car parts and tools covered the desk, bed, and floor. Ugly black stains spotted the carpet, completely overwhelming its three-tone pattern. The only positive thing about the room was that it had its own door leading outside.

"This place really isn't big enough for two people," Race said as he joined me in the scrap emporium. "But it'll do for the summer. By fall I oughta be able to afford an apartment."

I grunted and dropped onto the bed, where I sunk into the flabby mattress.

Oblivious to my culture shock, Race secured the bottom of an old Valvoline box with duct tape then began tossing cans of spray paint into it. "I shoulda done this before you got here, but I've been kinda busy. I'm putting a roll cage in a guy's car, and he wants it done by Monday."

This time I couldn't even muster a grunt. Paralyzed by apathy, I watched my uncle chuck stuff into boxes and milk crates. There was no way this could work. If the guy couldn't take the time to clean out a room for me, what made him think he'd be able to put up with all the other things about a kid that would cramp his style?

I stared down at the flecks of orange paint that had spattered my favorite jeans the other night. I still couldn't fathom why the cops had let me off. Dad refused to discuss it. All he'd seemed to care about was getting rid of me.

"Wanna help me load this stuff into the van?" Race asked.

I lifted my shoulders noncommittally, still staring at my jeans.

"Hey, the sooner we get this place cleaned up, the sooner you can make it yours."

Now there was some incentive. I sighed and pushed myself up off the bed. Maybe it would be easier if I cooperated. I grabbed the nearest box and followed him out to the van.

Within half an hour everything was loaded up. Race had even vacuumed the carpet—with a Shop Vac—and found clean sheets for the bed. They were green and yellow striped. I glanced sideways at him.

"University colors," Race explained, blushing as if I'd accused him of some sort of perversion.

"You went to the University?"

"Yeah. For a year."

"You flunk out?"

"Nope. The parental gravy train dried up. Seems you've gotta read the fine print if you want to get an education out of our family."

You had to read the fine print if you wanted to get anything out of our family.

My uncle's shop, in an industrial complex on the west end of town, was spotless compared to the trailer. The one exception was the area right inside the doorway. A frat house reject couch and chair sat beside a table built from milk crates and plywood. The surface was buried under a roach's fantasies: Coke cans, Taco Time wrappers, and the remains of stale 7-Eleven burritos. After stepping through that mess, the rest of the shop shocked me. It was crammed full of boxes, tools, and spare parts, but everything was organized. I walked around, giving it a casual once-over.

Even though I figured the least bit of interest would invite a landslide of enthusiasm from my uncle, I couldn't resist the pull of the race car. Scuffed, battered, and painted basic black, it sported yellow eights on the doors and roof which were shadowed with red to give them a three-dimensional pop. Both front fenders advertised Rick's University Video, while the trunk promoted Willamette Electrical Supply. "Eugene Custom Classics" was stenciled across the hood under a sky blue pentagon with a skinny white star in the middle. I thought I recognized it as the logo for some car company. Dodge, maybe?

"A lot of work goes into one of these things."

Race's voice startled me, but I managed not to jump. With a grunt, I turned away. He took the hint and got busy unloading the van.

A second car sat at the back of the shop. The roof had been chopped off and the interior stripped. Inside, a structure of steel tubing was beginning to take shape. I figured that was the roll cage Race had mentioned. I could see why it was called a cage, since it hugged the outside contours of the car, forming a skeleton to protect the driver.

More exploration revealed an assortment of toolboxes and equipment. On one shelf, beside a row of car manuals, I spotted some trophies.

Race was good enough to win trophies?

I glanced over my shoulder. He was still stacking boxes, so I wandered closer. Several of the awards bore the date and the inscription "Trophy Dash Winner." Others boasted a "Main Event" victory.

"How 'bout some lunch?"

I jerked back, hoping Race hadn't noticed what I was looking at. Fat chance of that. He grinned at me, probably thinking he'd scored some points.

"You hungry?" he asked.

I shrugged. Was he for real? It was almost two o'clock.

"McDonald's okay?"

"Sure."

"Then let's go."

I followed him outside.

Trophies. I wouldn't mind winning a trophy for something. I wondered what it would be like to drive a race car. I bet it was a rush.

Race seemed surprised when I ate three Big Macs, a large order of fries, a milkshake, and an apple pie. What did he expect? Dad was sending him money. Why should I go hungry?

I had to endure that same Jimmy Buffett tape the whole drive back to the trailer. As soon as we got there, I retreated to my room. Even with the car parts gone, it reeked of oil.

Margaritaville was still bouncing around in my head, so I busted out my CD collection. Race had been way off with that crack about heavy metal. Sure, I listened to that stuff with my friends, but what I really dug was older rock. Stuff like Jerry Lee Lewis and the Beatles. Almost anything from the '50s, '60s, and '70s. Chuck Berry seemed like a good bet right now. I stuck the disc in my boombox and cranked up *Maybellene*, wondering if Race would nag me to turn it down. Probably not. He seemed like the type to go out of his way to get along with people. I bet I could get away with a lot if I worked it right.

Secure in my protective bubble of music, I started unpacking. The majority of my boxes went straight in the closet—there wasn't anyplace to put most of my stuff—but I did jam my clothes into the dresser and slide my posters out of their mailing tube.

I had to stand on a milk crate to tape the upper corners of the artwork to the walls. One of the curses of being short. I kept hoping someday I'd have a growth spurt, but I figured it was a lost cause. Dad was only five foot seven.

When I finished putting my personal stamp on the place, one thing remained. An old drawing of Race's. I wasn't even sure why I'd brought it. Maybe because it reminded me of the only memory I had of him, from when I was a little kid and we'd visited Grandma and Grandpa for Thanksgiving.

It had been one of those bleak November days where everything outside was gray and dripping. The scenery in the house had been just as dismal. Grandma decorated in every shade of white, sticking expensive, breakable things where you couldn't be a kid without knocking them over. I'd wandered through the house until I came across Race's room—a colorful refuge, just messy enough to be interesting.

Race must've been about fourteen then. He was sitting at his desk, putting together a model of a car with the number 43 on the doors and lots of lettering on the sides.

"What's that?" I asked, standing in the doorway.

"Richard Petty's 1970 Plymouth Superbird."

There wasn't even a hint of impatience in Race's voice, so I took that as an invitation to keep talking.

"Why's it got that big thing on the back?"

"The wing? That helps hold it down on the track. It's a superspeedway car and it can go over 190 miles per hour."

I was five years old. I had no idea what 190 miles per hour meant.

"That's more than three times as fast as you guys went on the freeway coming here," Race explained, setting the car down and swiveling in his chair to face me.

"Wow. Can I have it?"

"No, but I'll draw you a picture." He fished a pad of paper and a pencil out of his desk and scrawled for a few minutes, creating a totally cool replica of the Superbird. When he was done he ripped the page from the tablet and handed it over. "How's that?" he asked, shooting off a grin that would have made me follow him into the bloodiest battle.

When we went home later that night I stuck the sketch up on my wall, where it had stayed for almost ten years. I hadn't seen Race after that, and for months I'd wished he'd been my big brother, instead of my uncle. But I was kidding myself if I thought that he was gonna fill that role now.

I stuck the Superbird drawing in the top drawer of the desk. Then I broke down the boxes I'd emptied and slid them under the bed so I wouldn't have to get new ones when Race kicked me out.

With my unpacking finished, I rooted through the closet until I found the box Race had made a crack about. Good thing he hadn't pressed the issue. It wouldn't have done much to promote my bad-ass image if he'd figured out I liked to read.

In my crowd it was acceptable for a guy to check out the occasional comic book or dirty magazine, but I read *real* books. Current authors like Alden R. Carter and Chris Crutcher, and even the stuff they taught in school. I totally got into how a writer could pull you away from the world and manipulate your feelings. It was like painting, except the pictures were created with words and ideas instead of watercolors or oils.

I flopped down on the bed with my dog-eared copy of *Stotan*. The mattress drooped seriously in the middle, folding around my sides like a taco shell. No matter. Within minutes I was drawn in by the story.

"Hey, Cody, come out here and get some dinner."

Race's voice jolted me. I slapped my book shut and shoved it under the pillow.

"Cody?"

"I'm coming."

In the kitchen, I found my uncle ferreting through the cupboards for clean plates. "Turn on the TV," he said. "There oughta be something good on cable."

I picked up the remote—complete with duct tape to hold the batteries in place—and flipped through the channels until I found MTV.

The plate Race handed me a minute later held nothing but a huge, orange mound of macaroni and cheese.

"Real balanced meal, dude."

"You don't expect me to wash more than one pan, do ya?"

From the appearance of the kitchen, it looked like it had been a long time since he'd washed *any* pans.

Race grabbed a second plate off the counter and sank into a chair that was covered with clean laundry.

"I probably oughta get you enrolled in school tomorrow," he said, "but maybe you could use a few days to get used to things first."

"Sure." I kept my focus on the Guns and Roses video I was watching.

"Somehow, I expected a little more enthusiasm than that."

"I appreciate it, dude. Seriously." To show I meant it I gave him a few second's eye contact before loading up my fork. You can get a lot of macaroni on a fork if you stab it instead of scooping it. The noodles all squish up and compress.

Race sighed. "Your dad sent some money. If you need anything, we could go get it tomorrow."

"Cool."

"You a big Guns and Roses fan or something?"

I shrugged.

"Do you always talk this much?"

"No."

He gave up and pulled a magazine out from under a couple of beer bottles on the coffee table. It had race cars on the cover.

We ate in silence until my plate was empty. "You got any more of this stuff?" I asked.

"Sure. Over there on the stove. Finish it up if you want."

There wasn't much left, so I sat down with the whole pan. My lack of manners, which would have made Mom go nuclear, didn't attract a glance from Race.

Somewhere in the distance a train whistle sounded. I didn't think much of it until it wailed again, this time much closer and accompanied by the clatter of wheels. As the noise got louder, the trailer began to shake. Dishes rattled in the cupboards. Beer bottles jiggled off the edge of the coffee table. Race sat quietly on the couch, flipping the pages of his magazine.

"Holy shit!" I hollered. "How often do those things come through here?"

"I dunno. I don't hear 'em anymore."

"You don't *hear* them?"

"Not really." Race kept his eyes on the magazine. "It's not so bad now, but before I had cable, they used to really mess with the TV reception."

I stared at my uncle, unable to believe people actually lived like this, then got up to drop the pan in the sink. As I headed for my room, I hesitated.

"You gonna give me your list of rules?"

Race blinked at me. "Uh—yeah. If you go someplace, let me know where you'll be, and if you're gonna smoke, try not to burn the trailer down."

"That's it?"

"Well, aside from not doing anything illegal. But I already told you about that."

I couldn't believe it. Back home there were tons of rules. The problem was they changed from week to week, so I'd developed a policy of doing whatever I felt like and not getting caught.

Race seemed pleased to finally have my full attention. "You wanna go see a movie tonight or something?"

What did he think this was, a *Brady Bunch* re-run? Still, something about the way he wouldn't quit with the nice guy routine almost made me want to give him a break.

"Not really," I said. Then, before he had a chance to suggest anything else, I retreated to my room and cranked the music.

In bed that night the full force of reality hit me. I was in a whole different town—a total burg compared to Portland—away from my friends and everything I knew. Dad might not be on my list of favorite people after banishing me to the nether regions of the state, but at least I was used to him.

I thought of my mother, off partying in Phoenix. A familiar anger gnawed at me, and I hated myself for caring. You'd think by now I would've learned she wasn't gonna change. You'd think I could've let it go. But some hopes keep springing back to life, no matter how many wooden stakes get driven through their hearts.

If I'd had any brains I would've considered myself lucky when she left. It was better than being criticized all the time—reminded I was weak and worthless like my dad. But something in me couldn't see past the injustice of her sneaking off and leaving things unresolved. You can't start a fight then walk away from it.

Shutting my eyes, I drifted back to the biggest mistake of my life. I felt the nozzle of the rattle can under my finger, heard Mike shouting, "*Cops!*" I saw red and blue lights spill over the sidewalk as beer surged through me, fanning my anger until it roared up like a grass fire.

And there in front of me, the dripping orange paint spelled out what I couldn't say to my mother's face: *Saundra Everett is a worthless bitch.*

Chapter 2

The next morning sunlight fought its way through the trailer's grimy windows to burn away the previous night's doubts. But I was still in Eugene and it still sucked.

The thing was, I didn't really mind my uncle. There was something about his puppy-dog friendliness that was hard to blow off. I could see myself getting to like him, but what if I gave in to that feeling and he decided I was too much trouble? Even worse, what if he didn't like *me*?

After experiencing a new level of hell trying to wash up in a shower that wasn't big enough to turn around in, I moussed my hair into its proper spiked form then went to confront my new life.

Race snored away in the front room. I found half a box of Cap'n Crunch in the cupboard, poured it into a pot, and dumped milk on top.

With Race monopolizing the couch, the only place to sit was the chair with the laundry on it. I picked up the remote and hunted till I found a channel that was showing a *Teenage Mutant Ninja Turtles* cartoon.

Race groaned, blinking at me across the room.

"You snore, dude," I said.

He grunted, worked an arm out from under the blankets, and squinted at his watch. "I don't think I've been up this early since the last time I was up this late."

"It's seven-thirty," I informed him, fixing my attention on the TV, where Raphael—the coolest of the Turtles—was kicking some bad guy's ass. "This is the time most people get up." I steam-shoveled my spoon into the pan, bringing it up fully loaded and dripping. A couple pieces of cereal escaped, disappearing into the pile of clothes underneath me.

Race burrowed back under his covers. "Turn it down," he said. "I don't get up till nine."

After having those damned trains rattle me awake several times during the night, I wasn't feeling particularly sympathetic. I clicked the volume down exactly two notches. Race didn't fight for more.

The Cap'n Crunch didn't do much to stave off my hunger, so when the cartoon was over I got up to search the kitchen. I didn't find any cereal, or even bread for toast, but I did discover some eggs in the fridge. As I mixed about half a dozen with the last of the milk, Race woke up again.

"What are you doing?"

"Cooking breakfast."

Race rubbed a hand across his face, sighed, and hefted himself up, wadding his blankets into a ball and tossing them to the far corner of the couch. "You already ate all the cereal," he pointed out, waving a hand at the empty Cap'n Crunch box on the kitchen floor.

"So?" There'd hardly been enough in that box to satisfy a three-year-old.

"So somebody has to pay for that stuff." Race edged around the coffee table to shut off the TV then pull a clean shirt from the pile of clothes I'd had been sitting on. A semi-clean shirt, anyway. He had to pick bits of soggy Cap'n Crunch off it.

"Any food left?" he asked, padding barefoot through the kitchen.

"Dude, there wasn't any food *before* I ate."

"Guess it's time for a grocery run." Race opened the freezer and pulled out a carton of Twinkies. He tipped out the last cake then tossed the box toward the garbage can. It missed.

"Very nutritional breakfast you've got there," I said, watching him tear open the wrapper with his teeth and devour the Twinkie in two bites.

"Don't knock it till you've tried it."

*   *   *

That afternoon Race dragged me to the grocery store, where he loaded up the cart with all sorts of healthy foods like Twinkies, potato chips, and microwave burritos. He seriously altered the structural integrity of everything in the pile by tossing a six-pack of beer on top. Not normal beer, like Budweiser or Miller, but some weird brand called Guinness.

On the way home, I had to draw the line when I heard Jimmy Buffett start in on *Margaritaville* for the fourth time in two days.

"Don't you have any other tapes?"

"Sure, there's a box around here somewhere. I just can't ever find it."

"Y'know, there's this amazing device called a radio receiver, and it's built right into your stereo."

Race turned to grin at me. "No kidding?"

I pulled my feet off the dash and scouted the floorboards until I found a shoebox full of cassettes. After popping the offending tape out of the stereo, I glanced at its title. *Songs You Know By Heart.* Now wasn't *that* the truth.

We didn't get back to the trailer until after three.

"Look, kid," Race said. "I gotta go to the shop and put in some time on that roll cage. You wanna come along?"

"Nah, I think I'll stay here."

Something in Race's posture went slack, like he'd just found out the cop who'd pulled him over for speeding was gonna let him off with a warning. "Okay. Well, if I'm not back by six, go ahead and fix yourself something to eat."

I spent the afternoon vegging in front of the tube. It was nice having the place to myself, at least until my channel surfing landed me on *Lord of the Flies.* It's this story about some British schoolboys who get stranded on an island. The society they form slowly disintegrates until they start killing each other. I didn't know what it was about that movie, but even though it spooked the hell out of me, whenever it was on I had to watch it. The idea that little kids could treat each other that way didn't surprise me. People were messed up. The whole world was messed up. By the time it was over I was thoroughly depressed.

Six o'clock came and went, but Race didn't show up. I didn't feel like cooking, so I ate a bag of Doritos. That only took the edge off. A half-gallon of chocolate ice cream helped, but I had to break down and cook a frozen pizza before I filled myself up.

Race still wasn't home by a quarter after seven. No big surprise. There had to be a hundred things he'd rather do than hang out with some strange kid.

Around eight I got up to snag a Pepsi. As I moved Race's beer aside I thought, why not? It wasn't like he was here to stop me.

I'd never had Guinness before, but I figured beer was beer. *Wrong.* Guinness was nasty. It tasted *burnt.* Still, it was alcohol. Race hadn't appeared by the time I choked down the first bottle, so I got myself another. The second one wasn't quite as bad. The third tasted almost decent.

As the alcohol percolated through my body, satisfying every brain cell and muscle fiber, the stress of the past two weeks melted away. I lit up a smoke and explored Race's music collection. Not a single CD in all those cassettes. It was rock, though, and respectable stuff at that: Queen, CCR, Van Halen. I selected Pink Floyd's *The Wall* and stuck it in the tape deck, cranking the volume and slumping on the couch with my fourth beer.

With the TV on mute, I whizzed through the channels until I came to a *Gilligan's Island* rerun. The contrast between the goofy castaways and the dark music felt satisfying. I flopped back, inching my feet up the wall and tracing the wood grain pattern of the paneling with my toes. Then the alcohol turned traitor on me. My blissfulness fizzled as I thought about how quick my dad had been to send me away. Sure, I'd been getting into trouble for a long time—since clear back in fifth grade. But it had never been anything serious until the deal at the zoo. How could Dad give up on me so easily? Pitiful as he was when it came to confrontation, why was *that* the thing that had finally made him take a stand?

Not that I wasn't used to him bailing. He'd sat back and watched Mom tear me a new one for as long as I could remember. And sometimes he even blamed me for it, like on my ninth birthday.

We'd been getting ready to eat dinner when Mom stormed into the kitchen, yelling about a notice I'd gotten from the library and stashed in my sock drawer. A bill for ten dollars in fines. I'd hidden it because I didn't want to get ragged on about reading instead of going out for Little League like a normal kid. Usually I was good about taking books back, but I'd been short on bus fare, and I sure as hell couldn't ask Mom for a ride.

"When are you going to learn to be responsible?" she ranted. "Do you think I'm made of money? You're going to pay for this yourself."

"How?" My allowance was practically non-existent. I was always getting docked a dollar for not taking out the trash, fifty cents for talking back, a quarter for each piece of clothing I left on the couch.

"Well, if you don't have money, I guess I'll have to return this." She dropped a package in front of me, wrapped in dinosaur paper that might have been cool if I'd been turning five. Dad glanced at the gift, but he kept his mouth shut.

My skin flashed hot and my body turned to concrete. Not for a second did I doubt Mom would make good on her threat.

"Go ahead," she said. "Open it."

"I don't want to." It was better not to know what I was missing.

"I. Told. You. To. Open it." She shoved the package across the table, the acid in her tone a warning that there were worse things than losing a present.

With my face rigid, I yanked off the paper. A set of walkie talkies, the ones I'd been wanting for months. An extravagant gift because my birthday was December 31st and we were always broke after Christmas.

My hand lingered on the box until I forced myself to pull it away. "Take 'em back. I don't care."

My feigned indifference set her off. She slammed back from the table, telling me what an ungrateful brat I was as she went to the counter to grab my cake. "You can just forget about having any of this," she said, stepping on the lever that opened the trashcan.

I watched as the cake I'd been waiting for all day slid into the garbage. Mom ceremoniously pulled her foot away. The lid slapped down to imbed itself in chocolate frosting. "Get your own dinner," she said, turning to leave the room. "I'm too upset to eat."

Dad got up and pulled his jacket from the peg by the door. He always made himself scarce when Mom went ballistic. My eyes caught his from across the kitchen, begging him to take me along just this once. He gripped the doorknob and his gaze shifted to the floor.

"Don't look at me. You know better than to rile her."

Even now, the memory made me want to slug him. I guess it shouldn't have been any surprise he'd shipped me off, with a history of crap like that. I got up and went to the fridge for another beer.

I was halfway through the last one and well into side two of the tape when my uncle came home. By then it was dark. Blue ghosts of TV light haunted the walls, reflecting off the insides of the windows.

Race made it across the trailer in two steps. He snapped off the stereo, abruptly ending *Comfortably Numb*.

"Hey, Speed Racer!" I said, saluting him with my bottle.

"What the hell do you think you're doing? Are you *drunk*?" Race flipped on the overhead light.

My pupils zipped down to pinpoint size so quick I could practically feel the recoil. "Ahh!" I hollered, throwing my arm across my face. "Turn it off!"

He left it on.

"Did you drink that whole six-pack?"

Slowly, I drew my arm away from my eyes and blinked at him. "Nah, I saved half this last one for you." Beer dribbled out of the bottle I held, splattering off the edge of the coffee table and down to the floor. The sight of it got me giggling so hard I slid off the edge of the couch. Five other bottles, which I'd balanced on the edge of the overcrowded table, avalanched over me, along with several dirty dishes and a stack of racing magazines.

"Dude," I said. "I'm so shredded."

"I noticed," Race said dryly. Then, with a note of annoyance he added, "Do you have any idea how much that stuff cost?"

Oh, sure, I get wasted and the only thing he can think of is the price of his precious imported beer.

"Hey, buddy, don't sweat it, I'll buy you another six-pack. Hell, I'll buy you a case." I levered myself between the couch and the coffee table, sending another wave of crap cascading to the floor. It took several tries to pull myself up. Race stood quietly while I made my attempts, his jaw tensed and irritation flickering in his eyes. I thought sure he was gonna let me have it. Then something gave way in his expression, and resignation replaced the anger.

"Kid," he said, "this was not the best thing you coulda done the first time I left you alone."

That was it? A feeble reprimand was the best punishment he could come up with? "Maybe you shouldn'a left me alone," I said. "You ever think of that?"

"Maybe I thought you could handle it," Race countered, his voice still eerily calm. "You're fifteen years old. That's plenty old enough to be trusted to look out for yourself for a few hours. I can't babysit you every minute. I've gotta earn a living."

"I thought you were an artist."

"Do you have any idea how many graphic artists there are in this town? If I didn't do a little welding on the side I'd starve."

"And that's *my* problem?"

Race's tone stayed level. "It is if you want to stay here."

"Who says I wanna stay here?"

Several long seconds passed as Race studied me. "All right, if that's how you feel, I'll call your dad tomorrow. I was hoping we could make this work, but I'm not gonna force you. My life would be a lot less complicated without a teenager in it."

A cold jolt cut through my buzz. "You'd like that, wouldn't you? You'd be happy if I left. You prob'ly never wanted me here to begin with!"

"Kid—"

"Fine. I'll go pack my stuff right now. I'll leave you to your race car, and your fancy beer, and your crappy-assed stink-hole of a trailer!" I staggered around the coffee table, slipping on one of those damned magazines. Race caught my arm before I could do a face-plant.

"Le'go!" I said, fighting his grip. "Damn it, let me go!"

Race's left hand clamped my other bicep. I struggled, but it didn't do any good. Soft as my uncle might come across, he was plenty strong. He got right down in my face.

"Cody, listen to me. I know being here must be tough on you, but it's the only reasonable choice you've got. I don't want you to go."

He was lying. He had to be. If my own dad could throw me out, why should some guy I hardly knew be willing to keep me around?

"I want to make this work," Race said.

Why did he have to be so damned understanding? Why couldn't he give me hell, like any normal person?

"What do *you* care?" I demanded, the mellow of the beer winning out over my anger and leeching the fight from me.

Something hard glinted in Race's eyes, then he sighed. "Let's just say I've got my reasons." His grip slackened, but I was too wiped out to break free.

"How 'bout you go crawl in bed and sleep this off?" Race said. "We can start over tomorrow, okay?" He released me then draped his arm over my shoulders to steer me across the room. The gesture cut straight through my emotional Kevlar, but somehow I managed to suck it up as Race led me down the hallway.

The wheezed-out bed groaned as I fell onto it. Race tossed a blanket over me, then, not yet familiar with the cast-iron nature of my stomach, he stuck a wastebasket beside the bed.

"Goodnight, kid," he said. "I hope to hell you don't have a hangover tomorrow."

Chapter 3

I wasn't hung over the next morning, but I did sleep late. Race was already up when I slipped into the kitchen to forage for breakfast. Using a half-eaten Twinkie as a pointing device, he gestured at my T-shirt, which read, *Please forgive me, I was raised by wolves.*

"Well, that explains a lot," he said. "And it calls to mind such an accurate image of my sister."

The comment stirred a tiny feeling of camaraderie in me.

"You feeling okay?" Race continued, studying me as if he genuinely cared.

"Sure." I ducked around him and went for the cupboard. His attention was making me feel twitchy.

"Good, because we're leaving for the speedway at two. We'll meet Kasey at the shop first. There's one last thing I've gotta do to the car."

"Who's Kasey?"

"My crew chief and biggest sponsor. So try not to live up to the slogan on your shirt."

At the shop, I flipped through a book about engines while Race fiddled with something under the hood of his car.

"So where's this big sponsor?" I asked, tossing the book onto a workbench and pulling out my smokes.

"Probably slaving away over a car. Kasey's a workaholic. Hardly ever takes a day off. I understand that's how it's supposed to be when you own a business, but I wouldn't know from personal experience." Race gave me a conspiratorial grin. "I'm kind of a slacker."

The crew chief still hadn't arrived when Race finished his repair. He hooked his trailer to the hitch on the van then backed up in front of the Dart. He'd just gotten the thing loaded when a mean-looking '60s car with a deep purple paint job roared into the parking lot. The engine was so loud—so powerful—that I felt the vibration in my chest and through the soles of my shoes. It stirred something primal and vaguely reminiscent of the rush that goes through me every time I catch a glimpse of a hot girl.

The door of the car opened and a woman stepped out. A rush-inducing woman. Her eyes echoed that perfect blue of an Oregon September day, and the hair pulled back from her face gleamed a rich cinnamon color.

She let loose with a smile that could've melted every glacier on Mt. Hood. "You must be Cody."

"Kid, meet my crew chief, Kasey McCormick," Race said.

"Your crew chief's a *chick*?"

He raised an eyebrow at me. "Got a problem with that?"

"Heck no." I glanced at Kasey, who seemed to be enjoying my stupefaction. Abruptly, I turned back to Race. "It wasn't an oversight was it, your not telling me she was a she?"

Race answered with a monstrous grin.

Kasey took off on her own, while Race and I detoured through the Burger King drive-thru before heading to the speedway, which was located a mile or so west of his shop. A green and yellow sign—no doubt a tie-in to the town's University theme—marked the entrance. From the highway, the place didn't look like much, just a grandstand with an asphalt oval stuck in the middle of a field. Dust billowed behind us, covering the race car in a fine powder as we bumped along the gravel driveway.

Up close, things looked even worse. A few small buildings and the wall that backed the grandstands were constructed from sheets of plywood. Weathered white paint, which must have dated back to the age of black-and-white TV, flaked from every surface. The parking lot was nothing more than a mowed field.

My uncle pulled up to a little shack at the end of the driveway. The grandmotherly-looking lady inside greeted us. "Well, hello, Race! Rumor has it you're planning to take the points lead away from Addamsen tonight."

Race chuckled. "I think that's a little optimistic, Cheryl."

"You'll do it, sooner or later. I have complete faith in you." The lady gave him a smile that made me think she was only a step away from ruffling his hair.

After Race introduced me, Cheryl had us sign some kind of release—probably so my parents couldn't sue if a chunk of flying metal took my head off. Then she stamped my hand and gave me a slip of paper. "That's your pit pass, hon. Don't lose it, okay?"

The track looked as sorry as the buildings, with its asphalt cracked and patched down low in the corners. A cement block barrier, topped by a battered chain-link fence, protected the grandstands, but the only wall to keep cars out of the infield was along the front stretch.

In the pits two strips of asphalt provided access to and from the front straight and separated the rows of cars, which sat amid powdery dust and close-cropped weeds. A third paved road, full of potholes, led to the backstretch. That was about all there was, other than a run-down concession stand, a few light posts, and a Porta-potty.

We found Kasey leaning over the fender of a Camaro that sported a two-tone blue paint job. The number 4 was stenciled on the roof and doors. A skinny guy with dark hair, who looked a few years older than Race and Kasey, hung over the opposite fender. I figured he must be the driver because he was dressed just like Race in a one-piece outfit that I'd been informed was called a firesuit.

31

I wanted to grab my food and go see what Kasey was doing, but Race wouldn't hand it over until I'd helped him unload the van. Famished, I finally tore into my first Whopper. Race plopped down on a stack of tires and fished a small order of French fries out of the bag.

"Hey, Kasey," Race called. "I got you a chicken sandwich."

"Just give me one second." Kasey adjusted something, and suddenly the Camaro was purring like the proverbial kitten. The skinny guy grinned and thanked her, clapping her on the shoulder.

"You know," Kasey told me as she came over to join us, "you're lucky Race remembered to feed you. When I first met him, he never ate anything before getting out onto the track."

It didn't look like he planned on eating much now. Other than Kasey's sandwich, the fries were the only thing he'd ordered. It was none of my business, though. I reached for my second Whopper and, because Race was ignoring them anyway, helped myself to his fries.

"Hey, those are mine!" he hollered, grabbing my wrist. Startled, I dropped them.

Race shot me a smoldering look. "Don't you have enough food without stealing my dinner?"

"I wouldn't exactly call an order of French fries *dinner*."

"What are you, the nutrition police? Excuse me if I refrain from getting my dietary advice from the human garbage disposal."

"Don't tell me you were actually considering eating something?" Kasey teased. "In a half hour or so, you'll be climbing into that car."

Race stopped glaring at me long enough to glance in her direction. "I was trying not to think about that," he admitted. He pulled a couple fries out of the bag and took a defiant bite.

I heard a bark of laughter and turned to see the driver of the 4 car giving Race a devilish look. "Is that so?"

He sauntered over to lean against the van. "You mean you're ignoring how knotted up your stomach's gonna feel when you're waiting for the main event to start?"

Race eyed him warily. "Yeah."

"And you're forgetting the way your car jolts when you hit that rough patch of asphalt right before you pull onto the track?"

"That's right." Race folded a couple more fries into his mouth.

"And you're just putting it out of your mind, how all those fans will be hollering your name while Addamsen bangs away at your bumper and tries to stuff you in the wall?"

Race's jaw faltered in mid-chew.

"And *heaven forbid* you should think about what's gonna happen when we get the green and fourteen cars try to jam into turn one all at once."

Race swallowed hard. "Guess I better take the van back out to the parking lot." He got up and dropped the rest of his fries in my lap. "Have at it, kid."

The driver of the 4 car laughed.

"Cody," said Kasey, "I'd like you to meet your uncle's closest friend, Jim Davis."

Stock car racing mostly seemed to be a lot of waiting around. Waiting to go out on the track for practice laps, waiting to qualify, waiting for a turn to compete. Throughout all this, Race kept trying to strike up a conversation with me, commenting on someone's car or offering an explanation I hadn't asked for. It was hard to keep my mind from drifting. I couldn't see the attraction of sitting around a dusty field, enduring endless noise and watching a bunch of guys drive in a circle.

Even if I had been interested, it was impossible to make sense of what was going on. The classification of cars was the biggest mystery. Some of them looked like they'd come straight off the street—other than being beat to hell—while others had bodies fashioned entirely out of flat sheet metal panels. The one thing I could tell was that a lot of the stock-looking ones were Camaros. I'd never been a gearhead like my buddy Mike, but I knew what a Camaro looked like because he drove one. Even though he was only a freshman, he already had his license. There were advantages to being held back in first grade.

The mind-numbing tedium didn't seem to bother Race and Jim. They sat around talking carburetors and camshafts and other stuff that made no sense to me. Race had one of those little blue Nerf footballs and was making an unsuccessful attempt to spin it on an outstretched finger.

Occasionally Kasey glanced in my direction and smiled. Every time she did, I thought my bones would liquefy.

"So, Kasey," I said, wanting her to fix those blue eyes on me again. "That car you were driving earlier. What was it?"

"A '68 Charger RT." Another smile. My bones slipped one more notch down the scale from solid to liquid.

"Is that, like, a Ford or what?"

Jim snorted.

"It's a *Dodge*, kid," said Race. He tossed the football in the air.

"Looks like you've got your work cut out for you with this one, Morgan," Jim said.

"How about the race car?" I asked, hating that they were stealing Kasey's attention and burning me in the process.

"It's a '74 Dodge Dart," said Kasey.

"Which is also a Mopar," Race added. "Kasey's crazy about 'em."

"Mopar?" Jeeze, couldn't they speak English?

"Miscellaneous Odd Parts Assembled Ridiculously," supplied Jim, smirking at Kasey.

"It's a name for Dodge and Chrysler products," she explained. "And, Jim, it must shame you immensely to be beaten by inferior equipment every week."

"Ha!" said Race, chucking the football at his "closest" friend.

Jim ducked. The ball bounced off the side of his race car, leaving a dusty mark right in the middle of the number 4.

"Sportsman 'A' dash! Time to get lined up!" A guy wearing a black and white striped shirt and sporting a Paul Bunyan-style beard bellowed as he strode down the asphalt strip that separated the rows of cars.

Jim leaned over to get the football, spiraled it expertly into the back of the Dart, then got up and slipped through the window of his own car. The seconds it took my uncle to navigate through the bars of the roll cage to retrieve the ball was all it took to get Paul Bunyan on his case.

"Move it, Morgan, or I'll bump you out of this race!"

Kasey handed a battered helmet into the #8 Dart, where Race was hastily belting himself in. Race jammed it on his head, fumbled with the strap, and—almost before Kasey had finished hooking up the netting that covered the driver's window—roared off to join the other cars. A pungent aroma lingered behind the Dart, familiar yet different. It was like gasoline, but a more gourmet version, sweeter and packed with excitement.

"So who's the Nazi?" I asked.

"Ted Greene," said Kasey. "He's the chief steward. It's his job to make sure everything goes smoothly in the pits, and he takes it very seriously."

"No shit. That dude needs to learn how to chill."

Even though I found the whole racing bit boring, I couldn't help seeing that my uncle fit into that world like a geek at a Star Trek convention. Everyone seemed to know him. A spike of longing caught in my chest as I stared at his car, lined up with the others near the back pit exit. It must be so cool to have everyone treat you like a hero. Race didn't hide anything about himself, and yet the people at the track liked and respected him. I'd never have the guts to let it all hang out like that.

Kasey and I watched the Dart and three other cars pull out onto the track. They circled slowly for a couple of laps, arranged in two rows of two, weaving back and forth.

"Why are they doing that?" I asked. We'd moved to the concrete wall up by the front stretch, where we could get a good view of the start-finish line.

"They're warming their tires so they stick to the track better."

Race's Dart, on the inside of the back row, bore down on the bumper of Jim's #4 Camaro. The pack bunched together as it came down the backstretch and into the corner at the north end of the track. Engines revved, getting serious. The cars thundered out onto the front straightaway and the green flag snapped in the flagman's hand.

Clustered tighter than the fingers in a fist, the pack tore into the first turn. On the outside of the front row, the yellow #9 car let the slightest gap emerge between itself and Jim's Camaro. Immediately, Race swooped into the opening. The last car, a black Camaro with a glittering silver #1, followed as if sucked by the vacuum Race left behind. Within seconds my uncle was in the lead, the black car directly behind him. Jim trailed by a few yards, and the yellow car fell into last place.

The driver of the black #1 was as aggressive as a pit bull and twice as fast. Every lap he pulled almost even with Race on the straightaways and rode the Dart's bumper so close through the corners that you couldn't see daylight between the two cars. Race managed to stay ahead of the black Camaro, but just barely. After four laps the race was over.

As Race pulled up to the start-finish line to collect his trophy, another pang of envy flared inside me. I reminded myself of how he and Jim had joked about my automotive ignorance, and a surge of resentment swept the ache away. How was I supposed to know the difference between a Ford and a Dodge?

I hung back when Race came into the pits. Kasey's smile brightened and she congratulated him, but she didn't get all gushy like most girls would've. I was beginning to get the idea that it would take a lot more than winning to get a reaction out of her.

"Good run," Jim said, even though he'd been beaten by inferior equipment again.

While Race worked his way out of the car, I kicked back on a stack of tires and lit up a smoke, taking a slow, cool drag to calm the churning inside me.

"So, how do they figure out who runs what?" I asked Kasey. I dropped my attention to the top of the toolbox, where a faint layer of dust had formed, and doodled with my free hand. I could feel Race's eyes studying me, but I didn't look up.

Kasey launched into an explanation that left me totally confused. The only thing I caught was that there were three classes and Race was in the middle one, Limited Sportsman.

"That last event was the Sportsman 'A' dash," Kasey said, as if I was supposed to know what that meant now that she'd bombarded me with information. Then she said something even a normal person could understand. "Your uncle had the second fastest qualifying time tonight."

Of course he did. I glanced at Race as he guzzled a quart of orange Gatorade. "So you're telling me he kicks ass?"

"He's second in the points right now."

"Huh." I took a final pull off my cigarette, threw it down, and crushed it with the toe of my shoe. Kasey watched like she couldn't figure out why I wasn't jumping at the chance to join the Race Morgan fan club. Fortunately, my stomach gurgled just then and bailed me out.

"I'm starved," I told Race. "Got any money?"

The glow of victory faded from his face as he dug a few crumpled ones out of his firesuit. I stuffed the money into my hip pocket and took off for the concession stand.

Race couldn't have been *that* good because he only took third in the heat. Jim won and immediately shot Kasey a smart-assed comment about his superior equipment coming through for him. The dude in the black car had a flat and finished last.

While the first Super Stock heat was getting underway, a young guy ambled into our pit to hit Race up for some advice on how to get his car to stop "pushing." I would've told him to take a hike, but Race didn't seem to mind giving away his secrets.

"If you want help with your set-up," he said, "you should ask Kasey—she's the brains behind this operation—but you can compensate for the car being tight by changing the way you drive it."

"I can?"

"Sure." Race pulled a sketchpad out of the top of his toolbox then drew a diagram of the track, showing the guy how to enter the corner to compensate for the way his car was handling.

I shook my head and walked away. Why would he want to help the competition like that?

We waited some more. It got dark, and then cold. My uncle's class lined up for their big finale, but a string of crashes in the race before it caused another delay. A spicy odor hung on the wind—a scent I wouldn't normally associate with cars.

"What's that smell?" I asked Kasey.

"Wild mint. There's a big patch of it in the infield off turn three." She handed me a cup of hot chocolate she'd gotten from the concession stand. "So are you having any fun tonight?"

"It's been a thrill a minute. I can hardly wait to do it again next week."

Kasey laughed. "The waiting can be frustrating," she admitted. "Especially when the officials can't seem to get their act together and restart the race after a wreck. But you'll like it once you learn more about the sport and start meeting people. Racing gets in your blood. You'll see."

I sincerely doubted that.

"You'll also see that your uncle isn't nearly the chump you seem to think he is."

I blew on my hot chocolate. "I never said he was."

"You didn't have to. The fact that you've ignored him the whole evening has spoken volumes."

I studied Kasey through the steam that wafted from my drink and dissipated into the night air. Didn't she know I could do a lot worse than ignore him?

"He's a good person, Cody, and he's only trying to help."

Right. Like the guy from Big Brothers and Sisters back in junior high who blew me off every week with some asinine excuse. Or my English teacher last fall. He'd acted like my best buddy because I could string a few coherent sentences together, but the first time I actually asked him for something, he couldn't spare two minutes of his precious time.

"I don't need any help," I said.

The waiting continued. I lit another cigarette. Boredom had forced me to burn through nearly an entire pack that evening. I'd have to be careful. The twenty I'd snuck out of Dad's wallet the night before I left Portland wasn't gonna last long, and there was no way in hell I could beg money off Race for smokes.

Finally, the chief steward waved the Sportsman class onto the track. The cars waited on the front stretch while the announcer blazed through a rapid-fire series of introductions for each of the drivers. This time Race was in the last row of a pack of fourteen cars. The guy in the black Camaro was right beside him.

"If Race qualified so good, why's he at the back?" I asked.

"They run an inverted field here," Kasey said. "It makes for a better show when the faster drivers have to work for a win."

The flagman waved the green flag and, as Jim had predicted earlier, the cars tried to slam through the first turn all at once. Row after row, they rushed into the corner two and three wide. It was amazing that no one bit it.

After the first couple of laps the chaos sorted itself out. The slower cars settled into position, and the faster ones worked their way forward. The black #1 Camaro, which had slipped ahead of Race at the start, began to snake its way to the front of the pack. Race was right on his ass. It got a little dicey a couple of times when the two of them came up on slower cars that were engaged in a battle of their own. Some of those guys wouldn't give an inch, and the black Camaro, like an overpowered bulldozer minus the scoop, threatened to plow right through them.

Finally, the #1 car took the lead. Race cranked it up, bearing down on the guy's bumper so hard it looked like he wanted to park his Dart in the Camaro's back seat.

For the first time I noticed that my uncle's car looked different than the others. There were a few that weren't Camaros, but none like Race's. Why had he decided to drive a Dart?

Lap after lap, Race dogged car #1, looking for a way around him but not finding it. The crowd went ballistic as the announcer delivered the blow-by-blow in auctioneer-fashion.

"Jerry Addamsen has that Camaro dialed in tonight, folks, but Morgan sure is giving him a run for his money. If the first few races are any indication, Addamsen's really gonna have his work cut out for him this season."

Race pulled even with the black car on the front stretch and once again tried to pass going into the corner. The same thing happened in the next turn. He kept coming so close, and each time, I found myself holding my breath, thinking this was the lap he'd pull it off.

"Oooh, almost. That little Dart just doesn't seem to have quite enough power for an outside pass. Meanwhile we've got a great battle going on for fifth place. There goes Tom Carey! Doesn't look like Whalen's gonna let him keep that position for long, though. Oh! And Jack Benettendi hits the wall!"

Benettendi's loss was Race's gain. As the guy's car glanced off the barrier, it spun in front Addamsen, who was about to pass. When Addamsen's black Camaro slowed and dodged to go around Benettendi on the left, Race hit the gas and dove around the spinning car's right side with so little room to spare he left a black streak on the wall.

"And, once again, Race Morgan steals the lead from our three-time points champion, Jerry Addamsen!" shouted the announcer. "Those of you who were with us last season will remember that Race took home Rookie of the Year honors and managed a third place finish in the points. And he did it in a Dodge, folks. Now *that's* something you don't see every day."

Addamsen put the squeeze on Race, but it was no easier for him to get by the 8 car than it had been for Race to pass him. When the checkered flag fell, Race was still in the lead.

Winning a stock car race must be a total rush. My uncle chattered like a kid on the first snow day of winter from the time he got out of the car until the Super Stock main ended almost an hour later. Several people congratulated him on sticking it to Addamsen. Every time they did, the catch in my chest corkscrewed tighter.

When it came time for the drivers to collect their payoff, my uncle dragged me along with him. Kasey had to retrieve the van and trailer to load things up.

"After last night, I'm not about to leave you alone," Race said.

I followed him and Jim across the track and up the bleachers to the announcer's booth. All the drivers were there, waiting for their money. The guy in front of us—a behemoth who would've dwarfed me even if I wasn't the size of a seventh grader—turned around as we came up behind him. He looked like he was maybe forty, and his brown hair stuck out at all angles from under a yellow ball cap silk-screened with the number 9.

"You must be the infamous nephew," he said in a voice almost as big as he was. He held out a huge, grubby paw. "Name's Denny Brisco. I've known your uncle since before he could see over the steering wheel."

I shook his hand. "I'm Cody."

Denny grinned. It wasn't one of those three-hundred-watters that Race could blind you with, but it was pretty close. As he opened up his mouth to say something else, a harsh voice interrupted.

"Morgan!"

The shout came from a guy in a black firesuit a little ahead of us in line. The salt and pepper hair and beard that outlined his weathered face made me guess he must be pushing fifty.

"Yeah?" Race said.

The guy pointed a Hamm's beer cup at my uncle. "You were damn lucky tonight."

"And how's that?"

"If I hadn't blown that tire in the heat, you'd still be seven points behind me."

"Six," said Race.

The guy seemed momentarily stumped by the correction. "Well, you're lucky you got the chance to make 'em up."

"Lay off, Addamsen," said Denny.

"Yeah," Jim added. "I didn't see you having any tire problems in the main. What's your excuse there?"

A couple of guys hooted. Addamsen muttered something under his breath. The driver ahead of him finished at the payoff window, and Addamsen took the guy's place, making out like he was too busy signing the sheet to concern himself with the rest of us.

"Next week we'll see," he said, brandishing his cup at Race again as he turned to walk off. "You just wait till next week."

"Hell, if you're gonna get serious, maybe I oughta hook up those other four plug wires," Race said.

Denny chuckled and slapped Race on the back with a hand that could have leveled an elephant. "You tell him, buddy. You drove a damned good race." He stepped up to the window and signed the sheet, then picked up his envelope. "'Course that means there ain't as much money in here as I might like."

Race grinned as he squeezed past to collect his own payoff.

"So are we gonna see you at the Little R tonight?" Denny asked.

"Yup."

"Good. You can buy my dinner."

Laughter erupted around us.

"Hell, Denny," Race said, giving the guy a rueful look, "it's not like I just won Darlington."

More laughter.

Denny winked at us. "I'll be lookin' for ya, Race."

Something told me he wouldn't be the only one. Addamsen watched us over his shoulder as he descended the bleachers. The thunder in his expression made me really glad that I didn't race in the Limited Sportsman class.

Chapter 4

Even though it was after eleven when we left the speedway, Race dragged me to a cafe called the Little R. Kasey followed in the Charger.

Trucks with car trailers filled the parking lot, overflowing into the business across the street. Inside, the place was packed full of guys in firesuits and women and kids wearing T-shirts that advertised their favorite driver.

Race motioned to a booth that backed up to the one occupied by Jim and his family. I waited to see where Kasey would sit then slid in beside her, earning a raised eyebrow from my uncle as he settled in across from us.

A scrawny, dark-haired kid, maybe eight years old, scaled the back of the booth and wedged himself between Race and the wall.

"Robbie Davis!" scolded the woman sitting across from Jim. "You sit your butt right down, and don't ever let me catch you doing that again!"

Giggling, the rug rat slithered southward until his chin was resting on the tabletop.

Jim reached over the back of the seat to ruffle his hair. "Where'd that traitor son of mine go?"

Robbie snickered.

"Well, Morgan, it looks like you've got yourself a kid."

"Yeah," Race agreed. "That's seems to be happening to me a lot these days."

Robbie beamed at my uncle. "Got any quarters?" he asked.

Race stood to check his pockets, plopped two coins on the table, then ducked out of the way when Robbie snatched them up and bolted for a candy dispenser by the door. As Race resettled himself, the waitress came by distributing menus. I opened mine with interest. The speedway burger I'd eaten earlier was feeling pretty lonely all by itself in the depths of my stomach.

"Order whatever you want, kid," Race told me. "But don't expect to make a habit of it. I don't win all the time."

"And it's a good thing," said Jim. "If you did, you'd probably wake up one morning to find my son camped out on your doorstep."

Robbie returned with a handful of fruit-shaped candy and shot his dad a sassy grin as he waited for Race to let him back into the booth.

"So how much is it worth to win a main event?" I asked, looking at Kasey.

"I believe it's around three hundred dollars this season."

"Cool. I guess I'll have the steak, then."

"Just one?" asked Race, swiping a lime green candy from the pile in front of Robbie. "Are you sure that's gonna be enough?"

While we were waiting for our food, Robbie slid a napkin and a red felt pen in front of Race.

"Draw something," he said.

"Like what?"

"Surprise me."

Race scribbled on the napkin. Within seconds a cartoon emerged of the black #1 Camaro stranded a few feet from the finish line. Steam shimmered up from its hood as Addamsen's fist shook from the driver's window.

Jim, who was watching over Race's shoulder, chuckled. "In your dreams," he said.

Race finished the sketch and pushed it toward Robbie.

"Cool," the kid said, a grin sliding over his face.

An image flashed momentarily through my mind. A pencil drawing of a 1970 Superbird. Something suspiciously like jealousy swelled inside me, but I smothered it. Why should I care who Race buddied up to? I eyeballed the little suck-up, but he was too busy studying the cartoon to notice.

"My kid must have a couple dozen of those damned things pinned on his wall at home," said Jim.

"When Race is a famous Winston Cup driver his drawings are gonna be worth a million dollars," Robbie informed us. He folded the napkin and stuck it in his pocket.

"In your dreams," I muttered, echoing his dad.

Our food came, and I dug into my steak, absently listening to the conversation. It had drifted to the topic of sponsorship. Drivers financed their addiction by weasling money out of business owners in exchange for plastering that company's name on their race car. Apparently, this wasn't something that was easy to do.

I looked at Kasey. "So what made a successful business woman such as yourself wanna team up with the likes of ol' Speed here?" I asked, waving my fork at Race.

Kasey toyed with a tomato in her chef's salad as she considered the question. "Oh, he just impressed me, once."

"Impressed you?" Jim quipped. "Race did that?" He looked at my uncle and shook his head.

"In the Enduro two years ago," said Kasey.

"Oh, yeah," Race said, "you decided to sponsor me that same night. That impressed you?"

"Hell, Morgan, I think that one even impressed Addamsen," said Jim.

I skewered my steak with my fork, lifting it and tearing a chunk off with my teeth. "What's an Enduro?"

Jim laughed. "Someone's idea of a bad joke, if ya ask me."

I glanced at Kasey, knowing she'd give me a real answer.

"It's a long race, usually about a hundred and fifty or two hundred laps," she said. "But the drivers aren't allowed to make any modifications to their cars. All they can do is strip them of the glass and interior."

"That's supposed to be impressive?"

"Not generally," Kasey said, "but it *is* an opportunity for the average person to race. And the purse is a thousand dollars."

"Radical," I said. "So, what happened?"

Kasey hesitated, casting a look at Race that was a little too sentimental to be purely professional. I wondered what the real story was between them. I had a pretty strong suspicion Race had the hots for her, but Kasey was harder to read.

"Well, your uncle was driving a Pinto—"

Laughter derailed my attempt to swallow, and a piece of steak caught in my throat.

"It might help if you chewed first," Race suggested.

"Thanks for the tip."

Kasey raised an eyebrow at me but continued her story. "He was driving a Pinto, and actually doing fairly well with it. Out of fifty cars, he and two others were the only ones on the lead lap. Race was in third place."

"In a Pinto." I shook my head.

"The fourth place car was two laps down," Kasey continued, "and the rest of the pack was even further back. There was really no reason why Race shouldn't have finished third. No one else could have caught up to him."

"But someone did," I guessed.

"Nah, kid, some over-anxious punk spun me out."

"On lap 198," Kasey added, "which meant there were only two laps left. The Pinto went sailing off the top of turn three and high-centered. Race managed to dislodge it by shifting into reverse, but when he tried to put it back in first, the linkage apparently jammed."

"So what did he do?"

"He finished the race in reverse."

"Yeah, right."

"She's telling the truth," said Jim.

"In reverse?"

Jim nodded.

"He couldn't get up to a competitive speed," Kasey said, "but he was two laps ahead, so it really didn't matter. All he had to do was keep out of the way of the remaining cars—there were about twenty still running—and finish the race."

"So, did he?"

"Almost. On the last lap, as Race was coming out of turn four, the fourth place car caught up with him. The driver tried to pass on the inside, but he came out of the corner a bit too fast and his car began to fishtail. He hit the Pinto in the right front fender. Race must have seen it coming because he steered into it. Instead of spinning him off to the side, the other car pushed him across the finish line."

"No way."

"It's true," Kasey said. "And if that wasn't dramatic enough, another driver came out of the turn, saw the checkered flag, and decided *he* was going to win it."

"He wasn't even on the same lap," Race added. "He just saw that flag and went after it like a bull."

"And?" I asked, directing the question at Kasey.

"This new car, a Chevelle, hit the water spilled by the car that ran into Race. It spun out and slammed both of them into the wall."

"Plastered that Pinto against the concrete like a bug on a windshield," Jim said.

"And it didn't explode?" I asked, remembering all those old stories I'd heard.

"No," Kasey said. "It didn't have to. Everyone in the crowd thought it was all over for Race, anyway."

"Yeah," Jim said, "those Pintos aren't much more than an engine wrapped in tin foil. And that was before the insurance

48

company started getting serious about making people put roll cages in Enduro cars."

"My Pinto had a roll cage," said Race, slightly insulted.

"Yeah," Jim said, "and that's the only reason you're still here. Hell, I bet they didn't even have to crush that thing when they got it to the wrecking yard."

Race laughed. "It wasn't *that* bad."

"It was bad enough," said Kasey, frowning. "The crowd let out this horrific roar, then the other cars reached the finish line, and it was worse than a demolition derby. When the dust and steam finally cleared, only two or three cars were still capable of moving.

"The Pinto's passenger side was wrapped around the front end of the Chevelle, and the driver's door had been flattened against the wall. With the poor lighting, the dust in the air, and the steam rising out of all the punctured radiators, no one could see what was happening."

"It was a regular zoo," Jim added.

"Well, obviously he didn't croak," I said.

"Of course he didn't *croak*." Kasey's eyes reflected her opinion of my cavalier remark. "The flagman and some other officials tried to get through the wreckage to the car. But before they could, Race crawled through the passenger window out onto the hood of the Chevelle. He stood up, gave the crowd that smart-aleck grin of his, and took a deep bow."

I looked at Race doubtfully. He shrugged in response.

"I had to do *something*. All those people were staring at me."

"It was a riot," Jim said. "The crowd loved it."

"I'd had my eye on Race for awhile, even though I'd originally intended to sponsor a car in a higher division," Kasey said. "It was plain he was a hard charger who had a real rapport with the fans. The Enduro clinched the deal. Anyone that crazy and determined to win deserved all the help I could give him. I went down to the pits at the end of the night and asked him if he wanted a sponsor."

"And all this time I thought it was because I was driving a Dodge," Race said.

"Well, that didn't hurt," Kasey admitted.

Race tipped his Pepsi glass at me. "Just so you'll know, having people track you down to offer you sponsorship doesn't happen very often in the racing world."

Like I cared. "You're crazy," I said, stealing one of his fries.

"Yeah," Race grinned. "And you know something? Your mom *knew* that when she sent you to live with me."

Robbie snickered.

"It woulda been a better story," I said, "if the Pinto had exploded."

Chapter 5

Race slept like a cat in a coma the next morning, but I woke up feeling like I'd swallowed a porcupine. It made no sense. There was nothing to envy. I didn't give a damn about racing, and it wasn't like my uncle lived a glamorous lifestyle. So why did I feel snarky about last night?

I fixed some breakfast then turned on MTV, not bothering to lower the volume when Ozzy cut in with *Bark at the Moon*. Race didn't twitch. Didn't anything faze him? I inhaled the cereal then retreated to my room to find something to alleviate my boredom.

Reading would've been my first choice, but none of the books I'd brought were new, and I wanted something fresh. Until I started school or figured out how to get to the public library, I was out of luck.

Nintendo would've been my second choice, but Mom had rendered the machine useless when she'd confiscated my games as punishment for drinking out of the milk carton. She was always over-reacting like that, and Dad never did anything to stop her. He'd just hide behind his newspaper while she reamed me a new one then grounded me for three weeks for not wiping up the orange juice I spilled on the counter.

I rummaged through my boxes in the closet and came up with a dartboard and a handful of shuriken. Cool. It had been a long time since I'd gotten any practice.

I hung the dartboard on the closet door, lit a cigarette, and stepped back to take aim. The expertly balanced oriental throwing star whizzed through the air, penetrating the board. *Thwack*!

The noise startled me, and for a second I hesitated. Not even my uncle could sleep though that. But when I thought about last night—how popular Race was, how everyone at the track seemed to love him—something dark stirred inside me and I *wanted* to wake him up. I followed with a second star, and then a third.

"What the hell's going on back there, Cody?"

"Nothin', Speed. Don't let it concern you." The darkness swelled as I thought about my uncle's flawless driving skills, and his hot crew chief, and little Robbie Davis worshiping the ground he walked on.

I threw another shuriken.

"Cody!"

I threw a few more.

"Please, kid. I'm trying to sleep."

"Don't let me stop ya, Speed."

"My name's not Speed."

A moment later, Race appeared in the doorway, looking ridiculous in only a pair of U of O Fighting Ducks boxers. His hair stuck up in tufts, and his eyes smoldered with annoyance.

I let fly with a shuriken before pulling the cigarette from between my lips. "What's wrong with Speed?" I asked, flicking the ash at a cereal-encrusted bowl on the dresser. "It's just as good a name as Race."

"God, kid, do you have to hassle me so early in the morning?" He glanced at my *Beer, it's not just for breakfast* T-shirt. "And don't you think you could find something a little more appropriate to wear?"

"Nothin' in your rules about a dress code," I said. "What the hell kind of name is Race, anyway?" I let loose with another star. It missed the board and penetrated halfway through the thin paneling of the closet door. Race winced.

"Grandma and Grandpa didn't actually *name* you that, did they?"

I knew they hadn't. But nobody would be caught dead with his real name, and I wanted to see him squirm when he said it.

"They named me Horatio," he said evenly. "Not that it's any of your damned business."

I turned around, giving him a look of undivided interest. "Horatio? Ho-*ra*-tio? Well, now. Isn't that original."

"Not especially. They've been naming the firstborn sons in our family that since God was a little boy. You're lucky Saundra's your mother, instead of your father."

"What?" And then I got it. The accident of one misplaced Y chromosome had spared me that fate and saddled him with it instead.

"Forget it," Race said. He'd regained his composure, and now looked more burned-out than pissed.

Somehow, the fact that I couldn't set him off made me want to do it that much more. I took one final drag off my cigarette and crushed it out in the bowl. "So," I said, "You score with Kasey yet?"

Race gaped at me like I'd shot a puppy. Then his mouth clamped shut and his jaw knotted tight. Bingo. Almost entirely by accident, I'd discovered his Kryptonite.

"Listen, you little—"

"Nope, I guess you haven't."

"—if you *ever* say anything like that around Kasey, you'll wish your parents had shipped you off to military school."

The surge of pleasure I got from his reaction would've been sweeter if it hadn't come with a side order of guilt. I glanced away. "Jeeze, dude. Don't get so excited."

"I'm serious, Cody."

"Okay, okay." Obviously he was completely gonzo about her. I shot another star at the dartboard. It missed.

"And what the hell do you think you're doing? My trailer might be a dump, but you don't have to make it worse. If you wanna play with your little stars, take 'em outside."

I glanced at him disdainfully as I stepped across the room to collect my weapons. "These are not 'little stars'," I said.

"They're shuriken. Don't you know anything about the martial arts?"

"No, but then I never expected you to know how to tune up a race car, either."

I wrestled a shuriken out of the door. The paneling squeaked and cracked as it pulled free. "What makes you think I *want* to know how to tune up a race car?"

Race didn't answer, but as he watched me retract the remaining weapon, the anger in his expression drained away and a sort of understanding took its place. "I guess you're really into that martial arts stuff, huh?"

I shrugged.

Race contemplated me for a few seconds then turned and left the room. He came back almost immediately with the Yellow Pages.

"What's that?" I asked.

Race flipped it over in his hands, examining both covers. "Looks like a phone book," he said, holding it out to me.

"Oh, real perceptive, dude. What do you expect me to do with it?"

For a second I was sure he was going to suggest something vulgar, but he resisted the obvious, even though I'd left myself wide open.

"Look up a karate school. Sign up for classes."

For once, my rapier wit failed me. I stood staring at him, momentarily stumped, and then a surge of anger welled up. How the hell could he go on being nice to me?

Part of me wanted to tell him to piss off, but I'd been begging my parents to let me study karate for years. Mom flat out refused, saying it was too violent, and Dad wouldn't cross her even though he thought she was being ridiculous.

"You know how much that would piss off my mom?" I asked.

Race grinned wickedly. "That makes it even better."

*   *   *

Left alone in the bedroom, I studied the torn, graffiti-embellished book. Could it be that easy? Just look up a school and make the call? What if he was messing with my head?

I couldn't believe he was offering me something I'd always wanted. Why would he do that? All I'd done was give him shit. And then it hit me. Race was gonna go on being nice no matter what I did. That's just who he was. The kind of guy who thought to buy a sandwich for his crew chief, and took the time to draw a cartoon for a little kid, and gave advice to a competitor, even though it might bite him in the ass later. The kind of guy who'd take in his loser nephew, sight unseen.

I dropped down on the bed, flipped through the phone book to the "k's," and spent the next fifteen minutes comparing ads for karate schools. When Race reappeared in the doorway, he was fully dressed and munching a Twinkie.

"Don't you ever eat real food for breakfast?" I asked. But this time it was an honest question, not an accusation.

"Not if I can avoid it. Twinkies are fast energy. Just what I need in the morning."

"I thought that's what coffee was for."

"Can't stand the stuff. That's Kasey's poison." Race licked sugar-infused shortening off his fingers. "I'm gonna be changing the oil in the van if you wanna go in the front room and make some calls." He turned and left me alone.

I phoned several karate schools. One had beginner classes starting the first of June and was located in the University neighborhood. I knew that was pretty close to the trailer park, so I jotted down the information and went outside.

Race was lying under the front of the van. I sat down beside him in the gravel.

"Find a class?" he asked.

"Yeah. I guess I need to go check it out."

"We can do that." Race reached up to twist an orange canister. Oil oozed over the sides and trickled down his wrist into the pan below. I gave him one of the rags at my feet. With a look of surprise, he accepted it and wiped his hands.

"What made you think I'd want karate lessons?" I asked as Race twisted a bolt into a hole on the bottom of the oil pan and snugged it up with a wrench.

"I dunno. What made you think I'd want a grease rag?" He worked a fresh orange canister out of its cardboard box and screwed it into place.

A few long moments passed in silence as I arm-wrestled my pride. I hated giving in, hated being wrong, but how could you go on slugging a guy who kept turning the other cheek?

"Sorry about giving you shit."

The apology came out as a mumble, but Race managed to decipher it. "That's okay. I know it can't be easy, leaving home and moving in with a stranger."

I took a deep breath and blew it out, steadying myself against the emotional ripple his empathy caused. "So . . . did it take you a long time to learn this stuff?"

"What, changing the oil? Nah, that kind of thing is pretty basic. But I've been hanging around racers and working on their cars since I was ten."

"Huh." I stood up and leaned against the driver's door, running the toe of one of my Converse high tops through the gravel till I'd dug a groove.

Race wiggled out from under the van and lifted the hood. One by one, he opened several bottles of oil and poured them into the engine. "Kasey's coming over tonight," he said as he finished with the last of them. "You wanna go see a movie?"

"Wouldn't you two rather go alone?"

"I would, but Kasey wouldn't. And I don't mind you coming along."

I pushed the gravel back into place with the side of my sneaker. "You really like her, huh?"

Race glanced at me a little suspiciously as he stuffed the empty bottles into a plastic bag. "Kid, even if I do it doesn't matter. She's not interested. She's my friend and my sponsor, and that's it."

"You ever ask her out?"

"Are you kidding? She'd shut me down in a heartbeat."

Thinking of the way Kasey had looked at him when she was telling her story the night before, I wasn't so sure. Not that I was gonna argue. "Well, if she's coming over, we better clean the place up."

"Definitely," Race agreed.

We spent the afternoon trying to make the trailer a little less rank.

"I'm not doing this for you, y'know," I told Race as I washed the dishes. "I'm just embarrassed to have a cool chick like Kasey know I live in a dump like this."

"I understand completely."

The place still looked pathetic at seven o'clock when the Charger pulled into the driveway, but at least you could see the floor.

"Wow," Kasey said as she sat down. "I don't think I've ever seen this chair without a pile of laundry on it."

"Actually," said Race, "it's a little better looking with the laundry. I need some new furniture."

"Dude, you need a new house," I said.

The minute the two of them got comfortable, the conversation turned to racing. They might as well have been speaking Klingon.

"Ah, hell," I said, flopping down at the far end of the couch and leaning back into the cushions. "Am I gonna have to hear about race cars again all night? I thought we were going to a movie."

"We are," Race said. "It doesn't start till seven forty-five."

Sighing, I slid down until my butt was balanced on the very edge of the couch.

"Kid, if you're that bored, you can go wash my van."

I considered flipping him off but didn't want to be that crass in front of Kasey. "I think I'll go down by the river." The previous morning I'd noticed that there was a trail leading along the bank. I'd wanted to explore it, but there hadn't been time before we'd left for the speedway.

"Well, just stay within earshot," Race said. "We're gonna leave in about half an hour."

Outside, I saw a kid pushing Matchbox cars around the roots of a cottonwood tree directly across from the driveway. He looked Robbie Davis's age, maybe eight or nine.

"Hey," he said. "I haven't seen you before. Did you just move in?"

I wasn't in the mood to be chatted up by a third-grader, but you can't bite a little kid's head off. "I'm staying with my uncle," I told him, jerking a thumb over my shoulder at the trailer.

"Race?"

"Yeah."

"He's cool," the kid said, sitting back on his heels. "He gives me all his cans and bottles to take back for the deposit."

Now why didn't that surprise me? I told the kid I'd see him around then continued toward the river.

As dumpy as the trailer park was, there was still something wild and soothing about the stretch of the Willamette that ran behind it. I slipped along the bank, pushing my way through the shrubs and clumps of fern that intruded on the narrow pathway. Above, clouds clustered, shafts of sunlight glinting against their sinister gray. The scent of impending rain and the sweet smell of cottonwood hung in the air, pushed along by a faint, damp wind.

I hoped that if I got far enough downstream, out of sight of the bridge that crossed the river into Springfield, I might find a peaceful retreat. A place I could sit and read without being discovered. A place where I could pull out my notebook and engage in a little creativity.

The truth was, reading was only half my secret. The thing I really kept under wraps was my ambition to be a writer. Since the summer after sixth grade, I'd spent a good part of my free time messing around with short stories and song parodies— stuff like Weird Al sang. I'd have been mortified if anyone found out. Mom had hassled me enough when I was younger for being a geek. She had this idea that creative, bookish guys were destined for a pathetic life of working minimum wage jobs and having their asses kicked regularly by real men.

There was only one person I'd talked to about my writing— my English teacher last fall. After he'd shoveled on the praise about the first couple essays I'd turned in, I mustered up my courage and showed him one of my stories. It took him most of fall term to get it back to me. Even then, he didn't give me any real feedback. He just corrected the spelling and grammar in hateful red pen, taking all the art out of it. And he put the dialog in proper English, not getting that I wanted to write it the way my characters would really say it. When I tried to explain that to him, he said, "You have to learn the rules before you can break them, Cody." The memory of it made me feel like I'd been caught walking buck-naked through the school auditorium.

I made it about a quarter mile downstream before I realized it was time to be getting back. A couple places looked promising for a hangout—a cluster of boulders, forming giant stepping-stones down the bank, and a downed tree, which jutted out into the river. Even though things were looking up a little with my uncle, it was a relief to know there was someplace I could escape to.

As I neared the trailer park, the curses and shouts of a fight overpowered the whisper of the Willamette. I scrambled up the bank to see the kid who'd been playing under the cottonwood getting the snot beat out of him by a guy as big as me. With as much trouble as I'd been in, I thought twice about getting involved. Somebody else's fight is somebody else's problem. But I hate bullies. Being on the left side of the bell curve for sheer bulk, I'd gotten clobbered too many times when I was younger.

The big kid had the little one backed up against a tree. Most of the real damage had already been done. Now he was just tormenting him, poking him in the shoulder and ribs with two rigid fingers to emphasize his threats.

"Hey, leave him alone," I said.

The bully, gripping the bloody T-shirt of his victim, shot me a disbelieving look. "You gonna make me?"

"Only if you ask nice."

The kid sneered, shifting his weight slightly to include me in his circle of menace. With prey-like instinct, the little guy took advantage of his distraction and pulled a Houdini.

"Son of a bitch!"

I should've guessed that, deprived of his quarry, the bully would turn his aggression on me. Still, when he head-butted me in the ribs, the attack caught me off guard. Rage soared up like a summer squall as we hit the ground, floundering in the dirt. I unloaded on the kid, slamming my fist into his cheek, his ribs, his eye. Shouts filled the air around us, but they barely registered. The bully got in a few good licks before I felt someone pulling me away.

"What the hell do you think you're doing?"

Race's voice cut through my fury. The bully, restrained by another guy, was just close enough to catch me in the shin with the toe of his Nike. I lunged against my uncle's grip but wasn't able to break free.

"Damn it, kid, lay off!" Race shouted.

"I didn't start it!"

"I don't care. That's no excuse for beating up a twelve-year-old!"

Race's words drained the rest of the fight out of me.

"He's *twelve*?" I'd been getting my ass kicked by a sixth-grader? I shook off Race's grip and wiped my nose with the back of my hand. It came away bloody. Humiliation rolled over me in a cold, sick wave. Then I saw Kasey and discovered a whole new meaning for the word.

"Get back to the trailer," Race said. The disappointment in his eyes hit harder than anything that stupid kid had thrown at me. How could he be so ready to believe the worst?

"But—"

"Now!"

He was just like everyone else. Washing his hands of me, not even waiting for an explanation. The crappiest thing about it was that I should've known better. I'd sold my soul for a few karate lessons, and he'd wadded it up and tossed it in the trash.

"Piss off!" I said.

"Cody—"

Turning toward the river, I ran.

Chapter 6

The path along the river had been tricky enough to navigate while walking. At a full run, I tripped over rocks and lurched down the muddy bank, soaking myself to the knees. None of that slowed me down. Neither did Race shouting my name, or the dampness in my eyes that meant I was close to losing control in a way I hadn't since I was little.

Panting hard, I finally collapsed against the rough bark of a Douglas fir, steeling myself against tears that I'd be damned if I let fall. I cursed myself for being so weak. Much as I'd scorned Race for his softness, it was me who was the real wimp. Mom used to ride me about it all the time. "Big boys don't cry, Cody," she'd say whenever I started sniveling.

The crazy thing was, stuff like falling off my bike or not getting my own way didn't faze me. I just seemed to feel things nobody else did. It was like my emotions were an instrument the universe could play at will. Every time I saw a dead animal beside the road, or heard my mom screaming at my dad, I'd get all weepy.

"Stop being such a baby," Mom would say.

Somehow I'd gotten a grip by the time I started school. Kids wouldn't put up with a crybaby, and since I was short and scrawny, bullies already had enough reason to single me out. But the feelings never stopped, I just found ways to disguise them. Getting mad was easiest. No one questioned the manliness of a guy who lost his temper, and it was satisfying to channel that onslaught of emotion into a good rage.

The blood drying on my face started to itch, so I stumbled to the river. Wet jeans clung to my calves as I squatted to wash. Even though my shoes and pant legs were saturated, I wasn't about to go back. Not with Kasey there. Instead, I slumped against the Douglas fir and stared out at the water.

I couldn't believe I'd done it again. Let down my guard. Got suckered in. How pathetic could I be? For over an hour I sat there, hating myself and wondering what to do next. After what had happened, I couldn't stay.

Eventually, a plan began to form. I'd pack my stuff, sit tight until Race fell asleep, and slip out. I could hitchhike south. Go someplace cool like L.A.

I waited until dark before returning to the trailer, then snuck in through the back door—the one that led directly into my bedroom. Race heard me and came down the hall, but the confrontation I expected didn't happen. Instead, he stood outside my door, not even pushing it open.

"Cody?" he said. There was no anger in his voice, just a high, questioning note.

"Go away."

Race hesitated, then his footsteps retreated to the front room.

Once I was sure he was gone, I jammed my writing note-books, some clothes, and my favorite books into my duffle bag. Then I pulled out *The Outsiders* and read it for the fiftieth time. It seemed like forever before Race finally turned off the TV.

After giving it another half hour to be safe, I eased open the back door. Cool night drifted in, smelling of cut grass and river mud. The rain that had threatened since late afternoon still hung back, but something in the wind told me it wouldn't be long before it fell. I stepped cautiously down the squeaky stairs and made for the road outside the trailer park, where I'd seen a sign pointing to I-5.

The hike to the freeway turned out to be only about a mile and a half. Getting there was the easy part. Catching a ride was a bitch. I stood at the base of the southbound on-ramp for half an hour, but the few people out at twelve-thirty on Sunday night didn't trouble themselves on my account. At last, an old dude in a pickup stopped and offered to take me as far as Creswell. With rain beginning to spot the asphalt I didn't bother to ask where that was. Only about ten miles south of Eugene, it turned out. Fifteen minutes later I was back on the side of I-5, rain pelting me with a vigor that Race's shower could only wish for.

I started walking. My leather jacket kept most of me dry, but my hair and shoes soaked up the water. Cars whizzed by, trailing red streaks that shimmered on wet asphalt before fading into the night. No one even slowed down. Still, I didn't let myself think this might be a bad idea. Sure, it was wet and cold now, but by this time tomorrow I'd be in sunny southern California.

Another hour and a half passed as I trudged southward. Finally, I spotted a sign announcing a rest area. I could sleep there and catch a ride in the morning.

Finding a place to lie down in that dripping, deserted scrap of civilization was a challenge. The bathroom was dry and relatively warm, but it reeked. The map kiosk offered a little protection from the rain, but it was too exposed. Finally I decided on a hemlock about a hundred yards from the parking lot. The spreading, densely-needled branches almost swept the ground, offering a decent amount of shelter. I curled up under it using my duffle bag for a pillow. Within five seconds, I knew how much sleeping on the ground was gonna suck.

Shit, maybe this whole idea had been a mistake. But how could I have stayed? Race had bitten my head off, jumping to conclusions just like Dad. If I hadn't left, he would've thrown me out anyway. Anyone could've seen that from the look on his face. At least this way it was my decision.

You'd think that at 2 a.m. a person could sleep anywhere, but it didn't happen. My body ached from the fight, the ground dug into my hip and shoulder, and my feet felt like I'd been wading through a Slurpee machine. Around me, darkness closed in despite the lights in the parking lot. The thought of all that farmland and wilderness bordering the rest area gave me the creeps. Who knew what kind of wildlife was out there, waiting to snack on a city boy? Cursing the chain of events that had led me to be shivering under a damn tree in the middle of nowhere, I curled into a ball and waited for the sun to come up.

A wave of anger rolled over me as I thought of my mother in Phoenix, no doubt snuggled up in some warm, cozy bed. I hoped she suffocated in her goose down comforter. I hoped she flunked out of the bartending school Dad said she'd enrolled in. The idea of her lending a sympathetic ear to some wasted boozehound made me laugh. She never listened to *my* problems. For years now her attitude had been, *you've got a roof over your head, food in your belly, and clothes on your back. Don't expect me to take a personal interest in your life, too.*

Resentment bubbled and roiled as I remembered all her screw-ups. But a tiny, honest voice told me to get real. I wouldn't care so much about the mean things she'd done if I didn't have good things to compare them to.

When I was really little, maybe two or three, Mom had been my best friend. She'd been so beautiful, so charming, and I'd been willing to do anything to make her happy. Every night when she tucked me into bed, she'd snuggle close and tell me stories. She didn't read them from a book. She made them up— fairy tales in which she was the beautiful queen and I was her brave and noble prince. But somewhere along the line that changed. I guess I stopped being cute and sweet enough for her. Or maybe I wasn't brave enough. Maybe she was right, and I was too much like my dad. By the time I was in kindergarten, it seemed like I couldn't do anything right. I was too noisy, too thoughtless, too moody. Every once in awhile the old magic would come back, but then I'd do something to set her off again.

For years I tried to win back that closeness, stuffing my feelings away, giving her treasures I'd found, setting the table without being told. But none of it worked. Even now there was a part of me that hoped she'd wake up one morning and start loving me again. Sometimes, for a second, I almost thought she had. But whenever we started to form a real connection, she made some offhand comment that told me she didn't have the first clue about who I was. *Since when aren't you good at math? You've always loved math!*

I tried to sweep the thoughts of her from my mind, but they swarmed back like mosquitoes, only scattering when the sky started to brighten in the east and I finally dozed off.

Traffic pulling into the parking lot woke me a couple of hours later. The sun had emerged, coaxing wisps of steam from the asphalt. Stiff and cold, I brushed hemlock needles off my clothes. The mirror in the bathroom was one of those sheets of polished metal that don't give you a real image, but I could see that sleep had smashed my hair into a ridiculous wedge. Wetting the gel in it, I tried to get it to stand up and arch the way it should.

I wondered if Race had figured out I was gone yet. He'd be getting up fairly early to enroll me in school. What would he think when he found out I wasn't in my room? Would he consider himself lucky, or would he get that hurt look in his eyes? Maybe it wasn't too late to go back. Maybe . . . no. I wouldn't suck up to him. I'd made my decision and I was gonna stick with it.

My empty stomach protested as I scouted the parking lot. Hunger had become my mortal enemy way back in seventh grade, but there wasn't anything I could do about it now. I spotted a young guy in a battered Honda Civic and hit him up for a ride. He was a college student at Southern Oregon

University, on his way back to school after a wild weekend in Eugene, and though he proved a little too chatty, at least he didn't ask stupid questions. Unfortunately, something was messed up with the engine of the Civic and it wouldn't do more than fifty. It was almost noon by the time we got to Ashland. My shoes still hadn't dried out, and I was ready to pass out from the gnawing in my gut.

I broke my only twenty for lunch. What was I gonna do for money when I got to LA? Would anybody hire me? No way could I pass for sixteen. Doubt swelled in my chest, but I forced it down. It was warm in southern California. I could sleep outside, maybe find work in the orchards and fields where the winter produce grew. I called up my resolve and hiked back to the freeway.

A frustrating hour passed as I stood along I-5, fatigue pulling at my outstretched arm. The sky, which had started the morning clear and blue, was clouding over. I lit a smoke and started walking. I didn't know how far it was to L.A., but waiting for a ride sure wasn't cutting it.

By now Race would've called my dad. Maybe he'd even taken my boxes to the Greyhound station to ship back to Portland. He must be relieved to have me gone. Hadn't he said his life would be a lot easier without a teenager in it? Now he could get back to his regular routine. He wouldn't have to worry about the beer disappearing from his fridge, or some punk kid embarrassing him in front of his wanna-be girlfriend.

Dad wouldn't be the least bit surprised I'd screwed up. He'd probably already bought a bus ticket to Colorado. And when Mom found out—if she bothered to talk to me at all—she'd tell me what a loser I was for blowing yet another opportunity. An opportunity she'd slaved away to give me.

One of those old Jeeps that look like a jacked-up station wagon on steroids pulled to the shoulder, kicking up gravel. It sported a homemade camouflage paint job in various tones of green and brown. I practically needed a ladder to crawl up into the front seat. Once inside, I almost wished I'd stuck with walking. The driver, a crew-cut guy in Army fatigues, wore a knife the length of my forearm on his thigh. The back end of the vehicle was loaded with ammunition and freeze-dried food. Three guns that looked like they were meant for hunting critters of the two-legged persuasion sat snuggly in a rifle rack that straddled the rear windows on the driver's side. If I hadn't been afraid of breaking my leg on the plunge to the ground, I might've bailed right then and there.

"Where ya headed?" the guy asked.

"L.A."

"Bad idea. The big cities are gonna be the first hit."

I didn't know how to respond to that, so I kept my mouth shut.

For the next thirty minutes, the guy lectured me on getting away from civilization if I planned on living through the nuclear meltdown that was sure to come any day. I kept my hand on the armrest, inches from the door handle, just in case. I'd read that these survivalists tended to be loners, but I didn't want to take a chance of being whisked off into the woods to live on nuts and berries.

In Yreka, a miniscule town maybe twenty miles south of the Oregon-California border, the dude exited the freeway and pulled to the side of the off-ramp.

"You're on your own from here," he said. "Be careful. No telling what kind of pervs and weirdos you're gonna run across hitchhiking."

I couldn't have said it better myself.

Three forty-three, and I'd only made 200 miles. At this rate, it would take a week to get to LA. I was starving again, so I bought a small bag of Doritos at a gas station, feeling vaguely uneasy as I parted with the money.

Had Race even bothered to look for me? Maybe he'd just gone to the shop to work on that roll cage, grateful to have me out of his hair. I thought of the disappointed expression on his face when he'd broken up the fight. I was used to looks like that, but Race's had been a sucker-punch.

I shook my head. Why should I care what he thought? He was just a two-bit race car driver at a speedway no one ever heard of. He lived in a dump rats would run screaming from and lacked the sense to find a real job. Hell, he didn't even have the guts to tell his crew chief he liked her.

I trudged down the freeway on-ramp, wondering if I was pushing my luck. That last ride had been freaky and, growing up in Portland, I knew there were people even weirder and more dangerous than that. Maybe I should turn around before something really crazy happened. But a bob-tail semi eased onto the shoulder, so I climbed into the cab.

The driver, a pot-bellied guy with a scraggily beard, wore a ball cap with a black and silver race car embroidered on the front. "Where ya goin'?" he asked.

"L.A." Somehow, there wasn't as much resolve in my voice as there had been when I'd said it earlier.

"I can take you as far as Sacramento."

"Sounds good."

The truck driver turned out to be the quiet type. The country music I had to endure blaring from his radio seemed a worthwhile trade-off for that. I kicked back, relieved to sit and enjoy the scenery. I-5 wound crazily through the mountains in a series of twisties that angled either uphill or downhill but were never flat.

My stomach rumbled and I glanced at my watch. Five-twenty. Was Race still at the shop? Maybe he was working on the Dart. I'd forgotten to ask Kasey what the big deal was about him driving a Dodge. Now I'd never know.

I thought about the smart-assed smirk Race had given me when he handed me the phone book the day before. Too bad about those karate lessons. I could've leveled that stupid kid in five seconds if I'd known a little karate.

My stomach growled again. As the hunger grew it reminded me of my dwindling funds. Maybe I should've raided my uncle's wallet before I left. Just thinking about that made guilt prickle my conscience. It hadn't bothered me to take my dad's money, but stealing from Race would've been like kicking a dog.

I glanced over at the truck driver. The car on his hat displayed the number 3. Just above it, the name Dale Earnhardt was stitched in silver thread.

"You a stock car racing fan?" I asked. Spurred on by doubt or loneliness, the words slipped out of my mouth before I realized I was gonna say them.

It was like flipping a switch. Mr. Quiet launched into a blow-by-blow of the previous day's Winston Cup event, whatever *that* was.

"How 'bout you?" he asked. "Got a favorite driver?"

I shrugged. "I don't know much about it. My uncle races, though."

"Yeah? Where at?"

"Eugene Speedway."

The trucker scratched his beard. "Never heard of it. He any good?"

"He won two races Saturday night. His crew chief told me he's second in the points."

That earned an appreciative nod. "You watch him race a lot?"

"Nah, this week was the first time. I prob'ly won't go back."

"Didn't do anything for you, huh?"

I shrugged again. I wasn't really sure *how* I felt about it. Much as all the waiting around had sent my brain into hibernation, there was something about seeing the Dart slam past that spinning car and leave a streak of paint on the wall that had given me a rush. Maybe talking about it would help me sort things out. I described the main event to the trucker.

"Sounds like your uncle's quite a driver."

"I guess. But he's crazy. He eats frozen Twinkies for breakfast, and he's got a girl for a crew chief." I was surprised to feel a smile spread over my face as I remembered how Race had neglected to tell me Kasey was a woman. One thing I had to admit—my uncle didn't lack a sense of humor.

"So, you got kin down south?" the trucker asked.

"Not really."

"Just strikin' out on your own, huh?"

I glanced at him uneasily, wondering if he was gonna bust me. "Pretty much."

The trucker nodded. "Tell me more about this uncle of yours. He sounds like quite a character."

Since there was nothing else to do, I humored him, relating everything I knew about Race, Kasey, and the guys at the speedway. The more I talked, the more I realized that some part of me wondered what was gonna happen to them. Would Race take the points lead? Would he get up the nerve to tell Kasey how he felt about her? And what about Addamsen? Was he gonna make good on his threat to pull something nasty next week?

"How'd you end up with your uncle, anyway?" asked the trucker. It was the type of question I usually ignored. But something about his friendliness, or maybe the fact that I knew I'd never see him again, led me to tell him the whole story.

"Shame it didn't work out for you," he said.

"Yeah, I guess."

"Did you try to explain about the fight?"

"No."

"Maybe he would've understood."

"I doubt it." But as I thought back to last night, when Race had stood outside my door, I realized the trucker might have a point. Race hadn't sounded mad. He'd sounded worried.

We rumbled along for several miles without speaking.

"You know," the guy said finally, "It strikes me that someone like your uncle probably wouldn't ask too many questions if you were to have a change of heart."

"I can't go back."

The trucker let my statement hang there unchallenged. On the radio a country singer wailed about his lost love.

"Everyone makes a bad decision now and again," the truck driver said after a few more miles. "Only time it gets to be a problem is when you don't admit to it and set things right. Be a damned shame if you blew your one chance at something good because of misplaced pride."

"You don't know what you're talking about."

"Don't I?" he glanced at me across the cab of his truck. "You think you're the first kid to ever run away?"

I turned toward the passenger window, staring down at Lake Shasta, which stretched out beneath the bridge we were crossing.

"I left home when I was thirteen," the trucker said. "Knew from the minute I set foot out the door that it was a mistake, but it took me two whole days to come to my senses and go back. Can't imagine where I'd be now if I hadn't done that." He hesitated, letting the words sink in. "In about ten, fifteen minutes we'll be in Redding. If you're interested, I could probably hook you up with a northbound ride."

The lake disappeared behind us. Trees flashed by, firs and pines giving way to oaks as the elevation dropped. The trucker seemed to feel he'd made his point, and he didn't say anything else.

He was probably right about Race. My uncle wasn't the type to rub a person's nose in their mistakes. Maybe I'd given up on him too soon. The fact was, I was tired. Tired of fighting, tired of always having to act tough, tired of being on the road. Just once I wanted to be able to let down my guard.

I thought of how Race had volunteered to take me when the rest of the family couldn't be bothered. How he'd held his temper and stayed friendly no matter how hard I'd pushed. If there was anyone I could trust it had to be him.

"I guess it wouldn't hurt to try," I said. "California's not going anywhere."

When we got to Redding the trucker found a driver who was headed up to Medford and didn't mind giving me a ride.

"You might be able to find someone there who can give you a lift the rest of the way to Eugene," he said, slipping me a twenty, in case I ran out of cash. "Good luck with your uncle. You mark my words, he's gonna be glad to see you."

But when I got to Medford I found myself stranded. Everyone I approached at the truck stop was either done for the night, headed south, or skittish about giving a kid a ride. After a few tries I lost my nerve and started second-guessing my decision. What if Race didn't want me back? What if he stuck me on the first bus to Portland?

I grabbed a burger in the truck stop restaurant then stepped out into the parking lot. Daylight had given way to dusk and a light mist chilled the air. After walking back to the interstate, I had to make a decision. North or South?

I headed down the northbound off-ramp and stuck out my thumb. In spite of what the trucker had said, I worried I was setting myself up for disappointment again. Even someone as soft as Race would have to be crazy to give me another chance. But foolish as I felt, I stood there in the growing drizzle, waiting for a ride.

I was still standing there half an hour later, only now it was pouring. I looked up at the big green sign above me. Exit 30.

The one in Eugene had read 189. Almost a hundred and sixty miles. That would be a long walk.

Water from my hair dripped under the collar of my leather jacket and trickled down the back of my T-shirt. I didn't know if I could put up with another night like the last. My shoes hadn't dried out fully until after three o'clock, and between the fight and sleeping on the ground I still felt stiff and sore. Maybe I should call Race. I could stand here all night and not get another ride. Would he drive all that way, though? Maybe he'd tell me to get lost.

I waited another twenty minutes, but no one stopped. Finally I turned around and headed back to the truck stop. My cold, wet fingers fumbled through my duffle bag for the notebook where I'd written Race's number. I had to force myself to dial the phone. What if he wasn't home? What if he hung up on me? I almost hung up myself after the second ring, but before I could, Race answered.

"Hello?"

I couldn't get my voice to work.

"Cody, is that you?"

"Yeah."

"Where are you?"

"Medford."

The line went momentarily quiet, then, "Want me to come get you?"

In spite of my hopes, in spite of Race's kindness, it was hard to believe those words. "You . . . you would?"

"Of course, kid. You think I'd just leave you there?"

I didn't know what to think. "What about Dad?"

"What about him?"

"Isn't he pissed about me taking off?"

"Nah, he doesn't know. I was hoping you'd come back and we could pretend it never happened."

My throat went tight. After all I'd done, he still hadn't given up on me.

"Tell me where you are," Race said, "and I'll be there as soon as I can."

That was it. No lecture, no demands for better behavior in the future. I gave him the exit number and the name of the truck stop.

While I waited I sat in the restaurant, writing about the day in my notebook and feeling totally relieved. Since I no longer had to worry about money, I stuffed myself with pie and drank cup after cup of coffee. I remembered Race saying he couldn't stand the stuff. It wasn't my favorite thing, either, but at least it was hot and they gave you free refills.

"Ready to go?"

I looked up, startled. It had only been two hours. I'm no math whiz, but it wasn't any trick to figure that Race must've done close to eighty to get there so fast. Was it just his racer's instincts coming out, or was he that anxious to see me?

His dark eyes peered into mine, trying to figure out if this was for real. Then, shaking his head at the four plates flecked with crumbs, he picked up the bill.

"Let's go. It's late."

The van was warm when I climbed into the passenger seat. I had to slam the door twice before it latched. Settling back against the well-worn vinyl, I rested my feet on the dash.

Race started the engine. The wiper blades squeaked lightly over the rain-sprinkled windshield and Jimmy Buffett, having found his way back into the stereo, reminisced about being the son of a son of a sailor. I guess Race must've felt pretty comfortable around me because he sang along. Or at least he tried to. His voice held all the appeal of a spoon in a garbage disposal.

"So . . . do you, like . . . want me to apologize or something?" I asked.

Race signaled his turn onto I-5 then glanced across the cab. "Do you want *me* to?"

"What for?"

"For not listening to you. Marty told me what happened."

"Marty?"

"The little kid you were sticking up for yesterday."

I snorted and turned away. "It wasn't any big deal."

"Maybe not, but I could've given you a chance to explain. It just threw me to see you whaling on a little kid."

"He wasn't that little."

"No. I guess I tend to forget that, since I know he's only twelve." Race cast me a sympathetic look. "I'm sorry, Cody. I saw you laying into him and lost it. You might act like an obnoxious jerk sometimes, but it shocked me to think of you as a bully. I should have known you'd have more integrity than that."

Integrity. Nobody had used that word in reference to me before. I let my head fall back against the seat. This was so weird. I'd been expecting a lecture, and instead I'd gotten an apology.

"It's no biggie," I said.

"It is to me. The last thing I want to do is act like my father."

I glanced over at him. "Grandpa's a real hardass, huh?"

"You might say that."

The bitterness behind the comment was so far from Race's normal easy-going nature that for a second all I could do was stare at him. I didn't know my grandpa very well. We'd stopped doing the holiday thing in Eugene the year after Race had drawn the Superbird for me. Dad had put his foot down for what must have been the only time in his life, saying he didn't want to drive a hundred miles twice a year just to eat turkey or open presents. Mom still visited to bum money or go shopping with Grandma, but she never took me. If it hadn't been for the trek Grandma made to Portland each summer to see me, I wouldn't have had any contact with my grandparents at all.

"I haven't talked to my folks in five years," Race said. Even across the dim expanse of the cab, I could see a faint flicker in the muscle of his jaw. "Dad was always a tyrant, but when he cut off my college fund because I wanted to study art instead of business, it was the last straw."

"So you dropped out?"

"Nah, I transferred to Lane Community College and put myself through the graphic design program. Took me three years to get a two-year degree. It humbles me to think Kasey got her bachelor's in engineering in the same amount of time."

"Wow."

"Yeah, Kasey's a regular genius."

I studied the dark highway in front of us. It was late now, after eleven-thirty. Traffic on the interstate was sparse.

"What about Grandma?" I asked. "She seems kinda strict, but I never got that she was mean."

Race gave a caustic little grunt. "Let's just say she always does what's proper, no matter how it affects anyone else."

I knew exactly what he meant. Grandma was totally caught up in appearances—an uptight, high-society woman who knew her position in life and never failed to act accordingly. If any warmth lurked beneath her drill-sergeant posture, I hadn't seen it.

For a good ten miles, we rode in silence. "Race?" I said finally.

"Yeah?"

"Why'd you let me come live with you?"

For a second I thought he wasn't gonna answer. He stared out the windshield, his face faintly lit by the glow of the instruments in the dash.

"I guess I didn't want you to go through what I had to," he said. "The family made my life hell when I was a kid. When I found out Saundra might be doing the same thing to you, I couldn't turn away."

"Is that why you've been putting up with my crap?"

"Pretty much."

The white lines on the freeway flashed by. Jimmy Buffett was now wishing he had a pencil thin mustache.

"Maybe I've been cutting you slack because I figured with Saundra for a parent, you had good reason to be angry and defensive." Race glanced across the cab of the van. "Look, I know she's your mom and you care about her, so I probably shouldn't run my mouth, but if it was up to me, I wouldn't trust her to raise a stray dog, let alone a kid."

"I don't care about her," I corrected. "You can say whatever you want."

Race choked off a laugh. "Sorry, but I don't believe that. I remember what she's like." His eyes locked briefly on mine before he returned his attention to the road. "Saundra was the coolest, most charming big sister a guy could ever want. But she was Daddy's Little Princess, and she squashed me like a bug every chance she got."

I gaped at my uncle. He'd been through it, too? No one ever seemed to get that while Mom looked perfect on the outside, she was like a beautifully painted Easter egg that had been left behind the TV for three months. I could hardly believe Race understood.

"It sucks," I admitted, my voice so quiet it got lost in the murmur of the engine.

"Well, you can't change her, kid, but you can damned sure refuse to let her change you."

Leaning my head against the passenger window, I puzzled over what he meant by that. How could Mom change me? She was over a thousand miles away.

Chapter 7

While it was no happily-ever-after when we got back to Eugene, over the next week Race and I managed to fall into a pattern that both of us could live with. I started school—which was torture since I was the new kid—and he worked. Then in the evenings he put in a few hours at the shop. Even though he gave me the option of staying home, I usually went with him. I could do my homework there just as easily as at the trailer, and it gave me an excuse to see Kasey. Sometimes Jim or Denny would drop by. They were both easy to like, but for different reasons. Jim had a wicked sense of humor, while Denny was quiet and radiated a calm, solid sort of vibe, maybe because he was older.

When he wasn't working on his own car, Race spent the evening hours earning money. Now that he had the roll cage finished, he was lettering some guy's Super Stock. Envy needled me as I watched his brushstrokes transform into a recognizable logo, and I wondered if I'd ever be able to write stories with that kind of confidence and talent.

Though I wasn't sucking up to Race, I stopped going out of my way to piss him off. Not that I didn't end up rattling his cage almost daily. Like Wednesday afternoon, when I took off and left the trailer unlocked. I didn't see why it was any big deal—I was only down by the river—but Race reacted like I'd left a big welcome sign for every thief in the neighborhood. As if anybody would want his crap.

Sometimes irritating Race wasn't completely unintentional. He was just so damned gullible I couldn't resist doing stuff to get him going. Thursday was a prime example, when he was late coming home from the shop.

"Oh good, you're here," I said as he walked though the door. "You can pay for the pizza."

"Pizza?"

"Yeah. I ordered one for dinner, since I couldn't find any clean pans to cook with." I gave him an innocent look. "You don't mind, do ya?"

Race sank into the chair by the door, which in only four days had already resumed its former status as his closet. "It never occurred to you to wash some pans?"

"We're out of soap."

Race frowned a little, like he wanted to object, but couldn't find a way to argue with such impeccable logic.

When the Domino's guy showed up, Race paid him, all the while grousing about the need to educate me on where to get a decent pizza. Apparently Track Town, over by the University, made a pie that was the stuff of legends.

"Tell me, kid," Race said a few minutes later, as I devoured the remains of my first slice and licked the sauce off my fingers. "If I hadn't shown up, how were you gonna pay for this?"

I still had that twenty the truck driver had given me, but he didn't know that. "You've got a checkbook over there on the counter."

"You have to sign checks, y'know."

"Yeah," I agreed, "but I coulda done it before the delivery guy got here and said you'd signed it for me."

Race gawked like he actually believed I would. "Kid, forgery is a Federal offense."

"Only if you get caught."

While it was never hard to mess with my uncle, the easiest way to do it was to mention Kasey. Race's confidence dried up like a snowflake in southern California every time I talked about her in a way that didn't relate to racing. And God help me if I said anything he could interpret as the least bit disrespectful. Sometimes I had to get creative to string him along.

Other times the opportunity just fell into my lap, which was what happened Friday morning.

I was rummaging through the kitchen for breakfast when I knocked a dirty pan off the counter. Race gave me his usual glare from the couch.

"Sorry," I said as I opened the fridge to grab the milk.

"Right."

"You working here or at the shop today?" I never knew where he was gonna be. A couple days before, he'd walked in on me scribbling in my writing notebook. Luckily, he seemed to think I was doing some homework.

"Here," Race said. "I've got a logo to finish."

I opened the milk and held it up to take a chug.

"Hey, get a glass! I didn't pay a buck fifty for that milk so you could slobber in it."

The instant the liquid hit my tongue I knew something wasn't right. It took a second for the sour taste to really register, then I was running for the sink, spitting and leaning my head under the tap to run water in my mouth.

"Why all the melodrama?" Race asked.

"The milk's sour."

"Can't be. I just bought it two days ago."

"Well, you taste it, then." I thrust the carton at him.

"I think I'll take your word for it." Race crawled off of the couch and hunted through the laundry on the chair for a pair of jeans. Coming up empty-handed, he pulled some from the dirty clothes mound that had rematerialized under the coffee table. They looked like they'd been used to mop up Prince William Sound after the Exxon Valdez ran aground.

"Just have a Pepsi instead," Race said.

"On my cereal?"

"Eat it dry. I'll get more milk later."

I reached into the refrigerator. "Hey, this stuff's warm." I checked in the freezer and discovered a couple pounds of hamburger, some microwave burritos, and Race's Twinkies lying in a melted half-gallon of mint chocolate chip ice cream.

"Gross. I hope you don't expect me to clean this up."

"You could use that ice cream on your cereal," Race suggested.

I didn't honor the comment with a reply.

"Well, let me take a look."

"Oh, yeah, the great mechanic. What makes you think you can fix the fridge if you have to get a chick to work on your race car?"

"Hey, none of that sexist bullshit in my house." Race looked in the fridge, smacked it a few times, then wiggled it forward to check the cord. It was still plugged in.

"So, like, what's the diagnosis?" I asked, perching myself on the counter where I could get a better view of his futile attempts.

"It's, like, broke."

I gave him a look of mock surprise, ignoring the dig at my grammar. "Really? God, Race, you're a freakin' genius."

"Hell, I don't know anything about refrigerators."

"Guess we'll have to get a girl to fix it."

Race scowled at me. "Go to school."

Laughing, I hopped down from the counter. "Hey, don't let it getcha down, dude. While Kasey's fixin' the fridge, you could always sew some curtains for her living room."

Race cocked an ear toward the door. "Isn't that your bus I hear?"

I glanced out the window. "No," I said. "It's a garbage truck. And I think there's a woman driving it."

It had rained most of the week, but Saturday morning a stiff wind blew away the clouds. Kasey stopped by to look at the fridge before we left for the track. She laughed when she saw my *Radioactive cats have 18 half-lives* shirt. Then, in about thirty seconds, she figured out why the refrigerator wasn't working.

"The condenser coils are filthy," she told Race.

"Imagine that," I said. "And in such a surgically sterile environment."

When Race went out to the van to get the Shop-Vac, Kasey eyed me in a way that made me want to crawl under the nearest large object.

"You're a smart kid, Cody, and I realize Race plays right into your hand, but just because you know how to push his buttons doesn't mean you should."

"It was a joke! It's not like he doesn't know how to sling it right back."

Kasey patted my shoulder. The gesture sent a tingle surging along my spine. "I'm just suggesting you might want to tone it down," she said, smiling to take the sting out of her reprimand. "Try using your gift of intuition for good instead of evil."

At the speedway that night, my uncle qualified faster than everybody in his class. It was apparently the first time anyone but Addamsen had done that since halfway through the previous season. The announcer made a big deal about it, and about the fact that Race was now only two points behind his rival. The idea must've torqued Addamsen, because he smoked Race in the trophy dash. Fortunately, the dash wasn't worth any points. That was one thing I'd learned this week.

"So when are you gonna let me take this baby out for a few laps?" I asked later, patting the hood of the Dart where I sat scarfing down a hot dog. Out on the track, another trophy dash was heating up.

"Maybe in thirty years or so."

"Aww, c'mon. I won't wreck it."

Race gave me a measured look. "Do you even know how to drive?"

83

"Nah, Mom wouldn't let me get my permit."

"Well, that's just a crime. On Monday, I'm taking you to the DMV right after school."

"Seriously?"

"Seriously. I can't have it getting out that my fifteen-year-old nephew doesn't have his driver's permit."

A couple of the Super Stocks tangled and smashed into the wall. Within seconds the stomach-turning stink of burnt rubber drifted into the pits. Both tow trucks scrambled toward the track and a big black car rumbled past us through the cloud of dust they left behind.

"What's that?" I asked.

"The track ambulance."

"It looks like the Ghostbusters car."

"Almost," said Race. "It's a '67 Cadillac hearse. You're only off by about eight years."

"Isn't that kinda morbid, having a hearse for an ambulance?"

"Well, it's not like it's a real ambulance. If anyone ever got seriously hurt they'd call 911."

"Still," I said. There was something warped about the idea.

Race's heat began with a snarl-up that slammed him against the outside wall. In spite of it, he immediately gained three positions when they got the race restarted. Then after a couple of laps, something began to change. Each time Race went into a corner, the back end of the Dart would hang out so far that the car was sliding almost sideways through the turn. It looked way cool.

"Why's he doing that?" I asked Kasey.

"It's not intentional. I think he has a tire going down." She glanced at me, weighing my level of interest. "When the rear end wants to come around that way, it's known as being 'loose.' I just hope he makes it through the next three laps."

One advantage to having the Dart handle like that seemed to be that it took up an awful lot of the track in the corners. The car directly behind Race, a white Camaro, didn't have a chance of getting around him. When I mentioned that to Kasey, she pointed out that the slightest tap from the Camaro would send Race into a spin.

"Driving at the limit like that, he wouldn't have a prayer of getting it back under control."

Addamsen hovered right behind the Camaro. If he passed it, I knew Race would have a real problem on his hands. Last week I'd seen how closely Addamsen could ride a guy's bumper. After the threats he'd been slinging around at the payoff window, I figured he wouldn't be above spinning Race intentionally. I spent the last two laps holding my breath.

Race managed to keep his position, coming in third behind Denny and Jim. Then, just after he crossed the finish line and headed into turn one, a loud bang made me jump damn near into the next county. The Dart spun toward the top of the track. Addamsen and the white Camaro swerved under it, but the guy behind them plowed into the right front fender.

"Ouch!" cried the announcer, "doesn't look like that'll buff out, folks. Let's hope Morgan can get that car back in shape for the main. He's dead even with Jerry Addamsen, now. If Morgan can finish ahead of him tonight, it'll be the first time anyone's taken the point lead from Addamsen in three years."

The Dart limped back into the pits, its front fender digging into the tire and shaving off rubber with every revolution. Since the wheels didn't seem to want to turn properly, Race had to bully the 8 car into its parking spot.

Almost before the Dart stopped, Kasey was inspecting the damage.

"How bad is it?" asked Race as he fumbled with the window net.

"I'm not sure yet." Kasey rolled the jack under the front end, lifting the Dart off the ground before Race even had a chance to climb out. Then Jim and Denny appeared. Finishing ahead of Race, they'd missed all the action.

"What happened?" asked Jim.

"Blowout. Carter nailed me when I spun."

"It's amazing it didn't happen sooner," Kasey said. "That tire was a ticking time bomb. You should have brought her in."

"Hell, Kasey," Jim said. "You oughta know by now that Race isn't gonna bring a car in off the track as long as it can make another lap."

"I wouldn't be surprised to see him *push* one across the finish line," Denny added.

"Well, one of these days he's going to break something I can't fix."

Race laughed. "You always say that, but it'll never happen. I have complete faith in your automotive genius."

"Can you fix it this time?" I asked.

"Fortunately, yes. I'll just have to replace the two tires and an outer tie rod end."

While Kasey and Race got to work putting the Dart back together, I wandered down to the north end of the track where the tow trucks and ambulance were parked. Creepy as the hearse was, it was pretty cool. One of the paramedics was kicking back beside it in a lawn chair, eating a cheeseburger while his partner rooted around in the Cadillac's back end.

"Can you guys get the poltergeists out of my attic?" I asked.

"'Fraid not," said the guy with the cheeseburger. "All my training is with the living."

"Where'd they get this car?"

"Dunno. It's been here as long as I have."

I circled the Cadillac. How awesome would it be to drive this thing around town?

"Your dad one of the drivers?" the guy asked. I noticed that his name, *Alex*, was stitched on the front of his uniform.

"No, my uncle. Race Morgan." I checked out the enormous chrome grill.

"Ah. You're practically royalty."

"I guess. Is this a pretty exciting job? You see a lot of blood and guts?"

"Not here. There's plenty of that on the highway, but racing's pretty safe. I don't think I've seen a serious accident in the five years I've worked this gig."

"There was Greg Shackleford last year," said the second paramedic, slamming the back door of the ambulance and coming around to join us. He was a heavy dude, and his nametag read *Steve*.

"The guy busted his leg," countered Alex. "I'd hardly call that life-threatening."

I hung out with the paramedics for most of the Street Stock main, trying to weasel gory details out of them about their work. Steve indulged me a little, but Alex said it was serious business, not a source of entertainment for the bloodthirsty.

When I saw the Sportsmen lining up for their main, I jogged back over to Race's pit. Kasey was finishing some kind of adjustment under the front of the car.

"Okay. That should do it," she said.

"You wanna check the toe again?" Race asked.

"There's no time. Get in the car."

"Let's move it, Sportsmen!" hollered Ted Greene, making his way down the row. Race scrambled through the window.

"Did you get it fixed?" I asked Kasey.

"Yes. Of course it's always a little unsettling, sending a car out without a few test laps, but that can't be helped."

Hearing Kasey sound doubtful was what unsettled *me*. In just a week I'd come to admire her assertive, businesslike attitude. She wasn't the type to stew over something without good reason. I realized what I was thinking and almost laughed. How could I be nervous about a stock car race?

"Why's Race so popular, anyway?" I asked as I watched the cars pull out onto the backstretch. "Doesn't Addamsen win more?"

"It's not just about winning. Jerry Addamsen may be a successful driver, but he's a mean-spirited bully. Your uncle, on the other hand, is the most kindhearted person I know. And he's got a sense of humor. Fans like a driver who's willing to laugh at himself. It shows humility. That's something Jerry doesn't even know the meaning of."

I felt like asking her why she wanted to keep their relationship all business if Race was such a great guy, but I kept my mouth shut. I had no doubt that Kasey would verbally flatten me if I gave her any crap. Besides, I wasn't gonna go around playing matchmaker like some twelve-year-old girl.

"The thing you have to realize, Cody, is that in spite of Jerry's talent, he has a lot of enemies at this track. Most people don't like a rough driver. Personally, I find the way he treats women distasteful. I've seen him with one arm around his wife and the other hand goosing the trophy girl."

The word that popped immediately into my head was 'ambidextrous,' but I didn't share the thought.

In spite of Kasey's doubts, the Dart performed flawlessly in the main. Race drove it like he'd just committed a double homicide and had the cops from four counties after him. Even so, Addamsen got a better start and zipped ahead. For eight laps, Race fought to pass him, but the slower guys kept getting in the way.

Halfway through their ninth time around, Addamsen ducked by the lead car. Race followed, zeroing in on his bumper. For six more laps Race nagged the Camaro through the turns and pulled even with it on the straightaways.

"Can you see the line Jerry's taking through the corners?" Kasey asked. "It's just high enough that Race can't get around him on the outside, but not so high that he can slip underneath. Race's only option is to sit back and wait for Jerry to make a mistake."

Race seemed to have a different opinion about his options. Instead of backing off and dropping down behind Addamsen the next time they went into a corner, he kept his foot in it. The black Camaro drifted up into the side of the Dart, and I thought sure Race was gonna lose it and skid off the top of the track. Worse, the Dart looked lined up to smack head-on into the leading edge of the wall. But somehow Race squeaked through the dwindling gap between Addamsen and the concrete barrier. The Dart roared onto the front stretch only a fender length behind the Camaro. Kasey let out a breath and shook her head, muttering about dumb luck and a lack of good sense.

Edging ahead of Addamsen on the straightaway, Race dove into the first turn to claim the lead. The grandstands exploded with shrieks and applause. But Addamsen wasn't giving up that easy. He hounded Race down the backstretch and played woodpecker with the Dart's back bumper as the cars plowed through the corner at the north end of the track.

"He's gonna spin him out!"

"No, he won't," Kasey said. "Jerry has better sense than that."

I shot her a skeptical look. "You didn't hear what he said last Saturday."

"Cody, Jerry's been racing for a long time. He knows how much he can get away with without being black-flagged. What he's doing now is known as intimidation. It's a very effective tactic with nervous or inexperienced drivers, but it won't faze your uncle in the least."

"But—"

"Trust me," Kasey said.

Addamsen went right on with his intimidation routine, but as Kasey had predicted, he didn't spin Race. Five laps later, the two cars tore out of turn four neck-in-neck. Race beat Addamsen to the checkered flag by a bumper.

The Dart circled the track and parked on the start-finish line. I didn't think the crowd could get any rowdier, but when Race climbed out of the car the noise level jumped a good twenty decibels.

"And here he is," the loudspeaker blared. "From *YOU*-gene, Oregon, sponsored by Eugene Custom Classics, Rick's University Video, and Willamette Electrical Supply, your new points leader, RACE—MORGAN!"

Race shook both fists in the air and the crowd cranked it up another five decibels. It was a good minute before the announcer could get on with details about the Dart and Race's one-woman pit crew.

As the photographer tried to usher my uncle and the trophy girl into position for a picture, Race turned and gestured to Kasey and me.

"What's he want?"

"It's customary for a driver to have his family and crew join him for the photo."

Race thought of me as family? I mean, I knew I was, but I didn't expect him to act like it meant something.

Kasey gave me a gentle shove toward the wall and I balked. "I can't go out there!"

"Yes, you can." Kasey latched onto my wrist as she climbed over the concrete barrier, dragging me with her.

I felt like a dope walking out onto the track. But as I stood with her and Race, listening to the fans whoop and holler, my embarrassment began to fade. I couldn't help wondering—what would it be like to have all those people cheering for me?

Chapter 8

I couldn't let Race think I was getting completely soft, so the next morning I woke him up by shooting a bottle rocket down the hallway. It was sort of a ritual I'd created, finding new and creative ways to get him off the couch before 9 a.m. For sheer reaction, the bottle rocket was the best thing I'd thought of yet. But it lacked the finesse of my prank a few days earlier, when I'd set the clock ahead two hours. Race was up, dressed, and on his way out the door before it occurred to him that at nine-thirty, I should be at school.

Over the next couple of weeks, as I waited impatiently for my karate class to begin, I settled into life in Eugene. I was even sorta starting to like the place, especially the university area, which was always a whirl of people and activity. Downtown was cool, too. In one part, the streets were paved with brick and closed to traffic. I liked to take the bus down there to explore quirky shops, listen to street musicians, and watch kids play hacky sack. The town had a whole different energy than Portland—beatnik and artsy and way more close-knit, with the college acting as a rallying point. It seemed like every business had "Go Ducks!" painted in a window.

As time went by, Race and I managed to find our groove. He quizzed me on the Driver's Manual we'd picked up, and I learned to sleep through the trains that rocked the trailer at all hours of the night. I tried to keep in touch with my friends back home, but Tim's parents wouldn't let me talk to him, and Mike always sounded like he was trying to find an excuse to hang up. A couple of times my dad called, but I let Race do the talking.

At school, the work wasn't much different than it had been back home, but somehow it seemed easier. Maybe because I didn't have any friends yet, so there wasn't much to do in class but pay attention. While the friendlessness got to me, I lacked the energy and nerve to do anything about it. I'd spent my entire life in the same house, going to school with the same kids, and now everything was different. With all that change, I couldn't deal with trying to get to know people, too. Besides, school would be out in a few weeks.

The third Wednesday in May, Race dragged me out to the speedway for practice—something infinitely more boring than a regular race. The next morning it started to rain. The drizzle continued Thursday, Friday, and Saturday. My uncle, a guy who could shrug off mouthy drunkenness, shuriken embedded in his closet, and an unscheduled trip to Medford, got grumpy when it came to being rained out.

"If missing one race makes you this miserable, what do you do in the winter?" I asked when I got sick of hearing him grumble about the weather.

"Suffer."

"Jeeze, just drink a beer or something. Or better yet, take me out for a driving lesson."

"It's raining," Race protested.

"No shit. This is Oregon. If you expect me to wait for the roads to dry out, I'll be old enough to vote before I have a license."

"All right," Race sighed. He took me to Lane Community College, where the upper parking lots were practically deserted because it was a weekend.

"Okay," Race said when I was belted in behind the wheel. "First of all, put your left foot on the clutch and your right foot on the brake."

"Which pedal's the clutch?"

"The one on the left."

"So the brake's in the middle?"

"Yeah."

I pressed down the two pedals. "Okay, now what?"

"Crank her over."

I turned the key. The engine rattled to life.

"Good," Race said. "Now, take your foot off the brake and very slowly let out the clutch."

The van lurched forward and died.

"I said *slowly*."

"That *was* slow!"

"Well try slower."

For the next twenty minutes he made me practice again and again until I got it right and could motor around the parking lot in first gear.

"Now, let's try shifting. This van is what you call a three on the tree. You've got three forward gears, plus reverse, and the shift pattern forms sort of an 'H'."

"What's a shift pattern?"

Race looked at me like I'd asked what the alphabet was. After he'd explained the concept, detailing where the gears were, he told me to try shifting from first to second. When I did, I jammed the linkage so bad Race had to get out, crawl under the van, and work it loose by hand.

"Okay, this is important," he said as he slid back into the passenger seat. "All the bushings on the linkage are wasted, so you have to be very precise when you shift. Pretend you're back in first grade, drawing a nice, square 'H' when you work the lever. Last time you rounded it off, like an 'S'. That's why it got stuck."

"Well, why didn't you tell me that to begin with?" Crap, did he expect me to be born knowing all this?

"Sorry. I never tried to teach anyone to drive before."

Another half hour passed. I jammed the linkage, lugged the engine, and then over-revved it. Finally I blew up. "This is impossible! You expect me to just know this stuff! I'm not a freakin' race car driver!" I slammed my fist against the steering wheel.

"Hey, calm down. It's no big deal. You'll get it." Race's words were patient, even sympathetic, but he clutched the door handle in a death grip.

"Don't you ever get pissed?" I demanded, glaring at him.

"Not usually."

"Shit." I rubbed my sore hand.

"Losing your temper doesn't do anybody any good, Cody."

"That's easy for *you* to say."

"Maybe so," Race agreed. "Now give it another try."

We spent the rest of the afternoon practicing. I must've killed the engine a million times, but Race never lost patience or suggested we quit. By the time we headed back to the trailer he was soaked from crawling under the van to free the linkage, but I could shift through the gears flawlessly.

"Good job, kid," he said. "I'm buying you a pizza."

I felt like I'd won a Nobel prize.

The cool thing about Race was that he didn't act like a parent—more like a brother, or an older friend. He never gave me grief about the petty stuff Mom had obsessed over. That's why it irked me when he got on my case about stealing the street sign.

It had tempted me every time we went into Springfield for groceries. Located at 4th and Main it said simply, "Police." An arrow indicated the direction to the station a mere two blocks away. Who could resist a challenge like that?

Rationalizing that in the middle of the week there'd be less traffic, I waited until Tuesday night. I borrowed some tools from the box Race kept in the van then hoofed it across the bridge at about 2 a.m. The heist was easy. I shinnied up the pole, busted the sign lose, and hightailed it. Not a single car interrupted me.

It wasn't until I got home that I had trouble. When I turned the handle of the trailer's back door, I realized I'd locked myself out. No big deal. Race kept a spare key under a brake drum near the carport. I retrieved it and stuck it in the knob, but it wouldn't turn. The front door must have a different lock. Okay, I could deal with that. Race slept like a zombie. A parade of hippopotami could sneak by him.

Maybe if I'd been a hippopotamus, I'd have had better luck.

"Cody?" Race mumbled as I pulled the door to a quiet *click* behind me. I froze.

"Where've you been? What is that?"

Too late I realized the lights that illuminated the trailer park were shining through the windows, glinting off the reflective paint on the sign.

"You're dreamin', dude," I said softly. "Go back to sleep."

Race didn't buy it. He sat up, pawed for the lamp on the end table, and knocked it to the floor.

"Let me see that."

I kept moving.

"Cody!"

I stopped.

"Kid, what do you think you're doing? You wanna wind up in juvie?"

"It's just a street sign."

"Yeah, and it's against the law to take 'em home with you."

"Oh, I suppose that's something you'd never do, huh?" I stared pointedly at the wall above the TV where an East 8th Avenue sign hung. It had taken me a while to make the connection. Eight was his car number.

"I was in college when I got that."

"So you're saying I'm too young to steal a street sign?" Hell. I got that crap from everyone. I was too young to smoke, too young to drink, too young to understand. Did everyone over the age of twenty-one think teenagers were complete morons?

"No, kid, it's just . . ." Race's voice trailed off. He rubbed his face as if he'd suddenly been stricken with the monster of all headaches.

"Well, that's what it is, right? You don't think I'm old enough. But it's perfectly okay that *you* did it."

"Cody," Race pleaded.

"What the hell is it with people? Don't you think kids have any rights?"

"Listen—"

"No, I'm not gonna listen! I'm not a baby! Either it's right or it's wrong. It's not okay just because you were older!" I kicked his drafting table. An assortment of pens and pencils fell off, rattling to the floor.

"Okay, you're right!" Race said. "It was just as bad when I did it. But you can't take these chances. You've already had one run-in with the cops."

"So?"

"So maybe I like having you around."

I glowered at Race across the living room. Then, slowly, I sank down into the laundry chair. He liked having me around? I mean, I knew he didn't mind me being there, but he actually *wanted* me?

Race looked steadily at me. "You can't keep doing this, Cody—taking stupid chances and losing your temper. Actions have consequences. You can't go around doing whatever you want and expecting to get off scot-free."

It was too much—the seriousness in his eyes, the reasonable tone of voice, the admission that he liked having me around. I couldn't look at him. "So . . . what do you want me to do?" I asked, staring down at my Converse high tops. "Put it back?"

"Hell no. You'd get busted for sure. But if you ever do something like this again I'll kick your ass." Race flopped back down in the tangle of blankets on the couch. "Now go to bed."

I got up and headed for my room. Behind me, Race muttered in exasperation. "When people pawn a teenager off on you, they oughta send along an owner's manual."

Chapter 9

Cool as Race seemed to be, I wasn't ready to let him in on my secrets, so I did my writing down by the river or while he was at the shop. I never let him see me with a book, either. But a couple of days after the street sign incident, the front door opened without the usual warning rattle of the van pulling up in the driveway.

Startled, I jammed the book I was reading down between the seat cushions. Race leaned through the doorway, too preoccupied to notice.

"Hey, kid, you wanna give me a hand? I need help pushing the van."

"Why?"

Race grinned sheepishly. "I ran out of gas."

"And of course you didn't drive past a single station on the way home."

"Just help me get it out of the road, then you can give me all the crap you want."

Rain sprinkled us as we hiked out to the main drag, where the van sat in the turn lane, blocking anyone who might want to make a left into the trailer park.

"Let's just get it into the driveway," Race said, "and I'll walk down to the gas station when the rain quits."

Sure, that would be easy. It was all we could do to get the thing moving. Then, when the front wheels hit the ramp where the street met the sidewalk, the van balked and threatened to roll back on us. If I didn't wind up with a hernia, it would be a miracle.

"Good enough," Race hollered as we pushed his monstrosity up in front of the dumpster. The skies unloaded on us before we could make it back to the trailer.

"There's this little thing on the dash called a gas gauge," I told Race as I sprinted up the steps. "You might want to consider looking at it some time."

"Doesn't work."

"What, you can build a race car, but you can't fix a simple thing like that?"

"Don't you ever give it a rest?" Race asked. "I swear you could try the patience of a saint."

"You're the one who said that if I helped push the van I could give you all the crap I wanted."

Sighing loudly, Race sank onto the couch and began rifling through the junk on the coffee table. Whatever he was looking for, he didn't find it. I cringed as he proceeded to hunt through the wadded up blankets, inches from the spot I'd stashed my paperback.

"You seen the remote?" he asked

"Uh, no." I scanned the room distractedly in hopes I might spot it before he proceeded too much further with his search.

Race reached down between the cushions. His eyebrows arched upward in surprise when he pulled out my book. "Hey, I remember reading this."

For a moment shock overshadowed my sense of self-preservation. "You read *To Kill a Mockingbird*?"

"Sure. In freshman English. I know it may come as a surprise, but I *am* literate." He held the book out to me, resuming his search without another word, and I realized I'd been given the perfect alibi. As long as school was in session, Race wasn't gonna look twice at me for reading.

Once I learned I could hide behind the guise of studying, I stopped worrying about Race discovering I was a freak. I even quit being paranoid about working on my stories when he was around. As a result, every time he caught me with my notebook, he got more curious about what I was doing.

"You're still working on that assignment?" he'd say. "What is it, a journal or something?"

"Notes for the CIA," I'd tell him. Or, "Addamsen's paying me to document your racing secrets." I knew he'd never sneak a look. He was too pathetically honest. But I kept my notebook stashed whenever I wasn't writing in it, anyway.

That Saturday we got rained out again. I took up hermitage in my room with Neal Shusterman's latest book, not because I was afraid of Race seeing me with it, but because his gloomy attitude was too contagious.

"It's just a race!" I said. "They'll have another one next week."

"Someday you'll understand, kid."

"God, I hope not." The day I let a bunch of beat-up cars rule my life was the day I'd throw myself in front of a bus.

One of the best things about living with Race was hanging out with Kasey. She seemed to know a little bit about everything, and if she didn't know something, she knew where to find out about it.

Kasey had breezed through high school in three years, then college in another three. She'd designed some kind of timber processing machinery in her final year, sold it to a logging company, and made a pile of money. That money was what she'd used to start her business, Eugene Custom Classics. Race called it a restoration shop, but Kasey explained that she also modified old cars, swapping engines or making changes to the bodies. And lots of people brought their cars to her for general repairs, since it seemed to be getting harder to find mechanics who'd work on stuff from before 1970.

Race took me over to Kasey's shop a lot the first month I was in Eugene, but it wasn't until the beginning of June that I got to see her house. It was a Friday night, and she was having a barbeque.

"There's a certain irony here," Race explained as we drove through a woodsy neighborhood on the butte behind the University. "This street sort of peters out a little ways past Kasey's, but it starts up again on the other side of 30th Avenue, and that's where my parents live. In the ritzy part of town, naturally."

"I take it we won't be going there any time soon."

"Not hardly."

That was fine by me. While I had to give Grandma credit for taking the time to come see me once a year, I'd never looked forward to her visits. Three days of etiquette lessons, forced cultural experiences, and mind-numbing shopping expeditions were not my ideal way to spend a summer weekend.

Kasey's place was all brick and cedar. A long staircase led from the driveway to a deck that ran the entire front length of the house, providing an awesome view of downtown Eugene.

Jim was there when we arrived, sitting at a picnic table with his kid and his wife Laurie.

"Cool shirt," Robbie said.

"Thanks." I'd found it at a crazy little shop on 13th near the U of O bookstore. It read, *Don't make me release the flying monkeys.* Amazingly, Race had started giving me an allowance after the pizza incident, providing me with funds to supplement my wardrobe. I guess he wasn't convinced I wouldn't forge a check. His generosity surprised me a little because he could hardly afford to pay his bills, and I knew he'd never ask my dad to send more money.

"Cody, would you like something to drink?" Kasey asked. "The cooler's full of pop. And I picked up some Guinness for you, Race. It's in the fridge."

"I say, will we be having the Guinness tonight?" mocked Jim in the worst Irish brogue ever to pass through human lips. He held up his Budweiser as if to offer a toast.

"Forgive me for not being able to choke down that swill you drink," Race said. "It's a damn shame they allow people to waste good hops that way." He went to collect his beer, nearly tripping over an enormous tabby cat that scrambled out the screen door under his feet.

"This is Winston," Robbie informed me, leaning over to drag the animal up onto his lap.

I tapped a cigarette out of my pack and was about to light up when I saw Kasey frowning at me. She never said anything about my smoking, she just eyeballed me like I'd blown a spelling bee by messing up on the word "dog." I tucked the Camel filter away and helped myself to a Pepsi.

"So how are things down at the shop?" Jim asked Kasey. "You ever get it sorted out with that employee who was giving you trouble? What was his name—Harley?"

"As a matter of fact, I had to let him go yesterday."

"So now you've just got Jake," Race said. He sat down beside me at the table.

"And a Mustang that needs to be wrapped up by Friday. It's going to be a busy week. But if I work through the weekend, I think I can manage."

"You need some help?" Race asked.

"I can't ask you to bail me out. You've got customers of your own."

"You're not asking, I'm offering."

Kasey smiled. "And I appreciate it. If I run into trouble, I'll give you a call."

A car pulled into the driveway and a couple minutes later Denny and his family joined us on the deck. It surprised me that Denny hung out with Jim and Race, because he seemed to be a lot older—probably forty. His kids were younger than Robbie, though. I hoped nobody was expecting me to entertain the little ankle biters.

As it turned out, they were pretty good at entertaining themselves. In fact, it looked like they were having more fun than I was. While they ran around the property playing hide and seek, I hung out on the deck with the adults. Naturally, all *they* talked about was racing. I had to amuse myself by plowing through a bowl of Doritos and trying to sneak occasional swigs off Race's beer.

"So what's this rumor I hear?" asked Jim, tipping his chair back on two legs.

For the third time, Race slid his bottle of Guinness out of my reach. "Which rumor is that?"

"The one about Addamsen having you stuffed into the wall tomorrow night."

Kasey looked up from the grill where she was flipping burgers and chicken. Winston wound around her legs. I could identify with the cat—my stomach was growling at the rich, smoky smell of the meat.

"I haven't heard anything about it," Race said.

"The way I heard it, he was gonna pay Tom Carey fifty bucks to do it," Jim continued.

"Fifty bucks!" said Race. "I'm only worth fifty bucks? Hell, when Chris Ackerman got stuffed into the wall last season everyone said Tom got paid a hundred."

Kasey didn't even crack a smile at Race's comment. Closing the grill, she came over to sit with us. "Where did you hear about this?"

"After practice Wednesday night," Jim said.

"For heaven's sake," said his wife, Laurie, "the man was drunk. You know how he gets when he's drunk."

"He didn't look any different than usual to me." Jim's comment earned a chuckle from everyone but Kasey.

"So what did he say?" Race asked.

"Oh, he just mentioned that crack you made awhile back, about hooking up the other four spark plug wires." Laurie was obviously trying to dismiss it. "He had an audience, and too much to drink, so he was bragging."

"If it bothered him that much, you'd think he'd have taken me out the following week. He had plenty of opportunity."

"Well, everyone knows that's not what's really got his knickers in a twist," Denny said. "Fact is, you shamed him good, taking the points lead. But he's got better sense than to wreck you."

"That's why he's hiring Tom to do it," Jim said.

Laurie smacked her husband's shoulder. "Just stop! You're not funny." She glanced at Kasey, then at Race, like she was trying to read whether they were the least bit freaked by the news. "Nothing's going to come of it," she said. "You hear this sort of thing all the time."

"You scared, Race?" I asked, smirking at him.

"Hell, no. And leave that beer alone."

"Laurie's right," said Kasey. "Nothing will come of it. And if it does, Race is perfectly capable of dealing with whatever happens on the track." She got up to check the food again. I studied her as she piled the meat onto two plates. Her expression was as calm and businesslike as ever, but there was something in it, some little hint of preoccupation, that told me she was worried. And Race thought she didn't care.

On the way home that night, I brought it up, but Race laughed it off.

"Kasey doesn't worry, and even if she did, it wouldn't be about some stupid rumor."

"I'm telling you, she likes you. She bought you Guinness. Doesn't that count for anything?"

"Yeah, good taste on her part. Generosity and friendship. Anything beyond that is your imagination, kid."

I gave up. She could probably send him an engraved wedding invitation, and he'd find a way to write it off.

Chapter 10

The following evening, Addamsen took fast time. It must've appeased him because nothing out of line happened in the trophy dash, which Race won. Nothing much happened in the heat, either, other than Denny's carburetor going south. Addamsen took that race, bringing himself back up even in the points.

"You gonna get the lead back in the main?" I asked Race a little later. He was sitting on his toolbox, sketching one of the Street Stocks that sat across the pit road from us. Taking advantage of the fact that Kasey had wandered over to the concession stand, I lit up a cigarette.

"I'm gonna try." Race coughed and waved away the cloud of smoke I'd accidentally sent in his direction. "That is, if you haven't killed me off by then, getting toxic waste in my airspace."

"Whiner," I said. But I blew my next lungful away from him. "So, you think Addamsen's gonna try anything?"

"Nah, it's just a rumor."

"But a few weeks ago he said—"

"Kid, people shoot their mouths off all the time. It doesn't mean anything."

"He seemed pretty serious to me."

Race gave me a speculative look, a grin slinking slowly across his face. "You're *worried* about it."

"I am not!"

"You think he's gonna try to do me in. You actually *care*."

My face went hot and I looked away. "Get over yourself."

Before my uncle could taunt me any more, Denny stepped up beside us, smelling strongly of that high-tech gasoline. "Hey, Race, you still got your old carb?"

"Sure. If I can find it." Race closed the sketchbook and got up to root through the parts boxes. "Here it is."

"Thanks, I'll get it back to you next week."

"Why'd you do that?" I asked as Denny rushed off. "What if he beats you tonight?"

"Then I'll congratulate him on driving a good race."

"But—" it didn't make any sense. Why would you want to help the competition, especially if you were so close to losing the points lead?

"Look, kid, it's just the way things are. Racers help each other out. If I needed something, he'd be the first guy to give it to me. Hell, I've seen him lend out his spare race car so people could keep up their points when they wrecked."

"He's got a spare race car?"

"Yep, Big Red, a '69 Chevelle. It's the car he drove before he built his Camaro."

For a few seconds I pondered how fanatical a person had to be to have a whole extra car. Then something occurred to me. "How can that carburetor even work on Denny's car if he's not running a Dodge?"

"Because it's not stock, it's a Holley. All the Sportsmen run the same kind of carb."

I shook my head. "I'm never gonna figure out this racing stuff."

Race laughed. "I didn't think you wanted to."

The Street Stock main took forever. Every time they got the race restarted someone wiped out. Usually when things were slow, Race and I tossed around his blue Nerf football, but the Sportsmen were already lined up, so I was on my own. I cruised over to BS with the paramedics.

"Back for more stories of blood and gore?" Alex asked as I boosted myself up onto the hearse's fender.

"I thought you said you wouldn't talk about that stuff."

"I won't." Alex checked out my T-shirt. "'As is.' Cute. I need to get one of those for Steve."

"One of what?" asked Steve, returning from the concession stand with a couple of hot dogs, a Pepsi, a bag of Fritos, and a red licorice rope.

Alex indicated my shirt.

"Hey," Steve said. "I might be fat, but at least all the parts are in working order."

"Are you trying to insinuate something?" asked Alex.

"Me? Of course not. Why, is there something to insinuate?" Steve hefted himself up beside me. The fender sank a couple inches under the added weight.

While we waited for the Street Stocks to finish, I listened to Steve and Alex swap insults. There was one final wreck—a nasty collision in turn three that sent the fragrance of wild mint wafting through the pits—and I had to hop off the fender so the paramedics could zip onto the track to check things out. They were back almost immediately.

"No dead bodies," Steve reported. "No severed limbs or spurting blood. You disappointed?"

"Only a little."

"You two are sick," Alex said.

The Street Stock Main was finally cut short due to time constraints, and as twilight faded the Sportsmen pulled onto the track. It took Race nine laps to get up to fifth place. Tom Carey, in the white #68 Camaro, dawdled half a lap behind, so he didn't worry me, but Addamsen was coming up on Race like Jaws on a shoreline full of swimmers. One more circuit of the track left him tapping at the Dart's back bumper.

Race, busy working an intimidation act of his own on #43, ignored the threat. After a few laps with the Dart hounding him, the driver of 43 got nervous and drifted high in turn one. Race slipped expertly into the groove. As the 43 car slid up the track, Addamsen wedged his Camaro between it and the Dart.

He cut low coming out of the turn, trying to slam the door on Race, and clipped the Dart's right front fender. Another driver might've backed down and let Addamsen have the position, but Race kept his foot in it. Slick as hot oil, Addamsen's Camaro spun off the front of the Dart, pirouetted across the backstretch, and came to a rest in the infield.

"Uh oh," I said. "That's gonna torque him."

"Race didn't have much choice," Kasey said. "If he'd let off or tried to steer out of it, they both would have spun."

"You think Addamsen's gonna see it that way?"

"Of course not."

When the race restarted, Addamsen tore up the track like he had a solid rocket booster strapped to the roof of his Camaro. But with only eight laps to go and a pack of slow traffic to fight his way through, he didn't have a chance of catching up to the Dart. Race crossed the finish line in second place. Addamsen barely squeaked into fifth, his engine howling in annoyance at being outrun.

Throttling back for the cool-down lap, the Dart slowed through turns one and two. The Camaro didn't. It rammed into Race's car, catching the left rear wheel and lifting the back end off the ground. The Dart skittered across the backstretch and slammed into a big tractor tire at the edge of the track.

While the rest of the pack scrambled to get around Addamsen's limping Camaro, the Dart sat motionless. A tow truck bounded out onto the track, yellow lights flashing through the darkness. Catcalls from angry fans echoed through the bleachers. Race was out of the car within seconds, surveying the damage. I was so busy watching the wrecker hook up to the Dart that I almost missed seeing the black #1 Camaro skulking past me down the pit road.

"You son of a bitch!" I launched myself at the car, whaling on the roof and kicking the door. Kasey's grip on the back of my jacket was the only thing that kept me from diving through the passenger window to rip Addamsen's head off.

"Cody, stop! You'll just make things worse."

I spun around to face her, fists clenched. "How the hell could things get worse?"

"You could get yourself thrown out, that's how. The officials have absolutely no tolerance for fighting."

"But it's not fair! They didn't even black flag him!"

"It wouldn't have done any good. The race was over. Now get a grip on yourself." The no-nonsense edge in Kasey's voice put a dent in my outrage, but it was the appearance of the wrecker, pulling up beside us with the mangled Dart in tow, that stopped me short. They'd had to hook up to the back bumper because the impact had jammed the left rear tire up against the wheel well. The front end didn't look much better. The hood was buckled, the fender was twisted up like some crazy metal sculpture, and even I could see that the angle of the right front wheel was all wrong. Race jumped down from the cab of the tow truck, stormy and a little dazed.

"Are you all right?" Kasey asked.

"Yeah, but the car's a mess." Race glanced from the Dart to Kasey with hint of weary humor. "I know, I know . . . one of these days I'm gonna break something you can't fix."

Kasey shook her head. "I wasn't going to say that. But I won't have much time to help you put her back together. Finishing that Mustang is really going to cut into my evenings."

My anger flared. How could they be so matter-of-fact about the whole thing? It wasn't like it was an accident. "You're not gonna just let Addamsen get away with this are you? You need to go kick his ass!"

Race swiveled to face me, the muscles in his jaw hard as concrete. "Cool it."

"Aren't you pissed? How can you not be pissed?"

"Of *course* I'm pissed, kid. Why do you think I'm not over there hashing it out with the officials? You wanna see me deck someone and get us all tossed outta here?"

I felt Kasey's fingers tighten around my upper arm in a subtle but distinct warning.

"Shit," I said, pulling away and kicking a stack of tires.

Kasey's eyes pinned me for a few seconds, then she must've realized I had enough sense not to be the spark that set off Race's dynamite.

"Well, let's take a look and see how bad it is," she said.

It was bad. One by one, Kasey listed the damaged parts: a tweaked spring shackle, a broken axle, two cut tires, a bent wheel, an irreparably twisted fender and front bumper, a mangled upper control arm, and a couple wasted tie-rod ends. None of it made sense to me, but it sounded like someone was in for a lot of work and expense.

Kasey and Race had just finished wrestling the rear end back into place and swapping out the two flat tires when Ted Greene appeared.

"So?" asked Race, wiping his hands on a grease rag.

"I know what you want to hear, Morgan, but I don't have an answer for you yet."

"What's that supposed to mean?" asked Race.

"It means that until we look at the videotape, all we've got to go on is what the flagman saw. And he said you were both being pretty aggressive."

"What?" Race's controlled expression dissolved into disbelief.

"You *did* spin him, Morgan."

"He cut down on me!"

"If he did, I'm sure it'll show up on the tape."

Race's fingers clenched white over the grease rag. It was seeing that, more than feeling Kasey's Spock-like grip on my shoulder, that kept me from telling Greene where he could shove his video.

"You mean to tell me a little bumping can justify deliberately wrecking a guy after the race is over?" Race demanded. "If that's the case, what's to keep him from slamming into me in the pits?"

Ted sighed, stroking his long and generous beard. "Look, I'm sorry, but we don't have a rule that specifically covers an incident like this. It's never happened before."

"Never?"

"Well, not as long as I've been here."

"So now what?"

Ted gave Race a steady look. "We'll watch the tape tonight and try to come up with an appropriate penalty. I'll give you a call in the morning."

Race eyeballed the chief steward for a long moment, then nodded curtly and turned away.

I had to hand it to him. He sure had a handle on his temper.

Chapter 11

Sunday morning I hooked my boombox up to the speakers in Race's stereo system and stuck in a CD sampler from five years before, when the technology was still new. Selecting the appropriate track—the roar of a low-flying aircraft—I maxed out the volume and pushed 'play.' A fighter jet blasted through the trailer, rattling the windows.

"Son of a—" Race bolted upright, gripping the back of the couch with one hand and clasping his chest with the other.

I collapsed on the laundry chair, laughing so hard no sound came out.

"Very funny," gasped Race as I slid to the floor to roll around. He hoisted himself off the couch and hit the 'stop' button.

"Dude!" I panted, finally able to catch a breath. "The look on your face!"

"It would be a mistake to think I'm merely writing off all your little pranks," Race said. "A big mistake."

The phone rang and Race stepped over me to answer it. It occurred to me that Race's revenge might include confiscating my only source of tunes, so I scrambled up, yanked the speaker wires out of my boombox, and reattached them to his stereo.

"You're kidding!" Race said into the receiver. "That's it?" He scowled as he listened to the response. "So that's the last word?" Another lengthy pause. "All right. Well, thanks for letting me know." Race dropped the phone into its cradle and looked up to see me watching. "That was Ted Greene. The officials decided Addamsen's gonna lose his payoff for last night, but he'll get to keep his points."

"What? That is so bogus! He coulda killed you!"

"Hardly," Race said with a hint of a smile.

"But what about your car? It's gonna take a lot of work to fix. Doesn't that count for anything?"

"Yeah, probably every waking hour of my time this week. Which means we better get a move on." Race pulled a T-shirt and jeans from the pile on the chair. "I'm gonna grab a shower, then we'll hit the wrecking yard, okay?"

"But how can they do that?"

"It's called politics, kid. You better get used to it because you're gonna run into it anytime you participate in an organized activity. Try to fight it and you just get pegged as a troublemaker."

"So Addamsen's gonna get away with it?"

"Looks like."

"That's not fair!"

Race shook his head as he turned to lumber down the hallway to the bathroom. "Kid, don't tell me you've reached the ripe old age of fifteen still believing life is fair."

Since I'd passed the written test and gotten my permit a few days before, Race let me drive to the wrecking yard. It was closed on Sundays, but Kasey got special privileges because she did a lot of business with them. She'd called ahead so the owner's son, Phil, would know to expect us.

Barefoot, shirtless, and smoking a cigarette, the guy answered the door of the trailer outside the gate. "Don't let the dog scare ya," he said, handing Race a key and gesturing at the Rottweiler chained to an old Jeep by the fence. "He can't get loose, he just likes to run his mouth."

"Right," said Race.

"Chryslers is down that-a-way." Phil indicated the northwest corner of the yard. The cigarette bobbed from his lips as he spoke.

"Yup—been here before."

Dropping his smoke, Phil crushed it with his bare heel before going back into the trailer. I raised an eyebrow at Race, who shrugged and started walking.

If you had to waste time scrounging in a junkyard, it was a good day for it. The sun was warm, a breeze swayed the tall grass surrounding the cars, and birds chattered like a playground full of out-of-control third-graders.

"Whoa, dude! Check it out." In front of me sat the coolest car in the world. It was big and boxy with tons of chrome, and square taillights the size of afterburners on a jet. The headlights—two on either side—sat back under fenders that arched up like the brows of a bird of prey. "This is totally choice."

"Needs a little body work," Race commented.

"What is it?"

"A '65 Ford Galaxie."

"How much do these things go for?"

"A boat like that? Hell, I wouldn't pay more than three, four hundred dollars for it even if it had a straight body *and* an intact windshield." Clearly, Race wasn't appreciating the coolness factor of the Galaxie. I gave him a look of strained patience before sticking my head through the driver's window to check out the interior.

"You don't seriously want a car like this?"

"Sure I do. It's a classic."

"It's a boat," Race corrected. "You've gotta measure the gas consumption in gallons to the mile."

"So?" I pulled my head out of the Galaxie. "Just look at the size of that back seat. Y'know, if I had a car like this, you could borrow it and take Kasey for a little drive—"

"You don't know when to quit, do ya, kid?"

I rubbed my hand over the roof, the chalky red paint coming off on my fingers. "Maybe you're right," I said. "Anyway, you've got a van."

Race raised his hand, pretending he was gonna smack me, but I ducked out of the way, laughing.

"C'mon, let's get to work," he said. "We've got a lot of parts to pull."

I followed him down the dusty path, casting one last glance over my shoulder.

"Tell ya what, kid—if you quit with the smart comments about Kasey, maybe I'll buy you one of those gas guzzlers for your birthday."

"Seriously?"

"Well, either that or a moped."

"Yeah, right." For a second there, I'd almost thought he meant it.

When we got to the Chryslers, Race located a Dart and stomped down the grass in front of it.

"No yellow jackets, that's always a good sign," he muttered as he dug a can of WD-40 out of the toolbox he'd brought along. "You wouldn't believe what I've found living in some of these wrecks." He wiggled under the front of the car to spray lubricant on the bolts that held the bumper in place. The stuff had a minty, almost medicinal smell.

"Hand me the 9/16ths wrench," Race grunted.

I dug through the toolbox, wondering how I was gonna figure out what a 9/16ths wrench was until I realized they all had little numbers engraved in them.

"Here." I crouched down in the weeds beside him. "So, you're just gonna let Addamsen off the hook?"

"Well, I'm not gonna wreck him, if that's what you're getting at."

"Why not? He wrecked you."

"That's his style, not mine."

I sat back in the grass and lit a smoke. The sun felt good, almost intoxicating. Only two more weeks and school would be out. It wasn't like I had anything better to do with my time, but I was still looking forward to summer.

"So what's the big deal about this championship, anyway?" I asked. "You act like it's more important than winning an Oscar."

"It is."

"Why?"

Race worked quietly for so long I thought he hadn't heard me. "It's just something I've wanted since I was a kid. Winning a championship—well, it's the ultimate way of saying you've made it. And there's the added benefit of sticking it to my dad. He never thought I'd be successful at anything."

"Didn't you win the Street Stock championship?"

"Nope. Missed it by two points the last year I ran in that division."

Two points. Man, that must've been a pisser. I leaned back in the grass, cushioning my head with one hand. "So how'd you get into this racing stuff, anyway?"

Race chuckled. "That one I'd have to blame on my uncle Ernie. He was a big NASCAR fan. Saundra and I loved him because he was such a kick in the pants, but my parents couldn't stand the guy."

"What was wrong with him?"

"You mean besides having the audacity to be blue collar and proud of it? Mostly it was marrying Dad's baby sister. And it didn't help that he corrupted me. When he'd come to visit, we'd catch whatever bits and pieces of a race they were willing to show on *Wide World of Sports*."

"And that got you hooked?"

"Pretty much. Ol' Ernie took great pleasure in annoying Dad by nurturing my interest in racing. He was the one who gave me my nickname."

"I'll bet Grandma and Grandpa loved that."

"Not nearly as much as they loved it when I started talking about racing, myself." He broke the final nut loose then slid out from under the car to bully the bumper off the front end. "It was bad enough, me watching that stuff on TV, but the idea of their kid driving one of those things—well, it was enough to get me excommunicated from the family."

"I thought you excommunicated yourself."

Race dropped the bumper at my feet. "I just finalized the deal. My parents had already made it clear I wasn't acceptable Morgan material."

Noting the harsh glint in my uncle's eyes, I decided it might be a good idea to change the subject. "So this championship," I said, snubbing out my cigarette on the bottom of my shoe. "Wouldn't it be easier to win if you drove like Addamsen?"

Race snorted. "Addamsen's got no class. I'd rather finish last than stoop to his level. There's no way I'm gonna have little kids thinking I'm some kind of cheat or bully."

"You're so noble."

Race shook his head. "You can give me all the crap you want, kid, but there's something to be said for knowing what you believe and sticking by it."

After dropping me off at the trailer, Race went to work on the Dart for the rest of the day. When the phone rang late that afternoon, I ignored it. Since there wasn't one at the shop, I knew it couldn't be my uncle. The answering machine picked up and I heard Dad's voice. "Uh, yeah, Race, with Cody's karate lessons starting this week, I just wanted to be sure that last check was going to be enough. Let me know if you need more. And Cody, if you hear this message, how about giving me a call? I'd like to know how you're doing."

Yeah, right. It would take more than a stupid phone message to make me believe that.

Race didn't make it home until after nine o'clock that night, and on Monday he only came back to the trailer long enough to grab something to eat.

"You okay with making dinner for yourself?" he asked, slapping together a PB & J. "I've gotta get down to the shop."

"Isn't that where you've been?"

"No. I was helping Kasey with the Mustang. She can't afford to be late with that job. She's still trying to build her business." Race put all the sandwich fixings away, stuffing the peanut butter in the fridge and the jam in the cupboard in his rush.

"Don't you have your own customers to worry about?" I asked, swapping the jam with the peanut butter. I was a little peeved about having to cook for myself again.

"Yeah, there's an ad I'm working on for one of 'em, but it doesn't need to be done until Monday. And I don't want you mentioning it to Kasey. If she knew, she wouldn't accept my help."

Race was gone all evening, and I didn't wait up for him. It was after eleven-thirty when I heard the door creak open. I got up and padded out to the front room. Race stood in front of the open fridge, examining its contents.

"Kinda late, isn't it?"

The bite of my tone attracted a vaguely guilty glance.

"I've gotta get the car back together," Race said. He pulled a half-gallon of milk from the top shelf and poured himself a glass.

"You didn't forget about tomorrow, did you?"

"What's tomorrow?"

"I've only been talking about it all week!"

Race turned and sagged against the counter. "Look, Cody, I'm beat. Just tell me so I can go to bed."

"It's my first karate lesson."

Race grimaced. "That's tomorrow?"

Typical adult. "I guess you're gonna bail on me, huh?"

"I didn't say that."

"What about your stupid car?"

"I'm sure it can spare me for a couple hours."

"Right." I wasn't like I hadn't been through this kind of thing a million times with Mom.

"Look, kid. I said I'd take you, and I'll take you. Understand?"

"If you say so."

Race's jaw tightened and he closed his eyes, taking a deep breath before he responded. "Go back to bed. We've both gotta get up early if I'm gonna give Kasey a hand tomorrow."

Yeah, I'd believe *that* when I saw it. The only time I'd witnessed him in a vertical position before seven-thirty was the day I'd set his clock back.

Amazingly, Race was up, dressed, and wolfing down a Twinkie when I wandered into the kitchen the next morning.

"Your class is at seven, right? I'll be here no later than six."

Make that 6:47. I was battling hurricane force nerves by the time he showed up. Fortunately, the dojo was only a few miles from the trailer and Race managed to avoid the cops in spite of setting his own speed limit. After all the fuss, my class was a lot less exciting than I'd expected. Mostly, we went over the dojo rules and practiced some basic exercises and stances. The sensei talked a lot about breathing and oriental philosophy, but I just wanted to get to the good stuff, where I could learn to kick somebody's ass.

At eight, Race picked me up and dropped me off at the trailer.

"I've gotta put in a few hours on the Dart," he said. "I'll probably be late, so don't wait up."

"Yeah, okay, sure." I'd be glad when that damned thing was fixed so I could stop living in solitary confinement.

Race wasn't home when I went to bed, and I never did hear him come in. The next morning I found his blankets lying crumpled on the couch, exactly the way they'd been the night before. I peered out the window into the driveway. No van. I didn't know whether to be pissed or scared.

Not sure what else to do, I called Kasey, who told me she hadn't seen Race since he left her place the day before.

"I'm sure he's fine, Cody. I'll drive over to his shop and see if he's there. Just go to school, okay? If there's any problem I'll call the office."

As I sat through classes that day, my annoyance boiled into an all-out rage. How could Race not come home? Didn't he know how much it would freak me out?

At three o'clock, instead of going home, I flipped through the bus schedules at the nearest convenience store and plotted how to get to Kasey's shop. Race's van was sitting out front when I got there, but the building was locked up and no one was around. I smacked the door then slumped against it, fuming. Where was everybody? It wasn't even four o'clock. Shouldn't Kasey's mechanic, Jake, be there at least?

I checked the van. It was open. Good, maybe I'd hotwire the damn thing and take it for a joy ride. I was contemplating how I might pull that off, considering my lack of mechanical expertise, when I saw the keys dangling from the ignition. Bingo!

The van rumbled to life under my touch and Jimmy Buffett kicked in with *Cheeseburger in Paradise*. Mashing the eject button, I jerked the tape out and tossed it into the back of the van. I glanced at the gas gage. Half a tank. Cool. I'd have myself some fun, and this time Race could be the one to feel a surge of panic when he came back and found out his ride had disappeared.

While Race had let me drive a lot, I'd never gone any place interesting like the hill above the University, where the roads were twisty and fun. I decided to swing up that direction to give myself a little challenge. Feeling vaguely uneasy without Race in the passenger's seat, I coaxed the van out onto the road.

The streets on the butte were winding and narrow, and the van swooped around them in an abrupt, rolling way that felt dangerous. The sensation sent a tingle through my muscles. Was this what it felt like to drive in competition? No wonder Race dug it so much.

I wound my way up the hillside, making it a contest to see how fast I could go. Then out of nowhere a car was coming at me. I swerved to the right. The shoulder gave way, and suddenly the van was plunging down an embankment, shrubs and undergrowth rushing by. A single thought echoed through my head as the van came to a stop, slamming into a Douglas fir.

Race is gonna kill me.

Chapter 12

As I sat on the front steps of the guy whose Douglas fir I'd dented, Race pulled up in the Charger. I expected a tirade. Instead, he gripped my shoulders hard and looked me over, his eyes finally stopping to peer into mine.

"Are you okay?"

I glanced away. "Yeah."

"He seems to be all right," said the guy who owned the house. "I don't think your van's too bad off, either, though I imagine you'll need a winch to get it out."

Race wound up having to call for a tow truck, but at least the homeowner didn't seem bothered by the damage I'd done to his shrubbery. And there wasn't much wrong with the van other than a dented grill, a tweaked fender, and a broken headlight.

"I probably oughta ground you or take away your driving privileges," Race said as we drove home. "But if you're willing to fix the van, I'll let it go at that." His tone lacked its usual lightness, but I didn't detect the hard set to his jaw that usually warned me when I'd pushed him too far.

Back at the trailer I retreated to my room. Race banged around in the kitchen, fixing dinner. I couldn't believe he was letting me off so easy. Maybe he felt guilty for leaving me home alone all night. Maybe he thought he got what he deserved. I wanted to believe that, but the rationalization left an uneasy feeling at the back of my mind.

"Cody—dinner."

I went out and dished myself up some Hamburger Helper. As I flopped down in the laundry chair, Race flicked the remote to bring the TV to life.

"About last night," he said, tossing the device onto the coffee table. "I sat down to rest for a few minutes and fell asleep. It was almost nine when I woke up this morning. I called from Kasey's shop, but I guess you missed the message I left on the answering machine."

My eyes locked on my plate, focusing on the green beans Race had mixed in with the meat and noodles. "I went straight over there from school."

"I should've left a note when we ran out to get parts."

Pissed as I was at him for ditching me, I couldn't see why he was rattling on about it when I'd screwed up so big. "Don't you even care?" I demanded.

"What—about the van?" Race poked at his food, scowling. "Of course I care, kid. I'd like to wring your damned neck."

"You don't act like you care."

"Why, because I'm not yelling at you?"

I shrugged.

"Look, Cody, even though it was a stupid way to deal with the situation, I know what inspired your joy ride. Maybe I'm messing up by not coming down hard on you. Maybe you'll go on to a life of crime and it will all be my fault. But I'd like to think you've got the sense to see what you've done wrong—that if I give you the opportunity, you'll make things right."

It couldn't be that easy. I'd screwed up and gotten caught. I was supposed to pay. Wasn't that how it worked?

"It doesn't make sense. If I was you, I'd kick my ass."

Race laughed. "I guess you're lucky you're not me then, huh?"

His amusement was like gasoline fueling the fire of my temper. "You think this is some kind of joke?"

Race studied me for a long moment. He sighed and set his plate down on the coffee table. "Okay. I didn't want to have to dredge this up, but here's the deal: When I was seventeen I wrecked my dad's Mercedes."

"Seriously? Man, Grandpa musta freaked."

"That's putting it mildly."

"So what'd he do?"

A rarely revealed hardness swept my uncle's face. "He sold my car." Race worked his mouth as if the words tasted bad. "It was just an old beater Nova, but I'd bought it with my own money. He said maybe I'd learn to respect other people's property if I lost something I cared about."

I stared at Race, thinking Grandpa had to be the world's biggest asshole.

"I'm not going to be like him," Race said with the determination I always saw before he went out on the track. "I refuse to believe that's the only way to raise a kid."

After school the next day, Race picked me up and took me to his shop. "The new fender and grill are in back," he said, gesturing over his shoulder into the rear of the van. "Some of the bolts are gonna be rusty. Make sure you spray 'em good with WD-40, or you'll never break 'em loose."

Leaving me to my own devices, he went to work on the Dart. I didn't have the slightest idea of how to begin, so I popped the hood. The shadows of the engine compartment made it impossible to see the bolts that held everything in place.

"There's a trouble light hanging under the work bench," Race called, anticipating my problem. I retrieved it, but all it did was illuminate my ignorance.

"Uh, Race? What am I supposed to do first?"

Patiently, he pointed out all the bolts and told me the best order in which to remove them if I wanted to save myself some grief. I dug a handful of wrenches out of the toolbox.

"No, kid, you want a ratchet." Race got one and showed me how it worked. "A job's always easier if you have the right tool."

I spent the rest of the afternoon grazing my knuckles and shearing off bolts. But I didn't complain. No way was I gonna let Race know how miserable I was. He commented on my swearing, saying I had the perfect vocabulary to be a mechanic, should I ever consider such a career path. As if.

I almost had the fender off when, reaching for a bolt, I sliced my finger. The thick smear of grease on my hands failed to staunch the oozing blood. "Hey, Race," I hollered. "We got any Band-aids around here?"

"Not exactly." He grabbed a roll of duct tape from the workbench and brought it to me, tearing off a piece. "There," he said, wrapping it around my finger. "All better."

"You coulda let me wash it first."

"Nah, germs can't live in grease."

"Is that a scientific fact?"

Race grinned. "Maybe."

I got back to work and the dented fender finally gave up its struggle. Sweating and shoving the hair out of my eyes, I pulled the new parts from the back of the van. I was glad to see that Race had thought of getting some replacement bolts. I'd busted off two of the originals.

The fender and grill went on a lot easier than they'd come off. As I fit them into place, a twinge of pride caught me off guard. *I'd fixed a car.* It wasn't like I'd rebuilt an engine or anything, but still. It was the first time I'd really used tools, and it surprised me how comfortable they felt in my hand.

"Nice work," said Race as he came up behind me. "I noticed you adjusting the fender. Pretty smart, thinking of a detail like that."

Embarrassed, I shrugged. It wasn't rocket science. The bolt holes were slotted, and it just made sense.

Race rested his hand on my shoulder. "You need to learn how to accept a compliment," he said. "You've done a great job here, and I'm proud of you. Now let me show you how to adjust that headlight, then we'll go get the obligatory celebration pizza."

"Can I have a beer this time?" I asked, craning my neck to look back at him.

Race squeezed my shoulder.

"No."

On the way home that night, I asked Race what he had left to do on the Dart.

"Mostly fine-tuning the set-up and replacing that bumper and fender."

I stretched out my feet so they were resting on the dash. "By an amazing stroke of coincidence, I just happen to have some experience replacing fenders."

Race looked at me across the cab, the surprised tilt of his eyebrows barely noticeable in the glow of the streetlights. "Are you volunteering to help with my car?"

"You don't have to make it sound like I offered to give you one of my kidneys."

Race chuckled. "My mistake. Sure kid, I'd really appreciate it."

Chapter 13

When I got up Saturday morning, Race was at his drafting table working on the ad he'd been neglecting all week.

"Would you believe I've been up since six?" he asked as I scrounged through the cupboards for cereal.

"Going by looks alone, I'd say you've been up all night."

We'd stayed at the shop until almost midnight the day before. Kasey had made her Friday deadline with the Mustang, but she'd gone down to Cottage Grove after work for her brother's graduation. Race was left with only me to help him finish the Dart.

I'd figured it would be a simple thing to swap out the parts, but that was before I knew they had to be modified. We had to trim the fender for clearance then roll the sharp edge so it couldn't cut the tire. Plus, the bumper needed to be welded to the fenders with metal straps. If it wasn't, Race said two cars could get locked together.

There was also the matter of straightening the buckled hood and setting up the front end. I proved to be about as useful as racing slicks in an ice storm. Race had to educate me, along with doing most of the work. The car was ready though, and it was a good thing because Race had a lot left to do on that ad before he could show it to his customer.

Kasey met us at the track that evening. First thing, she handed Race a check.

"What's this for?" he asked, studying it wide-eyed.

"You didn't think I was going to let you work all week for free, did you?"

"You don't owe me anything." Race held the check out to her.

"Just accept it graciously. I couldn't have finished that Mustang on time without your help, and I know putting the Dart back together must've taken a toll on your finances."

"Kasey—"

"End of discussion." She turned and walked away.

"Ha! You gotta love a chick who knows her own mind," I said, faking one of the punches I'd learned in karate at Race's chest. "Anyway, at least now you can pay the rent."

Race scowled as he caught my fist. "Kid, I could do without the commentary."

As the Street Stocks lined up to qualify a little later, Denny strolled into our pit, an open two-liter bottle of Coke in one of his big hands and Race's spare carburetor in the other. He handed the carb to my uncle then took a swig off the bottle, wiping his mouth with the sleeve of his firesuit.

"Thanks for the loan," he said. "You ever get word back from the officials on what's gonna happen to Addamsen?"

"They're taking his payoff and letting him keep his points."

"Typical," Denny said, shaking his head and taking another slug of Coke. "Guess we'll just have to work things out for ourselves."

Race gave him a warning look. "I don't want him wrecked."

"Wouldn't dream of it," Denny agreed. "Anyway, it's more humiliating if you just outrun him."

Ted shouted for the Sportsmen to line up and Denny hotfooted it back to his car.

"I've never seen anyone treat a two-liter as their own personal Big Gulp," I commented.

"That's nothing," said Race. "You should see him when he's walking around the pits with a gallon of milk."

*   *   *

Jim had developed some kind of engine trouble during practice, and Kasey was helping him sort it out, so I helped Race get ready to time in.

"Whoa, kid," he said as I jammed the window net into place. "Don't be in such a hurry. I need my helmet."

I dutifully went to get it. "This thing looks like it's been through a war," I said as I handed it to him.

"Yeah, I know. I need a new one. They're just so damned expensive."

"I bet Kasey would buy you one."

"Kasey's already put enough money into this team."

Much as I wanted to note that that was the whole point of sponsorship, I held my tongue. Money was a subject he wouldn't budge on, same as the non-existent romance I kept prodding him to pursue.

"You think the car's gonna run all right?" I asked.

"It felt fine during practice."

"Then I expect you to take fast time."

"That *would* be a nice way to stick it to Addamsen."

Race didn't take fast time. He didn't even make it into the top five, which meant he missed out on the trophy dash. That was something that hadn't happened all season.

"Do we need to make adjustments?" Kasey asked. "You looked a little loose out there."

"Nah, it's me, not the car. I just don't have my edge tonight."

"I wouldn't doubt it, after the week you've had."

"It's been no worse than yours."

"The difference," said Kasey, "is that I don't have to go out there and compete."

Without the dash to participate in, Race had more time than usual on his hands. I offered to toss the Nerf football around with him, but he was too tired. When he failed to pull out his sketchbook, I knew he must really be beat.

I shut the lid of the toolbox and parked myself on top of it, lighting a cigarette and flipping though the drawings. There must've been one of damn near every car in the pits, as well as several of Jim, Denny, and Kasey. There were a lot of Kasey.

"Hey, I don't remember you drawing this," I said, studying a sketch of myself leaning against the Dart. Did I really look that cool? I took a pull off my cigarette, and *BANG*, it exploded in my face.

"Holy shit!"

Race howled, hunching over and practically falling off the stack of tires he was sitting on. It took me a second to figure out he was more than just an innocent bystander.

"You—you!" I sputtered, throwing down the shredded remains of my smoke.

Race grinned wickedly. "Told ya it'd be a mistake to think I was writing off your pranks." He dug a tin of Cigarette Loads out of his firesuit pocket. I'd used the tiny explosive devices on my friend Mike, so I recognized the package immediately.

"I think I'll hold onto these," Race said. "Just in case."

Without Race to provide competition, Addamsen won the trophy dash. In the heat, Race drove like he was operating under some kind of weird two-second time delay. He made all the right moves, just not at the right time. I'd never been able to put a finger on exactly what was so cool about the way he could maneuver a car around the track, but whatever it was, Race didn't have it tonight. He barely managed a fourth place finish, and that was only because Jim, who'd been second, blew his engine.

Addamsen won again, sneaking up to within two points of Race's lead. It wasn't a very big margin.

"Something better change before the main," Race said as he crawled out of the car. "Or I'm in trouble."

Kasey looked at him sympathetically. Even though she didn't say anything, I could tell what she was thinking. Unless Addamsen had a four-tire blowout or was abducted by aliens, Race was gonna lose the points lead.

Between the Super Stock heats, Jim and Denny sprinted across the track. They came back fifteen minutes later towing a car I'd never seen before. It sported the same number 9 as Denny's Camaro, but instead of being school bus yellow, it was red.

"Big Red?" I guessed, looking to Race for confirmation.

He nodded.

Jim went to work with a roll of duct tape, transforming Denny's 9 into his own familiar 4. Then he and Denny began checking tire pressures and gassing up the car. Engaged in an animated discussion, the two of them glanced occasionally toward Addamsen's pit.

"Isn't Jim third in points?" I asked as I watched.

"That's right," Race agreed.

"And Denny's fourth."

"Uh huh."

"That's just plain nuts, throwing away a chance to move up."

"No, kid," Race corrected. "That's what's known as class."

While the Sportsmen got into position, Kasey and I found ourselves a good viewing spot along the pit wall.

"He's not gonna be able to hold off Addamsen, is he?" I asked.

"Most likely not."

"He's crazy. I can't believe what he puts himself through for that stupid championship."

Kasey smiled. "He's no different than any of the others," she pointed out.

"Well, they're all crazy, then."

Race started the main event mid-field. It was strange seeing him there instead of in the last row, but at least it gave him a buffer against Addamsen. Since Jim was driving a different car than the one he'd qualified with, he'd been bumped to the back of the pack. He got a good jump, though, because Denny, who sat directly in front of Addamsen, seemed to forget where his accelerator was. Surging up beside Denny's yellow Camaro, Jim left Addamsen all by his lonesome.

Pandemonium reigned for the first few laps until the pack began to thin out. Race gained a couple positions on slower cars then lost one to Tom Carey, settling into sixth place. Toward the back, Denny made a move on the 22 car, while Jim used up the whole track in his fight to get around Denny's Camaro. It seemed to be a futile battle, but Addamsen hadn't found a way around either one of them.

Race squeaked by another of the slow guys then dropped back to sixth a lap later when Randy Whalen ripped past him coming out of turn two. Holly Schrader challenged the Dart next. I was so busy worrying about Race that it took me a while to catch on to what Jim and Denny were up to. They'd moved into eighth and ninth place, but Addamsen still hadn't passed them. As Denny put the heat on Schrader, I began to see the reason. Each time Addamsen made a move on Jim, Jim would slide up or down the track, so he couldn't get by. Big Red wasn't as fast as Addamsen's Camaro, but with Denny right in front of it helping to block the track, it didn't need to be.

"Are they running interference for Race?"

"It looks that way," Kasey said.

"Won't they get black-flagged?"

"No. It isn't the most sportsman-like behavior, but it's not illegal."

"That is totally cool." It occurred to me that Denny, who'd had second fastest time, was sacrificing his chance at winning the main. I pointed that out to Kasey.

"Sometimes it's the principle of the thing," she said. "Jerry Addamsen's been shoving people around for years, and I can guarantee you those two aren't the only ones who'd like to put a stop to it."

"Don't you think it's gonna piss Race off? He's got such a weird sense of honor."

"Race isn't the only one they're doing this for. Besides, Jerry took the matter beyond the normal rules when he wrecked the Dart. If Race hadn't put in overtime repairing that car, he wouldn't be so exhausted that he needed someone to run interference for him."

I worried Addamsen would take Jim out, but after last week he seemed to be watching himself. While he rode Big Red's bumper hard, and even nudged it a couple of times, he kept his driving clean.

When Jim and Denny came up behind the Dart, their forward progression stopped. They finished in seventh and eighth place. Addamsen once again trailed Race by four points.

The cars slowed and exited the track. Kasey stopped me as I turned to head back to our pit. "I know it's a point of pride for you, coming up with new ways to get Race up every morning," she said. "But you might take pity on him and let him sleep in tomorrow."

I laughed. "I think I can do that." Anyway, I was gonna have to reconsider my strategy now that I knew he'd fight back.

Chapter 14

On Sunday, Race managed to get his ad finished and life dropped back into a less frantic pattern. It was the last week of school and I was glad to be almost done with it. When you don't know anybody, school is a pretty lonely place.

Still, no homework meant no excuse for my reading habit. I figured Race was used to seeing me with a book, and I was sure he'd never say anything to hurt me, but I couldn't stomach the idea of him thinking I was some kind of geek. The worry lurked at the edges of my mind Tuesday afternoon as I kicked back in the laundry chair, reading *The Red Pony* for probably the sixth time. It was one of my favorite stories, even though it depressed the crap out of me and gave me the creeps every time I read the part about the buzzard plucking the dead pony's eye out. Something about the way Steinbeck used such simple language to say so much really got to me.

A sudden movement caught my eye and I glanced up. Race, who was allegedly working at the drafting table, had abandoned his project in favor of one of those ever-present sketchbooks. I shrank down in my chair, knowing I was the focus of his artistic outburst.

"What are you doing?" I asked, a little cranky because that kind of attention always made me feel like I wasn't wearing any pants.

"Just a quick sketch."

"Again?"

"You make a good subject."

I snorted.

"Seriously," Race said, scribbling on the pad. "You're visually interesting."

"What's *that* supposed to mean?"

"Well, there's your hair, for starters. That rooster tail of yours is a real attention grabber."

Almost unconsciously, I reached up to touch my bangs, which, with the aid of a great deal of super-hold gel, arched out over my forehead.

"Hold still," Race said.

"Wait, I just remembered something."

Apparently sensing I wasn't gonna hold the pose much longer, Race quickly scratched at the sketchpad. "What is it?"

"You're supposed to make an appointment with my guidance counselor."

"What's that about?"

"How should I know?" My tone might have been a tad too defensive. There'd been a couple of pranks, but I couldn't see how anyone would've found out. Most likely it was just some routine end-of-the-school year bullshit. Or at least I hoped so. I got up, causing Race to sigh, and retrieved the note from my backpack.

"You're supposed to give him a call," I said, handing it over.

"You haven't done anything wrong, have you?"

"No!" I swear Race could see right through me.

He let out a second, more exaggerated sigh. "Then why do I have this feeling of impending doom?"

On Thursday afternoon, Race met with my adviser. I was surprised at how nervous I felt, waiting for him to get back from the school. Not wanting him to know, I chilled in my room and didn't come out when I heard the van pull into the driveway.

Race knocked on my open door before walking into the room where I was sprawled on my bed, pretending to read. He eased himself down in my desk chair wearing a poker face that would have made him rich in Vegas.

"So what did the counselor say?" I asked casually.

Race swiveled the chair back and forth, grinning. "Oh, we just had a nice little talk."

"About what?"

"Don't you know?"

"It didn't have anything to do with a fetal pig, did it?"

"A fetal pig? No, not that I recall." Race flashed me a broad smile. "But maybe you'd like to tell me about the fetal pig."

"Another time." Like in twenty years. The way that substitute had shrieked when she'd found the formaldehyde-infused pig brain in the top drawer of her desk had been hilarious, but I wasn't sure if my uncle would appreciate the humor.

"Actually," Race said, "it wasn't anything bad. He was impressed that you'd pulled the D's and F's you were getting at your old school up to B's and C's. He just wondered if putting you in an advanced English class next year would be too much pressure."

Slightly dazed by this turn of events, I stared at Race.

"What *I'm* wondering is why you never told me any of this," Race said. "I'd think you'd be proud of your accomplishments."

I shrugged. "You never asked."

Race sighed. "Well, it's obvious you're no idiot. I told him to put you in whatever classes he felt were appropriate."

"So in other words, I have to work harder next year."

"The advantage to that," Race said, "is it'll give you less time to mess around with fetal pigs." He pushed away from the desk, hesitating as something in one of the piles of papers attracted his attention.

"You still have this?"

I propped myself up on one elbow to see what he was holding. It was the Superbird sketch he'd done for me that Thanksgiving we'd spent in Eugene.

Race studied the picture and shook his head. "I must've drawn this—what—eight or nine years ago?"

"More like ten."

"Times sure change." He returned the paper to the stack. With another slight shake of his head he looked at me and smiled. "I can't believe you haven't thrown that away."

I couldn't believe I hadn't put it on the wall, where it belonged. When Race left the room I got up and pinned the Superbird drawing to the cheap wood paneling above the desk.

I don't know whether Race was in complete denial or didn't trust the local weather forecasters, but he always seemed shocked and insulted when the races got rained out. Saturday, the first day of summer vacation, was no exception. It didn't help that my dad called again.

"Why won't you talk to him?" Race asked. "I can understand you being ticked off at your mom, but your dad's a decent guy."

"That's your opinion. He had his chance while I was living with him."

"You didn't exactly make a good case for yourself, staying out till all hours and flunking half your classes."

I looked away. "That's no excuse for kicking me out." Why did Race have to take his side of it, anyway? He hardly knew my father.

"Kid, you got busted for vandalism. Your dad felt like he had to take drastic measures to keep you from messing up your life."

Right. "He coulda tried listening to me."

"He's making an effort now. You oughta take that into account."

I gave Race a pointed look. "Let's see, you last talked to Grandma and Grandpa what—five years ago?"

"That's different. You know what my dad's like. And Mom hasn't even tried to keep in touch."

"Yeah, I'm sure you left her a forwarding address."

Race scowled. "She has connections. If she wanted to know where I live it wouldn't be that difficult for her to find out. Your mom managed to."

By Sunday morning, Race had recovered from his rainout blues. "I've gotta go meet Kasey to run an errand," he told me through a mouthful of frozen Twinkie. "You okay here by yourself?"

I paused in the middle of the karate punches I was practicing. "Can I come with you?"

"No."

"Then why'd you ask?"

Ignoring my question, Race pawed through the usual chaos on the coffee table for his keys.

"Is this a date?" I persisted.

"Get real, kid."

"Well, why not? When are you gonna tell Kasey how you feel, anyway?"

"Did it ever occur to you that maybe I have?" Race located his key chain and pulled it free.

"You did?" I couldn't believe he'd given me a serious answer. Usually he told me to mind my own business.

"Yeah. She's not interested. And I'm not gonna push it. I'd rather have her friendship than nothing at all." Race pulled a sweatshirt over his head. The rain was still falling, and the temperature hadn't broken sixty-five degrees in two days. He reached for the doorknob.

"Dude, you can't give up hope."

"I appreciate your support kid, but it's a lost cause."

Once Race was gone, I spent an hour practicing the stuff I'd learned in karate that week. My second lesson had gone a lot better than the first. Even though the sensei had rambled on about respect, balance, and self-control, I'd kind of dug what he was saying. I liked the idea of having the discipline to stick with something until I was excellent at it. The things he and the more experienced students could do were pretty intense.

When I got bored with the punches and kicks, I sat down at my desk to work on a story. Time disappeared, and suddenly Race was leaning through my bedroom door.

"Hey," he said, startling me. "Let's go down to the shop."

I glanced at my watch, shocked to see that it was almost five o'clock. "Now? It's dinner time."

"We'll grab a pizza at Track Town. I've got something to show you."

Never one to let anything stand between me and a pizza, I stuffed my notebook into a drawer and followed him to the van.

While we ate, I pestered Race to tell me what he had down at the shop, but he refused.

"Does it have something to do with the Dart?" I asked.

"No."

"Is it alive?"

"Of course not. I have enough trouble feeding you."

"Is it bigger than a breadbox?"

"Definitely."

At the shop, a light mist fell, slicking my leather jacket as I stood waiting for Race to unlock the door.

"Close your eyes," he said.

"You've gotta be kidding."

"Nope. Close 'em or I won't show you."

Groaning, I complied. Race led me inside.

"Okay. You can take a look."

It took a second to get my bearings. Then I saw it. Tucked away in the back corner sat a pale yellow '65 Galaxie. For a minute all I could do was stare.

"Dude . . ." I said softly, shaking my head as a stampede of emotions ran roughshod over me. I slipped closer and touched the fender, needing proof the car wasn't some kind of mirage.

"It doesn't run," Race said. "But Kasey can get us a good deal on an engine kit. I'll show you how to do a rebuild then help you go through the brakes and check the suspension. By the time you get your license in December, we oughta be able to have it on the road."

I stroked the Galaxie like it was some kind of living thing, the metal cool and smooth beneath my fingers. No one had given me anything like this in my life. Race could hardly pay his bills—I couldn't believe he was willing to spend the little money he had on me.

Blinking hard, I turned to him. His face was lit with a satisfied grin.

"Why?" I asked, my voice cracking.

Race shrugged. "I just wanted to."

"I can't believe this . . ." My throat tightened around the words.

Race spared me the embarrassment of losing it in front of him by stepping forward to lift the hood. "How 'bout dragging that toolbox over here? If we get on it, we might be able to pull this engine tonight."

"Morgan thinks he has this race all wrapped up, folks, but in a brilliant surprise move Cody Everett screams past him to take the lead!"

It was nearly midnight, and Race and I had stopped at the supermarket to pick up some groceries on the way home. Still stoked about the Galaxie, I challenged my uncle with an empty shopping cart.

"It's a true battle," I said. "Engines scream down the straightaway, tires squeal through the corners—"

"Everett cries out in terror as Morgan stuffs him in the wall." Race swerved his cart at mine.

"But as always, Everett is undeterred by this terrible set-back! He regains control and chases Morgan down the front stretch."

Race tossed a bottle of dish soap into his cart, squashing the bread. "And the crowd roars in laughter, watching Everett try to race with two flat tires, a bent frame, and half his suspension scattered across the track."

"Minor mechanical difficulties are no problem for a driver as talented as Everett," I countered. "It's a bitter fight, ladies and gentlemen. Both drivers are tough and experienced. But in the end superior skill wins out and Everett takes the checkered flag!"

Letting go of the shopping cart's handle, I pumped both fists in the air. The cart was traveling pretty quick, and like any good stock car, it pulled to the left—straight into a display of Charmin. Packages of toilet paper cascaded over the tiled floor.

"Nice victory lap, Everett," Race said. "Remind me never to let you drive the Dart."

Dumbfounded, I gaped at the mess.

"Y'know," Race commented, looking around to see if anybody had witnessed the incident. "I think what we *really* need now is some produce." He snagged the sleeve of my leather jacket and quickly directed me to the other end of the store.

Out in the van, we laughed like idiots. I was still feeling giddy and revved up when we turned off the highway into the trailer park.

"Did you check the mail yesterday?" Race asked.

"No. I thought you did."

Race pulled alongside the bank of mailboxes. He handed me the key so I could open ours. I dug out the wad of mail and began sorting through it.

"Bill," I tossed an envelope at Race. "Another bill. Latest issue of *Circle Track*—"

"Hey, watch it," Race groused as the magazine bounced off his shoulder.

I flashed him my cockiest grin and continued slinging mail. "Bill. Occupant. Something from the DMV . . ." I froze, my eyes locked on the remaining envelope. Familiar billowy handwriting screamed up at me.

"What is it?" Race asked.

"A letter from Mom."

I hadn't heard from her since the day she'd left Portland. Even when I got in trouble, it was Dad who'd talked to her. All the arrangements had been made for me to move to Eugene without a single word passing between us. What could she possibly have to say to me now?

Feeling Race's eyes on me, I didn't risk looking up. I thrust the keys in his direction. "We gonna sit here all night?"

As soon as I got to my room I tore open the letter. It was short and to the point. Mom was done with her bartending classes and had found a great job. She'd heard from Dad that I was no longer quite the juvie-bound punk she'd given up on back in April. It was time to get a fresh start. She wanted me to move to Phoenix.

Chapter 15

I couldn't sleep that night. The letter, like a beacon rotating in my head, kept drawing my attention. The worst part was, of all the stuff that could've gone wrong with my living arrangements, this hadn't even been on the list. I tried to convince myself that I could refuse to go—that Mom had given up her right to tell me what to do when she left. But deep down, I was afraid she had the power to make me move.

Race had enough sense not to ask about the letter the next morning, and I didn't tell him what it said. Maybe if I didn't respond, Mom would give up the idea. She was flighty. She didn't like inconvenience. Unfortunately, she was also stubborn. When she decided she wanted something, she usually got her way.

I tried to figure out why she wanted me back. Maybe she was angling for child support. Maybe she needed to impress a new boyfriend by playing the Good Mommy role. The one thing I wouldn't let myself believe was that she might actually miss me. I'd been through a lifetime of her intermittent bursts of attention, and they always ended in disappointment. It was easier to be ignored.

"You okay, kid?" Race asked when I'd been up for a good twenty minutes and still hadn't said anything.

"Sure."

"I've got a welding job at the shop this morning. Fuel cell can for a Street Stock. I should be home by two at the latest. You can come if you want."

I shook my head.

"Don't let her get to you," Race said, punching my arm lightly as he headed out the door. "It isn't worth it."

Now that school was out, I had plenty of time and nothing to spend it on. I tried finishing the story I'd been writing but got stuck on the ending and couldn't figure out a way to fix it. On any other day I could take a walk along the river to kick-start my brain, but it was still raining, and I couldn't stop obsessing about the letter. I pulled it out of the envelope and stared at the words. She'd said to give her a call. Maybe I should do that. Just confront things head on and tell her I wasn't coming.

I picked up the phone and dialed, but it didn't go at all the way I'd planned. From the get-go she commandeered the conversation, droning on about her new life and job. I could hardly get a word in.

"Mom," I interrupted. "Mom! I need to talk to you about coming to Phoenix."

"I'll send you a ticket," she said, barely stopping to breathe. "But not from Eugene. I refuse to pay the extra fare just for the sake of convenience. Get Race to drive you to Portland. It'll give you a chance to say goodbye to your dad before you leave."

"Are you high?"

"What did you say to me?"

"I'm not gonna make Race drive a hundred miles just because you're too damned cheap to pay a few extra bucks!" God, how inconsiderate could she be? "Anyway, I'm not moving to Phoenix. I like it here." I was sort of surprised to hear myself say that. Coming back after running away had seemed like the only decent choice I had. But now it was more than that. I couldn't stand to think of what my life would be like without Race in it.

A long, slow silence oozed out of the phone. "Maybe I didn't make myself clear," Mom said. "You're my son, and you'll do as I say."

"Make me!" I slammed the handset down so hard that pieces of the phone's base busted off and flew across the room.

144

Shit! How was I gonna explain that to Race?

Maybe I could fix it. He must have some glue somewhere. I dug through all the drawers in the kitchen, then through the little compartments at the edge of the drafting table. Finally I found a bottle of Elmer's under the sink.

It took me a good ten minutes to locate the broken pieces. Knowing Race could walk through the door at any second, I tried to stick them all together at once. But the glue wasn't drying fast enough to hold them, and they kept falling apart. I was about to throw the stupid phone across the room in frustration when Race pulled up out front. Damn!

"What happened?" Race asked as he discovered me trying to shake sticky bits of plastic from my fingers.

I might as well have had glue on my lips, too, for all I could answer.

Race went to the kitchen, opened a drawer, and pulled out a roll of duct tape.

"What did I tell you about using the right tool?" He tore off a piece of the sticky silver webbing and used it to bind the plastic together. "There. That thing's good for up to two-hundred miles an hour."

An unexpected twist of a smile darted across my face. I shook my head. Race probably thought duct tape could cure cancer.

"There's only one person who could piss you off enough to mutilate my phone," he said, sitting down on the arm of the laundry chair and giving me a serious look. "What did she say that got you so upset?"

I didn't answer. No way was I gonna tell him.

Race sighed, running a hand through his hair. "Cody, if she bothers you that much, don't talk to her."

"You're not mad about the phone?"

"No. But I'm starting to worry about you. It's like your temper doesn't have an 'off' switch. You're always running wide open. One of these days that's gonna get you into real trouble. You just got lucky with the van."

"It's not like I do it on purpose! It just happens. Usually I don't even see it coming." It was the first time I'd said anything about the anger that ambushed me out of nowhere. It was embarrassing, admitting to it.

"I get that, kid. I know you think I don't understand because it's so easy for me to let stuff go, but I can see it's a real struggle for you. I wish there was something I could do to make it easier."

Race went quiet, looking at me, then he got up and clapped his hand solidly on my shoulder. "C'mon, let's go down to the shop and work on your car. That'll make you forget about all this."

My car. That was just one more thing I'd have to leave behind if Mom got her way. It wasn't the most important thing, but I was sure gonna miss it.

Chapter 16

I didn't call Mom again, and over the next few days the urgency of the letter slowly lost its grip on me. Practicing my karate and working on the Galaxie served as good distractions. Race seemed impressed with how easy it was for me to remember all the stuff he taught me. He even told me I was mechanically inclined, imparting this like he thought it was more important than being the next Dalai Lama.

Much as I expected Mom to call me back, it didn't happen. Each day that passed left me a little more at ease. I didn't want Race finding out what she was up to. It wasn't that I didn't believe he wanted me with him. I was just afraid that if he knew, he'd agree Mom had a right to take me.

By the end of the week, I was pretty much back to normal. I decided that unless I heard from my mother again, I'd pretend I'd never gotten her letter. That was easier than trying to control the anger that blazed up whenever I thought of her. My sensei kept talking about centering yourself and not letting your emotions control you, but it seemed impossible. How could I get a handle on something that huge?

On Saturday, cloudless skies and temperatures in the 70s erased the dismal weather of the past ten days. Race was revved up after the previous week's rainout and easily creamed Addamsen in the trophy dash. We spent the lag time between events playing catch.

"Look alive, kid!" he hollered, drilling the Nerf football at me. I nearly tripped over a toolbox making a dive for it.

"Hey," I said, tossing it back. "You never did explain why you drive a Dodge. Doesn't it make it harder when something breaks here at the track and you can't borrow it from Jim or Denny?"

"Sure, but there's advantages, too." Race tossed the football toward one of our parts boxes, apparently sensing another teaching opportunity. He never said it outright, but I knew he was jazzed about me getting interested in cars. He tugged the floor jack through the infield dust and used it to raise the front end of the Dart.

"Okay, look at this." Race crouched down to point at the underside of the car. "See how it doesn't have springs? Instead it's got these torsion bars. They provide the spring action by twisting. The cool part is you can make an adjustment to how high the car sits off the ground by turning this bolt, here. Not such a big deal in a Sportsman, where everyone uses weight jacks to adjust the ride height, but it was important in a Street Stock."

I hunched down beside him, breathing in the mingled scents of hot oil and speedway dust as I studied the suspension. "So why doesn't everyone in Street Stocks run a Dodge?"

"Because the whole amateur racing industry is centered around Chevys. They're cheaper and easier to get parts for. People seem to think there's some mysterious magic about how Chrysler suspensions work, but that's a bunch of crap. The laws of physics don't change just because you're running a Dodge."

"Exactly," said Kasey, coming up behind us. She'd been off checking out Jim's new engine.

"Is the lesson over?" I asked. "I'm starving."

"You're always starving," Race said.

"So?"

Not bothering to argue the point, Race dug some money out of his wallet and handed it over.

I snagged a cheeseburger from the concession stand then took it over to the hearse so I could watch the next race with Steve and Alex. I'd gotten into the habit of hanging out with them for a little while every Saturday. Even though Steve had been the one to entertain my ghoulish curiosity that first night, it was Alex who was turning out to be the coolest. He knew Tae Kwon Do, so we had a lot to talk about. I told him what my sensei had said about keeping your emotions in check, and how impossible that seemed.

"It's like everything else. It just takes practice," Alex said. "You didn't expect to split a board after your first lesson, did you?"

"Of course not."

"Well, controlling your emotions is no different. Just keep practicing, and over time it will get easier."

When I looked at it that way, it gave me a little hope.

Addamsen behaved himself in the heat, in spite of the way Race had shown him up earlier. Maybe Jim and Denny's lesson in manners two weeks before had made an impression. Surprisingly, there hadn't been any fallout. I guess Addamsen knew he'd end up looking like an ass if he tweaked about it.

Denny pulled off a win, with Race coming in second and adding another point to his lead. The cars filed into the pits, and I jumped down from the hood of the Cadillac. "Catch you guys later," I told the paramedics. "I gotta go see if my uncle needs anything."

I dashed back over to the Dart, drawing the pungent odor of racing fuel deep into my lungs and reveling in how the shriek of Super Stock engines reverberated in my chest. It was a perfect night to be at the speedway.

"Nice of you to let Denny win one for a change," I said as Race wiggled out of the Dart.

"Let him, hell. I'm not the only one out here who can win a race, y'know."

"Yeah," I said, slugging him in the shoulder, "but you're the only one who could take the points lead away from Addamsen."

While we waited for the next event we tossed the football around, squinting against the sun until it dropped behind the grandstands. A breeze wafted through the infield, stirring a strange exhilaration inside me. I had my own car, the coolest uncle in the world, and a Mom who was way off in Phoenix, where she couldn't bother me. I was finally in sync with the universe. From here on out, anything was possible.

Ted Green hollered for the Limited Sportsmen to line up, prompting Race to put the football away and slide through the window of the Dart.

"Addamsen's gonna blow his engine on the first lap of the main and you'll gain ten points on him," I said.

Race cinched up his belts. "Now where's the fun in that? I'd rather have it be neck-in-neck right up to the finish. It's more exciting for the fans that way."

Maybe so, but there was nothing like a good points buffer to make you feel secure. I dropped my cigarette and ground it out in the powdery dust, reaching to hook up the window net. As Race cranked the engine, I crouched and hollered at him through the nylon webbing. "Now remember, I'll settle for nothing less than total victory, so get out there and kick some ass!"

With fast time, Race held the outside position on the back row. I let out a whoop as he rocketed between Tom Carey and Jim at the start. Before Addamsen could file in behind him, Jim swung down low, slamming the door on the black Camaro. For the next eight laps, the four of them snaked their way through traffic, gradually picking off slower cars.

Addamsen managed to squeak around Jim, but he seemed to have his hands full with Carey. That was fine by me. The further Race could stretch out his points lead, the better I'd feel. The four cars zigzagged around lapped traffic, and Race zeroed in on Holly Schrader, challenging her for third place.

Half a lap ahead, one of the slower cars began spewing steam. The second place car, trying to pass the leader, got squirrelly when it hit the trail of water in the high groove. Its driver regained control, but Race wasn't so lucky. As he swooped around Schrader's Mustang in turn one, the back end of his car broke loose. Carey, directly behind, clipped the left corner of his bumper. The back of the Dart lurched up off the ground. The rear tires left the asphalt and the engine revved. The dark underbelly of the car flipped into view and, smooth as could be, Race's car rolled up on its roof.

There wasn't time to do anything but think *oh shit* as Carey swerved to the right, launching himself off the top of turn two. Addamsen dodged low, spinning to the grass of the infield. Then the rest of the pack piled into turn one. Jim, in the lead, had nowhere to go. He tried to throw his car sideways, but was too close to pull it off. In front of him, the Dart completed its roll, slamming down on all four wheels.

Jim's Camaro slid around to a three-quarter angle.

Then it plowed right into Race's door.

Chapter 17

A cold, sick feeling clenched my stomach as I watched Jim's Camaro slam into the Dart.

"Oh my God," Kasey said, her whisper cutting straight through me. Then she was dragging me across the infield. Yellow tow truck lights sliced the darkness as we ran.

Jim had already backed his car away from Race's by the time we got to turn two, where the unsettling reek of overheated brakes hung in the air. With all the dust, I could hardly see.

Ted Greene stood at the edge of the asphalt, trying to restrict the growing crowd of crew members. "Get back," he shouted. "Nobody but track employees and paramedics out here!" He seized my shoulders as I tried to shove past. "Kasey!"

Her arms went around me, pulling me close. "He's right, Cody. We need to stay back."

The ambulance braked at the top of the track. Before Alex and Steve could get out, Race crawled through the window of the Dart. Relief rushed over me. *He was okay.*

Swaying, Race gripped the top of the door then leaned over and retched.

"You should've stayed in the car," Alex said, sprinting to his side. "You could have a spinal injury."

"I'm fine—just a little dizzy."

"Better safe than sorry. Now hold still. No, stop moving your head. You want to end up paralyzed? Steve, get me a cervical collar."

Steve brought it to him, then leaned into the Dart to grab Race's helmet.

"Did you lose consciousness?" Alex asked as he immobilized Race's neck.

"I don't know."

"You don't know?" Alex led Race to the back of the ambulance and made him sit down.

"I don't remember," Race snapped.

"Can you tell me who the president is?"

"Abraham Lincoln."

Alex frowned. "Are you trying to be funny?"

"Yeah, but apparently I'm not being very successful. Look, I told you I'm fine. Why don't you go ask Jim who the president is?"

"Jim isn't the one with a big crack in his helmet," Steve said.

Race tried to stand up, but Alex restrained him. "You're going to the hospital to get checked out."

"I don't wanna go to the hospital."

"Steve, radio for an ambulance."

"I don't need a damned ambulance!"

An uneasy feeling crept over me. It was totally unlike my uncle to give the paramedics such a hard time.

"Race, you're showing classic signs of head trauma. If I don't—"

Race clutched suddenly at the door of the ambulance, and Alex steadied him as he started to sway. "Oh, shit. . . . I feel really—" He slumped forward into the paramedic's arms.

Fear squeezed my chest, forcing out the air. What the hell was happening? He'd been fine just a second ago! Kasey's grip tightened around my shoulders, and it was that, more than the damp breeze sweeping in from the surrounding wetlands, that chilled me.

"He's going to be all right," she said, her voice soft in my ear. It seemed like she was trying to reassure herself as much as me.

As Steve pulled a stretcher out of the back of the Cadillac, and Alex tended to Race, Ted went into drill sergeant mode, barking at the people who still crowded the edge of the track. "Get back! Anyone not helping with these cars, clear out!"

All those times I'd watched shows like *Cops* and *911* I'd never thought about what must be going through the minds of the people involved. It seemed sick, now, that they could put that stuff on TV. That was my uncle Alex and Steve were working on, and I didn't want anybody watching. Finally, I understood why Alex refused to talk about his job.

A siren wailed far away down West 11th. I shivered, my knees going wobbly. Kasey's grip was the only thing keeping me upright.

Amber light from the tow trucks bathed the wrecked cars, the track, and the backs of the paramedics. The yowl of the siren got louder. I began to shake as the real ambulance pulled onto the track, its flashing red beams bleeding together with the yellow ones.

"It's going to be okay," Kasey repeated, but the trembling in her voice made a lie of her words.

The new paramedics took charge. Seeing us pressed against the front of the crowd, Alex slipped over to join us, his eyes solemn.

"What happened?" I demanded. "He was just talking to you! What's going on?"

"Sometimes with head injuries it's like—"

"You told me no one ever gets hurt out here! You said!"

"Cody—" Alex reached out, but I shoved his hand away.

"You lied to me!"

"Kasey?" Denny was suddenly there. "Give me the keys to the van. I'll make sure all Race's stuff gets back to the shop."

"They're in the toolbox."

I tore away from Kasey's grasp. "Who gives a shit about his stuff? What about Race? What's gonna happen to him?"

Kasey swung me around to face her, drawing me close with a little shake that cut through my panic. "He's going to be fine, Cody," she said, looking me right in the eye.

But what if he wasn't? What if . . .

Ted touched Kasey's shoulder. "The ambulance is ready to leave. You two should go. I'll help Denny get things sorted out." He looked across the track at the crumpled Dart and shook his head. "I'm so sorry, Kasey."

It was the only time I'd heard him say anything in a civil tone.

The emergency room at Sacred Heart was glaring bright compared to the darkness outside. I shifted restlessly behind Kasey as she tried to give the lady at the admittance desk the information she needed.

"And your relationship to the patient?" the woman asked. Something in her tone made me nervous. Didn't they only let family see you when you got hurt bad?

"They're engaged," I said.

"That's right," Kasey agreed. I'd never heard her lie before.

"So you can provide contact information for his parents?"

"Just their names, but they live here in town."

How did Kasey know their names? Race hardly ever talked about his mom and dad.

"Don't call them," I told the lady. "They won't come, anyway."

"Cody, they have to be notified," Kasey said. "They're his parents."

"And that's supposed to mean something?" My voice rose to an agitated squeak. Why did we have to go through all this crap? Why couldn't someone just tell us what was wrong with Race?

The lady at the desk asked about a hundred more questions that neither of us knew how to answer, then she told us to sit down and wait.

"When are they gonna tell us something?" I asked, pacing in front of Kasey's chair. I really needed a smoke, but I was afraid to leave the ER.

"They're doing the best they can. Just sit down, all right?"

"I can't." I felt like I'd swallowed a dozen NoDoz. Besides, I knew that if I tried to chill, I'd disintegrate into a blubbering idiot. My thoughts strayed toward the edge of a dark path and I yanked them back before they could explore it any further.

"Cody?"

I swung around, startled to find Grandma behind me, even though I knew she couldn't live more than ten minutes from the hospital. She'd cancelled her visit the previous summer, so it had been almost two years since I'd seen her. The one thing about her that had always stood out in my mind was how perfectly put-together she seemed. She didn't look that way now.

"You shouldn't be here," I said, glancing between her and my grandfather.

"Cody." Kasey took my hand, giving it a warning squeeze.

"No! They don't have any right. They don't even care about Race!"

"They're his parents," Kasey said firmly. She got up and introduced herself, explaining how she knew their son. Grandma's jaw twitched as she listened to what had happened, but she reacted to the news with her typical stoicism. Grandpa stood rigid, glaring at me like the whole thing was my fault.

I slumped into a chair and glowered as my grandmother pestered Kasey for details we didn't know. Why couldn't she sit down and shut up? Kasey didn't need the stress of having to comfort her. Especially now, when I knew damned well she was as scared as I was.

It seemed like a year before a doctor called for my grandparents. If I hadn't been so freaked out, I would've been pissed he assumed they had some claim on my uncle. I wedged myself between him and everyone else. "Is Race gonna be okay?"

The doctor looked past me toward Grandpa with a seriousness that made the bottom drop out of my stomach. "He's all right, isn't he?" I demanded. "Can I see him?"

"I'm afraid not, son." The doctor glanced at me and then away. "You're the parents?" He directed the question at my grandfather.

"I want to see him!"

"That's not possible—" Before the doctor could finish, panic kicked in, jacking up my heartbeat till I could practically hear it. If Race was all right, why were they trying to keep me away?

"He's dead, isn't he?"

"No."

"Then why can't I see him? You've gotta let me see him!"

Hands clamped around my upper arms. I jerked my head around to see my grandfather's face inches from mine.

"That's enough!" he said.

"Leave me alone!" I yanked free, whipping around to face him. When he raised his hand I swung on instinct. Two months earlier, I probably would've hit the stupid son of a bitch, but somehow I caught myself in time, slamming my fist into the wall instead. Pain seared through my hand.

"Don't touch him," Kasey told my grandfather, her arms going around me. My eyes welled with tears, but I refused to let them fall. "Can't you see that he's upset?" Kasey voice was fierce. She pulled my head against her shoulder and stroked my hair, like I was some scared animal she was trying to comfort. "Cody," she said softly. "You're going to have to calm down or they'll make you leave. Okay?"

I took a deep, shaky breath. "Yeah." I pushed away from her, stifling a whimper as I bumped my sore hand.

The doctor seemed to be waiting for the family drama to end. I knew he was gonna tell us something we didn't want to hear.

"What's wrong with my son?" Grandma asked.

The doctor's eyes met hers and he cut to the point. "The CT scan shows bleeding, and it's causing pressure to build up within his skull. We can relieve that pressure surgically, but I need your consent."

"What will happen if you don't operate?" Grandma asked.

"The intracranial pressure will continue to rise, resulting in extensive brain damage and, ultimately, death."

Grandma paled. "But with surgery he'll be okay?"

"It's not quite that simple. Certainly, it will improve his chances, but the mortality rate for this type of injury is upwards of 60 percent. Even if your son survives, I can't guarantee there won't be permanent brain damage."

It was all happening so fast, I couldn't process one idea before the next one hit. Surgery? Intracranial pressure? Brain damage? And then that big one: a mortality rate upwards of 60 percent. I didn't think I could handle fear this huge. I was sure it would knock me out. But it didn't. In spite of it, I was still standing there with my hand throbbing and Kasey's fingers digging into my arm.

"What do I need to sign?" Grandma asked.

The doctor held his clipboard out to her, indicating multiple places on the form. Grandma scribbled her signature.

"What now?"

"Someone will show you to the proper waiting area. We'll let you know when he's out of surgery."

When the doctor left, Grandpa said he was going for a cup of coffee. He didn't ask Grandma or Kasey if they wanted one. I eased myself into a chair, cradling my hand against my stomach. It hurt like hell.

"Let me see," Kasey said. She tried to be gentle, but I yelped.

"This is really swollen, Cody. I think you might have broken something."

"Good thing we're at the hospital." Laughter came over me suddenly, and I couldn't make it stop. Race would've appreciated the joke.

"Shhh." Kasey pulled me close. "It's okay."

The doctor's words snuck back into my head. A mortality rate upwards of 60 percent. What did that mean? Sixty-one percent? Sixty-nine? What if Race died? What if—I couldn't let myself think that. He was gonna be okay. He had to be.

"I'm scared, Kasey." The words came out in a quaver.

"I know. Me too." She held me until I stopped shaking. "Now let's go get your hand taken care of."

It wasn't broken, just bruised. A doctor bandaged it and gave me a shot for the pain that really messed with my head. As I leaned against Kasey in the surgery waiting area, time slowed to a trickle, but my thoughts raced along at a hundred miles an hour. They always came back to that same terrifying idea. Whenever it crept into my head, I swatted it away, not allowing myself to consider what exactly it might mean.

"Kasey?"

I looked up. Denny, still clad in his grungy firesuit, filled the doorway with his bulk. He covered the distance between us in three long strides.

"They wouldn't tell me anything at the front desk—said I'd have to speak to the family." He sized up Grandpa with a scowl and nodded at Grandma with sympathetic respect. Whoa. Denny knew my grandparents?

Kasey stood up, fixing on Denny like a stranded hiker catching her first glimpse of Search and Rescue. When he stepped forward, she allowed herself to be drawn into his mammoth embrace.

"How bad?" he asked.

Kasey pulled her head away from Denny's chest, shaking it slightly. "Not here." She led him out into the hall, away from the hostility that shimmered off Grandpa like heat from asphalt.

A few minutes later they returned. Denny sank down beside me. "Don't you worry, Cody," he whispered, leaning close. "Race knows how much you and Kasey need him. If he has any say in this, there's no way he's gonna leave the two of you." He patted my leg, and I realized he hadn't even stopped long enough to wash up. Grease embedded the creases of his hands, and the scent of it clung to his firesuit.

Time inched by. I sagged against Kasey. Absently, she rubbed my back, soothing me with a sort of comfort my mother hadn't offered in years. I tried to force my mind to be still, but it kept rattling on like it was following lines of code from the basic programming class at my old school. *If* Race died *then* . . . I cut off the thought. Race wasn't gonna die. He couldn't.

It was almost two when the surgeon finally came out to talk to us. "The surgery was successful," he said. "We were able to evacuate the hemorrhage using a minimally invasive procedure. He's in recovery now, but they'll be taking him up to ICU shortly."

"Is he going to be okay?" Grandma asked. Like she hadn't heard the other doctor. Like she was hoping he was wrong.

"It's too early to make a prediction," the surgeon told her, his compassionate tone not taking the sting out of his words. "The thing you have to understand is that in cases like this there are two types of injury. The first occurs with the initial impact and the second results from swelling. It's this secondary damage that we're worried about now. We'll attempt to minimize it with drugs and by keeping your son sedated and on a ventilator, but the next twenty-four hours will be critical."

"When can we see him?"

"It may be some time yet. You can go up to the ICU waiting room if you'd like, but I'd advise you to go home and get some sleep. It's late."

"That sounds like an excellent idea," said Grandpa, glancing at the clock.

"William—" Grandma protested.

"I know this is difficult," the doctor said. "It's only natural that you want to be with your son. But you won't do him any good by wearing yourselves out."

Grandma nodded and unfolded herself from her chair. "Let's go, Cody."

"What?" Her words cut right through my drug-induced stupor.

"You're coming home with us, of course. I'll call your father in the morning. Even if—well, let's just say it will be a long time before Race is able to take care of you again."

Bam. There it was. The thought I hadn't allowed myself. The conclusion to that *If-Then* statement. I stared at Grandma, stunned.

"I'll take care of him," Kasey said. Her arms closed around me with a firmness that told me going home with Grandma was the last thing I needed to worry about.

"I hardly think that's appropriate."

"And I hardly think it's appropriate to add to Race's trauma by taking away someone he cares so much about." Kasey's voice cut like a torch searing through steel. "Don't you think he's already lost enough tonight?"

Grandma eyed her with astonishment. Clearly, she wasn't used to people talking to her like that. "You may be right," she said softly. "I'll be back in the morning. We can discuss it further then."

"What about you?" asked Denny as my grandparents filed through the doorway.

"I have to see him," Kasey said.

"I'll come with you."

"Denny, no. It's after two. You need to go home to your family. They won't let you into ICU anyway."

"And they'll let you?"

A sad smile twisted Kasey's lips. "They think I'm his fiancée."

Denny shook his head, a hint of amusement temporarily eclipsing the haunted look in his eyes. "If you need me to stay . . ."

"We'll be all right."

He told us he'd be back first thing in the morning and gave both of us a hug. When he was gone Kasey took me upstairs, where she picked up the phone on the wall and spoke to one of the nurses in ICU.

"Just a few more minutes," she said, leading me to one of the couches in the waiting area. "Will you be all right out here by yourself?"

"I want to see him, too."

Kasey shook her head. "I don't think that would be a good idea, Cody."

"But—"

"Just wait here. I'll be right back, okay?"

The ten minutes Kasey was gone seemed like an hour. When she returned, pale and trembling, I knew she'd been right not to let me go. Whatever it was that had shaken her up that bad, I didn't want to see.

"I don't want to leave," I said.

"Me either. I'd just lie awake all night listening for the phone." Kasey sat down and pulled me close. "We'll stay here, okay?"

Exhausted, I huddled in her arms, the pain in my hand cutting right through the stuff they'd given me. All night long, Kasey had been trying to reassure me, telling me everything was going to be all right, even though I knew she didn't believe it herself. Now she cried, barely making a sound as the tears spilled down her cheeks.

Seeing that scared me more than anything else.

Chapter 18

The underside of the car—the part that's never supposed to see daylight—rolled momentarily into view, then the Dart crashed down on all four wheels. Jim's Camaro hurtled toward the yellow number 8 on the door.

"No!"

"Cody, it's just a dream. Cody!"

My eyes jolted open to the harsh light of the ICU waiting room. Kasey's arm curled around my shoulders and my head rested in her lap.

"Race. . . ?" I said, blinking up at her. The skin around her red-rimmed eyes was swollen. It looked like she hadn't slept at all.

"He's still holding his own."

Relief washed over me, but it was only temporary. Twenty-four hours, the doctor had said. It had been only—what—maybe four? The clock on the wall read a quarter to six.

The residue of the stuff they'd given me for my hand still clouded my head, but the pain had come back full-force. I felt groggy and at the same time like I hadn't slept in a year. A weird sort of numbness clawed at my stomach. Suddenly, my eyes filled with tears.

"Big boys don't cry," I whispered as Mom's old mantra popped into my head.

"What?"

"Mom used to say it. 'Big boys don't cry.'"

"That's horrible," Kasey said, stroking my hair. "What a cruel thing to tell a child."

"But it's true." I was shaking now, fighting hard to hold back the tears. Quick as they always were to spring to the surface, I hadn't let myself give in to them since I was a little kid.

"Oh, Cody. No wonder you're so angry. It's not a crime to have feelings."

"My mom thinks it is."

"Well, she's wrong."

I shuddered in Kasey's arms. One whimper escaped, then sobs wracked my body. Once they started, I couldn't make them stop. What if I never got to see Race again? What if he died?

Kasey held me tight. "It's okay, Cody. You have nothing to be ashamed of. Someone you love is hurt, and you're allowed to cry."

Kasey went to check on Race again before getting herself a cup of coffee and me a hot chocolate from the vending machine.

"We should go down to the cafeteria and have some breakfast," she said, sitting down beside me.

My stomach cinched up at the idea. "I don't think I could eat anything." Who'd have thought those words would ever come out of my mouth?

"I know. I feel the same way."

We ended up staying in the waiting area because we were superstitious about leaving together, and neither of us wanted to go to the cafeteria on our own.

Kasey tracked down the ICU doctor after his morning rounds and got an update. Nothing had changed. She used the opportunity to ask questions, though. Lots of questions. It was almost like Kasey thought she could help Race get better just by understanding what was wrong with him. I heard more than I wanted to know about possible complications. The surgery put Race at risk of infection. Being on the ventilator made him susceptible to pneumonia. But the biggest concern was still brain swelling. If it got too bad, he might need more surgery.

Even if none of those things happened, no one could say for sure if there'd be any lasting damage.

"You should understand that people are never quite the same after a traumatic brain injury," the doctor said, explaining that Race could have mobility problems, difficulty thinking and speaking, even personality changes—if he woke up at all.

"He'll get through this, Cody," Kasey said when we were alone again. "I've never known your uncle to give up without a fight."

"That's a lot of stuff to fight."

"They have to tell us about the possibilities so we'll be prepared, but it doesn't mean any of those things will happen."

"They could."

"Yes, and he could be just fine, too. You aren't doing yourself any good by focusing on the worst."

Wasn't I? If I was ready for the worst, it couldn't catch me off guard, like Mom's letter had, or seeing Jim's car slam into the Dart.

"You heard that doctor. He said people are never the same after something like this."

"He'll be okay," Kasey repeated, and I wondered how anyone could look so exhausted and still so fierce. It hit me suddenly that she could be staying with Race in ICU—and that she wanted to—but she wasn't because that would mean leaving me by myself.

"You care about him, don't you?"

"Well, of course I do, Cody."

"No, I mean you *really* care."

Kasey didn't answer, but her eyes told me I was right.

"I knew it. Race keeps saying you don't, but I could see it all along. You've gotta tell him, Kasey."

"I know." Her voice was less than a whisper, and her expression echoed the question running through my own head. What if she didn't get the chance?

When Denny showed up, Kasey filled him in on what the doctor had said.

"Damn," he muttered, shaking his head as he settled beside me. He asked a few questions, but I shut the conversation out, wondering where Jim was. Shouldn't he be here, too? It wasn't like I blamed him for what happened, but he was supposed to be Race's best friend.

The morning dragged by, the minutes not blurring together like they normally would, but each one separate and distinct. Grandma got there a little after nine and Denny gave her a curt but respectful nod. Apparently he didn't hold her in as much contempt as he did Grandpa. When Kasey repeated the list of complications, I focused on the throbbing in my hand, trying to ignore the words. Every time I heard them, they got more real.

It was the longest morning of my life. Having Grandma there only made it worse. She agreed to let me stay with Kasey, but that was the only good part. She and Kasey got caught up in this odd verbal dance, like they weren't sure whether to resent or respect each other. It didn't help that Grandma insisted on referring to Race as 'Horatio,' making him sound like some kind of geek.

"Stop calling him that," I finally snapped.

"It's his name, Cody."

"Yeah, well it's Grandpa's name, too, and you call him William."

"Your grandfather's always gone by his middle name."

"So? How come he gets to choose what to be called and Race doesn't?"

My grandmother's eyes locked on mine, challenging my insolence, but after that she dropped the Horatio bit.

Time continued to crawl. Every hour Kasey or Grandma would go in to spend a few minutes with Race. His condition wasn't improving, but it also wasn't getting worse. My head buzzed with fears and unanswered questions, and now that Grandma had made an issue of it, I couldn't help wondering what was gonna happen to me. If Race didn't make it, or if he was so messed up that I couldn't stay with him, where would I end up? I couldn't stomach the idea of moving to Phoenix or living with Grandma, and I didn't think Dad would be willing to take me back.

At about noon, a middle-aged woman joined us in the waiting room. She had a girl my age at her side who looked like Kasey, only with freckles and hair that was more brown than cinnamon. Guilt drilled into me when I realized I was sizing the girl up. Sure, she was cute, but how could I be thinking about something so shallow when Race might be dying?

Kasey hugged the woman hard. "Mom." There was a note of relief and sadness in her voice that, just for a second, made her sound ten years old.

We went through the whole medical update again for Kasey's mom and her little sister, Brooke.

"They can only tell so much from the CT scan," Kasey said. "One indicator for determining the severity of the injury is to see how long it takes him to wake up once he's no longer sedated. Even then, they really won't know how bad things are until he's fully alert and strong enough to do the things he'd normally be able to."

Brooke sat beside her mother, listening wide-eyed. Her fingers coiled around the paperback she'd brought with her, twisting it into a cylinder. When Kasey went on to list the things that could still go wrong, I leaned forward in my chair and buried my face in my hands.

"Brooke," Kasey said. "Why don't you take Cody down to the cafeteria? He hasn't had anything to eat since last night." Her eyes met mine and I understood. Kasey had to talk about it to stay sane.

*   *   *

In the cafeteria, Brooke got French fries and a turkey sandwich. Nothing looked appetizing to me. My stomach was a clenched fist. I finally chose broccoli cheese soup, something that could slide down my throat pretty much on its own without causing any major upsets.

"Poor Race," Brooke said as we found a table and sat down. "I can't believe this is happening to him." She set her book beside her tray. It was a romance novel, the historical kind with a roguish-looking guy on the cover, his shirt ripped open to expose muscles nobody but Arnold Schwarzenegger actually possessed.

"You know Race?"

"Sure. I stayed with Kasey for a couple of weeks last summer. I got to help out at the speedway." Brooke smiled as if that were some great honor. "Race is sweet—and he's got such a cool sense of humor. I like him better than any of the other guys Kasey's dated."

"She's not exactly dating him."

"No, but she's interested."

I steadied my soup cup with my bandaged right hand, stirring the lumpy mixture with the other. "Seems like everybody but Race has that figured out. And I think Kasey only realized it this morning."

"My sister's not big on romance." Brooke tore the top off of a pack of ketchup and squirted a puddle beside her fries. "She was always too busy helping Dad at his shop, or taking care of us younger kids, or studying so she could win a scholarship. My theory is she never got comfortable with the dating scene, so she tries to avoid it."

I pushed my soup around in its paper bowl. It was starting to congeal. Raising the spoon, I took a bite, but the glop just sat there on my tongue. I almost gagged when I tried to swallow.

"Race said he asked Kasey if she was interested in dating him, and she told him no," I said. "But it's obvious she really cares."

"You know what I think?" Brooke asked, popping a French fry into her mouth. "I think she's always been crazy about him, but she was afraid of scaring him away. She does that, you know. With every guy she dates. The minute it starts getting serious, she sabotages the relationship."

"Why?" That sounded totally neurotic—not like the Kasey I knew at all.

Brooke shrugged. "Maybe she can't stand not being 100 percent in control."

"Maybe." I pushed my soup away. As shaky as I felt from not eating, I couldn't get my stomach to cooperate.

Brooke looked at the barely-touched soup and reached across the table to slip her hand over mine. Her blue eyes pulled me in like a hug. "He's going to be okay, Cody. Race is a fighter."

"That's what Kasey said."

"Well, she's right. Just because he's mellow doesn't mean he can't dig his claws in."

My eyes got hot and I blinked hard, staring down at the table. "That's how it was with me. Race decided he was gonna save me from myself, and no matter what I did, he never gave up."

Brooke's hand squeezed mine.

"I gotta go back upstairs, Brooke. It makes me nervous, being down here."

Kasey's mom and sister had to get back to Cottage Grove, but Grandma and Denny stayed with us the rest of the day. While Kasey and Grandma alternated sitting with Race, Denny hung out in the waiting room with me. He didn't say much, just thumbed through magazines and offered occasional words of encouragement, but having him there made me feel better.

The lack of sleep caught up with me late in the afternoon. Slumping against Kasey, I dozed in a weird twilight state. I wasn't fully awake or asleep, and I could hear everything going on around me. Grandma talked about what Race had been like as a kid—how she was always butting heads with him. She chose her words carefully, but it was clear she believed Race had been slumming when he hung out at the track. I wondered what Denny thought about that. He hardly said a word when Grandma was around. Kasey tried to explain the appeal—how the people at the speedway were like family—but Grandma didn't seem to get it.

Then the tone of the conversation shifted. "I can't stop thinking about that helmet," Kasey said. "I almost bought him a new one, but he's so stubborn about accepting money, even for the car."

"You shouldn't have to take responsibility for his choices," Grandma said.

In that half-conscious zone, with the world buzzing around me, I felt warm and safe. I wanted to stay there so badly that I closed my mind against their words. But a tiny finger of misgiving wiggled its way into my thoughts. Was there something that could have prevented all this?

At dinnertime, Denny had to leave, and Kasey dragged me down to the cafeteria. I hesitated in the buffet line, rejecting all the possibilities until she started making choices for me. She stuck a cup of chicken soup on my tray, then a bowl of green Jell-O and a carton of milk. When we sat down I poked at the food, making an effort so Kasey wouldn't have to worry about me, too. I noticed she was having as much trouble as I was trying to force anything down.

"Is it true about the helmet?" I asked, toying with my Jell-O.

"What?"

"If Race had a better helmet, maybe this wouldn't have happened?"

Kasey sighed, regarding me with a frown that said she wished I hadn't asked. "It's possible. Or at least it wouldn't have been as bad."

I chopped at the Jell-O with my plastic spoon. "Then it's not just an accident."

"Cody, the thing you have to understand is that probably half the drivers at the speedway are guilty of some sort of safety violation. They use harnesses that have sat out in the weather for years. They wear firesuits that have been washed so many times they're no longer flame resistant. Some of the roll cages in the Street Stock class are practically cobbled together with bailing wire. Safety is the last thing most drivers worry about."

"It should be the first thing."

"I know. But racing is expensive, and if it's the difference between a new helmet and a better cam, the cam is going to win every time. It doesn't help that young men—and race car drivers in particular—have a tendency to think they're invincible."

I shoved the Jell-O away and reached for my milk, struggling to open it one-handed. "Then why don't the officials do something about it? Aren't they supposed to inspect all the equipment?"

"Yes. But a lot of times it doesn't happen the way it should." Kasey leaned across the table to help with the carton. "At any rate, none of that matters now. It won't change what's happened."

But it did matter. Race had taken a chance he shouldn't have. He had gambled, and all of us had lost.

Chapter 19

At around nine-thirty that night, Kasey came back from ICU wearing an expression that was a mixture of exhaustion and euphoria.

"He's doing better. They think they'll be able to take him off the ventilator sometime tonight."

Relief washed over me the way cold water does when you plunge into a river on a scorching summer day. I felt weak, like the only thing that had been holding me together was my fear. Then at the back of my mind a little flare of anger blazed up. Kasey and I shouldn't have had to go through all this.

Grandma was long gone, attending some charity dinner, so Kasey called and left her a message before sitting down beside me.

"I should take you home. We both need sleep, and we aren't likely to get much of it here."

"I want to stay."

"So do I, but it's not practical."

Kasey drove me to the trailer so I could get some clothes. Walking through the front door was spooky. Everything was exactly as we'd left it Saturday afternoon. The thirty hours that had passed since then felt like a lifetime.

By the time we got to Kasey's house I was so tired I stumbled as I followed her down the hall to one of her spare rooms. I collapsed on the bed and stared up at the ceiling, focusing on a shaft of light that poured in from the hallway. Kasey's cat, Winston, hopped up and stretched out alongside me. Warmth and comfort radiated from his body as he purred.

Out in the living room Kasey played back the messages on her answering machine. There must've been a dozen of them, all from people at the track. One was from Alex. I thought about how I'd yelled at him and felt a prickle of regret. None of this was his fault.

I closed my eyes and told myself it was okay to relax now, that Race was getting better, but the inside of my head buzzed like a busy freeway interchange. I knew a cigarette would help. I hadn't had a one since I'd left the speedway the night before. There'd been plenty of times I'd been desperate for one, but I'd been too scared to leave the hospital, even to go out to the parking lot for a few minutes. I considered sneaking out onto the porch now to light up, but I was too wiped out. Besides, I didn't want Kasey to catch me at it.

Sleeping that night wasn't any easier than eating had been, even with Winston snuggled up against my side. My hand ached, and my mind was stuck in a groove, rehashing thoughts I'd spent the whole day trying to avoid. What if Race didn't wake up? What if he did, but he wasn't Race anymore?

When I finally managed to drift off, images of the wreck kept jerking me awake. At six o'clock I gave it up and went out to the kitchen, where Kasey was sitting at the table drinking coffee.

"I called the hospital," she said. "Race is breathing on his own now, but he's still unconscious." She studied the dark liquid in her cup then looked up and forced a smile. "Would you like me to make you some breakfast?"

I shook my head.

"You have to eat."

"You're one to talk."

Kasey sighed. "I know. I feel like my stomach is staging a rebellion. Let's just get something at the hospital. I don't want Race to wake up alone."

"What about the shop?"

"I called Jake yesterday. He'll take care of things."

The ICU waiting area had a sick sort of familiarity. It was like I'd spent weeks there instead of hours. Denny had to work, but Grandma showed up just after we did, looking impatient and annoyed.

"I talked to your mother last night, Cody. She said she told you a week ago that she wanted you to move to Phoenix. You might have mentioned that yesterday."

"Why? I'm not going." I slumped in my chair, wishing she'd leave me alone. I was numb from lack of food and sleep, but the daze felt almost good. It slowed down the rush of thoughts in my head, and I didn't want to be wrenched out of it.

Grandma settled herself in a chair across from us, her tailored skirt falling neatly into place. "When I told her about Race's accident, she was particularly insistent."

"So? That's her problem."

"It may be yours, as well."

"Cody can't leave," Kasey said. "Doesn't she understand what that would do to Race?"

"Saundra's not thinking of Race, or Cody for that matter. She's thinking of herself," Grandma said.

I snorted. "As if that's anything unusual."

Grandma's eyes skewered me. "Your mother has her issues, but when push comes to shove she comes through for you. You wouldn't be here now if she didn't."

"That's what I don't understand," Kasey said. "She sent Cody here. What made her change her mind?"

"With Saundra, who knows? She gets an idea into her head, and no matter how ridiculous or impractical it may be, she does whatever it takes to get her way."

One thing you could say for Grandma—she was equally harsh with everyone. It gave me a little rush of satisfaction to learn that even though my mother was her favorite, she wouldn't hesitate to call it like she saw it.

"Frankly, Saundra's feelings are the least of my concerns," Kasey said. "What will it take to get her to let Cody stay?"

"I'll talk to her," said Grandma, totally shocking me. "She doesn't listen to most people, but she'll listen to me. She has to if she wants to stay on the good side of my checkbook."

Later that afternoon, Kasey came back from sitting with Race and eased herself down beside me. I looked up from my book. After reading the same page about five hundred times, I still had no idea what it said.

"He's doing much better," she told me. "They're going to transfer him to a regular room."

"Is he awake yet?"

A faint look of uneasiness flickered in Kasey's eyes. "Cody, people with this type of injury rarely wake up all at once."

"I know. You keep telling me. But has he woke up at all?"

"Yes, in a manner of speaking. Only for a few minutes at a time, though."

"Is he. . . ? Can he. . . ?" I couldn't come right out and say what I wanted to, but Kasey must've been worried about the same thing, because she figured it out.

"He's still Race."

The words released something in me that had been tangled up in unworkable knots, but they also brought a fresh surge of anger.

"He's having some trouble speaking, and he's not particularly lucid, but the doctor said that's normal. It doesn't mean he won't get better." Kasey's eyes gently probed me. "Do you want to see him?"

My heart pounded, and suddenly there wasn't enough air in the room.

"No," I said quickly. I didn't realize I was shaking until Kasey put her hand on my arm.

"I know it's frightening."

"I can't," I said. How could I explain? I didn't want to see Race hooked up to a bunch of tubes and machines. I didn't want to see him weak and helpless and maybe not knowing who I was.

Kasey patted my arm. "There's no hurry. Maybe tomorrow."

On Tuesday things were a little better because Race had been moved to a regular room, but hanging around the hospital still creeped me out. Kasey went down to the cafeteria with me at lunchtime. At least my appetite had returned.

"He's retaining more of what the nurses and I are telling him, and that's a good sign," Kasey said. "The briefer the period of post traumatic amnesia, the greater the likelihood for a full recovery."

I stirred my pool of ketchup with a French fry, annoyance building in me like lava pulsing toward the mouth of a volcano. I was so sick of medical jargon.

"I'm just thankful I don't have to keep telling him what happened," Kasey added. "You'd think it would get easier, but it's more difficult each time."

The thought of her going through that really pissed me off. "Why should you have to tell him? Let the nurses do it."

"Would you want to hear something like that from a stranger?"

A comforting flood of anger washed over me. "I wouldn't have to, because I wouldn't have been stupid enough to get in that car with a crappy helmet."

Kasey stared at me, her fork motionless in midair, but something kept her from telling me off. Feeling calmer as the anger flowed back and displaced my fear, I glared at her. Kasey could gawk at me all she wanted. It didn't change the fact that this whole thing was Race's fault.

On the way home that night, Kasey looked like she'd pulled a week of all-nighters, but a dash of her confidence had returned. Denny'd shown up after work—though there was still no sign of

Jim—and he and Kasey had spent an hour with Race while I sat in the waiting room thinking I should be at karate practice. Even though Kasey would have taken me, I hadn't mentioned it to her.

The angled rays of evening sunlight glanced off the hood of the Charger as we cruised up Alder. I caught a whiff of roses from someone's garden and marveled at the contrast between what was happening at the hospital and out in the real world.

Beside me, Kasey rattled on about how well Race was doing. "He's in remarkably good spirits, all things considered. Though I don't think any of it has really sunk in yet."

I stared out the window on my side, watching trees and houses flash by. The stronger Race got, the madder I felt. What right did he have to put us through all this?

"He said he'd finally broken something I couldn't fix." Kasey made a funny little noise, halfway between a laugh and a sob. "He's such a smartass. I suppose I should be grateful he's still got that."

My sore fingers clenched the armrest on the Charger's door, sending pain surging through my hand in a way that felt ironically satisfying. How could Race joke about something like this? Didn't he understand how much it had hurt us?

"He wants to see you," Kasey said. "I know you don't think you're ready, but it would help both of you."

"No."

"He's worried about you," she persisted. "You're the first thing he asked about."

"What, not his car?"

Kasey bristled, eyeing me across the front seat. "I know you're hurting, Cody, but you could try being more compassionate."

"I could," I said. "But I won't."

Chapter 20

"I have to go to the shop today," Kasey said Wednesday morning. "There's too much for Jake to deal with on his own. But I'm taking you to see Race, first. He's worried about you, and he doesn't have the strength for it. He needs to know that you're all right."

Tired and irritable, I poked at the scrambled eggs she'd fixed me. My dreams the night before hadn't been as bad as they were right after the wreck, but they'd still cut into my sleep. "Why should I care what he needs?" I mumbled. "He never asked me what I needed when he got in that damned car with a lousy helmet."

A brief war played over Kasey's face. Understanding battled with annoyance, and finally a pained look of patience won out. "I know you're angry, Cody. On some level I am, too. But neither of us is anywhere near as angry with Race as he is with himself."

"That's his problem."

The look of patience evaporated. "I'm beginning to get tired of your attitude. The thing you have to realize is that you're staying with me for Race's benefit as much as your own. I love you like one of my brothers or sisters, but if you make me choose between you and Race, you're going to lose."

"You think that'd be anything new? I'm used to people putting me last."

Kasey gave me a hard look. "I might have a little more sympathy for you if you were the one recovering from a critical injury. Now finish your breakfast and get in the car."

"Forget it. I'm not going back there." My temper flared and the words spilled out before I could stop them. "Race should've known better. *You* should've known better! Why didn't you buy him a damned helmet? You've got money."

Guilt and pain flashed across Kasey's face. She sank heavily into the chair across from me. "Don't you think I've asked myself that question a hundred times since Saturday night?"

A tide of shame washed over me.

"I understand why you want someone to blame," Kasey said, her voice shaking. "You think if you can find somebody to hold responsible it will help. But it won't. Can't you see that? Even if you pin this on Race—or on me—it won't go away." Kasey pushed back from the table, drained and defeated. "Finish your eggs," she said quietly. "We need to go."

"Kasey—" I looked at her desperately. "I don't want to." My fury had burned out, leaving me with nothing but fear.

"I know. But what you want isn't as important as what Race needs."

As we drove to the hospital I slumped in my seat, ashamed of myself for yelling at Kasey and confused over how I felt about Race. It wasn't like I *wanted* to be mad at him, the anger just kept growing in me like a mudslide, huge and thunderous and out of control.

"I know you're afraid," Kasey said. "So I want to tell you what to expect. It isn't like when Race was in ICU. There aren't any machines—he's just got an IV. He's having some trouble finding words, though. It's called aphasia and it can be a little unsettling."

"Did they shave his head?" Somehow the idea of Race sporting the Mr. Clean look really bothered me.

"Only in two places, for the surgery and the ICP monitor." Kasey took her hand from the wheel, reaching across the seat to place it on top of mine. "It won't be as bad as you think."

At the hospital I lagged behind, scared of what I would see in spite of Kasey's reassurance. My heart thumped hard, doing that weird fluttery thing where it feels like it's tripping over itself. I kept my eyes fixed on the floor as I walked into Race's room.

"Cody." Race's voice exerted a strange power over me, drawing my attention from the speckled tile. Kasey was right— it wasn't as bad as I'd expected. But he still looked like hell. Just seeing him in a hospital bed would've spooked me, even if it hadn't been for the shaved patches, and the stitches, and the remnants of that reddish-yellow stuff they slather on your skin before they slice you open. The worst part was the rigidity in his face, telling me how much pain he was in and how hard he was trying to hide it. It made my stomach twist. Pissed as I was at him, I didn't want to see him hurting like that.

Race gave me a smile that was tired and pale in comparison to his usual smart-assed grin. "Hey," he said. Then he noticed my bandaged hand. "What . . . what happened?"

I glanced at Kasey. Not knowing what I should say, I shrugged.

"He bruised his hand. It's nothing serious." Kasey's finger-tips prodded my back, giving me a gentle push toward the bed. I ducked to the side and took refuge in the chair over by the wall.

Kasey shook her head almost imperceptibly, but she didn't tell me off. Instead, she stepped forward to fill the void at Race's side.

"I can't stay, but Cody will keep you company this morning."

"You're going to . . ." Race faltered, "to the . . ." A faint look of aggravation flickered in his eyes and he swore. At least he could remember the important words.

"To the shop, yes." Kasey's slender fingers curled around his. If Race couldn't tell how she felt about him from the intensity of her expression, then he really did have brain damage.

"I'm sorry, Race," she said. "But I have to."

"'S okay. . . . You should."

Even though I'd been warned, the halting pace of Race's words shook me up. I think some part of me had believed that once he woke up everything would be okay.

"Cody has money for the bus and he knows how to get to the shop," Kasey said. "Send him to me when you get tired." She squeezed Race's hand. "I'll be back this evening."

For a long moment their eyes locked and a current crackled between them. Then Race pulled his hand away, breaking the circuit.

"You need to . . . go."

A flutter of panic lodged in my chest as Kasey left the room. Race was gonna want to talk, and I was still so furious I knew I couldn't do it. How was it possible to be so worried about someone and still want to kick his ass?

"C'mere . . . kid," Race said, patting the blankets as if I was a stray dog that needed coaxing.

"I'm good where I am."

Race lay quietly for a minute, looking up at the ceiling. "I'm sorry. . . . This isn't what you . . . signed up for."

"Damned straight."

"I . . ." Race hesitated, searching for a word. "I . . . get it. You're . . . pissed at me. Hell, *I'm* pissed at me. . . . I totally botched my chance at . . . at the championship."

My rage, barely suppressed, came tearing to the surface. "Who gives a rat's ass about the stupid championship?"

"Kid—"

"There's more important things than a damned stock car race!"

"I know. . . . C'mere. . . . We'll talk."

"I don't wanna talk. Anyway, aren't you supposed to be resting? You look like shit."

"Cody—"

But Grandma appeared in the doorway then, saving me from further conversation. For the first time in my life I was glad to see her, in spite of Grandpa hovering in her wake.

While Grandma had come every day, it was the first time Grandpa had been back since Saturday night. He stood by the wall, back ramrod straight, scowling and glancing at his watch. Grandma shot him a warning look as she sat down on the edge of Race's bed.

"You're looking better today. The doctor said you're making remarkable progress."

Race clearly wasn't hearing a word she said. His eyes, narrowed in suspicion, were fixed on Grandpa. Grandpa stared back with equally intense distaste.

"William," Grandma cautioned.

"I don't know what you were expecting from me," he said. "I told you my coming here would be a mistake."

"For the love of God, he's your *son*. I know the two of you have your differences, but you could make an effort."

Grandpa broke free of his staring match to focus on Grandma. "And why is that, Noreen? It isn't as if this were unavoidable. I might be able to generate a little sympathy if he'd been hit by a bus."

"You'd probably . . . throw a . . . party . . . if I got hit by a bus," Race said.

"You see? Right there—nothing but insolence." Grandpa blasted Race with a glare. "You've been defiant your whole life. Running around with white trash, wasting my hard-earned money on art classes when you should have been studying business. And now you expect me to feel sorry for you?"

"I don't . . . expect a . . . a damned thing."

I shoved up out of my chair and stepped in front of Grandpa. "Why don't you get lost?"

His smoldering scowl made me shiver. "What did you say to me?"

That was one of my mother's lines and now I knew where she'd got it.

"I said you should get the hell out of here."

Grandpa's eyes impaled me before darting away to settle on Race. "As if it weren't bad enough that you've wasted your own life," he said. "Now you're exerting your negative influence over Saundra's son as well."

That was wrong on so many levels I didn't know where to start.

"Give me a little credit, Grandpa. Don't you think I could figure out how to be insolent and defiant all on my own?"

"Don't make the mistake of thinking you're too big to be taken over my knee."

"I'd like to see you try."

Grandpa lurched toward me and seized my good wrist.

"Get your . . . hands . . . off him," Race ordered, struggling to get up. Grandma held him back.

"William!" she said, her voice as commanding as Kasey's.

"I will not put up with that sort of disrespect."

"Then maybe we should leave."

Reluctantly, Grandpa's fingers unclenched, releasing me. Without a word he turned and left the room.

"I'm sorry, Race," Grandma said, patting his hand as she stood up to go. "I shouldn't have brought him."

Trembling with outrage and exhaustion, Race closed his eyes and sagged against the pillows.

The room was so quiet after Grandma left that I could hear people talking at the nurses' station down the hall.

"Thanks, kid," Race mumbled.

Suddenly it was too much. Race's gratitude, Grandpa's hatefulness, and most of all the way my uncle had been so ready to jump to my defense. But conflicted as I felt, the anger still burned in my gut, hot as the inside of a combustion chamber.

184

"I gotta go," I said. Not daring to look at him, I ducked out of the room and took off.

The heat of the sun felt good on my skin after the chill of the hospital's air conditioning. I knew Kasey would tweak if I showed up before noon, so I crossed the street to 7-Eleven and spent the next few hours playing video games one-handed while trying not to think about what happened that morning. Grandpa was such an asshole. Growing up with him would've been ten times worse than growing up with Mom. It was amazing Race hadn't wound up a delinquent like me.

When I got to the shop, Kasey put me to work.

"Things are really backed up and I need all the help I can get. Do you think you could wash parts? I'll pay you."

"You don't have to pay me."

Kasey found some rubber gloves big enough to fit over my bandaged hand then showed me the parts tank. I spent the afternoon cleaning stuff I couldn't identify.

The shop was a madhouse. The phone kept ringing, and mostly it wasn't business, but people wanting to know about Race. Kasey took pity on them. I would've hung up. Didn't they know she had work to do?

When I finished with the parts, hand throbbing from the activity, I went to see what else needed to be done. Kasey was lying under an old Ford while Jake hung over the fender, holding something for her. I decided it would be a bad idea to interrupt them, so I located a broom and got to work. It looked like the place hadn't been swept in a month.

Cleaning the floor made the counters and workbenches look worse, so I started picking stuff up. I was surprised at all the receipts I found, deposited on every available surface. I took them into the office where the desk was piled with cookies, homemade bread, and baskets of fruit. Casseroles and salads jammed the tiny refrigerator in the corner.

"Hey, Kasey," I called, leaning out through the doorway. "What *is* all this stuff?"

"Gifts from friends at the track. They figured we'd have enough on our hands without having to cook, too."

"People really do that?" I'd seen it in movies, but I never thought it actually happened.

"Of course," Kasey said, as if it took place every day in her world.

By six I'd scrubbed the bathroom, straightened the office, and started wiping down the tools I'd picked up. If the size of the pile was any indication, I figured the toolboxes must be empty.

"Thanks for all the help," Kasey said, giving me a one-armed hug. "Are you ready to go?"

"I've just gotta clean this stuff up and figure out where to put it."

"It's not that important. I'll get to it tomorrow."

"If he wants to help, let him," Jake said. "You go see Race. I'll stick around to give Cody a hand, then I'll drop him by the hospital on my way home."

"Are you sure? You've already put in extra hours this week."

"Of course I'm sure."

Jake was a muscular, crew-cut guy who looked like he'd make a good Marine. He was pretty old, probably old enough to have kids in college, but he'd always seemed cool enough. He showed me where the tools went then gave me a basic rundown on the projects he and Kasey were involved in.

"You did a good job today," he said, "but cleaning parts and sweeping aren't the only ways you could help."

"I don't know anything about cars."

"I'm not talking about cars. I'm talking about your attitude. You need to stop giving everyone such a hard time. Kasey's got her hands full between looking out for you, running this business, and taking care of Race. Do you have any idea how much pressure she's under?"

I thought about the scene at breakfast. It was the only time I'd given her any shit, and I still felt bad about it.

"I know Kasey acts like she's tough as nails, but she's only twenty-three—hardly more than a kid herself. You don't have any business adding to her stress by throwing temper tantrums."

The words seared me deep. I'd been worrying about Kasey for days. Wasn't it enough that I felt lousy for yelling at her?

But the more I thought about it, the more I realized Jake was right. As aware as I was of how shook up Kasey had been since the wreck, I hadn't considered that I might be part of the problem.

Chapter 21

The next morning Kasey dropped me off again at Sacred Heart. Apparently Race hadn't told her I'd run out on him the day before.

"So you . . . decided to give me . . . another chance," he said, focusing on me with a vagueness that proved he wasn't all there.

"I guess." I was torn between anger and the need to have things be okay between us. "Y'know, your hair looks like it was attacked by Mothra."

Race flashed a weary grin. "Maybe you should bring me a . . . mirror . . . so I can start working on a . . . a . . ." he fumbled for the word.

"A comb-over?"

"Yeah."

I dropped down in the chair, wondering why it was so hard to let go of being pissed. Kasey had told me to talk to him about it, but I didn't know how to start. I felt so furious, so betrayed. How could he go making me care about him then almost get himself killed?

Race shifted around, trying to see me. The effort made him wince, and I felt a twinge of guilt, but it wasn't enough to make me move the chair into his line of vision.

"Kasey said you . . . helped yesterday."

"Yeah." I traced a finger over the design on the fabric of the chair.

"That's good. . . . She works too hard."

I couldn't argue with that.

"She's . . . worried . . . about you."

"She said that?" I couldn't believe Kasey would tell him anything that might stress him out.

"No. But I can see it. You shouldn't . . . don't give her a hard time . . . okay?"

"I don't."

Race was quiet for a long time, and I didn't step in to fill the silence. "I owe you an . . . apology," he said finally. "I screwed up big time."

Some mean little part of me couldn't let him off the hook. I stared down at my feet. Noticing a bit of rubber pulling loose from the side of one of my Converse high tops, I tugged at it. "You can apologize all you want," I said. "But you're not getting any sympathy from me."

"Kid, I don't want your . . . sympathy. . . . I just want my life back."

"Actions have consequences." The sliver of rubber ripped away from my shoe, and I rolled it between my fingers.

"What?"

"That's what you told me when I stole that street sign. Actions have consequences." I flicked the rubber fragment at the floor.

Race sighed. "I sure was right about that."

"Well, it's not fair. How come me and Kasey have to suffer the consequences for your actions? It isn't right!"

Race was quiet.

All the pain, fear, and anger of the past few days swooped down on me at once. I knew I was about to start crying, and I'd be damned if I'd let him see me do it. Shaking, I shoved away from the chair and went to stand by the window.

"You didn't even think about us, did you?" I demanded, staring out at the traffic on Hilyard Street below. "All you cared about was that stupid championship."

"That's not . . . that's not true, Cody."

"It *is* true! If you cared about us, you never woulda got in that car. You had to know this could happen."

"I didn't."

"You should have!" With wetness on my cheeks, I swung around to face him. "You even admitted you needed a new helmet. How stupid could you get?"

"Cody—"

"You scared us!"

"Look, kid—"

"You coulda died."

"I didn't."

"You *could* have!" Quivering, I turned back toward the window. "You're such an asshole," I said, my voice fading to a whisper.

"I know."

I slumped against the wall, overpowered by tears. I couldn't have stopped them if I wanted to, and I was tired of trying. Race needed to take responsibility. He'd created this mess, and it was his job to make it go away.

"Cody," Race's tone was sharp with distress. "Come over here."

I stayed where I was.

"Damn it, kid . . . don't . . . do this to me."

What was he gonna do about it? He couldn't come after me.

"Cody—*please.*"

He could beg all he wanted. Let him be the one to feel scared and helpless for a change.

The crash of metal on metal made me jump, but it wasn't until I heard Race grunt and swear that I turned around. He was out of bed, clinging to the little wheeled table, and it was rapidly sliding away from him.

"Are you freakin' *stupid*?" I lunged forward to grab it before it could roll any further. But even as I spoke, I knew it was me that was stupid. How many times had I heard that lack of judgment was one of the problems after a head injury? How many times had I been told a repeat trauma in the first six weeks, no matter how minor, could be fatal? Race could've messed himself up big-time and it would've been my fault.

Shuddering at the thought, I pulled his arm over my shoulders and helped him sit down. Race collapsed onto the bed, his face damn near as white as the pillowcase. For several moments he lay still, struggling to catch his breath.

Shit, what if I'd really hurt him?

"Are you okay?" My voice came out wavery. "You want me to get a nurse or something?"

"No. Just . . . give me a minute." He stretched out a hand to feel for the blanket. I tucked it over him. Then I saw the IV needle lying on the bed, slowly dripping to form a wet spot. The pole was jammed sideways between the head of the bed and the wall.

"Damn it, Race." The words caught in my throat as I realized what he'd done. "You dumbass." I flicked the little valve that stopped the flow of liquid.

"I couldn't get the. . . . The stupid pole got stuck."

I reached for the button to call the nurse, but Race clumsily pushed my hand aside.

"Kid . . . stop. It can wait. . . . Just sit."

Tears blurred the room as I sank onto the edge of the bed. I couldn't believe what Race had put himself through for me. First the deal with Grandpa, and now this. I sure as hell didn't deserve that kind of loyalty.

"Kasey's gonna kill me," I said.

"Kasey's not gonna . . . find out."

Race squeezed my shoulder and I cried harder.

"I—" The word choked me. "I was so scared, Race." I pulled my feet up and dug the heels of my sneakers into the bed frame, burying my face in my knees.

"I'm sorry," Race said. "You just don't know how . . . sorry I am." He rubbed my back with clumsy, faltering strokes. "I know I was stupid, I just hope you can . . . forgive me."

I swiped at my face, brushing away tears. "Does that mean I can't be mad? Because I don't know if I can stop."

"No," Race said. "That'll just have to . . . go away . . . on its own."

Race finally let me call a nurse who fixed his IV and lectured him on the foolishness of getting out of bed without help. I felt guilty for letting him take the heat, but I didn't have the guts to admit to my part in it.

The exertion had wiped Race out, and I felt bad about that, too. It was my fault he was in so much pain. The stuff the nurse gave him seemed to help, but I could tell it didn't make it go away entirely.

As I sat there the rest of the morning, watching him drift in and out of restless sleep, I thought about how close I'd come to really screwing up. Again. Race had been right when he said my temper was gonna get me into trouble. I cringed as I thought of all the crap I'd given him since I'd moved to Eugene. Insulting him, running away, wrecking his van. He'd put up with it and hadn't held it against me. Hell, he'd bought the Galaxie in spite of it. As I considered that, another sliver of guilt needled my conscience. No matter how much a helmet might cost, it couldn't be as much as what he'd paid for the Galaxie.

Well, there was nothing I could do about that now. But I wouldn't let him down again. From here on, I wasn't gonna let anything come between us—especially not my temper. Somehow, I'd figure out how to get a handle on that. If my sensei and Alex both said it could be done, it must be possible.

At noon I took off to help Kasey at the shop. She made things more interesting this time by letting me assist her with some simple jobs. Even though it would've been faster to do them herself, she didn't seem to mind teaching me. My hand ached from yesterday's workout, but I managed to do everything she asked.

Late in the afternoon, the phone interrupted Kasey for probably the hundredth time.

"Cody," she said. "It's for you. Your mom."

I didn't want to talk to her, and it turned out I didn't really have to. In her usual fashion she babbled on about me coming to Phoenix as if my life hadn't come crashing to a halt Saturday night.

"Your grandmother seems to think you need to stay there, but I can't see how you'd want that. All that drama at the hospital, and then having to live with a stranger. Did she even ask what you wanted? Wouldn't you rather be here with me?"

"No," I said. "I want to stay with Race. He needs me."

"Race doesn't need anyone. Never has. He's snubbed the family his whole life."

"That's not true—you guys snubbed him. Don't you care about him at all? He's your brother. Damn it, Mom, he almost died!"

The line was quiet for a few seconds, then, "Well, what did you expect? He drives a race car. It's a dangerous hobby."

Outrage rippled through me and I throttled the phone, wanting to throw it across the room. It took all my willpower to reach out with one finger and push the button that broke the connection. I stood there for almost a minute with a dial tone buzzing in my ear and the handset clutched in a death grip. Then Kasey was beside me, one hand on my shoulder, the other patiently extended.

"Give me the phone, Cody."

I was clenching it so hard it hurt to relax my fingers.

Kasey placed the phone back in its cradle and put her arms around me. "I think it would be best if you didn't talk to her for a while."

No problem there. I never wanted to speak to my mother again.

*　　*　　*

Friday on her way to work, Kasey dropped me off to hang out with Race. He looked more alert than he had the day before, though he still seemed distracted, like part of him was caught up in dealing with pain. I noticed a couple of flower arrangements on the table and windowsill and wondered who'd visited last night. I hadn't seen anyone when I'd come back to the hospital with Kasey after dinner, but then I'd stayed out in the waiting area. Race was exhausted that late in the day, and I knew Kasey was the only person he wanted around when he felt that bad.

"So how's life in the Hotel Sacred Heart?" I asked.

"It sucks, kid. I wouldn't put it on my . . . on my vacation itinerary if I were you."

"I'll make a note of that." I tossed a package of Twinkies on the bed. "Here. I figured you'd be jonesin' for these by now. I was gonna bring your Jimmy Buffett tape, but I wanted to spare the nurses."

"Thanks." Race fumbled with the plastic, finally grabbing the bag with both hands and ripping it open with his teeth. "Hey, they're frozen."

"Well, yeah. That's how you like 'em, right?"

"Yeah, but—"

"Just don't let Kasey catch you with those. She'd prob'ly say something like 'Twinkies don't provide the proper building blocks for restoring neural pathways.'"

Race laughed as I slid the chair over to within view of the bed and sat down.

"Is it Friday?" he asked. "I keep losing track of time."

"Yeah. Kasey has to work tomorrow—she's got a bunch of mechanics to interview—but I'll come keep you company." I knew it was gonna really be rough on him, being stuck here while everyone else was at the track.

"You don't have to . . . feel sorry for me."

"Who says I do?"

"It's written all over your face. I can deal with the fact that there's a race tomorrow. Anyway, this is only . . . temporary. I'll be back out there this season, no matter what everybody thinks."

I believed him. He'd already defied the odds, and wasn't attitude half the battle? I didn't understand how he could be so optimistic, but it sure impressed me. I'd have been sniveling like a two year old if this had happened to me.

Race quietly finished his Twinkies, then his face went serious. "Cody, if I ask you something will you give me a straight answer?"

"Sure," I said, uneasiness swelling inside me.

"I want to know about the . . . wreck."

"Didn't Kasey tell you?"

"She told me it was nobody's fault, but I'd already guessed that. I need to know what happened."

I didn't much want to talk about it, and since Kasey hadn't told him, I wondered if I should. But didn't he have a right to know?

"It really *was* an accident," I said, explaining how he'd gotten sideways and Tom Carey had clipped him.

Bewilderment clouded my uncle's face. "Tom Carey?"

I swallowed hard. "White #68 Camaro." No matter how many times I had to fill the holes in Race's memory, it never got easier.

"Getting hit by him isn't what messed you up, though. It was when—" and now I realized why Kasey hadn't told him, "—when Jim hit you in the driver's door."

Race closed his eyes, drawing a long, slow breath. "Well, that explains a lot. Denny and some of the other guys have been here to see me, but not Jim. I wondered . . ."

"It wasn't his fault," I said, even though I wanted to kick Jim's ass for bailing on Race. "He tried to throw his car sideways, he just didn't have a chance."

"Things happen on the track. A lot of times it's nobody's fault."

I realized we'd made it through a whole conversation with him stopping only a few times to search for a word. Maybe he'd be lucky and skate out of this without any lasting problems.

I heard a noise in the hall and glanced up to see Grandma standing in the doorway.

"Good morning," she said as she came in. Looking at Race she added, "I'm sorry about your father. I shouldn't have brought him. He cares, he's just too stubborn to show it."

"Somehow I find that hard to believe," Race muttered.

"I know it's not easy for you to see, but he never meant to be cruel. All those times he was harsh when you were growing up he was only trying to protect you—to teach you how to survive in a difficult world."

Grandma eyed me meaningfully, and I realized she expected me to be a gentleman and give her my seat. I relinquished the chair.

"I suppose that's how you . . . justify . . . never standing up to him," Race said.

"He never hurt you. You were never abused."

"And that makes what he did okay? Damn it, when are you gonna stop . . . defending him?" Race's eyes flashed like the sparks from a welder.

Grandma sighed and shook her head. "I know I've made mistakes. I'm trying to make up for them now. But I can't change the past."

"I'm not asking you to. I just want you to stop making excuses for him."

Grandma met Race's eyes, saying nothing, but giving him the slightest nod.

"Maybe you should go," he said. "I don't have the energy for this."

"No, Race. We need to talk."

"About what?" The note of irritability in Race's tone deepened.

"About where you and Cody will live once you've left the hospital. Kasey has voiced some concern about the two of you going back to your trailer. I have to agree."

Race gave her a stony look.

"Even if that weren't a factor, there's the issue of money. Do you have any idea how far behind you can get by missing just a few weeks of work?"

"Mom, please."

"No." She held up a hand to silence him. "I can't in good conscience leave you and Cody alone in this situation."

Fear rose up in me. "You're not gonna let Mom take me to Phoenix, are you?"

"What's this about . . . Phoenix?" Race's voice was sharp as a Ginsu knife, and he looked from one of us to the other.

"Saundra suggested it might be better if Cody were with her. I set her straight, of course—you've done more for the boy than she ever has. But I have to know he'll be safe."

"I take good care of Cody."

"I know you have so far, but at this point you're not even capable of taking care of yourself."

Race started to protest, but Grandma talked right over him. "Kasey and I have discussed the situation and we've come up with a solution. You can move in with her for the next month or so, and I'll loan you whatever money you need to pay your bills until you get back to work."

Race scowled. He was starting to get that glassy-eyed look that meant his pain meds were wearing off. Grandma had picked the wrong time to tangle with him.

"No," he said.

"Race—"

"I'm not taking your . . . money. And Kasey's already done more than enough for us."

"Race, you have to be practical."

"It's out of the question."

Grandma continued to badger him, but he refused to discuss the subject any further. Finally, Grandma gave up and left.

"You're being stupid, y'know," I said.

Race gave me a warning look. "Kid, don't even start."

Late that afternoon Kasey was showing me how to do a brake job when Denny stopped by the shop.

"My wife thought you could use these," he said, handing Kasey a Tupperware container full of cookies.

"Thank you, Denny. I'll take some to Race tonight. He keeps telling me he's desperate for real food."

That wasn't exactly true. Race was usually too nauseated to eat much. He just didn't like us worrying about him, so he tried to make us think it was because the hospital food sucked.

Kasey passed the bowl to me and I hastily wiped my hands on my jeans before popping the lid. *Mmmmm.* Chocolate chip. Denny's wife had a new fan.

"So how's he doing?" Denny asked, parking his butt on the edge of the tire machine and stretching his enormous feet out over the dusty concrete. He hadn't visited since Tuesday because Kasey'd told him how wiped out Race was in the evenings. Too bad the other people from the track couldn't seem to take the hint. When they showed up Race felt obligated to talk to them, and that really drained his energy.

"Better than anyone expected," Kasey said. "So far there seems to be minimal impairment, which is amazing, considering how serious they initially thought the injury was. He's very fortunate."

Shaking his head, Denny laughed. "Leave it to Race to come from behind and surprise everyone. I'll try to get by to see him tomorrow, but if I don't, let him know that when he's ready, I'll help him get the car together, okay?"

"I appreciate the offer," Kasey said. "But it's not necessary. We can do the work during the off-season."

My mouth went dry around the cookie.

Denny frowned. "You don't think he'll be back this year?"

"It's highly unlikely."

I looked hard at Kasey, knowing better than to confront her with Denny around, but she avoided my eyes.

When Denny left, Kasey immediately got to work. "All right Cody, why don't you see if you can get these return springs back on." She handed me the brake spring tool.

I didn't take it. "Why'd you say that to Denny?"

"Because it's the truth."

"Race would be pissed if he found out you were telling his friends stuff like that."

"Race doesn't need to know." Kasey gave me a look that suggested she could make my life miserable if I told him. "I know you want things to go back to the way they were before the accident, but it isn't that simple. It can take months, even years, to fully recover from a brain injury."

"But it won't! He's a lot better already. You keep saying how lucky he is, how it could've been worse."

Kasey's face went stiff. "Cody, Race is in denial, and the sooner the two of you accept the fact that he's not getting back out there this season, the better it will be for everyone involved."

I felt like I'd been slapped. How could she say that? "You're the one who told me he never gives up without a fight," I reminded her. "You're the one who said it's in his blood. If Race thinks he can get back out there this season, who are you try and stop him?"

"It's not about whether he *can*, Cody, it's about whether it's safe."

I glared at her. I knew what this was about. She was scared. "You can't protect him by keeping him off the track, y'know. He

199

could get hit by a truck walking down the street. It's not fair, getting between him and his friends."

Kasey shook her head. "I don't know what I'm thinking. You're no more capable of seeing reality than he is."

"You're the one who can't see reality! If Race thinks he can do this, then he can. Why don't you believe in him?"

Sighing, Kasey got to work replacing the brake return springs herself. "I have to hand it to you, Cody, when you're on your game you're loyal to a fault. But Race has a lot of work ahead of him and it's not going to be easy. I just hope when things get rough, you'll be as supportive as you are now. I hope you won't give up on him."

I chilled her with a scowl. "You're the one who's giving up on him. You're wrong and he's gonna prove you wrong."

Kasey shook her head sadly. "I certainly hope you're right."

Chapter 22

The minute I walked through the door Saturday morning, Race started to laugh.

"Kid, where did you get that shirt?"

"Dad sent it," I said, looking down at the lettering. It read: *I have animal magnetism. When I go outside squirrels stick to me.*

It had come in the mail the day before, confounding my feelings about my father. He'd never given me anything except on Christmas and my birthday. I was still ticked at him, but after reading the letter that came with the package it was hard to go on hating him completely.

> *Cody,*
>
> *I saw this and thought of you. Sorry it took me so long to get it in the mail, but good job pulling up your grades. It seems like you've finally found what you need.*
>
> *I know I haven't done the best job as a father. Maybe if I'd stood up to your mom years ago things never would have come to this. I put myself first, and there's no excuse for that. I don't blame you for not being able to forgive me.*
>
> *I was sorry to hear about Race. Let me know if there's anything I can do to help and please tell Kasey to keep me updated.*
>
> *Dad*

"So Kasey's been picking up the mail?" Race said.

"Yeah."

"Good. I need you to bring me the bills. The end of the month's coming up, and I've gotta figure out how to get everything paid."

"Dude, the end of the month came and went. It's July first. Anyway, Kasey's taken care of that stuff."

"She paid my bills?" Race's brow furrowed in annoyance. One thing I'd noticed since the wreck was how much more emotional he was, flipping from one extreme to another. I hoped it was just stress, and not one of those personality changes the doctor had warned us about. I counted on Race to be laid-back.

"Chill, dude. She's keeping track of everything. She knows you'll wanna pay her back, she just thought it would be easier this way. She talked to Dad, too, and he's sending his checks to her now, so my room and board is covered."

Race shifted, trying to find a comfortable position. His face still had that tautness, but other than that he looked better today—stronger and less drained.

"Well, I've got a little money in the bank," he said. "Do you have any idea where my wallet is?"

"Kasey has it."

"Get it. I'll give you my ATM number. Just remember you've gotta leave five bucks in the account. The rest you can give to her."

I sunk down into the chair. "She's not worried about it and you shouldn't be, either."

The commercials that had been airing on the TV came to an end, allowing regular programming to resume. I cringed as Pee-wee Herman took over the screen, encouraging everyone to, "scream real loud!"

"Jeeze, Race, don't tell me this is one of your dirty little secrets," I said, glancing at him suspiciously.

"Nah, I'm not watching, it's just on."

"So why don't you change the channel? It's not like you've gotta get up. Here, hand me that remote."

Race grabbed at the device, fumbling like it was a wet bar of soap. Finally I took it away from him and silenced the television. I noticed some new flower arrangements on the windowsill and examined the cards. One was from the Davis family, signed by Robbie and Laurie, but Jim's name was in the same handwriting as his wife's. Stupid bastard. He couldn't even be bothered to jot down his own name. What kind of friend was he?

"Have you thought any more about what Grandma said?" I asked, plopping back into the chair.

"Not at all. And I'm not going to. You shouldn't either," he added, mocking me.

"So what are we gonna do about money?"

"I'll figure something out."

"How?"

"I just will. It's not your problem, okay?"

I noted the irritated twitch of his jaw and cut to the chase.

"Maybe I could help. Kasey's paying me for the work I'm doing at the shop. I told her she didn't have to, but you know how she is."

Race grimaced and rubbed his forehead. "Look, kid, I'm glad you're giving her a hand, but I'm not taking your money. Anyway, you're gonna need it for the Galaxie. It'll prob'ly be a while before I can help out with that. Okay?"

I shrugged. It bugged me that he had no realistic idea of how we were gonna handle things, but what could I do?

Not wanting to leave Race alone to stew about what was going to be happening at the track that night, I spent the whole day with him instead of taking off at lunchtime. As usual, he began to fade in the afternoon, another reminder that he was worse off than he wanted us to believe. The memory of what

Kasey had said the day before flared up, but I snuffed it out. She was wrong. Race would be fine.

I'd brought along my writing notebook, so when he started dozing, I pulled it from my backpack. I was working on a new story, my first attempt to write about racing. Words swirled in my head, drawing me in, and it was a relief to get lost in them.

Late that afternoon, Denny dropped by on his way to the speedway. Race pretended sitting out was no big deal to him, but he didn't fool either of us. I was glad when Kasey showed up at five-thirty, even though she was blown out from squeezing interviews into her schedule. In spite of the effort, she still hadn't found a decent mechanic. She didn't dwell on it in front of Race, but on the way home that night she gave me the details.

"The difficult part is finding someone who can weld as well as work on cars. That puts a lot of potential candidates out of the running. I suppose that's why I tolerated Harley's poor work habits for so long. He was a good fabricator."

I flexed my sore hand, feeling that stiff, itchy pain that meant it was healing. "Why don't you just hire a mechanic *and* a welder?"

"Because I don't have enough work for two people, and anyone with those skills isn't likely to be interested in a part-time position."

It seemed like everyone had problems that weren't easy to solve. Kasey couldn't find help, Race kept letting his pride overrun his good sense, and my mom couldn't get it through her thick skull that there was no way in hell I'd ever move to Phoenix. All that unfinished business left me uneasy. How was I supposed to relax when I didn't even know where I'd be living in another week?

As we cruised up Spring Boulevard, I told Kasey about my failed attempt to reason with Race that morning. "I don't know why he's so hung up about money."

"It's not that hard to understand," Kasey said. "Race sees money differently than you or I do. To him it's a form of leverage. His father gave or withheld it as a means of control, and even though his mother doesn't treat it the same way, it's clearly very important to her."

"He needs to get over it. How does he think he's gonna manage without help from you and Grandma?"

Kasey pulled into the driveway, silencing the Charger's mammoth engine with a flick of the key. "I told you, Cody, he's in denial. It's a natural part of the process. Sooner or later he'll get to a point where he can accept what needs to be done."

"I sure hope so."

The next morning Kasey went to the shop even though it was Sunday. Race scowled when I told him where she was.

"She's working too hard," he grumbled.

"It's all part of running your own business. Or at least that's what Kasey says."

"Maybe so, but I'm not making it any easier, sucking up all her time in the evenings."

"If you're that worried about it, you oughta take Grandma's advice. It would really take a load off Kasey's mind if she didn't have to worry about you." I knew Grandma had been coming by every afternoon and telling him the same thing, but I figured hearing it from a second source couldn't hurt.

"I don't wanna talk about it," Race said.

Since he hadn't said 'no' I figured I was making progress. I grabbed the remote and turned on the TV, not wanting to press my luck. It was too easy to make him cranky these days.

As I flipped through the channels, rejecting educational programming and fire-and-brimstone televangelists, Race changed the subject. "Seems like you haven't been smoking as much lately. You didn't leave once yesterday to have a cigarette."

I shrugged even though I was proud of my abstinence. "Kasey won't let me smoke at her place. I guess I could go out on the deck, but she gives me these disappointed looks that make me feel like I peed on the rug, so I'm trying to quit."

Race laughed. "If Kasey's disappointed looks are that effective, I need to get her to give me lessons."

I found an old movie that wasn't completely worthless, and the two of us settled in to watch. It was almost over when a familiar yet completely unexpected figure appeared in the doorway.

Jerry Addamsen.

"Well, now. You don't look so bad," he said. "Rumor has it that a few days ago you were swappin' paint with death."

Race and I stared at his nemesis in silence until I finally found my voice. "He was," I said, looking Addamsen straight in the eye. "But he ran the bastard off the backstretch into a tractor tire."

The driver of the black #1 Camaro regarded me for a long moment, a ghost of a smile tugging at the corners of his mouth. Then he laughed. "I see the apple doesn't fall far from the tree."

"What are you doing here?" Race asked, his eyes narrowing.

"Just paying my respects." Addamsen leaned against the door jam, looking strange in a T-shirt, work boots, and jeans rather than the black firesuit I was so used to seeing. "Denny said you had surgery."

"Well, it wasn't exactly something that could be fixed with duct tape."

"Amazing," said Addamsen. "I thought everything could be fixed with duct tape."

The two of them continued to stare at each other.

"I guess you've got the championship wrapped up now," Race said after several long moments. "Must be nice."

Addamsen's expression stiffened. "Well, I can see where you'd think that, but you're wrong. I like a challenge. You're the only one who's been able to touch me in years."

"If you like a challenge so much, why'd you run me off the backstretch?"

Addamsen laughed. "I didn't say I never lost my temper."

The silence resumed, Race still obviously not trusting his rival, and Addamsen looking like he thought it might've been a mistake to come.

"They're saying you won't be back this season," the older man said after the quiet had stretched out for a good thirty seconds.

"They're full of shit."

A grin spread over Addamsen's weathered face. Then he looked at the floor. "Y'know, Morgan, you probably think it doesn't matter to me one way or the other, but the fact is, I hate seeing this happen to you. This kinda thing shouldn't happen to anyone."

"You came here to tell me that?"

Addamsen nervously tapped the heel of one of his grubby work boots against the toe of the other, flaking dried mud onto the hospital floor. "I don't know why I came," he admitted. "I want to win the championship, but not like this."

"What does it matter? Isn't a win a win?"

"You know better than that."

Race grunted, but the wariness faded from his eyes.

"Well, I've gotta get going," Addamsen said, pushing away from the doorframe. "If you need help getting your car back together, give me a call."

Race's expression made it clear he'd sooner juggle cats than dial Addamsen's number. Stone-faced, Addamsen dug his wallet out of his back pocket and removed a business card.

"Here," he said, thrusting it at me. "I know your uncle's too damned stubborn to ask for my help, so you hang onto this."

Chapter 23

Monday morning Kasey needed me at the shop, so it was almost twelve-thirty by the time I got to Sacred Heart. Knowing how tired Race was getting of hospital food, I caught the bus that went down Franklin Boulevard so I could grab a pizza at Track Town. It was a good thing, too. Race looked like he could really use a pick-me-up.

"Here," I said, depositing the box in his lap. "It's a get-well pizza. I didn't want to be like everyone else and get you some lame card."

"You should market that idea," Race said.

Seeing him struggle with the cardboard flap, I reached out and popped it open, allowing the tantalizing scent of tomato sauce and hot cheese to waft up from the pie. I'd gotten it half and half because I believed pepperoni stood on its own, while Race preferred everything but the kitchen sink, including nasty stuff like mushrooms.

Race was already slopping sausage and bits of green pepper all over the bed—another reason to avoid overloading a pizza— so I grabbed him a towel from the bathroom to use as a table-cloth.

"Kid, I owe you my life," he said after consuming half a slice. "The only thing that would make this better was if we were eating it at Track Town. I am *so* ready to get out of here."

Race might think he was ready, but I knew he wasn't. Every time he stood up he got so dizzy he had to clutch the IV pole to keep from falling over. The vertigo was better than it had been a few days before, but it was still scary to see.

"Y'know, I appreciate you coming by every day to entertain me," Race said. "It must be pretty boring."

"That's all right. Nobody's charging me admission to get in."

"I wish I could say the same."

"Doesn't the track have insurance?"

"Yeah, but I have no idea how much it will cover, and Kasey refuses to talk about the subject. She keeps giving me her standard, 'You shouldn't be worrying about things like that,' line."

Race reached for a second slice of pizza. I was already working on my third.

"Denny came by after you left yesterday," he said, redirecting the conversation. "He wants to take you out to the track tomorrow."

"I think I'll stay here with you."

"You should go," Race argued. "You'll like it. The Fourth of July's the biggest event of the season. They've got fireworks, a demolition derby, double points in all the divisions . . ."

"Dude, you've gotta stop thinking about those points."

Race gave me a look that said, *yeah, like* that's *gonna happen.*

"I want you to go. You've been spending too much time here with me."

"It's my time. I can spend it however I like." I pulled a fourth slice away from the pizza. Race tossed the better half of his second back in the box. He still wasn't eating much, and it made me uneasy.

"Kasey thinks you should go," he said.

"Kasey thinks you should move in with her," I countered.

Sighing, Race looked up at the ceiling. "Would it shock you to learn I talked to my mother about that very subject last night?"

I stared at him. "Yeah. It would."

"Well, I did. I still don't like the idea, but she was making noises about having you move in with her."

"You gonna take the loan, too?"

Race's jaw tensed. "That was part of the deal."

Much as I knew it was the only practical solution, I felt for him. I pulled the pepperonis off my pizza slice, savoring them one by one. "It's only for a little while," I said. "By the end of the summer, we'll find ourselves an apartment. That was what you'd planned to do anyway, right?"

Race didn't answer.

"And I'll go to the speedway with Denny tomorrow. It'll prob'ly be fun."

"It'll be the first Fourth of July race I've missed since I was ten." Race studied the ceiling tiles again.

I'd seen him grumpy about rainouts and disheartened by Kasey's rejection, but never seriously bummed. How was I supposed to make him feel better? He'd always been the one reassuring me.

"Do me a favor, kid. Tell Kasey and have her take you to the trailer to pack up some of our stuff tonight. I don't want to have to go over it again with her."

"Sure." I jammed the rest of my pizza into my mouth and closed the box, saving the rest of it for Race. Maybe he'd eat more later.

"You wanna watch some TV?" I asked around a mouthful of pizza crust.

"I wanna take a nap. But go for it."

I decided to finish up the story I was writing, instead. Race slept for a couple of hours, long enough for me to work through the ending then go back and mess with some details I didn't like.

"Still scribbling in that notebook, huh?" Race's voice startled me out of my fictional world. "You're never gonna tell me what that's about, are you?"

"Prob'ly not."

Race watched me for a second then looked up at the clock. "Wow. It's almost four."

"You got a hot date or something?"

"Only with the physical therapist."

I shut the notebook and jammed my pen into the wire spiral. "I take it that's my cue to leave."

"No offense, kid, but I've gotta maintain my dignity."

Nodding, I got up. I was used to being booted out by hospital staff. "No problem. But I need you to sign something for me, first. There's this karate tournament up in Portland on Saturday. I'm not ready to compete, but the sensei says we should all go to show our support for the people who are." I dug a crumpled release form out of my pocket, smoothing it and placing it on the table, which I rolled in front of Race.

"Oh." I pulled the pen out of my notebook. "I guess you'll need this."

Race eyed it like it was road kill.

"What's wrong?"

"Nothing." He reached for the pen, knocking it onto the blankets.

"Don't you want me to go?"

"No kid, it's not that . . ." He groped for the ballpoint, shifting it into the proper position with his other hand.

"Well, what?"

The pen shook slightly in Race's grasp. His face was a mask hiding a riptide of emotion. Images from the last few days flashed through my head—Race wrestling with the Twinkie wrapper, pawing at the remote, fighting to open the pizza box. Suddenly it was obvious. Why had it taken me so long to see? Stunned by the revelation and the enormity of the loss it meant, I slipped the pen from his clenched fingers.

"Hey, don't worry about it. I didn't want to go, anyway. It's, like, a two-hour drive."

Race closed his eyes, leaning heavily back into the pillows as I signed his name to the paper. Crap, why did I have to go putting him on the spot like that? Why couldn't I use my damn head for once?

"It'll be okay. Really. I mean, that's what therapy's for, right?"

Race was quiet.

I didn't know what to do. It was like watching the Olympic flame go out and trying to compensate with a Bic lighter. Awkwardly, I reached out and gripped his shoulder.

"This ain't gonna beat you, dude."

Race's eyes flickered open at my touch. For a brief second, I saw everything he was feeling—the fear, the pain, the humiliation.

I would have given anything to make it go away.

As I rode the bus down Hilyard, I replayed the afternoon in my mind and wished I could erase it. It was bad enough for Race to miss out on the Fourth of July and have to take Grandma's money. Why had I pulled out that stupid release form and made things worse?

Kasey was putting together a set of heads when I got to the shop. When I told her what Race had said about the trailer, she set down the valve spring compressor.

"I'd better give him a call."

"No! He doesn't want to talk about it. He said we should take care of things."

Kasey frowned. "I have to discuss the details with him. How will I know what he wants us to pack?"

"I'll help you figure it out. Don't call him. He's had a really lousy day."

"What happened?"

I told her what I'd learned at the hospital, expecting a look of concern, but Kasey's face didn't register even the slightest surprise.

"I'm sorry you had to find out this way, Cody."

"What? You *knew* about it? Why does everyone keep hiding stuff from me?" Hurt and anger surged through me, fighting for dominance in a race too close to call. I could understand Race and Kasey keeping things from each other—I could even sympathize with Race for being too embarrassed to admit his limitations. But how could Kasey leave me in the dark?

"I wasn't trying to hide anything. I was hoping this would resolve itself and never become an issue."

"But it hasn't."

"No. Everything else is getting better, just not that."

"But he's an artist!"

Kasey nodded. "I'm sorry. I should have told you. I could have saved both of you some grief. But Race isn't dealing with this very well, and I suppose I was trying to protect him. He won't talk about it—not even to me."

A whisper of fear grew inside me, and I eyed her warily. "What else haven't you told me?"

"Nothing."

"What about the insurance?"

"That's not an issue. Even if there's a problem, Sacred Heart can't force him to pay. It's in their charter."

I scowled. "And you think Race is gonna take their charity?"

Kasey's lack of response was answer enough.

"That's why you won't talk to him about it," I said.

"Yes."

Couldn't she see she was making it worse?

"I know you're trying to protect him, Kasey, but you're doing it all wrong. He's stressed out not knowing, plus you're taking away the only control he has." I gave her a critical look. "*You* wouldn't like it."

Kasey turned back to the partially assembled head on the workbench. "I'll take that under advisement," she said stiffly.

Low rays of evening sunlight slanted through the grimy windows of the trailer as Kasey and I stood in the front room, looking at the mess. In spite of what I'd told her about helping, I didn't know where to begin. A lot of my things were already at Kasey's and the rest would be easy to box up. But Race's stuff was another story.

"What do we pack?" I asked.

"For now, just clothes and personal items. The rent's paid through the end of the month, so there's no hurry. I'll talk to Race about it in a week or two. By then he might be ready to let us put the rest of it in storage."

I nodded, my gut clenching at the sight of the drafting table, which I'd been trying to ignore.

"Go pack your things," Kasey suggested gently. "I'll take care of Race's."

It was better in my room, but not by much. I pulled a pile of collapsed boxes out from under my bed, shaking my head as I remembered how I'd saved them. I'd been so sure Race would kick me out.

Using the proper tool—duct tape—I reassembled the boxes and secured the bottoms. Then I began shoving things into them at random. Once the drawers in the dresser and desk were empty, I started on the walls. As I took the target off the closet door, my fingers traced the upraised edges of the paneling where the shuriken had penetrated. Race had been so pissed. I almost laughed when I thought of how he'd handed me the phone book. Typical Race. I'd been such an idiot, fighting him. How could I not have realized he was gonna be the best thing that ever happened to me?

Suddenly furious, I ripped down the rest of the posters and photos, oblivious to torn edges. Until I came to the Superbird drawing. Compared to the stuff Race had pinned above his drafting table, it was rough and unpolished—the work of an artist still discovering his talent. My fingers trembled as I removed the tacks that held it in place. I sank onto the bed, staring at the sketch.

"Cody? Are you about done in here?" Kasey spoke from the doorway, but I couldn't look up.

"It's not fair," I whispered, wiping the tears from my face. One fell on the paper, spotting the #43 on the Superbird's door. Gently, I brushed it away.

Kasey sat down beside me, tucking her arm around my shoulders. My hand shook as I held the drawing out for her to see.

"He drew this for me when I was five."

Hot tears obscured my vision as Kasey's arms drew me close. This time, she didn't try to find comforting words. Neither one of us would have believed them.

Chapter 24

Visiting Race the next day was awkward. Both of us tried to pretend nothing had happened, but it didn't work. I felt like I had a weird advantage over him, and it made me want to do something to balance the score. So when Denny came to pick me up I ripped the story I'd finished the day before out of my notebook and handed it to Race.

An uneasy feeling hung in the back of my mind as Denny and I drove to the track. Everyone was gonna ask about Race. What was I supposed to say? But Denny had that covered.

"You stick by me, Cody. Anyone starts asking questions you don't wanna answer, you let me handle it, okay?"

I nodded.

As we pulled into the pits, the biting scent of racing fuel drifted through the cab, bringing a tsunami of overpowering memories. Instantly I knew it had been a mistake to come. People were unloading cars, lifting toolboxes out of truck beds, and lining up for hot laps as if it were any ordinary Saturday. The activity struck me like a fist to the gut. How could Race's friends just go on like nothing had happened?

Holly Schrader came up behind me while Denny was backing his car off the trailer.

"Hi, Cody. I didn't expect to see you here today. How's Race?"

The two Whoppers with cheese Denny had bought me on the way to the track churned in my stomach.

"He's doing great," Denny said, hefting his girth through the comparatively small window of the Camaro. "Cody, you wanna climb up and unload those tires for me?"

I crawled into the back of the pickup, and Denny gave Holly the latest update, sparing me from having to say anything.

"I don't think I want to be here," I said after Holly left.

"It'll get better," Denny said. "You'll like the derby."

Yeah, just what I wanted to see—cars crashing into each other on purpose.

Though Denny did a good job of deflecting people's questions, I couldn't dodge all the well-wishing. I knew people were trying to make me feel better, but it didn't work. I just wanted them to leave me alone. The only one in the Sportsman class who didn't say anything was Jim.

After the trophy dash, which Addamsen won, I saw Steve making his weekly pilgrimage to the concession stand.

"I'll be right back, Denny. There's something I gotta take care of."

I found Alex by the hearse, chilling in the lawn chair he always brought. He smiled when he saw me.

"Cody, hey! I stopped by the hospital a couple of times last week, but I missed you. How are you holding up?"

I shrugged.

"Any word yet on when they're going to let Race go home?"

"Probably Thursday. He still gets pretty dizzy when he's up walking around."

Alex nodded. "They'll want him to be steady on his feet before they let him go. But from what I heard last week, he's doing really well."

Except that he wasn't. I thought of him clenching my pen—that walled-off look on his face—and a train wreck of emotions slammed into me. It was one thing to cry with only Kasey around, but I was mortified by the idea of blubbering in front of everybody. Knowing if I said a word I'd lose it altogether, I froze. Alex took one look at me, grabbed my arm, and led me around to the relative privacy of the back of the hearse. He opened the door and motioned for me to sit.

"Pretty overwhelming, huh?"

I nodded. "I feel like such a wuss."

Alex dropped onto the floorboards beside me, hunching forward and resting his elbows on his knees. He fixed his gaze on the smashed down grass at our feet, rather than me, and I appreciated him giving me that little bit of space.

"What you're going through is normal, Cody. Nobody expects the people they care about to get hurt. It's always a shock, and it takes time to work through. Believe me, I see it every day."

Trying to get control of myself, I looked out over turns three and four where the Street Stocks weaved back and forth, warming their tires in anticipation of the green flag. Golden, late afternoon sun blazed down on them from an amazingly blue sky, and the heat of the day still hung in the air. It was perfect Fourth of July weather—a rarity in western Oregon.

"I was a real jerk to you the other night. I—I said things I shouldn't have. I'm sorry."

Alex patted my knee. "Don't worry about it. That was hardly the worst emotional outburst I've seen. People say a lot of crazy things when they're upset."

"It's not just that. Race wouldn't be here if it wasn't for you and Steve. I owe you guys big time."

"You don't owe us anything. We were doing our jobs. I'm just glad it turned out the way it did. Sometimes, no matter what you do, it doesn't help."

"That must really suck."

"Yeah," Alex agreed, staring out over the north end of the track. "It does."

Jim avoided me through the heat races. At first I thought it was my imagination, but when I walked past him to go to the concession stand and he didn't say anything, it really torqued me.

"Hey, Jim," I said pointedly on my way back to Denny's pit.

"Cody," he acknowledged, nodding and shifting as if his boxers were riding up. "How's Race doing?"

"Maybe you should go talk to him and find out."

Jim blinked then mumbled something about how busy he'd been at work.

"You're his best friend, Jim. You're supposed to have his back. Hell, even Addamsen's been to visit him!"

That tidbit of information seemed to catch Jim off guard. "You don't understand."

"I understand just fine—you feel guilty. Get over it. Race already lost the championship. You think it's gonna make things better if he loses you, too?"

Jim glanced away from my deliberate stare, fiddling with the radiator cap on his car.

"Look, he knows it's not your fault. You're the only one who thinks it is. Just go see him, okay?"

Jim didn't answer. Disappointed, I walked away.

Kasey was waiting up when Denny dropped me off after midnight. Curled up on the couch with Winston, she smiled sleepily at me as I came through the door. "How was it?" she asked.

"The fireworks were okay."

A slow comprehension registered in Kasey's eyes. "You were miserable."

"I know you and Race were trying to help," I said quickly, "but it felt so wrong, being there without him."

Kasey nodded. "I should have realized that. I'm not sure what the trouble is with me lately, but I just can't seem to think straight."

I knew what the trouble was. She was exhausted. Between putting in ten-hour days at work, then spending the evenings with Race, she never got a break. The only thing that seemed to recharge her was when her mom would call or stop by the shop.

"Come sit down," Kasey said, drawing her legs up to make room for me on the couch. "There's something I need to talk to you about."

My stomach tensed and I froze. "What?"

Kasey's face softened at the panicked note in my voice. "There's nothing wrong. It's about the story you gave Race this afternoon."

"He told you about it?"

"Not exactly. When I showed up he was trying to decipher your illegible penmanship. He kept asking me to translate words for him." Kasey smiled. "Fortunately, with all my younger brothers and sisters, I'm fluent in chicken scratch."

"So what's the big deal?" The thought of her seeing some of the words I'd put on paper made me uneasy, but it wasn't like she'd read the whole thing.

"It was frustrating for Race. He understood how difficult it must've been for you to trust him with your private thoughts. He didn't want to disappoint you."

My uneasiness revved to a fast idle. "You read it to him, didn't you?"

Kasey nodded. "I had to ask several times before he let me. You need to know he didn't betray your confidence. If you want someone to be angry with, that someone should be me."

Humiliation warmed my face. I felt suddenly naked. "I'm not mad," I said, sitting on the arm of the chair beside the door. "I'm just embarrassed."

"You shouldn't be. You have talent, Cody. You ought to be proud of that."

"My story didn't suck?"

"No, it didn't *suck*." Kasey shook her head and smiled. "There's something else you might want to consider. I know you seem to regard your sensitivity as some sort of weakness, but it's not. It's a gift. Without it, you wouldn't be able to write the way you do. You're a smart, intuitive, young man. You'd be doing yourself a favor to recognize that."

I blushed harder and stared down at my dusty Converse high tops.

"Did Race like my story?"

"He was thrilled with it. I haven't seen him grin like that in days. He's very proud of you."

I felt a crazy little grin of my own slip over my face.

"It's getting late," Kasey said, disturbing the slumbering cat as she stood up from the couch. "We need some sleep. But remind me tomorrow and I'll get you set up to use the word processing program on my computer. With handwriting as atrocious as yours, you're going to have to learn how to type."

In spite of what Kasey said, I felt self-conscious facing Race the next morning. I had to remind myself that the whole point of giving him my story had been to level the playing field. I was *supposed* to be feeling like someone had pantsed me.

"Hey," Race said as I entered his room. "You're just the guy I wanted to see. I got the official word a few minutes ago— they're gonna let me out of here tomorrow."

"That's great."

"So how was it last night? Did Addamsen steal the show?" Race's upbeat attitude contrasted sharply with the downer he'd been on for the past two days. I felt like the world was starting to right itself.

"Not completely. Denny kicked his ass in the heat. He almost had him in the main, too." I tossed a package of frozen Twinkies at Race then straddled the arm of the chair.

"Where did Jim finish?"

Irritation churned inside me, and it was a struggle to keep my face from broadcasting it. "Fourth in the heat, sixth in the main."

Race nodded, pursuing his own battle with the Twinkie wrapper. "I take it Kasey talked to you last night?"

"Yeah."

"And you're not upset?"

"No."

The package burst open and a snack cake shot through the air, landing on the floor a few feet from me. I scooped it up. "You still want this?"

"Three second rule." Race held out his hand and I dropped the Twinkie into it.

"Well, I guess the floor's gotta be pretty clean."

"I wouldn't bet on that. I haven't seen 'em sweep it since I've been here." Race chomped the end off the Twinkie. "Y'know, that was a great story you wrote. I was impressed with the details. How'd you know what it would be like, getting spun out in the middle of a race? You've never driven anything but my van."

"Well, I *did* wreck it," I pointed out.

Race shook his head. "Still, it's pretty amazing. You really nailed what it's like to be out on the track."

I shrugged. It hadn't been that tough to figure out. I'd just watched him and the other guys at the speedway then put what they seemed to feel into experiences I understood. Like the satisfaction I felt that first time Race took me out for a driving lesson. Or the *oh shit* feeling I got when I lost control of the van.

"How long have you been writing?" Race asked, digging the second Twinkie out of the demolished wrapper.

"I dunno. Maybe three or four years."

"Your school counselor never mentioned it." Race's voice was muffled by snack cake. "He just said you did well on your essays."

"He didn't know. Nobody does. I tried showing a story to this one teacher last fall, but he flaked out on me."

"And of course you never told your mom or dad."

"Are you kidding? Mom thinks artsy guys are losers." *The same way grandpa does*, I realized.

Race gave me a sad little smile. "Our family isn't very big on encouraging creativity. Though I have a feeling your dad might understand. He was really impressed with your grades."

"I'm not showing it to him."

"Hey, no pressure. I'm just honored you showed it to me." Race's eyes caught mine in a solemn look, and for a moment he was quiet. "You've got a gift, Cody. You owe it to yourself to do something with it. Talent only goes so far by itself. You've got to train it. And you can't let anyone stand in the way—not even yourself."

I thought of Grandpa cutting off Race's college fund, and how he hadn't let that stop him. I pictured Race scrawling in his sketchbook without the least bit of self-consciousness, no matter who was watching. He wasn't afraid to let people see the creative part of himself. I didn't know if I had that kind of courage. But looking at him now, I understood talent wasn't something you should take for granted. In a second, it could get snatched away.

"I'm behind you 100 percent, kid," Race said. "I want you to know that."

Like there was any question.

Chapter 25

Thursday morning, while Kasey went to pick up Race, I stayed home transferring my story onto the computer in her basement rec room. It was a slow process of hunt and peck, and after about 15 minutes I decided that, come September, I was gonna sign up for a typing class at school.

The Charger growled into the driveway. I shut down the computer and went upstairs. After tapping the remote button to fire up the TV, I flopped on the couch to wait. I knew it would be awhile. Kasey's house was built on a hillside so the front door, which opened onto the deck, was a full story above the ground. All those stairs were bound to kick Race's ass. I could've gone outside to help, but I figured he'd prefer not to have two people witnessing his weakness.

A couple of minutes later Kasey opened the door. Race, pale and shaky, failed to look dignified as he sank like a stone onto the chair near the doorway. It rattled me to see how thin he seemed in regular clothes. It hadn't been that obvious when he was in bed.

"I never really noticed those stairs until today," Race gasped. "You know there's fourteen of 'em?"

"There's only seven the way I take 'em," I said.

Race glanced at the TV, which had just cut from a volley of commercials to a soap opera. "Jeeze, Cody, don't tell me this is one of your dirty little secrets."

I snatched the remote and changed channels.

"You should go lie down, Race," Kasey suggested.

"I don't wanna lie down. I've spent most of the last two weeks lying down."

The way he was slouched in that chair, he was practically horizontal, anyway.

"Do you need one of these?" Kasey asked, holding out the small pharmacy bag she'd brought in with her. "You look like you're really hurting."

Race scowled like an overtired two-year-old. "No. I told you, I'm not gonna take that stuff. It makes me feel like I'm in the Twilight Zone. I've got enough trouble trying to think straight without throwing chemicals into the mix."

"What's in there?" I asked.

Kasey set the bag down on the coffee table. "Vicodin."

"I'll take it off your hands."

"No, you won't, kid." Race nodded at Kasey. "Put those away somewhere. Just get me some aspirin."

"What's wrong with spending a little time in the Twilight Zone?" I asked, flipping through the channels.

Race closed his eyes and sank deeper into the chair. "The problem is when you can't make yourself come back."

Too stubborn to lie down, Race fell asleep where he was sitting. Winston, taking advantage of a warm, inert body, curled up in his lap. The cat had been sleeping with me since I'd moved in, seeming to sense I needed the peaceful vibe he radiated, but now he put his healing feline energy to better use.

Kasey told me to keep an eye on Race then headed for the shop. It was after six when she returned. Tired as she looked, she went straight to the kitchen to make dinner.

Race hovered in the doorway, leaning against the frame as he watched. "Can I help with anything?" He'd spent the afternoon alternating between sleeping and wandering restlessly through the house, looking for something to do.

"No, just relax. I've got things under control."

Race sighed and joined me on the couch, where I was playing Mario Brothers on my Nintendo. With my first paycheck, I'd replaced a couple of the games Mom had swiped.

"Kasey works too hard," Race muttered for probably the hundredth time that week. "Tomorrow we'll cook dinner for her."

I wasn't so sure she'd appreciate that.

Soon the tantalizing scent of beef stroganoff began drifting from the kitchen. By the time Kasey called us to the table, my stomach was rattling the bars of my rib cage.

"This smells delicious," said Race, pulling out a chair and sitting down.

"It's nice to have someone to cook for. I enjoy the process, but sometimes it seems like a bit of a waste for only one person."

I slid into a chair and, at Kasey's beckoning, grabbed the pan of noodles. After heaping some on my plate, I passed it to her and reached for the stroganoff.

Kasey took a helping of pasta then started to spoon some onto Race's plate. The heat of his glare stopped her short. She pushed the pan in his direction.

"Thank you," he said stiffly as he scooped into the container. Noodles wiggled off the spoon and plopped onto the table.

"Your plate's a little to the left," I said.

Race threw a noodle at me. It missed and landed in my milk.

"Do I have to drink that?"

Fighting a smile, Kasey reached for the stroganoff.

I dug into my food, pointedly ignoring Race as he concentrated on the pan of pasta. With great effort, he managed to get some onto his plate. The vegetables were another story.

"You have a mean streak in you," he told Kasey as peas rolled over the tabletop.

"I'm sorry. I should have thought."

"I'll say," I agreed, "peas shouldn't even be considered food." I'd been avoiding them, but Kasey put an end to that by lowering a spoonful onto my plate.

"Didn't you ever give this boy vegetables?"

Race gave Kasey an innocent look. "What're vegetables?"

"You know, dude," I said, "those green and red things that come on your side of the pizza."

"Oh, yeah. I never mess with those. I prefer the one-pan method of cooking."

Kasey shook her head, but her expression melted from exasperation into amusement.

"Y'know, I've been thinking," Race said. "Maybe we could run down to my shop some night this week and have a look at the Dart."

Kasey's smile faded. "I'm awfully busy. I still haven't found a mechanic, and evenings are the only time I have to catch up on paperwork."

"So how long do you think it'll take to fix?" Race asked.

"I have no idea." Kasey turned her attention toward me as I skeptically examined my milk. "Cody, if you're thirsty take mine. That noodle won't bother me." She leaned across the table to swap glasses.

"I know you're busy," Race persisted, "but I'd like to know what I'm up against. Maybe I could give Denny a call and have him run me by the shop."

"Can we talk about this another time?" Kasey asked. "I'm exhausted."

Race studied her, torn between hurt and understanding. As an expert in the fine art of manipulation, I had to hand it to Kasey. She sure knew how to disarm him.

I was shocked to find Race up when I entered the kitchen the next morning at six-thirty. Judging by how tired he looked, I figured he'd had trouble sleeping. That was something I could relate to. It had been several days since I'd woken in the darkness to the image of the Dart flipping through the air, but it had happened again last night.

"Are you taking Cody to the shop today?" Race asked, poking at his Cheerios. Milk sloshed out of the bowl and puddled on the tabletop.

"No," Kasey said. "I think for these first few days he should stay here and keep you company."

"I don't need company. The shop's more important. I feel bad enough already that you got behind because of me."

Kasey looked up from the morning edition of the *Register Guard.* Or the *Register Disregard,* as Race called it, since they tended to neglect printing the speedway results. "That's not your fault," she said. "You didn't tell Harley to quit."

"Yeah, but I was the one who gave you a reason to spend a good part of the last two weeks at the hospital."

"That was my decision."

"Take Cody with you," Race insisted. "He likes the work and you need the help."

"I don't think it's a good idea for you to spend too much time alone."

Race shoved away from the table, spilling more milk. "Damn it, Kasey, I don't need a babysitter."

Carefully, Kasey folded the paper and got up to take her bowl to the sink. "He's staying here today," she said.

It was awfully considerate of them to ask for my input on that plan.

"C'mon kid," Race said later that morning. "We're going for a walk. I'm not gonna get my stamina back by sitting here watching TV."

"Is that a Kasey-approved activity?" I asked, averting my eyes from the book I was reading.

"Do I look like I care?"

Race kept a firm grip on the handrail as we descended the fourteen stairs. Straggling down the driveway, he grumbled about the heat. Just the night before, he'd been freezing and Kasey'd had to turn off the AC.

"Dude, it's only, like, seventy-five degrees. Your thermostat's messed up."

"Along with everything else."

I had to reduce my pace to grandma-speed so Race could keep up. I entertained myself by practicing some karate kicks at mailboxes.

"I haven't seen you with a cigarette once in the past two days," Race said. "How goes the battle?"

"Pretty good. It's a struggle sometimes, but I haven't had a smoke since Sunday."

Race grinned. "Good work."

We got about three houses down the street before he had to sit down to rest on a huge boulder at the end of someone's driveway.

"I'm so out of shape."

"Well, no shit. Try looking on the bright side. You're alive, you can walk around, and you don't get dizzy when you stand up anymore."

"You're such an inspiration." Race heaved himself up off the rock. He only made it another half a block before giving in and turning back.

That little bit of exertion wiped Race out so much he retreated to his room, granting me a few hours of uninterrupted peace while he slept. When he returned to the living room he wore a pinched, pale look that meant he was struggling with another headache. He dropped into the chair by the door and stared at the blank TV, tapping his foot in boredom.

"It's more interesting if you turn it on," I said.

"I've had enough daytime television to last me the rest of my life."

"Well, read a book, then. Kasey's got tons of 'em down in the basement." The whole north wall of her rec room was floor-to-ceiling bookshelves. A lot of her collection consisted of college textbooks and big tomes about engineering, but she also owned quite a bit of fiction. Enough to keep me busy for the rest of the summer.

"Not that I have anything against it, but I never really got into reading," Race said.

"Maybe you should try it. It doesn't take any strength and it's a really good way to kill time."

When Race continued to sit there, I laid my book face down on the coffee table and got up. "C'mon," I said. "I'll help you find something interesting."

Race sighed and followed me downstairs.

"Here we go," I said, pulling a book from the shelves after surveying the fiction. "You'll like this. It's mystery, but it's got a lot of humor." I handed him the first of Robert B. Parker's novels about a private detective named Spenser. Kasey had the entire series, fifteen books so far, and I figured it would keep Race busy for a while.

Leaving him alone with the *The Godwulf Manuscript*, I went back upstairs. I briefly wondered how he was gonna manage to turn the pages, but decided not to risk annoying him by bringing it up. He must've figured it out because I didn't see him again until a quarter to six.

"That Spenser character's a real smartass," Race said when he emerged from the basement.

"Takes one to know one," I observed.

"We need to make dinner," Race said. "Kasey shouldn't have to work all day and then come home and cook for us."

"Have at it. I don't want her giving me crap for pawing through her cupboards."

Race disappeared into the kitchen. The banging and clatter he made distracted me, but it wasn't until I heard the sound of breaking glass that I figured I'd better help. The phone rang before I made it halfway across the living room. I detoured to grab it.

"Cody? Hi, it's Mom."

"Sorry, wrong number." I hung up and proceeded to the kitchen, where Race was picking the broken pieces of a Ragu jar out of an enormous puddle of spaghetti sauce. It was amazing how much square footage a quart of pureed tomatoes could cover.

"Who was on the phone?"

"No one. Here, let me do that. You're gonna cut yourself."

Race tossed the bigger shards of glass into the garbage can. "You have no idea how annoying it is when you and Kasey won't let me do things for myself." He grabbed for a paper towel and the entire roll pulled free of its holder, bouncing off the counter and spiraling across the floor through the spaghetti sauce.

The phone rang again. Wearily, Race tracked through the puddle on the floor to get to the wall-mounted one by the refrigerator. As he picked it up, I realized Mom was probably calling back. I wondered which would be worse, talking to her myself or letting him do it.

"Why, hello, Saundra!" Race's voice was a sing-song of false cheerfulness. "Oh, he did, did he? So that was you just now." Race glanced at me and I froze. "Yep, I'm still alive and kicking. Sorry to disappoint you." He leaned back against the counter, lifting one foot to examine the pungent red goo covering the bottom of his sneaker. "Well, judging by the limited nature of your conversation a minute ago, I'd have to conclude that he's not interested in talking to you. To tell you the truth, I'm not interested in talking to you, myself."

Relieved at Race's intercession, I sat down.

"If that's how you feel, maybe you need to talk to Mom about it," Race continued. "She and I have an understanding."

There was a long pause, during which Race motioned for me to slide a chair over so he could sit. "Yeah, yeah, I know he's your kid, but he's old enough to make his own decisions."

The rumble of a big engine sounded in the driveway.

"Oh, shit!" I scrambled out of my seat and snatched the roll of paper towels. Race barked an abrupt goodbye and hung up, joining me in trying to mop up the mess.

The floor was still a big red smear when Kasey walked into the kitchen. Worse, I noticed that tomato sauce spotted the cupboards, walls and refrigerator to about knee level. Kasey said nothing, just faded into a chair, her face creased with exhaustion.

"I'm sorry," Race said. "I didn't think you should have to come home from work and cook. We'll clean it up."

Kasey gazed wide-eyed at the mess.

"Look, you guys," I said. "Why don't you go watch TV or something? I'll take care of this."

"Kid, it's not your—"

"Just go." I motioned toward the living room. "And don't track that stuff on the carpet."

Race gripped the counter for balance as he kicked off his shoes, then he followed Kasey into the other room. When I heard the low tones of the evening news I got to work.

I guess on some level I'd been thinking that when Race came home everything would be all right. Now I knew it wasn't gonna be that simple.

Chapter 26

After the Ragu disaster, I took over the cooking and cleaning duties. Race insisted on helping. Figuring he needed something to occupy his time, I let him, but I didn't allow him anywhere near a jar of spaghetti sauce.

While Kasey put up with our interference, I could tell giving up that control bothered her. Her house, once spotless, took on a more laid-back appearance under our blundering care. Every night I saw a battle going on in her eyes as she noticed a crappy vacuuming job or a few crumbs on the counter.

"Let it go," I said. "You're stressing Race out, trying to do everything yourself."

I figured things would get better with time, but they didn't. Not even when Kasey loosened the reins enough to let me go back to work in the afternoons. She was making several trips a day, between running me back and forth and taking Race to Sacred Heart three times a week for outpatient therapy.

"It's not an inconvenience," she insisted. But Race harrumphed that he knew damn well it was. Still, when Grandma offered to take him, he refused.

"I wouldn't want to pull her away from her busy volunteer schedule," he said, making me realize that some grudges could over-ride even his deep-seated sense of honor.

"She's your mother, Race. She wants to help," said Kasey.

"All she wants is for people to see that she's doing her duty. If she really cared she'd start accepting me for who I am."

Unlike Race, I was getting used to having Grandma in my life. She was overly proper and domineering, but the one thing I had to appreciate about her was how she'd come to respect Kasey. She didn't understand her, but she respected her. Unfortunately, Grandma also agreed with her when it came to the Dart. Kasey claimed she didn't have time to work on it, and Race, overwhelmed by his indebtedness to her, didn't argue.

I was disappointed in Kasey. I understood how the idea of Race returning to competition freaked her out, but it wasn't right for her to cope by using his guilt against him.

Kasey and Grandma's meddling was only part of the problem. Things also weren't going well with Race's recuperation. He couldn't concentrate, his memory was crap, and fatigue leveled him if he pushed too hard. Along with constant headaches, he had trouble sleeping. It wasn't unusual to find him passed out on the couch in the early morning hours with the TV on. After two weeks, he still had trouble operating the remote and dialing the phone. And while he pretended to prefer the comfort of sweats over jeans, we all knew he just couldn't manage a zipper.

Reading was the only thing that seemed to help. "Now I understand why you've always got your nose in a book," he told me. "It's kind of a relief to live somebody else's life for awhile."

I agreed, but I knew my need to escape had been nothing compared to his. I thought about his artwork, how sketching for him had always been as natural as reading for me. How brutal was it to lose that? Race never mentioned it, and Kasey and I were careful to avoid the subject.

"He'll deal with that when he's ready," Kasey said.

The saddest thing was that Race just wasn't himself anymore. All traces of his former optimism were gone. His easygoing, devil-may-care wisecracking had disappeared, leaving nothing but sullenness and irritability. It was like he was turning into the old me. Kasey pointed out that moodiness was a common symptom of a traumatic brain injury. The thought didn't reassure me. Instead, it brought back the fear that some essential part of Race's character had been permanently erased.

I tried not to let Race's crankiness get to me, reminding myself of my vow not to disappoint him again. Karate was the one thing that helped with that. After neglecting to practice the whole time Race was in the hospital, I'd worked it back into my schedule. Every day after breakfast I'd go out to the flagstone patio behind Kasey's house, where the dappled sunlight filtered through the trees, spotting the rock with glimmers of pale gold. There was something refreshing about cool morning air, the birds chattering in the trees that covered the hillside. I could see now what my sensei was saying about developing the mind and spirit at the same time as the body. Repeating the simple moves while I concentrated on my breathing always calmed me. I thought it might work for Race, too, but he was rarely up at that time.

Denny tried to help, visiting several times a week in an effort to boost Race's spirits. "You just gotta keep on keepin' on," he'd tell him. But the encouragement was like rain on a freshly waxed car, beading up and rolling away.

A lot of other people stopped by, too. Holly Schrader, Randy Whalen, even Tom Carey. But never Jim. Race was nice to their faces then complained when they left. "Why can't they just leave me alone?"

One Saturday in late July, Kasey took desperate measures to stir Race from his funk. She came home early and confronted him as he sprawled on the couch reading *Early Autumn*, the seventh book in the Spenser series.

"We're going to the speedway tonight," she said. "You should get ready."

Race didn't look up. "Unless you've been putting the Dart back together on the sly, I have absolutely no reason to go."

"Yes you do. Your friends are worried about you. It would help if they could see that you're okay."

Race lowered the book and extended a hand to indicate his reclining body. "You call this okay?"

"I'm not in the mood to argue." Kasey shuffled through the handful of mail she'd collected on her way in. "There's a letter here for you, Cody. Your mother again."

Mom had continued to call, and I'd continued to hang up on her. Race did the same. Only Kasey took the time to speak to her, but she didn't try to force me to.

I accepted the envelope, ripped it in half, and tossed it in the nearest wastebasket.

"An appropriate response," said Race.

"You need to get ready," Kasey told him. "We're leaving in half an hour."

I didn't know if I bought into this speedway idea. On one hand I could see it being very effective. On the other, it might be a complete disaster. What if we ran into Jim? He still hadn't bothered to visit Race or even call. Besides, Race was always at his worst in the evenings—tired, crabby, and easily rattled. It didn't seem like the optimal time for his return to the public eye.

At the track, Race let Kasey pay the entry fee in order to avoid a spectacle at the ticket booth. Several people stopped us on our way to find a seat, wishing him well and wanting to know when he'd be back. Kasey fielded the questions, with Race mumbling an occasional answer and looking overtaxed. When a pack of Super Stocks screamed down the front stretch, he flinched at the noise.

"Race!" Jim's kid, Robbie, waved madly at us before sprinting down the bleachers. "Hey," he said, screeching to a stop in front of us. "You got a haircut. I liked it better the other way."

"So did I," Race said.

Kasey'd had the final word on that, convincing Race the Mothra look wasn't particularly becoming. He wasn't happy with how short they'd had to cut his hair to even it out. I'd suggested a Mohawk, hoping to spare at least some of it, but had been overruled two-to-one.

"Come sit with us," Robbie said, grabbing Race's hand to drag him up to the spot where his mother was seated. Irritable as Race had been lately, he seemed to draw the line at taking his problems out on a little kid. He trailed behind, releasing Robbie's hand and gripping the kid's shoulder as they navigated the bleachers.

Laurie scooted over to make room for us. "Hey, Race, good to see you," she said, smiling up at him. "I'm sorry Jim hasn't stopped by. It isn't that he hasn't been worried about you."

"I know." Race lowered himself with the aid of Robbie's shoulder.

Time trials got underway and Robbie jabbered at Race throughout them. It surprised me to see that talking with the little squirt seemed to recharge Race's batteries. But as the night wore on, I watched him sag. He hunched forward during the Super Stock heats, shutting his eyes and massaging his temples. I'd heard enough about brain injuries to know the noise and action were too much stimulation.

"I'm sorry, Race," Kasey said as the cars of the fast heat decelerated to leave the track. "I should have realized how overwhelming this might be for you. I just thought—"

"Well, maybe next time you'll listen when I tell you I don't wanna do something."

Kasey put her hand on Race's arm. "Let's go home."

"Are you kidding?" He straightened up, eyes pinning her. "I look pathetic enough to all these people. I'm not gonna wimp out and leave early on top of that."

"Race, you're not being reasonable."

"Tough."

He stuck it out through the rest of the night, giving in only toward the end of the Super Stock main, when taking off early to get a jump on the crowd became a legitimate excuse. Kasey stole worried glances at him the whole time, and Race seemed to take satisfaction in watching her squirm over his discomfort.

Somehow, I couldn't blame him.

Kasey's plan to kick-start Race's attitude backfired in more ways than one. The next morning he got up at a decent hour and came out to the patio where I was practicing a karate kata.

"Kid, I'm gonna need you today."

I didn't know what to make of that, but it sounded interesting, so I went inside and told Kasey I wanted to stay home.

"What's up?" I asked Race half an hour later as I stood by the window and watched the Charger disappear down Spring Boulevard.

Grinning, he held up the keys to the van. "We're going to the shop."

I wondered what unscrupulousness he'd stooped to in order to find those. Kasey'd had them stashed away in some personal Fort Knox. "Dude," I said, "you can't drive. The doctor said six weeks and it's only been like, four."

"So now you're the voice of reason? What irony."

I studied the sly smile on his face, torn between caution and the desire to keep that triumphant look from fading away. It was the first glimpse of the old Race I'd had in a long time.

"What if we have a wreck or something? You hit your head again and your brain could turn to mush."

"What makes you so sure that wouldn't improve my quality of life?"

I looked at the key ring again. What could it hurt? Kasey would kill us if she found out, but wasn't she pushing Race into it every time she weaseled out of taking him to the shop?

"Okay," I said, "but if Kasey catches us, you gotta take the fall."

"Naturally."

I trailed behind him down the steps. "You want me to drive?"

"No."

I began to have doubts when he struggled to fit the key into the ignition, but once he got the van started, things went pretty smoothly. At least until we reached West 11th. As Race navigated the downtown area with parked cars on one side and traffic whizzing by on the other, his face went rigid and his focus zeroed in. He looked as jittery as I'd felt that day he'd given me my first driving lesson, but we made it to the shop unscathed.

Race tussled briefly with the locked door then led me into cool darkness where the familiar scents of grease and racing fuel brought on a wave of nostalgia.

"Well, let's see what we're up against." Race switched on the lights.

The mangled Dart, still on the trailer, sat just inside the bay door. The roof was mashed down against the roll cage and bore deep gouges from its slide across the track. Door bars stuck out against sheet metal, like ribs on a starving dog. The hood had been torn off completely. It rested against the workbench, the baby blue Mopar emblem scuffed through to bare metal.

As I took it all in, an Ice Age unfolded in my gut, advancing glaciers through my veins.

"Wow," said Race.

My head buzzed and I took an awkward step forward, feeling suddenly off-balance.

"Cody?" Race grabbed my arm, steering me toward the couch, where he forced me to sit. "Jesus, kid, I'm sorry. I didn't realize."

The buzzing faded into anger. "What—that it was serious? That you damn near got yourself killed?" My voice shook as I yelled at him.

Race sat down beside me. "It never occurred to me that seeing the car would hit you like this."

It hadn't occurred to me, either.

"You okay?"

I stared at my shaking hands as if they were someone else's. "I think I need a cigarette."

"I'll take you home if you want." The look in Race's eyes told me he was hoping I'd refuse.

"What kind of wuss do you think I am?" I took a deep, slow breath to center myself, like my sensei had taught me, then stood up. "Let's get to work. We've only got a few hours if we want to make it back to the house before Kasey."

I didn't realize what we were up against. Even getting the car on the ground was a trial. It took Race several attempts to line the trailer hitch up with the van's receiver, something he could normally do on the first shot.

"Son of a bitch," he grumbled, pulling forward with a little squeal of the tires on his fifth or sixth try. He looked like Mt. St. Helens on the day of the big eruption by the time he finally he got it.

Before we could back the car off, we had to change both right side tires, which had been flattened by their impact with the track. It was no easy task. Maneuvering the jack on the bed of the trailer was a pain because the fender kept getting in the way. Race swore the whole time. After repeatedly dropping lug nuts and making me fish under the trailer with a broom to retrieve them, he finally growled at me to finish the job.

"Now what?" I asked after wrestling the second tire into place.

Race pushed himself up off the tongue of the trailer, where he'd been resting. "Now we see if she'll run. Crawl in there and crank her over."

The starter whined eagerly, powered by the battery we'd just charged, but the engine refused to fire.

"Pump the throttle a couple times," Race ordered. He gripped the top of the door with both hands, and though he tried to look nonchalant about it, I could tell he was running on fumes.

I squeezed the accelerator. The tantalizing zing of racing fuel tickled my nose.

"Not that much! You flooded her! Just give it a rest. She's not gonna start now." Race leaned over the fender and pulled a spark plug wire. Then, after wiggling the rubber boot back from the metal connector, he held it a fraction of an inch away from the plug.

"Try again."

I pressed the starter button and the engine spun.

"Enough!" he snapped. "We're not getting spark."

Race went to dig through a toolbox, coming back with what I now recognized as a circuit tester, thanks to my work at Kasey's shop. After a little more analysis, he told me to climb out of the car.

"Ballast resistor," he said. "Musta cracked in the wreck. I may be worthless at changing a tire, but at least I can still diagnose a simple electrical problem."

"So what do we do about it?"

"Buy a new one. But for now we'll use the come-along to get the car off the trailer."

Another task that proved easier said than done. I crawled under the Dart and wrapped one end of the cable over the axle. I hooked the other to a chain bolted around one of the steel I-beams that formed the skeleton of the building. Race's hands shook and sweat beaded on his forehead as he worked the handle on the come-along to take up the slack.

"You want me to do that?" I asked, impressed but worried by his stoicism.

"No," Race barked. "I want you to get in the car and steer. Be ready to brake when she starts rolling."

I'd had about enough of getting my head bit off, and it torqued me that Race didn't seem to realize I was on his side. But, clenching my teeth, I reminded myself of all the second chances he'd given me. Amazingly, even though I was pissed, it was like I was looking at my anger from the outside, instead of being completely at its mercy. Maybe Alex was right about emotional control being a matter of practice, just like breaking a board.

By the time we had the Dart off the trailer, it was almost four o'clock.

"We should go," I said. "You look like you're gonna pass out."

Ignoring my suggestion, Race picked up a couple of jack stands. The determined set of his jaw scared me. I grabbed his wrist, causing one of the supports to clang to the concrete floor.

"Race, you've gotta stop. You're gonna mess yourself up."

"Can't get much worse."

"You really want to take that chance?"

"Do you have any idea how damn tired I am of being useless? If I leave here without at least getting this car up on jack stands, I'm gonna feel like a . . . like a . . . complete loser."

Alarm prickled my skin. I hadn't heard him fumble for a word since a few days after the wreck.

"I'll do it," I said. "You sit down."

At last Race gave in, handing me the other jack stand then retreating to the couch.

When I was done with the car, I attempted to back the trailer in beside it. Backing a trailer isn't easy. When you cut the wheel the way you think the damn thing oughta go, it goes the other way. Even when I figured out I needed to steer the opposite direction, I had trouble. Eventually I got it by pulling forward until the trailer lined up behind the van, then making a straight shot in reverse.

"Good job," Race said as I released the lever and lifted the receiver off the ball. It surprised me that he'd sat there watching instead of insisting on doing it himself.

I drove the van forward and closed up the shop. "Let's go."

Race went for the driver's door.

"Uh-uh. Other side," I told him. "I wanna make it home alive."

For once, he didn't argue.

It was almost five by the time we got to the house, but, fortunately, Kasey wasn't home.

I helped Race up the stairs then ushered him inside, where he collapsed in the chair by the door.

"You want some aspirin?"

"No. Get the . . . the . . ."

"Vicodin?"

"Yeah."

After retrieving it, I glanced nervously out the window. Kasey could come home at any time. Had I parked the van the way it had been this morning? Was Race gonna be okay? What if I'd been an accomplice in him screwing himself up for good?

Race pulled gently on my shirt. "Kid, I'm sorry. I shouldn'a yelled."

I let the curtain drop back into place. "It's okay."

"No it's not. When you used to get mad, I never understood, but now . . ."

"Really, it's no big deal. I get it."

Race sighed, fading back into the chair cushions. "Every morning I wake up thinking . . . this is my life. What if it never gets better?"

It was the first time he'd said anything like that to me. "It's gonna get better. I'll help. We'll fix the car."

Race shut his eyes, dismissing my attempt at encouragement.

"You better get cleaned up," I said. "Kasey's gonna be home any minute and you're getting grease on her chair."

"Give me a second."

We didn't have a second. The tell-tale note of the Charger's exhaust sounded from Spring Boulevard. Race was so wiped out he didn't even flinch.

"Oh, shit. We're dead." I tugged his sleeve, but he didn't budge. "C'mon dude, she's gonna bust us."

"That's . . . inevitable."

Kasey's footsteps were uncharacteristically urgent on the stairs. The door swung open and her eyes met mine in a look that made my stomach stop, drop, and roll.

"Just where have you two been? I've been calling all day."

I couldn't answer.

"And don't even think about trying to lie your way out of this. The hood of the van is still warm."

God help the poor kid who ended up with Kasey for a mother.

"We were at the shop," Race said.

Ah, good tactic. Just fess up and catch her off guard.

Kasey glanced from me to Race, then her eyes zeroed in on mine. "Go start dinner. I'll deal with you later."

She took Race's hand in a way that seemed ironically gentle after the glare she'd leveled me with. "Come on, let's get you cleaned up," she told him. "You're getting grease everywhere."

In the kitchen, I dug through the cupboards, looking for something easy to fix. I located a couple boxes of macaroni and cheese, pulled them out, and put water on to boil. Kasey joined me few minutes later.

"He's okay, isn't he?" I asked.

Kasey got herself a glass of ice water then sat at the table, her eyes fixing on me with weary disappointment. "Of course—he just overdid it. He's exhausted."

There had to be more to it than that. "He was having trouble finding words," I said. "He took Vicodin."

"He'll be fine, Cody. He didn't do himself any permanent damage, though he'll no doubt spend the next few days regretting this little escapade."

I leaned against the counter, folding my arms across my chest and waiting for a lecture.

"I knew this would happen," Kasey said. "Frankly, I'm surprised it took him so long. But what the two of you did today
was foolish. Race's judgment is off right now, and I need to be
able to depend on you to use yours. He's not in any condition to
get behind the wheel of that van."

"I drove home," I said.

"You shouldn't have let him go to begin with."

"Why not? It's the first time I've seen him happy in weeks.
Everything woulda been fine if he hadn't pushed so hard."

"That's exactly my point. He doesn't know when to quit."

"Then I'll make sure he figures it out. You can't take this
away from him. He needs it."

Kasey rubbed a pathway through the beads of condensation
forming on her glass. "He shouldn't be driving."

"I'll play chauffer."

"It's too soon."

"No, it's not!" I pushed away from the counter, annoyed
that she couldn't see how she was contributing to Race's
frustrations. "Damn it, Kasey, you won't let him do anything,
and it's sucking the life out of him. He's always grumpy. He
never jokes around. What good is it that he lived through that
wreck if he's not Race anymore?"

My words seemed to shift something in Kasey. Her eyes
fixed on mine, and for a second I saw the fragile part of her that
cried the night Race was hurt. Then her gaze slipped past me,
out the sliding glass door, to focus on the hillside.

"I miss him!" I said.

Kasey nodded. "So do I."

Chapter 27

Race was worthless the next day. He looked like he couldn't make it off the couch, much less down to the shop, but Kasey wasn't taking any chances. She told me to stay home and keep him out of trouble. It was clear she didn't trust me entirely because as she got ready to walk out the door she held up the keys to the van.

"I'm taking these," she said. "In case either of you get any wild ideas." Then looking pointedly at Race, "Are you going to behave yourself, or do I need to pull the coil wire, too?"

"Nah. I'm not up to hotwiring anything today."

That evening at dinner Kasey relented and laid the key ring next to Race's plate.

"I still don't think you need to be down there working on the car, but if it helps, I'm not going to stop you. The only thing I ask is that you let Cody do the driving for the next couple of weeks."

"Kasey—" Race protested.

She held up her hand. "I'm not the one who put the six-week restriction on your driving. If you want to argue with someone, argue with your doctor."

Later that night Kasey came into my room, where I was lounging on my bed reading. She handed me an envelope with a Phoenix postmark.

"Cody, I know you've had your difficulties with your mother, and she hasn't been particularly sympathetic about Race, but I've spoken to her quite a bit lately, and I think she's truly sorry. She wants another chance."

That was one of Mom's tricks. If all else failed, she went weepy and apologetic. I'd fallen for it every time when I was little, and it always proved to be a mistake. Even now I wasn't completely immune. That was one of the reasons I'd avoided her calls and letters. She'd really blown it this time, and I'd be damned if I was gonna let her off the hook.

Kasey sat down on the edge of my bed. "I know she's hurt you, Cody. She has problems—that much is obvious. But she loves you."

Love, right. Mom always claimed she cared about me, but she put her own needs first. Was that love?

"Just think about it," Kasey said. "You've made a great deal of progress since you've come to stay with Race, and I think you're ready to handle this now." She propped the letter against the lamp on the end table and left the room.

Race still wasn't firing on all cylinders Tuesday morning, but he insisted on going back to the shop. He must've learned his lesson about pushing too hard because he was content to look the car over and tell me what needed to be done. We found more damage than we'd expected. The right side suspension had been tweaked and, worse, the K-member—that heavy structure that tied both frame rails together—was bent. Replacing it would be a major undertaking. The engine and most of the suspension bolted to it.

My lack of experience slowed our progress, and by the time I had to leave for work we'd barely made a dent.

"At this rate, the season'll be over before I get the car back on the track," Race grumbled.

"Don't worry, dude. I'll figure it out eventually." Now that his mood was starting to improve, I'd be damned if I let my incompetence mess things up.

The next morning I got back to it, torching away a damaged section of the roll cage. Operating the torch was one of those things Race couldn't do anymore. He set stuff on fire when he tried to use it. I wasn't exactly thrilled about doing it, myself. It was painstaking work because I had to be careful not to mess up the good bars.

While I stressed and sweated in leathers that dwarfed me, Race cranked up the welder and laid a test bead on a piece of scrap metal.

"Hmmm," he said. "Guess I'm gonna need a little practice."

I finished my cut then took a peek, carefully holding the torch away from anything flammable. "No kidding. That looks like it came out of a chicken's butt."

Race kept at it the rest of the morning, and we were both amazed at how quickly the quality of his welds improved. I wondered why he could do that when he couldn't dial the phone.

"Probably because welding's mostly a wrist action," Race guessed, explaining that his fingers were what didn't want to work. It was the first time I'd heard him admit to his dexterity problem, and I hoped it meant he was coming to terms with it.

My optimism didn't survive long. Race might be able to weld, but that didn't change the fact that even though he'd gained a lot of ground since he'd gotten out of the hospital, he was still operating on a fraction of his normal strength and stamina. If he worked for more than a few hours his productivity took a nosedive. And the more he fought it, the worse it got.

As the week passed and his limitations continued to hold us up, Race slipped back into his funk. Uneasiness smoldered inside me, nibbling away the dry tinder of my resolve. I wanted to believe I'd been right to fight Kasey about the car. I wanted to think that working on it would make a difference.

But what if it didn't?

Friday night, Kasey arranged for Denny to help with moving stuff out of the trailer. July was almost over, and Race was insistent about not paying another month's rent. Kasey told him we'd take care of the packing, but Race refused to let us deal with it ourselves.

"You don't have to do this," Kasey told him. "You should save your energy for more important things."

"Damn it, it's my stuff. Don't you think I oughta be the one to sort through it?"

"You can do that later. For now we'll box up everything and store it in the basement."

"You don't want all that crap in your house."

Kasey finally gave in, and the three of us met Denny at the trailer. After being locked up for a month with a bag of reeking garbage under the sink, the place smelled totally rank.

Race shouldered past me into the kitchen. "God, what a mess. We might as well haul this thing to the dump and tip it up on its side." His gaze locked onto the drafting table and the half-finished drawing taped to its surface. For several long moments he stood stone still, eyes sweeping the table, his art supplies, and the sketches pinned up beside the window. Then he surged forward, yanking the paper off the angled surface and tearing it in half. The pieces drifted to the floor as he ripped another drawing off the wall. Instantly, Denny was on him, latching onto his arms with those massive paws.

"Damn it, Denny, let go!"

On his best day, Race wouldn't have stood a chance against his friend. Now his resistance barely made a ripple.

"I'm not gonna let you do something you'll regret later," Denny said.

"It's my stuff!"

"That's right. And if you still wanna tear it up a year from now, that's fine by me. But you're not gonna do it tonight."

Race swore and twisted in Denny's grip until, exhausted, he sagged and gave up.

"Maybe we should go outside," his friend said gently. "Let Kasey and Cody get to work in here."

Race closed his eyes and gave one curt nod before allowing Denny to lead him out of the trailer.

A few nights later I woke from a nightmare, heart pounding out a hard rock rhythm in my chest. Compared to some, this dream would have been downright peaceful—if it hadn't been about a funeral.

My breath rasped in my lungs. I struggled to rein it in, sitting upright in a tangle of blankets as sweat cooled on my back and chest. At least I hadn't screamed this time. I was always afraid Race would hear.

For weeks I'd been so caught up in what *was* that I hadn't given much thought to what could have been. Except at night. Now the feeling of loss was so sharp and real my throat ached and my eyes prickled with tears. I fell back against the pillow, telling myself it was okay. He was alive. I was safe.

But there was no going back to sleep. Images of a coffin, and Kasey's teary face, and Grandma standing rigid before a gaping grave kept flashing across my closed eyelids. I got up and pushed open my door. The whisper of the TV drifted down the hall. I padded into the living room where Race was slumped on the couch, watching an old horror movie in spite of the fact that it was after three o'clock.

"Can't sleep?" I asked, shivering in my sweat-dampened T-shirt and boxers.

Race didn't look away from the screen. "Par for the course. How 'bout you?"

"I dreamed you were dead."

"What a cheery thought."

Rage swelled in my throat. "Can't you ever be serious?"

The jagged edge of my voice tore Race's attention from the movie. His eyes caught mine and held them. "Sorry, kid." He patted the couch. "Here, come sit and watch with me."

I swallowed hard. "I hate horror movies. They're depressing. Everyone dies."

"You're looking at it wrong. You gotta see it from the standpoint of how much crappier the people in the movie have it than you. A head injury is no picnic, but it could be worse. I could be a werewolf."

"Funny," I said, but I sat with him and watched. It turned out I was right. The movie was depressing and everyone died.

In the days that followed, Race's horror movie philosophy didn't help him. He got more irritable and moody as his level of self-loathing increased. But that wasn't the worst of it. The worst thing was when he started tuning me out.

It wasn't just me. He withdrew from Kasey, too, ducking away from her touch and ignoring her attempts to reassure him.

"How stupid can you get?" I asked as I drove him to the shop one morning. "Kasey's finally acknowledging your existence. You wanna blow that?"

Race scowled out the passenger window. "Kid, I don't have anything to offer her. And the more I think about it, the more I realize that was true even before the wreck."

"That's bullshit."

"Is it? I'm a loser. My trailer was a swamp and I've never had a steady job."

"Kasey loves you," I said.

"She'll get over it."

It was depressing being around so much negativity. The only time I got a break was when I was at the shop and on the few occasions Denny convinced Race to get out of the house for a few hours. Grandma, who'd been making twice-weekly visits, offered to take me out for dinner or a movie, but I declined. I wasn't that desperate.

As July melted into August, the situation deteriorated. Physically, Race was making steady improvements, but mentally he was a basket case. While he stayed committed to working on the car, he did it in a fatalistic way, speaking to me only when necessary. The littlest thing could send him into a rage that rivaled one of my old ones. Every day my fear compounded. What if the injury had shorted out something in his brain, and he never went back to being his old, agreeable self? I wasn't sure I could deal with that. I didn't want to give up on Race, but it was killing me to live with this ghost of who he used to be.

I remembered the way he'd always looked after a race. The grin that took over his whole body. The confidence that radiated like heat from an engine. Getting back out on the track would fix this—I was sure of it. But at the rate we were going it would never happen. We needed help, so even though I figured Kasey would shoot me down, I approached her about it one day at work.

"I know how you feel about the Dart," I said as we prepared to drop a newly rebuilt 327 into a '68 Camaro. "But we need you. Race can't do the stuff that has to be done, and I don't know how. It'll take us a year to get the car fixed."

Kasey lowered the boom and gave the engine hoist a shove to get the motor mounts lined up. "I'm sorry, Cody, but I have to say no. The minute that car's back together Race is going to want to drive it."

Annoyance drilled me. "Well, that's the point, isn't it? Maybe it's what he needs."

"He's not ready."

"But he will be in a couple weeks."

Kasey raised an eyebrow at me. "I'd tend to take your opinion more seriously if you had a degree in medicine."

And what made her such an expert? "That goes both ways, you know."

"Cody, it won't hurt him to sit out the rest of the season. If the two of you insist on spending your time working on the Dart I'm not going to stop you. But I also won't help."

While Kasey refused to listen to me about the car, she agreed that Race needed a distraction and encouraged him to do something—*anything*—other than hole up in his room and stew about his problems. She suggested he take classes at the college. She encouraged him to talk to a counselor. One night at dinner, she even asked him to come help at the shop.

"Oh, *that* would work," Race said. "You'd get about two hours a day out of me. Besides, I'd drop every tool you own."

"You couldn't hurt them. They're Snap-Ons."

Race ignored the quip. "Forget it. I can barely deal with my own car—hell, I can't even tie my damned shoes." His face twisted. "Do you have any idea how frustrating that is?"

"No, I suppose I don't," Kasey said, meeting the hostile stare with sympathy. "Do *you* have any idea how frustrating it is to see someone you care about this miserable and know there's nothing you can do to fix it?"

Race stared down at his plate, hands clenching on the table-top.

"I know how aggravating this must be," Kasey said. "But you've got to realize you're not the only one who's hurting."

Race's head jerked up. "And what have you lost? Your home? Your independence? The only talent you ever had?"

Kasey closed her eyes, pausing to draw a breath. "We're losing *you*."

The gentle response did nothing to cool Race's temper. The vein in his temple pulsed as he glowered at her, jaw knotted.

"You act like you're ashamed, Race, and there's nothing to be ashamed of. You're working as hard as anyone could at getting better. You don't need to keep hiding your problems. If you'd just talk to us—"

Race shoved away from the table, rattling the water glasses and making the chair legs screech across the linoleum. "I don't want to talk. Talking doesn't change anything."

Later that night I hunted Kasey down at the computer in the basement where she was catching up on paperwork for her business.

"What brings you down here?" she asked, fingers hovering over the keyboard.

I shrugged.

"That was quite a scene at dinner," Kasey observed.

"At least he *said* something. Mostly he sulks around acting like no one else exists."

A rapid burst of clicks resonated from the keyboard as Kasey finished what she'd been doing. "He's depressed, Cody. You shouldn't take it personally."

"I can't help it! He won't talk to me. He just keeps shutting me out." I slumped against the wall and slid to the floor. "I can't deal with this. I don't mind that much when he yells, but when he acts like I'm not even there . . ." An ache crept into my throat, choking off the words. I rubbed my hands over my face. "You know that stuff the doctor said about brain injuries—how people's personalities change and they're never the same again? What if that's happened to Race? What if this is just who he is from now on?"

Kasey swiveled to face me, eyes wide. "Oh, Cody, is that what you've been worrying about? It won't be like this forever. What Race is going through is a perfectly natural reaction to loss. He just needs time to process things in his own way."

"How much time? Weeks? Months?"

What if I couldn't hold out that long?

"I don't know. Maybe it would be a good idea for you to get away for a while."

I blinked at her, shocked, "I'm not gonna give up on him."

"That's not what I'm suggesting. I just think a change of scenery for a week or two might help."

"What kind of change? Dad doesn't want me, and I'm not going anywhere near Grandma's as long as Grandpa's there."

A faint *don't be silly* look flitted across Kasey's face. "You're wrong about your father," she said. "He's only trying to do what's best for you, but your mother's the one I had in mind. She wants you to visit."

The words hit me like a faceful of ice water. "Uh-uh—no way! You didn't hear what she said about Race."

"Cody—"

"She told me getting hurt was his own damned fault."

"I seem to recall you saying something similar."

"That's different!"

"How?"

I pinned Kasey with a glare, struggling to put what I felt into words. "She's not a kid."

"I'm going to let you in on a little secret, Cody. Just because someone's an adult doesn't mean she's going to act like it. Seeing how your grandfather and Jim have behaved recently should tell you that much."

And that made it okay? Adults had all the rights. They should accept the responsibilities that went with them.

"People have different ways of dealing with fear and pain," Kasey said gently. "Your mother reacted out of anger. That's something you ought to be able to understand."

"I'm not like her!"

Kasey sighed. "I didn't say you were, I'm just pointing out she's only human. Every time I talk to her, she tells me how sorry she is for what she said to you. She wants to apologize, but you and Race won't let her."

A protest caught in my throat as I remembered how many times the two of us had cut her off.

"You should give her a chance."

"She doesn't deserve it."

"I think she does. If it weren't for her, you might very well be in a detention center right now. Your mom is the one who kept you out of the system."

"Is that what she told you? It's gotta be a lie. Why would the cops listen to her?"

"They didn't. But she persuaded your grandmother to intervene. After a hefty donation, the zoo agreed to drop all charges."

"No way."

"Why do you think you got off without even having to do community service?"

I shrugged. "I just figured it wasn't any big deal."

"It was a *huge* deal. Fortunately, your mom cared enough to get involved. She asked your grandmother to take you in, and that's where you would have wound up if your grandfather hadn't been so dead set against it. Instead, your grandma offered to pay for military school, but your mom nixed that idea and called Race. You might consider what a concession that was, in light of how poorly they get along."

"That can't be right," I said. "Race woulda told me."

"Your mom's kept him as much in the dark about this as she's kept you. I can't claim to know her reasoning behind that, but I can say she's gone above and beyond in her duty as a parent."

The firmness in Kasey's expression made it impossible to look at her. "I don't believe it," I whispered, staring down at my knees.

"It's the truth, Cody."

I shook my head. How could it be the truth? It went against everything I thought was real.

When I went back to my room, Mom's letter was still on my end table. My resentment hung on me like an old, comfortable sweatshirt, the kind you can't get rid of, even when it's full of holes. I didn't want to believe Mom had bailed me out. But what if Kasey was right?

I picked up the letter and tore it open. It started with an apology—a list of all the ways Mom had screwed up. That was new. She'd said she was sorry in the past, but always in a way that skirted around admitting she'd been wrong. And there was something else about this letter. It seemed honest. Mom told me how miserable she'd been, living in Portland and being married to Dad. She even talked about what she'd done to fix her problems—going back to school, seeing a therapist. I wasn't sure I believed it, but part of me wanted to.

The letter ended with a final apology—this one to Race—and asked for just one thing: The chance to talk to me. I folded the paper and stuck it in the envelope.

What would it hurt to call? Leaving home had changed me for the better. Maybe it had done the same for her.

Chapter 28

Even with that little seed of hope, the call wasn't easy. I dialed Mom's number and stumbled through the conversation, my feelings as tangled as the wires that snaked through the engine compartment of Race's van. Some deep, desperate part of me wanted it to be different this time, wanted to believe Mom had changed. But the pissed-off part woke up as soon as I heard her voice, and it wouldn't let me do anything more than grunt.

Mom didn't seem to notice. "Kasey thinks you need to get away for a while," she said after apologizing again and telling me how things were going to be so much better now. "I'm coming to Eugene next week, and I'd like to see you. Maybe you can come back to Phoenix with me—just for a visit."

I stiffened at the suggestion then reminded myself I owed her one for sending me to live with Race.

"Please think about it," she said.

Please. That wasn't a word I was used to hearing from her. It snuck through the jumble of mismatched emotions and stung my conscience hard.

During karate practice the next morning, the conversation played back through my mind, in spite of my efforts to stay focused. In the end I'd agreed to consider a trip to Phoenix. But what if Race took it the wrong way? I didn't want him to think I'd abandoned him.

I'd stewed about his blow-up half the night and come to a conclusion that it was time to take matters into my own hands. If Kasey wouldn't help with the Dart, I'd find somebody who would. Like Denny. In spite of what Kasey had said to him that day at the shop, I figured I could talk him into it. But I wanted to do it in person, so he'd have a harder time saying no. That meant getting to the speedway.

"Guess what?" I said when I found Race in the kitchen eating breakfast. "It's been six weeks. Kasey can't give you any more crap about driving." I laid the van keys on the table.

Race exhibited all the enthusiasm of an earthworm on a wet sidewalk.

"We need to celebrate," I said. "Maybe we can go to the speedway tonight."

"What makes you think I'd want to?"

The question jolted me. I hadn't expected him to refuse. "I just thought it might be fun."

Race rolled his eyes. "Yeah, it's loads of fun watching people do something I can't."

"But you *can*, now. All we've gotta do is get the car back together."

"Why?" said Race. "So I can go out there and find out that I'm no good at driving, too? What makes you think I'd still have my edge? You figure somehow that's sacred?"

I stared at him, caught off guard by this new level of doubt. Even though we'd barely talked about it in days, I'd figured his commitment to working on the car meant he knew he'd drive it again.

"It's time to face facts," Race said, standing up and taking his cereal bowl to the sink. "I'm never gonna get back out there, and I'm sick of caring about it."

Race's words shook me, but they also confirmed my theory. Getting in that car was the only thing that would convince him he wasn't completely useless. I called Kasey at her shop and asked if she'd take me to the speedway that night, but she said she had too much paperwork to catch up on.

"Try Denny," she suggested. "I'm sure he could use an extra pair of hands in the pits."

Denny agreed to swing by the house on his way to the track. I waited for him on the bottom step, wearing my *I'm up and dressed. What more do you want?* T-shirt.

"Where do you get those things?" Denny chuckled.

I shrugged. "Here and there. Mostly at the mall. Dad sent me the squirrel one." I climbed up beside him in the cab of his old, beater pickup.

"Addamsen still leading the points?" I asked as he backed his trailer around and headed down Spring Boulevard.

"Yup. But I'm trying to give him a run for his money—'course I'll never catch up." He was quiet a few seconds, negotiating the narrow, twisty road. "Jim's dropped down to fifth. He just can't seem to get it together since the wreck."

"Cry me a river."

Denny raised an eyebrow. "He still hasn't been by to see Race?"

"Are you kidding? He's an asshole." Just the thought of Jim made me want to slam my fist into something. I rolled down my window and rested my arm on the top of the door.

"Well, some folks have a harder time than others dealing with the bad stuff life throws at 'em."

"Gimme a break. Race is the one who's got bad stuff to deal with, not Jim."

"That's what I'm getting at," Denny amended. "Some people don't know how to handle it when something lousy happens to a friend. I've been there myself. I was ten years old when my mom died. My buddies didn't know what to say. Some of 'em just acted strange, but others stopped talking to me altogether."

"Well, they were assholes, too." I slumped in the seat, suddenly wanting a cigarette. What was it about riding shotgun that triggered those cravings?

"Just because people *should* act a certain way doesn't mean they're gonna," Denny said, echoing what Kasey had told me the night before. "Fact is, this thing with Jim is complicated.

He's scared. He knows that if something like this could happen to Race, it could happen to anyone."

"*You* don't seem that shook up about it."

Denny laughed. "I'm good at fakin' it. Besides, I've got a few more laps under my tires than Jim does. It takes a lot to rattle my cage."

The conversation wasn't going the way I'd planned. I stuck my hand out the window and directed it into the wind, making it shoot up and down on the air currents. I wasn't sure how to approach the subject of the Dart, sensing I had only one shot at getting it right.

"Race's head is really messed up right now," I ventured.

"Yup," Denny agreed. "It's a shocker, seeing him like that. Must be hard to live with."

"It's getting worse. Today he didn't even want to go to the shop." I ran my fingers around the edge of the side mirror, rubbing away a layer of grime. "Working on the car's been the only thing keeping him going, but now he thinks that even if he gets back out on the track, he's not gonna be able to drive like he used to."

Denny glanced across the cab at me, and I knew what he was thinking. Maybe Race was right about that.

"The way I see it, there's only one way to fix this," I said. "He's gotta get out there and try."

"How's the car coming?"

"It's not. We got the suspension parts off and the engine pulled, but we still don't have the old K-member out. I don't know how we're gonna get a new one. It's one thing for me to do stuff like that at the shop where we have all the right equipment, but I don't think I could manage at the wrecking yard. And we've still got the door bars to deal with. Race had a guy bend some new ones, but I'm afraid I'll mess 'em up trying to fit 'em."

Some optimistic part of me hoped Denny would hear my list of woes and volunteer, but he stayed silent.

"We need your help."

Denny's sigh was audible even over the rumble of the pickup's lousy exhaust. "I know, and I'm sorry, but I gave Kasey my word."

"Kasey's wrong!" I said, jerking around to face him. "She's part of the problem. You know I'm right about this, Denny. You know he's gotta get back out there."

"If this was just about Race and his car, I'd help in a heartbeat, but there's something you've gotta understand. I've been watching this thing between him and Kasey for a couple of years. Those two belong together. Now that she's finally figured that out, I'm not gonna be the one to step in and mess it up. Sure, Race needs to get back out on the track. But not as much as he needs Kasey. Understand?"

"You wouldn't mess it up."

"Cody, I made a promise. Maybe it was foolish, but at the time it was what Kasey needed to hear. I don't go back on my word."

What was it with him and Race and their damned John Wayne ethics? Scowling, I turned away and fell back against the seat. "You're just as bad as Jim. If you really cared about him you'd help."

"Hold up there, buddy. You don't know the first thing about me and Race."

"Yeah, yeah," I said, perturbed that he seemed immune to my manipulative prowess. "You've known him since before he could see over the steering wheel."

Denny seemed surprised I remembered a comment he'd made almost three months ago. His serious expression melted into a smile. "That's right. Race musta been about ten when I met him. I was driving a Street Stock back then and didn't have a single win to show for it, but for some reason, he decided I was the one to pull for. By the end of the season he was helping me out on Saturday nights. Back then you didn't have to sign a stack of release forms to get a kid in the pits."

My annoyance was momentarily sidetracked by curiosity. "I didn't know you guys had that kind of history." It explained why Denny stuck by him, though, and why they were such good friends, in spite of their age difference.

"Sure," Denny said. "Who do you think taught him how to drive?"

I gawked at him. "Are you kidding?"

"Nope. His dad was giving him fits—too many rules, too much criticism. Race asked me for help. 'Course it was one of those deals where the student surpasses the master. Once he got out on the track it didn't take him long to start kicking my butt."

I smiled at the thought of that younger Race, at the talent lurking inside him, waiting to be discovered. "What was he like when he was my age?"

"Quiet, until he got to know a person, then that crazy sense of humor kicked in." Denny shook his head, his eyes going sad as a basset hound's. "Race was just an easy-going kid who never had a mean word to say about anyone. All he wanted was to be left alone so he could watch the races and draw his pictures."

"Well, Grandpa sure wasn't gonna let *that* happen."

"Nope, and I never could understand it. What kind of man rejects his own kid?"

"You don't know the half of it," I muttered, thinking about what Grandpa had said to Race at the hospital. "The more I learn about him, the more I wonder how Race could end up so laid-back."

Denny chuckled. "Race is hard-wired to be laid-back. But I think it helped that he found what he needed at the speedway.

Family is everything to us racers. If you lack one, someone just takes you into theirs."

I thought about what Denny had done for Race and, later, what Race did for me. Suddenly I saw how my life was part of a pattern. Then an even bigger idea hit me. Maybe it wasn't a coincidence that I had as much trouble with my parents as Race did with his. Maybe that was part of the pattern, too.

In spite of what Denny had said about Race's easy-going nature, I knew that didn't completely explain the differences in how we'd handled the abuse. Somewhere along the way Race had made a choice about how he was going to let it affect him.

My mind flashed back to the night Race had picked me up in Medford, and the memory of his words echoed through my skull. *"You can't change her, kid, but you can damned sure refuse to let her change you."*

At the time it hadn't made sense, but now I understood. I'd been letting Mom change me all my life.

As I watched the trophy dashes that night, I wondered who I could get to help us now that Denny'd refused. Jim was totally out of the question, and I didn't know any of the other drivers well enough to ask.

When the answer hit me I felt like an idiot for not thinking of it sooner. Addamsen. I'd been using his business card as a bookmark for weeks. But thinking of a solution was easier than implementing it. I felt like I was traveling behind enemy lines as I approached him after his heat.

"Good run," I said, trying to sound gruff and manly, but botching it when my voice broke.

Everyone in Addamsen's crew stared at me. They were rough, burly types—the kind of guys who could heft a bundle of shingles onto their shoulders and climb a ladder without breaking a sweat. I could practically smell the testosterone oozing out of their pores.

Addamsen turned away from his conversation when he saw me. "It's Cody—right? How's Race? He gonna be out here anytime soon?"

I looked from Addamsen to his crew. I hadn't planned on having an audience for this conversation, but it was too late to back out now.

"That's what I need to talk to you about. Remember how you said that if he needed help he should give you a call? Well, he needs help."

Addamsen chuckled. "I knew he'd be too damned proud to ask me himself."

"He doesn't even know *I'm* asking." I glanced nervously at Addamsen's crew again. I didn't want to broadcast Race's private business for them to hear.

Shifting his eyes from me to his friends, Addamsen caught on. "Let's take a walk," he suggested.

It helped, getting away from the others. As we made our way down the pit road, with Street Stocks rumbling past to line up for their main, I outlined what needed to be done on the car and why we were having so much trouble.

"What makes you think he can drive if he can't fix his car?" Addamsen asked.

"It's mostly his dexterity that's messed up. You don't need that to drive."

"Must be a bitch, him being an artist and all."

"No shit."

"So why haven't any of his friends helped? I know you gotta be scraping the bottom of the barrel to ask me."

I explained how Jim had been acting and the deal Denny had made with Kasey.

Addamsen barked out a nasty laugh. "Damn uppity women, thinking they've got some right to get between a man and his car. I can't believe Race puts up with that."

Now I could see why Kasey didn't like this guy. "Look," I said. "I'm not here to debate sexual equality with you. Are you gonna help or not?"

Grinning, Addamsen shook his head. "Sure, I'll get a couple guys together and come over tomorrow. Lord knows Denny's the only one who's given me a challenge in weeks. Jim's been worthless since that wreck—guess he's worried he's gonna be the next one to get his brain scrambled."

I pulled a concession stand napkin out of my back pocket, on which I'd jotted down the shop address. "Here. There's no phone, but we're usually there by nine."

"It'll take me a couple hours to get a K-member," Addamsen said. "I'll see you around noon."

Chapter 29

I got up the next morning to find Race crashed out on the couch with the TV on and Winston curled against his side. Kasey, having overslept, was in a hurry to get to the shop. It was no use protesting her seven-day workweeks. She didn't listen. Ironically, she refused to let me help out more than five afternoons a week.

I picked up the remote and silenced the television.

"You got more interviews today?" I asked Kasey as she bustled through the living room.

"Yes, though I don't hold out much hope. I swear I've spoken to every mechanic in Lane County." She paused to clutch at a ream of work-orders that were trying to slither out of her arms.

"Maybe your standards are too high. I keep telling you all you need is a regular mechanic. Race could do the welding."

Kasey glanced toward the couch. With typical cat arrogance, Winston assumed this attention was directed at him and meowed.

"I gave Race the opportunity to help two days ago, and you saw how that went. At any rate, I think you might be reading more into his abilities than he can deliver."

"Kasey, I've seen it."

"And just what do you know about welding?"

The words caught me like a roundhouse kick, and I gave her a scalding look. What did she think I was, stupid?

Kasey sighed, scooping her keys off the coffee table. "I'll tell you what, Cody, if you can get him to agree, we'll give it a shot."

Once Kasey was gone, I shook Race's arm.

"Wake up. We've gotta get down to the shop."

"Go 'way."

I let him sleep awhile longer, hoping he'd get up on his own. He'd be less grumpy that way. When he finally began to stir I glanced at my watch. Nine-thirty. It would only take fifteen minutes to drive to the shop, but I figured we needed half an hour to be safe.

"C'mon, dude. You gotta get moving. We're gonna waste the whole morning."

"Not much we can do without a new K-member," he mumbled.

"We can work on the door bars."

"Pointless waste of time."

I spent the next hour gently cajoling him, knowing if I pissed him off too much he'd never leave the house. My efforts had no effect on his leisurely morning ritual. By eleven o'clock I was desperate. I hadn't put all this together just to have him blow it off.

"Look," I said, sitting down across from him at the kitchen table. "If you don't want to work on your car that's fine, but I haven't gotten anything done on the Galaxie since before the wreck."

Race pushed his empty cereal bowl away and flipped the page of the Sunday comics.

"Maybe another time. I'm not in the mood."

Not in the mood? My temper revved and—like an engine screaming past redline—blew. I slapped my hand down on his newspaper.

"Damn it, Race, I'm getting sick of your attitude! I put up with your moodiness, I put up with you snapping at me—hell, I even put up with you acting like I don't exist—but I'll be damned if I let you quit. Now stop feeling sorry for yourself and get your ass out in that van."

Race gaped at me, staggered by the outburst. It was the first harsh thing anyone had dared to say to him since Grandpa's tirade.

"Welcome to tough love," I said as I turned to leave the kitchen.

Five minutes later, Race was ready to go.

I knew better than to say anything about Addamsen before we got to the shop. Race would just turn around and head home. But to spare everyone an awkward moment, I figured I had to give him a heads up at some point. I waited until I had the torch lit and was fish-mouthing a door bar, then broke the news. "Umm, I forgot to mention it earlier, but we might be getting a little help today."

Race glanced up from the measurement he was making. "Who, Denny?"

"Addamsen."

A mismatched assortment of emotions paraded across Race's face. Surprisingly, he said nothing. Ten minutes later a white Chevy pickup bearing the Addamsen Construction logo pulled up outside the open bay door. Race watched stone-faced as his nemesis and two crew members got out.

Addamsen gave my uncle a curt nod and went round to the bed of his truck to unload a goo-encrusted K-member. He dumped it at my feet. "Get this cleaned up," he said. Then he turned to Race. "So what needs to be done?"

It was weird, seeing the two of them regard each other with such stiff formality—the only sign they shared a less than amicable history. Without any indication that the circumstances were unusual or the least bit unexpected, Race said, "The old K-member has to be pulled."

"John, you wanna get on that?" Addamsen waved a hand at one of his friends then looked back at Race. "What else?"

"We need to fit these bars and make a new door skin."

Addamsen ordered his other crew member to take charge of the sheet metal work before settling in to help Race with the roll cage. Figuring it was best to fade into the background, I found a sheet of plastic and a couple cans of Gunk, then got to work cleaning the K-member.

It was a surreal afternoon, with everyone trying to act normal even though they must have felt as uncomfortable as I did. After a couple hours Addamsen sent one of his guys to Dari Mart to grab some food and a half rack of Hamm's.

"Have a beer, Morgan," Addamsen said, slapping a blue and white can down on the roof of the Dart.

I grinned at the idea of Race's first beer in six weeks being of the cheap, American variety. But he simply opened the can and took a drink, doing a decent job of not letting his disgust show.

As Addamsen and his crew plowed through the Hamm's, things loosened up. Race nursed his beer all afternoon, so I knew something other than alcohol was improving his spirits. By four o'clock the roll bars were in place, the new K-member was installed, the engine rested in its motor mounts, and a fresh door skin sat waiting to be painted. Race looked as confident as a guy with a twelve-car-lead on the last lap of Daytona.

"We've gotta get rolling," Addamsen said as he wiped his hands on an old T-shirt. "But I might be able to make it back over here Thursday or Friday night if you need help with that suspension."

"Nah, you guys have done enough. Cody and I can handle the rest."

"So we'll see you at the track on Saturday?"

"Better make it two weeks," said Race. "I want to get a few practice sessions in first."

Addamsen nodded.

"I appreciate the help," Race told him.

"Well, I had to do something to liven things up at the track. It's damned boring out there without you nipping at my heels."

As luck would have it, just as Addamsen's pickup backed away from the door, Kasey's Charger pulled up. I wondered what she was doing here. She hadn't been to the shop since before the wreck.

"What's going on?" she asked.

Race eyed her coolly. "Just getting a little help with the car."

"From Jerry Addamsen?"

"I'm hardly in the position to look a gift horse in the mouth. Anyway, you ran off everyone else."

Kasey peered accusingly in my direction.

"Don't look at him like that," Race said. "It wasn't hard to figure out for myself. Every time I mentioned the car to Denny, he changed the subject."

Without saying a word, Kasey shifted her gaze to the nearly finished Dart, a storm building in her eyes.

"We're getting close," said Race. "We might just have her back together for practice on Wednesday."

"No." Kasey spoke the word softly, more to herself than to Race. It wasn't an order—it was denial. She glanced around the shop, her eyes coming to rest on the new door skin, the tweaked K-member, and finally the beer cans Addamsen's crew had left scattered around.

"You were drinking," she said.

"Oh, come on. I only had half of one, and you can't even call that crap beer."

"It contains alcohol. Alcohol's a neurotoxin."

Furrows formed in Race's forehead as his newfound spunk gave way to agitation. "So how long do I have to wait before I can have a drink? Six months? A year?" He looked at her hard. "I don't think you'll be satisfied even then."

"You're not ready. You shouldn't be drinking, and you shouldn't be driving that car."

"Damn it, Kasey, haven't I lost enough without giving this up, too?"

"I don't expect you to give it up, I just want you to wait."

The last vestiges of Race's patience evaporated. "I've been waiting long enough!"

"It's too soon," Kasey said, the pitch of her voice rising.

"That's not your decision to make."

"You push too hard. That first day you drove the van—"

"Did it ever occur to you that you could have prevented that? I asked time and again for your help with the car. We could have taken it easy and done it your way, but you wouldn't even give me that much."

The two of them stared at each other like cats swishing their tails. Then Race's expression softened and he sighed.

"I know what you're trying to do, Kasey, and it's not gonna work. You can't control the world. You might think you're keeping me safe, but you can't protect me from everything."

"Race—"

"No, listen." Race's voice took a more soothing tone. "I understand how hard this has been. I know I scared the hell out of you. But I can't change what happened, all I can do is be more careful from now on. I owe it to you and Cody to make safety my first priority, but you can't ask me to stop racing. I won't."

Kasey shook her head, looked away, closed her eyes. For the first time I understood how big her fear was and how out-of-control it made her feel.

Apparently Race did, too. He stepped forward, resting his hands on her shoulders. "I'm sorry," he said as he pulled her close.

Kasey trembled in his arms, on the brink of tears, but not giving in.

"You don't know how sorry I am," Race whispered. He rested his cheek against her hair.

For several long moments Kasey let him comfort her. Then she pushed away, palms flat against his chest and face taut with sudden comprehension. "You're right," she admitted. "I *have* been holding you back."

"I understand."

Kasey's eyes reflected a rush of thought. "I need to go," she said. "I have to make a call."

"What?" Race blinked down at her.

"To Denny," she said. "To see if he'll lend us Big Red."

Chapter 30

After vowing that first thing Monday morning she was going to have a phone installed at Race's shop, Kasey went to Dari Mart to make her call. When she came back she told us Denny had to work late the next day, but he promised to load Big Red onto his trailer so Race could swing by and pick her up. Finally, she filled us in on what had made her drop by to begin with.

"I've hired a mechanic. His name is Eddie and he just graduated from the automotive program at Lane. He doesn't have much experience, but I'd rather train somebody myself than put up with deep-set bad habits. Besides, I like Eddie's attitude. He has a real passion for old cars."

"Can he weld?" I asked.

"He's taken a class, but I decided you might have a point, Cody. Maybe Race would be willing to take care of the welding." Kasey turned her attention from me to him, a question in her eyes.

"I'm still lousy at sheet metal," Race confessed. "Too much starting and stopping. My fingers don't wanna do it."

"Then teach Eddie," Kasey said. "That's another thing I like about him—he's eager to learn."

The next day, Race went with me to Kasey's shop to get an idea about what he was up against. We found her in the office, shuffling through a pile of payroll forms and receipts.

"Cody, why don't you show Race what we're working on. I need to get this finished so I can run it over to my accountant. I'm already facing a penalty."

Race cocked his head to study the papers. "Quarterly payroll taxes? Shouldn't you have filed those in July?"

"I should have, but I didn't."

"Kasey, you can't let that stuff slide. You've got enough problems without riling up the Feds."

"I know, I know." She held up a hand to ward off the criticism. "But paperwork bores me to tears and it's not one of my strengths. Why can't the government leave me alone and let me restore cars?"

"It's part of owning your own business," Race said, as if he were some sort of authority on responsible behavior.

I leaned heavily against the doorway. Being of like mind with Kasey, I was bored just talking about paperwork. "Isn't that what accountants are for?" I asked.

"No, accountants file taxes, they don't do bookkeeping," Kasey explained. "Or so my CPA keeps telling me. He said the next time I show up with an oil box full of work orders and receipts, he's locking the door and turning off the lights."

"This stuff doesn't bother me," Race said. "I can have a go at it if you want."

"How do you know about payroll taxes?" Kasey asked. "You've never had any employees."

"They covered that stuff in one of my business classes. So how 'bout it? It'll give you time to get caught up on the important stuff."

"I'd want to pay you."

Race rolled his eyes. "It's not enough that you're feeding us and putting a roof over our heads?"

"Cody's father compensates me for his room and board. Besides, if I paid you, you'd be able to buy the groceries for a change."

"All right," Race said. "You can pay me, but only if you start charging me rent."

That afternoon Kasey closed the shop at a normal hour so we could go out to the track. As Race and I were loading the jack and tools into the van, she came up behind us.

"You might find this useful," she told Race, holding out a Bell Helmet box.

His eyes went wide. "You bought this?"

"Not exactly. Your mother wanted you to have it, but she was confused by the choices. She asked me to order it."

Gaping like he'd learned Dale Earnhardt was hiring him as a relief driver, Race broke loose the cardboard flaps and pulled out a black, full-face helmet.

"She knows you better than you seem to think," Kasey said. "She predicted you'd be back out there before the season ended."

Race couldn't seem to find any words.

We swung by Denny's house on the way to the speedway. When Race backed up to the trailer hitch on his first try it was clear he was making progress.

"Are you scared of getting back in the car?" I asked as we pulled away.

"Not half as scared as I am of *not* getting in it."

At the track I unchained Big Red and backed her off the trailer while Race pulled his firesuit on over his clothes, resigning himself to letting Kasey help with the zipper.

"Maybe I oughta take her out for a few laps first," I suggested, leaning out of the car. "You know, just to make sure she's running okay."

"Let's not give Denny a heart attack," Race said.

Reluctantly, I wiggled through the window of the Chevelle. "You're gonna let me drive yours when it's finished though, right?"

"In your dreams. But maybe one of these days all the stars will line up and we can think about building you a Street Stock."

"Seriously?"

Race looked at me as if he were about to make a solemn vow. "I would never joke about something as important as a guy's first race car."

I stared open-mouthed as he maneuvered around me to climb into Big Red. While I'd fantasized about getting on the track, I'd never considered it happening in a car of my own.

Kasey waited for Race to belt himself in then handed the new helmet through the window. "Be careful."

With his eyes saying he knew how hard it was for her to watch him do this, Race gripped her fingers. Kasey smiled sadly and squeezed back then pulled away so she could fasten the window net.

"He'll be okay," I said as she stepped aside and Race cranked the Chevelle's engine.

"I know."

I understood what she was feeling. Even though I'd been pushing to make this happen, it was kinda freaky, seeing him get in that car. "What we want isn't as important as what Race needs," I reminded her.

Kasey raised an eyebrow at me, but a flicker of humor played across her lips.

As Big Red pulled away, my conviction wavered. What if I was wrong about Race getting back on the track? What if he couldn't do this? The disappointment might strip away his newly recovered confidence and make things worse than before.

The Chevelle whined down the backstretch, building up speed. I let the sound steady me as I sucked in a breath, hunting for my center. If Race had found the nerve to face that possibility, then I could, too.

For the first few laps he took it easy. I expected him to cut loose as soon as he had the tires warmed up, but after ten laps he was still backing off too soon going into the turns.

"You think he's scared?" I asked.

"Wouldn't you be?"

The Chevelle decelerated down the front stretch and pulled into the pits. Kasey dropped the window net.

"I don't even want to know what kind of times I was turning," Race said, his voice heavy with disgust.

"It'll come back to you," Kasey encouraged.

"It better do it soon, because I'm running out of steam."

Kasey helped Race wrestle off his helmet then offered him a bottle of Gatorade. He reached for it with a shaking hand.

"I feel like such a wuss."

"Take your time. Denny said you could borrow the car as much as you like. We can always come back tomorrow."

Scowling, Race thrust the bottle at her and jammed the helmet over his head. Kasey barely had a chance to help him with the chin strap and secure the window net before Big Red roared away.

"Way to get him psyched," I said as the Chevelle screamed toward the pit exit, stirring up a cloud of dust.

"That wasn't exactly my intention."

"Whatever. It worked."

Back out on the track Race pushed the car to the limit, slinging it through the corners like he still believed he was invincible. My nagging fear evaporated as it became clear he still had whatever it was that made him so good. Then, coming out of turn four, he got on the accelerator a little too soon and broke the back tires loose. The Chevelle's rear end whipped around, nearly smacking the wall. When Race tried to correct, Big Red spun, coming to rest facing backwards in the middle of the front stretch.

My heart felt like it was firing on all cylinders at once, then none at all. I glanced at Kasey, who looked equally rattled. Was this what we could expect every time he spun out?

The Chevelle sat quiet and motionless on the track, indicating Race was engaged in a struggle of his own.

"Well, that shook him up," I said as my heart fell back into its normal firing order. "But it's nothing a little pep talk won't fix."

I jogged onto the asphalt to peer through the square holes in the window net. "You okay?"

Race was gripping the wheel so hard I figured it would take a hacksaw to get it out of his hands. He turned to face me, too flustered to hide what he was feeling.

"Guess you've still got your edge," I said.

"I'm beat, kid," he stammered. "I'm ready to call it a day."

It wasn't like I didn't understand. Hell, I probably wouldn't have had the guts to get out there to begin with. Still, I was disappointed.

"All right," I sighed, making no effort to hide my feelings. "Come on in and we'll get her on the trailer." I turned and headed back to Kasey.

Behind me the starter cranked and the Chevelle pulled around, rumbling toward the pit entrance. At the last minute, it swung wide to cut through the grass at the edge of the infield. The tires gave a little squeal when they bit into asphalt. I grinned and shook my head as Big Red ripped through the turn, coming out onto the backstretch wide-open. Race was so easy.

"Apparently your pep talk worked," Kasey observed.

"It's all in the delivery."

For the next half hour Race abused that car as if it were his own. He pushed it to the edge and beyond, sliding, spinning out, and getting so close to the wall I expected to see sparks. The more he lost control, the less it bothered me. Finally, he pulled off the track. As Big Red growled to a stop beside us, it looked like the only thing keeping Race from sliding to the floorboards was the safety harness.

"Am I gonna have to use the come-along to get you out of that car?" I asked, watching his trembling fingers fumble with the helmet strap.

"I might take you up on that if I'd remembered to bring it."

Kasey motioned me aside so she could assist him. It occurred to me the attention she was giving him made up for the humiliation.

With considerable effort, Race heaved himself out of the Chevelle. Then, leaning against the car, he broke into shaky laughter. "Damn!" he said. "That's gotta be one of the most profound experiences of my life."

Kasey put her arm around his shoulders and directed him to the open side door of the van so he could sit down. "You looked good out there."

"I feel like I just won the Daytona 500." Race focused that crazy-assed grin of his on her and for few seconds they got lost in each other. "Thank you," he said softly, reaching for her hand.

Kasey smiled. "Welcome back."

After that workout, it was all Race could do to climb up in the passenger's seat, so I got Big Red back onto the trailer and Kasey drove the van.

"I owe you guys an apology," Race said as we pulled onto West 11th. "I know I haven't exactly been easy to live with."

"Race, you're a master of understatement," I observed.

He ignored the sarcasm. "I figured if I just worked hard, everything would come back, but that's not how it's been." He glanced apologetically at Kasey. "It's gonna take a lot longer than I thought."

"We don't care how long it takes," she assured him. "Cody and I are in this for the long haul. The only thing we care about is that you stop hiding yourself from us."

With a slight shake of his head, Race turned away. "It's not that easy. I know you guys think I should be okay with how things are different—how *I'm* different—but I feel like . . . like damaged goods." He hesitated, struggling with the words. "It seems like everyone's watching everything I do and feeling sorry for me. I hate it."

"We love you for who you are, not what you can do," Kasey said.

I figured humor stood a better chance of making an impact. "If you want, you can have my *As is* T-shirt. Then you wouldn't have to explain yourself."

"Cody!" admonished Kasey. But Race broke into exhausted laughter.

"That's a good one, kid. I might have to take you up on that."

The next day Race discovered a whole new meaning to the word "frustration" as he took a stab at organizing Kasey's books. Remembering the receipts I'd found the day I'd cleaned the shop, I gave him a heads up about Kasey's filing system. He made a broad sweep of the building, looking in every nook and cranny, but just when he thought he'd collected all the receipts, Kasey told him about the ones in the glove box of the Charger.

"That reminds me," Race said. "Where's your vehicle mileage log?"

"What vehicle mileage log?"

"The one you should be keeping to record the trips you make to get parts or haul cars. You can deduct that stuff, you know."

"Oh," said Kasey, "I didn't even think about that."

Race shook his head and retreated to the office, where he got to work transferring the information from the receipts to a spreadsheet he'd created on the computer. The keyboard presented a challenge to his compromised motor skills, and he swore at it under his breath until he came up with the idea of jabbing the keys with the eraser-end of a pencil. Creating ways to compensate for his limitations was one of the tricks he'd learned in therapy.

While Race was shocked by Kasey's lack of business sense, both Kasey and I were equally astonished at how good he seemed to be at that stuff. The irony wasn't lost on me.

"Grandpa would be so proud of you," I taunted.

Race snorted. "You underestimate his capacity for disapproval."

That night Kasey dropped me off at karate practice then went to Race's shop to help him and Denny work on the Dart. I was torn, wanting to be in two places at once, and expected to have trouble concentrating. It surprised me that once I got through the warm-up exercises, my thoughts zeroed in on the lesson.

"That's how it should be," the sensei told me after class. "You're developing harmony between your mind, body, and spirit. By practicing the moves and breathing, along with the philosophy, you're gaining control over your whole self."

The word "whole" resonated with me the rest of the night. Until all the pieces had started coming together, I'd never realized how scattered I used to feel.

Kasey and the guys got a lot accomplished, but not enough for the 8 car to make practice the next day, so Race borrowed Big Red again.

It was a small crowd Wednesday night—just us, Denny, Holly Schrader, and a handful of drivers from the other divisions. I didn't know half the people, but they knew Race and made a big deal about welcoming him back.

Considering how wheezed out the Chevelle was, Race turned some respectable times. To everyone else it must've looked like he'd taken up right where he left off back in June. Only Kasey and I knew what a struggle he'd had Monday. At least this time he wasn't quite so exhausted when he climbed out of Big Red at the end of the night.

On the way home we dropped off Denny's car before hitting the closest convenience store so I could get a sugar fix. Race bolted down a package of Twinkies under Kasey's disapproving eye then tried to bum some of my M&Ms.

"Forget it," I said, clutching the bag to my chest. "You coulda got your own."

"I only want a couple."

We tormented each other the rest of the way home, trying Kasey's patience with our banter. I was surprised Race had the energy to goof off, but like a turbo kicking in, the change in his mental state seemed to provide him with an extra boost of horsepower.

"So when's Addamsen taking you on a tour of the Hamm's Brewery?" I asked as we got out of the van at the house. "I hear they're giving out free samples."

"Nah, they stopped doing that after the government forced them to print the number for Poison Control on the cups."

I winged an M&M at Race as he started up the stairs. It missed and rattled off the handrail. He turned around, barely ducking in time to avoid having the next one hit him in the face. Instead, it bounced off Kasey's back.

"Stop it, you two," she said, going into mother-mode without even looking at us. "Someone's going to get hurt."

"Yeah. You could put an eye out with one of those things," Race deadpanned. With one hand clutching the railing in his only concession to fatigue, he ignored my ongoing barrage of candy-coated chocolate and plodded up the steps.

"That wouldn't slow you down any. You're The Legend. Race Morgan, the guy who can out-drive Death, who drinks Hamm's beer and lives to tell about it, who—" I reached the top of the stairs and Race snatched my M&Ms.

"Oh, that's nice," I said. "Stealing candy from a kid!"

Inside the house, the phone began to ring. As Kasey scrambled to get the door unlocked, I made a grab for my M&Ms, but Race yanked them away, backing against the railing and dangling them out of reach.

"If you want 'em so bad why don't you just take 'em?" he mocked. "Or have I been wasting your dad's money on those karate lessons?"

"I could, but I'd have to knock you on your ass, and Kasey'd kick me out if I hurt you."

"Guess you're outta luck then, huh?" Race shook the bag.

"Not necessarily." Foregoing karate, I resorted to a sneakier tactic—tickling. It caught Race completely off guard. He dropped the candy, grabbing at my hands to ward off the assault.

"That's enough!" Kasey stood in the doorway, something in her expression implying she was upset about more than our horseplay. I stopped in mid-tickle and Race pulled away from me, gasping.

"What's wrong?" he panted.

Kasey glanced from one of us to the other as if unsure of how to deliver the news. "That was your mother, Cody. She's coming into town on Friday. Somehow she seems to have gotten the impression you're going to Phoenix permanently. She said to be sure you had everything packed."

Chapter 31

Race stared at me, eyes wide with pain and bewilderment. "You're leaving?"

"No!" I swear, I would've rather been run over by a Super Stock than have him look at me like that. "She wanted me to visit, and all I said was I'd think about it. No way am I gonna go live with her." I turned on Kasey, feeling betrayed by both her and my mother. "You see? This is how she is. You can't trust her."

"Cody—"

"I shoulda known better! I can't believe I fell for it again."

"I think you're overreacting. She must have misunderstood you. Or maybe I'm interpreting this whole thing wrong."

"What's going on?" Race demanded.

Sighing, Kasey sank into one of the deck chairs. "I thought it might be a good idea for Cody to get away for awhile, just until you had more of a handle on things. When Saundra told me she wanted him to come visit, it seemed like the perfect solution."

"You were gonna send him to his mother? She ran out on him. She's a selfish, manipulative—"

"Race, you aren't helping matters, treating her as though she's evil incarnate. I realize she's let both of you down, but if it weren't for her, you wouldn't be together."

Race snorted. "One moment of misplaced kindness hardly qualifies her for Mother of the Year."

"She went to bat for Cody when he needed her. She didn't have to do that." Kasey filled him in on what she'd told me the other night.

"That's not the story I got," Race said, standing with his chin thrust out and his arms across his chest. "She never once mentioned my mother. According to Saundra, the thing at the zoo was a big fuss over nothing. She's always been an expert liar. She probably told you what she thought you wanted to hear."

"Except that your mom confirmed the story."

That zinger totally derailed Race. He eyeballed Kasey without saying a word, jaw clenched and shoulders rigid.

I didn't know what to think. I wanted to believe Kasey was right, but Race and I had experience on our side.

"The two of you need to give her a chance," Kasey said, staring hard into Race's eyes. "I've seen firsthand how obstinate you can be about your mother. I can only assume you're being equally unfair to your sister. It would hardly hurt Cody to stay with her for a few weeks."

Race's face was darkened by more than just the night's shadows. "You don't know what you're talking about," he growled. "Your family's normal. When you've got screwed up relatives butting into your life, the best thing to do is walk away."

"If you want to go on letting your resentment eat at you, that's your business," Kasey said. "But you're not being fair to Cody. That's something you might want to think about."

Kasey's reprimand hit home with Race. When I asked him for advice later that night, he wouldn't give me any. "You need to figure this out for yourself," he said. "I'm obviously not an impartial witness."

The next morning I tried to call Mom to clarify things, but she wasn't home. I left a message then spent the next few hours at Kasey's computer, typing up some old handwritten stories while Race was out running errands. He got back a little before noon.

"Hey, kid, c'mon up here," he called down the basement steps. "I got us some lunch."

286

The enticing scent of pepperoni greeted me as I hoofed it up to the kitchen, where Race had deposited two Cokes and a Track Town box on the table. He popped the lid, wiggled a slice loose, and dropped it onto a paper towel.

"This is an 'I'm sorry' pizza," he explained. "Second cousin to the 'get well' pizza."

I pulled out a chair and sat down. "You don't owe me any apologies."

"Yeah I do. Last night when Kasey said you were leaving . . ." Race hesitated, shaking his head as a sort of kicked-puppy look skulked across his face. "I guess that's the first time it really hit me, how much my attitude was affecting you guys. I can't say I'd blame you if you *did* want to leave."

"Well, I don't," I said, pulling the tab on my Coke. "And you haven't exactly got the monopoly on stupid behavior."

Race grinned.

I reached into the box, taking a slice of pizza from the center of my half so there was little chance of it being contaminated by mushrooms or green peppers. Gooey mozzarella trailed behind, forming lifelines back to the mothership.

"I've been a real pain in the ass," Race said. "You don't know how much I appreciate the fact you haven't given up on me. I'd like to think I can handle anything, but the truth is, I couldn't have gotten through this without you and Kasey. It shakes me up to think about what it woulda been like if this had happened a couple years ago. I wouldn't have had either one of you."

Race's words sent a flash flood of emotion through me. I was touched and embarrassed, but I didn't know how to respond, so I stuffed my mouth full of pizza and washed it down with a slug of Coke.

"You believed in me, Cody, right from the start. Even when Kasey and everyone else thought I was delusional. You didn't let me give up, and you called me on it when I got to feeling sorry for myself."

"Actually, I sorta enjoyed that last part," I said, ripping savagely at my second piece of pizza.

Race acknowledged my joke with a slight, lopsided grin as he picked up an errant sliver of green pepper and tossed it toward the box. "This thing with the car," he persisted. "It wouldn't have happened if it hadn't been for you. I know that, and I know you went to bat for me with Kasey. As for getting Addamsen to help—well, that was a crazy idea, but—it worked." He gave me an admiring glance. "It took guts to pull that off."

All the praise was making me feel guilty. Even if what he said was true, it didn't make up for the selfish things I'd done. "You're forgetting the part where I got mad at you for getting hurt. And how I yelled at you while you were in the hospital." If we were gonna make a list, it might as well be accurate. My eyes focused on a smattering of crumbs on the table. "I'm as bad as Grandpa."

"Cody, you're *nothing* like my father. You have a heart. And I don't hold that stuff against you."

"Well, I hold it against me. I was a jerk."

"So don't be a jerk anymore," Race said easily.

I didn't understand how he could make everything sound so simple—how he could *believe* everything was so simple—after all he'd been through. Then I realized that so many of the things my sensei had been trying to explain—taking the path of least resistance, accepting the world as it was, disarming an opponent without violence—were things Race did naturally. *The Tao of Race*, I thought, feeling myself smile.

I looked across the table at my uncle, knowing I'd done nothing to deserve having someone like him in my life. The question now, I realized, was what was I gonna do to *start* deserving it.

"I'm sorry," I said.

"I know."

"I've still gotta say it."

"I know that, too." Race regarded me with a quirky little smile—a gentler, more sentimental version of his typical smart-assed grin.

Still feeling like the wrong guy had initiated the apology, I looked away. "I shoulda been the one to buy the 'I'm sorry' pizza."

"Nah," Race said, finally picking up the slice he'd been neglecting. "I think I prefer hearing the words."

I tried to call Mom twice more that afternoon, but I couldn't catch her at home. Each time her answering machine picked up, my stomach knotted tighter. I wanted to believe it was all a misunderstanding, but it wasn't easy to give her the benefit of the doubt when I couldn't confirm the details. And it didn't help that she wasn't returning my calls.

"It'll be okay. You'll see," Kasey said.

I told myself she was right and tried to stuff the worry away. Fortunately, there were plenty of distractions. The change in Race's attitude was one of them. Getting out on the track had proved to be even better medicine than I'd expected. The more confident he got, the fewer problems he'd had with headaches, insomnia, and fatigue. He could now put in an afternoon at Kasey's and still be good for a couple of hours at night working on the Dart.

That evening I tried Mom again with no luck, then got up early Friday to catch her before she left Phoenix. No answer.

It'll be fine, I told myself. *You read the letter. Things are gonna be different now.*

Somehow, I made it through the day. The Dart was finally ready for its first practice session, so we hauled it to the track that evening for testing and final adjustments. When we got home, one of those new Thunderbirds was parked in the driveway, taking up the spot the van normally occupied. Race pulled over into the weeds at the side of Spring Boulevard.

"That's gotta be Saundra," he said. Her flight had been due at 7:10. Sure enough, the door opened and my mother stepped out, dressed in an outfit that was as costly as any of Grandma's, but a lot flashier.

When I saw her, my stomach went wobbly with a mixture of hope, anxiousness, and leftover resentment.

"Cody!" Mom said, expertly navigating the slope of the driveway in her 3-inch heels. She swept me into a flamboyant embrace.

It must've been five years since she'd hugged me, but as alien as it felt, there was something comforting about it, too. I hugged her back. The scent of her fitted leather jacket, mingling with the familiar, musky fragrance of her perfume, triggered a cascade of memory. For half a second I was three years old again, snuggled up beside her, begging for a story.

"It's so good to see you." Mom pulled away and held me at arm's length, granting me a rare smile. "I didn't think you'd ever get home. I've been waiting almost an hour."

Uneasiness whispered in the recesses of my brain. It was just past eight, and the airport was clear out in west Eugene, a good twenty minutes from Kasey's house. There was no way she could've been here that long.

Mom let me go and extended her slim hand to Kasey. "It's so nice to finally meet you. I owe you so much for taking care of my son."

"It was no trouble," Kasey said.

"You're looking good, Race," Mom noted.

He gave her a noncommittal grunt.

"Well," she said, returning her attention to me, "I'm supposed to meet your grandmother downtown for a late dinner. But I had to see you first. It's been ages."

"I tried to call," I said. "I left messages."

"I know. It's just been so hectic, getting things together for this trip."

The feeling of misgiving grew. "Mom, I can't move to Phoenix. I never agreed to that."

My mother's mouth stiffened at the corners, but her smile didn't falter. "I have a room all ready for you, Cody. I know things weren't good at home, but it's different with your dad out of the picture. We'll be a family again, just you and me."

"I like it here."

"You can come back to visit."

My apprehension mushroomed into alarm and disappointment. This was no misunderstanding. I looked at Kasey, wondering if she could see what I did. Her brow furrowed with puzzlement, but the remnant of her smile told me she was still buying into Mom's charm.

I glanced anxiously at Race, needing confirmation I wasn't imagining things. His eyes held a softness that said he felt for me. But he didn't step in.

With the flame rising under my fear, I turned on Mom. "I'm not going. All we talked about was a visit, and if you're gonna twist it around to make it sound like I said I'd move, you can forget the whole thing."

"Now, Cody, there's no need to be snippy."

"I'm staying here."

Mom eyed me with a hint of warning before shooting Kasey an *isn't it amazing what we parents have to put up with* look. "Well, we don't have to discuss this now," she conceded. "It's late, and I'm sure you're all tired. Besides, I'll be in town until next Friday. I'll come by then and we can talk."

"You won't be able visit with Cody before that?" Kasey asked.

Mom turned an apologetic smile on her. "I wish I could, but I'm pressed for time, and I have so much business to attend to."

I grunted. "Why doesn't that surprise me?"

Lightning flashed across my mother's face. Her fingers flexed, and instinctively I flinched. Then she forced another smile. "I'll see you Friday."

The next morning the phone rang while I was eating breakfast. Kasey was at work, and Race was still asleep, so I answered it.

"Cody, it's Mom."

I was tempted to hang up, but satisfying as that might've been, I knew it wouldn't fix anything. "What do you want?"

Mom didn't notice the catch in my voice. "I'm calling to warn you you'd better have your things packed and ready to go on Friday. I won't tolerate another display of attitude like the one you gave me last night."

Her complete about-face shouldn't have been a shock, yet it wrenched my gut like the plunge of a roller coaster. "I'm not going, Mom."

"Oh, yes you are. Let me tell you something, young man. Your little butt would be in jail right now if it wasn't for me."

Anger flared, strong and solid inside me. "You mean if it wasn't for Grandma. Anyway, you lied to me. You said things would be different. You haven't changed at all."

"You're the one who hasn't changed. Still back-talking me and showing no respect. I've been working hard to put my life back together. I won't let you ruin that for me. You're coming to Phoenix, and that's final."

"You can't make me."

"I most certainly can."

"Race is my guardian now. He won't let you."

"Race can't do a thing about it. All he has is a temporary piece of paper. I have custody."

The revelation struck like one of her slaps, knocking the words out of me.

"I'll be there at seven o'clock sharp," Mom said. "If you know what's good for you, you'll be ready."

Chapter 32

Mom's call haunted me all day. I knew she couldn't physically force me to leave, but I worried about her having the law on her side. Could she sic the police on me?

I wanted to tell Race about it, but I remembered how he'd said he wasn't an impartial witness. If that hadn't made it clear I was going to have to figure this out on my own, his failure to confront Mom last night should have. Anyway, Race had enough to deal with. He was preoccupied with the monumental task of sorting out Kasey's accounts. Even though he'd collected the receipts at the shop, we kept finding new ones at the house. They were stashed everywhere—on top of Kasey's dresser, in the kitchen junk drawer, under a stack of magazines on the coffee table. I even found one marking a page in a cookbook the night I made meatloaf. And it wasn't just a matter of figuring out the shop's expenses. Kasey had cobbled her books together in a way that left gaping holes. Race had to start from scratch designing a new, more comprehensive, system. Then came the real challenge—breaking Kasey of her bad habits so she wouldn't botch it up.

That night we went out to the speedway and sat with Denny's wife and kids. It was a whole different scenario from the last time we'd watched from the stands. Race didn't seem bothered that he wasn't out there himself. He spent the evening coaching me on driving techniques, using different racers as examples. By the end of the night I understood good passing strategy, the best line around the track, and how to avoid getting humiliated on a restart.

On the way home Kasey made an observation. "The Dart could still use a little fine tuning, but it was certainly raceable tonight. I'm surprised you didn't insist on getting out there."

"I'm not ready," Race said matter-of-factly.

Kasey shot him a look of surprise that slowly morphed into respect.

"I'm not completely stupid," Race added.

Kasey shook her head and smiled.

Race didn't seem particularly bothered about Mom's imminent return. "She might put up an argument next Friday, but she's not taking you anywhere," he said. "I won't let her."

While it was nice to finally have him take a stand, his confidence didn't put me at ease. He hadn't heard the things Mom said on the phone.

When Kasey noted how odd it was that Mom didn't seem to be interested in spending time with me, I told her that wasn't anything unusual. "She didn't come here to see me, she just wanted to hang out with her old friends and weasel some money out of Grandma," I said.

Kasey frowned. "Don't you think you're being a little hard on her? The whole purpose of her trip was to come get you."

That made it pretty clear whose side Kasey was on. And it confirmed my fear that she'd never believe me if I told her about Mom's call.

All that day and the next I worried, watching Race prepare the car and himself for Saturday night and wondering if I'd be there to see his comeback. A single question ran through my head on an endless loop: Could Mom force me to go? There was only one person who could tell me. Dad. The trouble was, I still didn't want to talk to him. He couldn't buy my forgiveness with one lousy T-shirt. I mulled the problem over all weekend, looking for another solution, but by Monday night I realized my only option was to swallow my pride and call.

Wanting privacy, I waited until the next morning then dialed his work number from the phone in the basement. Race always respected my space when I was down there.

"Hey, Dad," I said. "This is Cody."

"Cody?" he asked in a bewildered tone, like there might be another Cody in his life who'd address him as "Dad." I was tempted to fire back a sarcastic comment, but I bit my tongue. Unfortunately, that left me with nothing to say. The quiet dragged out for several seconds.

"I'm sorry—you never call me," Dad said finally. "What's up? Are things okay with Race? The last time I talked to Kasey she said he was having some trouble adjusting."

"He's cool now. He's gonna be racing this weekend."

"Really?" Dad hesitated. "Isn't that awfully soon?"

"It's been almost eight weeks. Look, Dad, there's something I've gotta ask you."

Silence. Man, he was pitiful at this.

"Mom's hassling me," I said. "She wants me to move to Phoenix."

Another silence, then, "Do you want to?"

"Are you kidding?"

"So what's the problem?"

"She said she can force me. She said she has custody."

Dad's abrupt laughter startled me. I rarely heard him laugh, and I sure didn't expect him to now. "I'm sorry, it just never ceases to amaze me the lengths your mother will go to in order to get her way. She's lying. I have custody. It was the one thing I insisted on when she asked me for a divorce."

My brain sparked and sizzled, processing this new information. He'd wanted me?

"So if you have custody, why'd you call her when I got busted?" I asked.

"Just because she doesn't have the last say doesn't mean she isn't your mother."

Right. Maybe in the technical sense.

There was another question buzzing in my head—the one I really wanted to ask. If having custody was so important to him, why'd he send me away the first chance he got? But I couldn't say the words, and wasn't sure I was ready to hear the answer.

"So she can't make me go?"

"No. If she gives you any more trouble just call me and I'll take care of things."

The conversation faltered.

"Is there anything else?" Dad asked.

"Uh, no."

"All right. Well, I have to get back to work. Call me again sometime, okay?"

That was something I'd have to think about.

With Mom's threat derailed, I could get back to important matters, like helping Race get ready for his return to competition. We went out to the speedway three times that week. He seemed confident, but I was a little worried. Running practice laps alone on the track with several breaks in between was one thing. Battling it out in traffic during a trophy dash, heat, and 30-lap main was another.

"It's no big deal," Race assured me. "I know my limitations. I'll take it easy all day and catch a nap in the afternoon. It'll be fine."

I figured he was right, but I couldn't help feeling nervous. It wasn't enough for him to get out there and merely make it through the evening. I wanted to see him kick some ass.

Thursday, after we got back from the speedway, Kasey poked her head through the door of my room, where I was scribbling down ideas for a story.

"Got a minute?" she asked.

"Let me check my calendar."

Kasey gave me her *I'm pretending you didn't say that* look and came in to sit on the edge of my bed. "I want to thank you for what you did for Race. I know I made it difficult."

I shrugged. "It's okay."

"No, really, it's not." She sighed and pulled at a bit of fluff on the bedspread. "You were right—maybe a bit overly optimistic, but still right. And I questioned whether you'd stick by Race. I'm sorry for that, Cody. If it wasn't for your stubbornness and insight, he'd still be sulking around here questioning his self-worth."

I turned around in the chair, hanging my arm over the back. "Are you saying I finally learned to use my gift of intuition for good instead of evil?"

Kasey pursed her lips. "Speaking of gifts, you're particularly adept at throwing a person's words back in her face." She studied me thoughtfully. "You know, at the beginning of May I wondered what Race had gotten himself into, but now . . . well, it's pretty amazing, the bond you two have."

It *was* pretty amazing. And for the first time, I understood it was what I'd been looking for my whole life.

Friday night we stayed home because Mom was due to show up. I'd toyed with the idea of not being there but rejected it because she'd called Kasey and told her when her plane was leaving. Kasey was still under the impression that Mom was being reasonable. She assured me that if I spoke respectfully and told my mother how much I wanted to stay in Eugene, she'd listen.

At 7:14 the bell rang. When Kasey opened the door my mother swept into the room, presenting her with a huge bouquet.

"These are for you. To show my gratitude for taking care of my son."

"I only stepped in recently," Kasey said. "Race is the one who's done all the work."

Mom threw a disdainful glance at her brother, who was sitting on the couch with me playing Mario Brothers on my

Nintendo. I'd convinced him to give it a try the week before, hoping it would help restore his fine motor skills, but so far the main result had been Race setting a world's record for getting Mario killed off.

"If he'd been doing the job properly, you wouldn't have had to step in," Mom said. "It's irresponsible to participate in a high risk activity like racing when you have a child depending on you."

Kasey's smile withered under the heat of Mom's tone. Her eyes darted at me, wide with sudden realization, but I looked away.

"Oh, yeah, it's *so* much more responsible to just run out on your kid," I muttered.

"I left you with your father," Mom said. "And though the man may be lacking in personality and ambition, the one thing you can say for him is that he takes his responsibilities seriously." She scanned the room. "Where are your bags? Our plane leaves at nine-twenty, and I still have to drop off my rental car."

I kept my eyes on the TV, where I was navigating Mario through a particularly difficult set of obstacles. "I'm not going."

"Oh, yes you are."

"Leave the kid alone," Race said. "The first time he gets inconvenient, you'll just send him back."

Mom shot Race a look that held all the warmth of a Midwest blizzard. "It wasn't particularly convenient for me to keep him out of jail, but I did it."

"And you'll hold it over his head for the rest of his life. Look Saundra, I've got to admit you came through for him, and you don't know how glad I am that you did. But he's happy here. Why don't you consider his feelings, for once?"

"I'm his mother," Mom said. "I love him, and I want him with me."

"Manipulation, coercion, inflicting guilt—you've got a funny definition of love," Race observed.

With an uncomfortable jolt I realized that, until I'd met him, it had been my definition of love, too.

"Get your things, Cody," Mom ordered. "Or I'll call the authorities."

I looked at Kasey—who was staying out of it in spite of her white-knuckle hold on the flower vase—then at Mom. "I don't have to. Dad told me you don't have custody."

"And you believed him?"

My temper kicked into gear, but with effort I managed to shift back to neutral. "The man may be lacking in guts and communication skills," I said, calmly mocking her, "but the one thing you can say for him is that he's honest. Unlike you." I put the game on pause, set down my controller, and got up. Race shot me a worried glance as I strode across the room to pick up the phone.

"What do you think you're doing?" Mom's voice shrilled upward.

"Calling Dad."

"I have no intention of talking to that man. Hang up and get in the car."

"No," I said, "I'm staying here." My finger hovered over the numbers as Mom knifed me with a wounded look.

"Are you *that* bent on breaking your mother's heart?"

Guilt tugged at me. I wanted to give in to it, but I knew I didn't have the strength to let her keep hijacking my emotions. Race was right. When screwed-up people butted into your life, sometimes the only thing to do was walk away.

I dropped the phone into its cradle. Focusing on it, I forced myself to work my feelings into words. "I don't want to break your heart, but I can't take this anymore. You're not gonna change. It's messing with my head to keep thinking you will."

I risked a look at her, hoping this time she'd get it. Willing my words to break through, so she'd finally understand.

"So we're back to this, are we? Poor little sensitive Cody. Better give him his way or he'll cry." A smirk twisted her lips. "You're pathetic, just like your father."

My brain buzzed with humiliation. I glanced at Kasey, hating for her to witness this. She shook her head faintly, and in that second it clicked.

Mom only had power over me if I gave it to her.

I turned to face her, calling on the inner calm I'd learned from my sensei. My scrawny, five-foot-five body felt like it had suddenly gained six inches. "No," I said. "I'm not. And I never have been. You don't get to tell me who I am."

In two strides Mom was across the room. Her hand flashed out and fire seared my cheek.

Instantly, Race was on his feet, grabbing her wrist and pulling her away. "If you *ever* touch him again, I'll have the state on you so fast you'll think you hit a time warp." His eyes blazed with a rage hotter than any I'd seen in those dark weeks following the wreck.

Mom drew back, the color draining from her face. She yanked her arm out of Race's grip, fingers massaging her wrist.

"I'm going to the police."

"You go right ahead."

The two of them glared at each other until Mom swung abruptly back to me, her gaze smoldering. "I'm giving you one last chance, Cody. If you don't come with me now, I'm through with you. Is that what you want?"

"No. But I'm not leaving."

The muscles in her jaw twitched, and her lips pulled into a bitter little smile. "Then I guess you've made your decision, haven't you?" Without another word, she turned and headed for the door.

My legs went shaky underneath me. I dropped to the couch. As Mom reached for the knob, my image of her blurred. I blinked and glanced down at my lap, bracing myself against the ache in my throat.

When the door slammed, I didn't look up.

Race rested his hand on my shoulder, and I jumped.

"Good job, kid," he said softly. "You really held your temper."

I looked up at him, swallowing hard—not caring if he saw the tears.

"I'm proud of you," Race told me.

My mouth slipped into a smile. What more could I ask for than that?

Chapter 33

The next morning Race woke me up—early. The sunlight on the branches outside my window looked so fragile and unripe that I immediately consulted my alarm clock. 5:49.

"It's not even six o'clock!"

"Yeah, I know. Kasey's gonna be up any minute. Come help me in the kitchen."

I pulled on cut-offs and the T-shirt Dad had sent me then followed him down the hallway. "I thought you were gonna take it easy today."

"I plan on going back to bed right after this. Believe me."

What I saw in the kitchen shocked me. Platters of pancakes, bacon, eggs, and fresh fruit adorned the table, which was elegantly set right down to the detail of two tapered candlesticks. In contrast, the countertops and stove were a disaster.

"It looks like an IHOP exploded in here," I said.

Race grabbed a sponge and began wiping down the stove. "I need you to load the dishwasher, pronto. It's gonna ruin the effect if Kasey sees this mess."

"Uh, yeah, about that. Don't you think a candle-lit breakfast would be more romantic without me around?"

"It's just for effect. Anyway, you need to be part of this. It's our way of showing Kasey how much we appreciate the trouble she's gone to."

I opened the dishwasher and pulled out the bottom rack. "If you wanted me to be part of it, maybe you shoulda got me up a little sooner."

"I would have, but things kinda got out of hand with the food. I'm not used to cooking with more than one pan."

Between the two of us, we got the kitchen cleaned up in seven minutes. I was closing the door on the dishwasher when Kasey walked in. She inspected the table with a smile.

"What's all this?"

"It's a 'thank you' breakfast," Race said, pulling out a chair for her.

Second cousin to the 'I'm sorry' pizza, I thought.

"I'm duly impressed."

Race lit the candles. "We wanted to show you how much we appreciate what you've done, taking us in and all. I know you must've had your doubts, considering what my trailer looked like."

"I hoped your sense of decency would overpower your distaste for picking up after yourself. And you didn't disappoint me." Kasey reached for the eggs, spooning some onto her plate before handing me the platter.

"Still, it's gotta be a pain, always having someone in your space. You can't even escape to the shop anymore, with me and Cody working there. I plan on getting an apartment as soon as I can, but I'm gonna have to pay off some debts first. When the insurance company gets their act together and figures out what I owe Sacred Heart—" Race saw the expression on Kasey's face and didn't finish. His stubborn refusal to accept the hospital's charity was one of the things they still disagreed on.

"Did it ever occur to you that I might like having the two of you around?" Kasey asked.

Race stared at her speechlessly as she stabbed a couple of pancakes and transferred them to her plate.

"I grew up in a large family. Sometimes I miss the chaos. This house has always been too big and empty for me."

"Really?"

"Really. You're welcome to stay as long as you like."

"I don't know if my ego could accept that."

Kasey smiled and passed the pancakes to me. "Tell your ego to get over itself."

When we were done with breakfast, I helped Race clear the table and load the plates into the dishwasher. After latching the door and pushing the button to start the load, I turned to find him watching me.

"You okay about what happened last night?" he asked.

"Sure. Why wouldn't I be?"

His lips twisted into an *I'm not buying it* sort of pucker, but he didn't call my bluff. "If she hassles you again, I want you to let me know right away so I can put an end to it."

"She's not gonna hassle me. She'll probably never speak to me again as long as I live."

And I'm fine with that, I told myself. *I've got Race and Kasey now. I don't need her.*

Race's eyes stayed on me, making it clear I wasn't fooling him.

"You gonna let me put the soap away?" I asked, shaking the box in his face.

He stepped aside.

"You did the right thing, kid," he said as I ducked around him. Then he gave my shoulder one quick squeeze before he walked away.

After breakfast, Race retreated to his room and slept until almost one. Kasey shocked me by staying home. For the first time in months, she was caught up enough at the shop to take a day off. She spent it doing yard work, and I helped.

At four o'clock, I put on the newest addition to my T-shirt collection. Race gawked at my chest as if I'd suddenly sprouted a pair of double D's.

"Where'd you get that?"

I looked down at the Eugene Speedway logo, still unblemished and smelling of fresh silk-screen ink. "Uh . . . the Museum of Natural History?"

Race grinned and shook his head.

We got to the track early, rattling down the dusty drive with the trailer squeaking against the hitch each time we hit a rut. The grass in the fields surrounding the track was dry now, its buff color warm and friendly against the sharp blue of the August sky. On the other side of the grandstands, engines howled. Super stocks—I could tell from the distinctive whine. They screamed into turn one as we got out of the van at the pit booth, and the vibration tickled my feet through the soles of my Converse high tops.

"Hey, Race, welcome back," said a guy in line to buy pit passes. Then everybody waiting began calling greetings and asking Race questions. When we got up to the booth, Cheryl, the lady inside, scrambled out to give him a hug. Race blushed at the flurry of attention.

"Must be pretty sweet to be so famous," I said as we got in the van and were given the go-ahead to pull across the track.

Race cocked his head back and smirked. "If you're nice to me, maybe I'll let you bask in my glory."

Once we were in the pits, Kasey and I took care of everything but the driving, including keeping Race on task for practice and time trials. We had to because everyone in Sportsman class, and a lot of guys from other divisions, kept distracting him by coming over to chat. The glaring exception was Jim.

Annoyed, I grumbled about his absence.

"Did you think you were the only one allowed to have a personal crisis over what happened?" Race asked.

"At least I got over mine."

"Jim will, too. Cut him some slack."

Proving he still had what it took, Race just missed setting fast time by three hundredths of a second. Our pit area was chaotic following that accomplishment, and Race got so side-tracked he neglected to line up for the trophy dash when he should have.

"It's good to see you back, Morgan," Ted Greene barked as he swept down the pit road, slinging threats. "Now get lined up, or I'll make you sit this race out."

"I always knew that man had a heart," Race told the Super Stock driver who'd been bending his ear.

Kasey and I went to watch from the pit wall as the four cars in Race's dash pulled onto the track. I felt so nervous I thought my stomach was gonna digest itself.

The Dart, always distinctive among those Firebirds and Camaros, now stood out for its crumpled roof and freshly painted driver's door. The #8 I'd fashioned out of duct tape completed the effect, contrasting with the expert graphics on the fenders.

"Next time around," I said, anticipating the start as the flagman brandished the furled green.

The cars blazed out onto the backstretch, bunched up tight. A tang of vaporized racing fuel drifted on the breeze, sending a surge of adrenalin through my bloodstream.

When the green flag flew, the pack charged into turn one as a single unit. Nothing changed for the first quarter lap except the speed of the cars. Then, slipping out of turn two, Denny edged ahead of Tom Carey to take the lead. Race followed in his wake, Carey to the outside and Addamsen falling directly behind.

With the white #68 Camaro still at his side, Race couldn't take the high line going into turn three. Instead, he bore down on Denny, whipping to the inside as the two cars pulled out of the corner. The Dart roared down the front stretch, its bumper inched up flush with Denny's door. It was enough to claim the groove. Race went into turn one hard and pulled ahead to take the lead coming out of two. The crowd practically went into meltdown.

After that, Denny didn't have a prayer of overtaking the Dart. Addamsen was another story. Race managed to hold him off for a lap and a half. Then, as they entered the north turn, the black Camaro squeezed by on the outside.

"Ah, crap," I said, knowing that with only one lap to go there was little chance of Race reclaiming the lead. He tried to prove me wrong, badgering Addamsen through the corners and pulling even with his rear quarter panel on the backstretch. But when the two cars screamed under the flag tower, the Camaro was a full fender-length ahead.

"Damn!" I said.

"Second place is impressive enough," Kasey pointed out.

"Hey, I'm not complaining."

The cars slowed for the cool down lap, then Addamsen pulled up to the start-finish line to claim his trophy. He grabbed the microphone from the announcer's hand and addressed the crowd.

"I'd like to thank my crew, John and Tony; my sponsors, Willamette Tire, Emerald City Subs, and Duke's Auto Wrecking; and most of all, my competitor, Race Morgan, for giving me a run for my money. It's good to have you back, Morgan." There was momentary silence as everyone tried to assimilate this new level of decency into their opinion of Addamsen. Then the crowd broke into a roar of approval.

Back in the infield, Addamsen parked his car and strolled over to our pit. "Morgan," he grunted. "That was the best challenge I've had in weeks. Your debt to me is paid." A hint of a smile indicated he wasn't entirely serious.

"Too bad you didn't tell me that sooner," Race said. "You could have saved me the public humiliation of buying you a case of Hamm's."

"It'd be even more embarrassing to have to return it," Addamsen said.

"Good point. Stop by my van after the races and I'll give it to you. Lord knows *I'm* not gonna drink that crap."

When Addamsen left, I followed Race to where the Cadillac hearse was parked at the north end of the track, so he could thank the paramedics.

"Just doing our job," said Alex.

"Yeah," Steve agreed through a mouthful of hot dog. "But do us a favor and try to keep the shiny side up tonight. I don't feel like breaking a sweat."

The heat wasn't as spectacular as the dash, but Race started out strong, stealing by Tom Carey on the first lap. Schrader and Whalen quickly overtook Jim, who'd had the pole. At least with them, Jim put up a fight. When Race challenged him, he ducked down low and gave up the groove. A weird combination of disgust and pity tugged at my gut. Was it guilt that made him do that, or did the idea of getting his car that close to Race's spook him?

In the remaining laps, Race managed to work his way up to third, but he couldn't find a way around Denny. He pulled into the pits after the race and parked the Dart.

"How are you holding up?" Kasey asked.

Race grinned. "I could do this all night." But he needed help with his helmet strap, and as soon as he got out of the car he planted himself on a stack of tires.

"You gonna be okay for the main?" I asked, handing him a bottle of Gatorade.

"Sure. My battery will be recharged by then."

A few guys came to talk to Race during the Super Stock heats, but by the time the Street Stock main began, the stream of well-wishers had dwindled. That made it doubly shocking when Jim slunk into our pit area.

"Hey," he said.

Race took a second to shoot me a *ha, I told you so* look before turning to acknowledge his prodigal friend. "Good to see you, Jim."

Jim stood with his hands jammed awkwardly into the front pockets of his firesuit, giving Race a cautious once-over. "You're looking good."

"Yeah, I'm through the worst of it. How're you doing?"

"All right." Jim glanced down at the cracked asphalt of the pit road, then back at Race, who was still resting on the stack of tires, but managing to look cool doing it.

"I feel like an ass for putting this off so long," Jim said, "but I want to apologize. I shoulda been there. I let you down."

Race smiled. "You're here now."

Guilt and disbelief glinted in Jim's eyes. I knew just how he felt, being let off the hook when he didn't deserve it. For a second, I could almost sympathize.

"I damn near killed you," Jim said quietly.

"No," Race said. "I damn near killed me. You just had the misfortune of being in the wrong place at the wrong time. Everyone tells me there was nothing you coulda done, and I believe that."

An incredulous half-smile flitted across Jim's face. He shook his head. "You're somethin' else."

Race grunted, dismissing the comment. "So what was that crap, letting me get around you in the heat?"

Even in the dim light, a flush of shame stood out on Jim's cheeks. He shrugged and looked away.

"Well, it better not happen again. I've got new door bars and the best helmet money can buy. You're not gonna hurt me."

Jim laughed, but before he could say anything he was interrupted by Ted Greene's growl. "Let's line 'em up, Sportsmen!"

"You heard the man," Race said, struggling to hide the effort it took to push himself to his feet. "And I better see some serious driving out of you."

As Jim walked away, I shook my head at Race's capacity to forgive. Much as I couldn't fathom it, I admired it. I didn't think I'd ever be capable of that kind of compassion.

Fatigue was beginning to sap what coordination Race had, so Kasey helped him with his helmet and belts. "Thirty laps is a lot to ask of yourself, especially this late at night," she said. "Just remember no one will look down on you if you drop out early."

Race reached for the ignition switch. "I'll keep that in mind."

"You're wasting your breath," I told Kasey as the Dart rumbled away.

"I know, but I had to try."

I turned toward the back pit exit. As I watched the cars line up, my confidence dropped a few hundred RPMs. What if Race couldn't do this? Even worse, what if he couldn't face up to the fact? In spite of what he'd told us about making safety his first priority, pride could easily wedge its way under his throttle and keep him from backing off.

The Street Stock winner collected his trophy and pulled into the pits. Ted Greene motioned the Sportsman class out onto the track. They circled around to the front stretch and parked on the start-finish line, then the announcer launched into introductions, rattling off car numbers and sponsor names in a machine-gun blast of words. He made it back to the final row in under a minute.

"And in the 8 car, from Eugene, Oregon, sponsored by Eugene Custom Classics, Rick's University Video, and Willamette Electrical Supply—he shouldn't even be out here tonight folks but why let a little thing like a near fatal injury stop him—RACE MORGAN!"

The crowd went nuclear, completely overpowering the announcer as he went on to sing Addamsen's praises.

The announcer finished his spiel by commanding the drivers to start their engines. With a ground-shaking roar, they obeyed. The pack pulled forward, building momentum as it circled the asphalt. Then, *snap*, the green flag was out and fourteen cars engaged in a free-for-all heading into turn one. Addamsen got the jump on Race, slipping between Denny and Tom Carey. Following his lead, Race shoehorned his car in behind the black Camaro.

For several laps, chaos ruled. Then speed and experience reshuffled the deck, sending the slower drivers to the back of the pack. Race clawed his way up to sixth place only to lose the position to Denny. Addamsen left both of them behind. By lap ten, he'd taken the lead.

During the next dozen laps, Denny picked off the slower cars, working into third place behind Schrader and Addamsen. Race couldn't keep up. He'd gotten stuck behind Johnny Quinn, a mid-pack driver, and was having no luck finding a way around him.

"He's getting tired," Kasey noted.

"Nah, he's still got plenty of fight in him," I said, even though I knew damn well that under ordinary circumstances, Race would've got around Quinn within two laps. "He'll pull out a top-five finish, just you watch."

It wasn't like it would take a miracle. He was still sixth, and there were eight laps to go. Then Tom Carey, who was always a strong runner, slipped into seventh and started banging at Race's back door.

"Now it's time to start worrying."

Almost before the words were out of my mouth, Benettendi, a lapped driver just ahead of Quinn, got squirrelly coming out of turn two. He nailed the guy he was trying to pass. Both cars careened down the backstretch in a cloud of tire smoke that stunk of burning rubber. Quinn avoided them by darting down low, but Race was too far to the outside to follow. Pulling wide and hanging two tires out into the weeds, he squeezed past Benettendi with a grating metallic shriek. So much for that new door skin.

As Race tore past the second car, the driver overcorrected, swinging abruptly to the right. His bumper dinged the Dart's rear quarter panel, knocking Race sideways in front of Carey. But before the 8 car could spin around completely, Race let off the gas. The tires bit, he gunned the engine, and the Dart rocketed into turn three to overtake Quinn.

A half-step behind the action, my heart went into jack-hammer mode as the spicy perfume of wild mint hit my nose. "Damn!" I said, trying to shake off the sudden adrenalin surge.

Then the flagman whipped out the yellow.

"Not good," said Kasey.

No kidding. The lineup would revert to what it had been before the wreck, costing Race the position he'd just gained. Even worse, an extended caution at this point would siphon his reserves, leaving his tank near empty for the restart.

The pack slowed to a crawl, making a wide sweep around the mayhem on the backstretch. Benettendi managed to get his car rolling, but a flat and a punctured radiator sidelined the guy who'd hit Race. In addition, two other drivers had skidded on the spilled water, crashing to add to the destruction.

Five full laps passed before the tow trucks got the damaged cars off the track. It took the clean-up crew another four to clear the debris and spread cat litter on the puddles.

"Could they move any slower?" I grumbled as one of the officials directed the line of cars through the clay granules to clear the dust. Race must be running on sheer determination by now.

After three more laps, the chief steward nodded. The flag-man held up the tightly rolled green. Cinching up like beads on a thread, the field of cars growled down the backstretch. I remembered what Race had told me the week before about restarts. The drivers had to hold their positions until the leader took the green, but after that, it was anything goes. This would be Race's best chance to gain some ground.

The green flag flashed. Addamsen's Camaro surged out of turn four. Race, noticing from his spot on the backstretch, charged past Quinn on the outside.

"Yes!" I shouted. Fifth place. Now if he could just hold onto it.

Easier said than done. Tom Carey had also gotten the jump on Quinn. His white Camaro might've been welded to the Dart's bumper, for as close as it followed. I sucked in a breath and held it. Just one screw-up, one moment of weakness, and it would all be over.

In those last laps, Race's strategy changed. He quit pursuing the fourth place car and put all his effort into keeping his position. Carey hounded the Dart through the corners, pulling up to within half a car-length on the straightaways. But Race held his ground. The checkered flag fell, and he crossed the finish line with Carey still trailing.

"I told you he could do it!" I swung around to hug Kasey.

The Dart growled down the pit road and pulled up beside us. It sported a gash that extended the length of the driver's door and bisected the duct-taped 8.

"I don't know whether to congratulate you or give you hell for staying out there," Kasey said, lowering the window net.

Race laughed. "I think I'd prefer it if you just handed me my Gatorade."

"You know you're going to regret this tomorrow."

Race flashed her an exhausted grin. "Wanna bet?"

He had to rest before climbing out of the car, but by the time the Super Stock main was over, he'd perked up enough to greet the fans that poured into the pits. The usual autographs were out of the question. Race could hardly hold onto his Gatorade bottle, let alone a pen. But Kasey had anticipated that problem, getting him to sign some photos of the Dart in advance. Even though the signature was barely legible, none of the kids swarming around him seemed to care.

I stepped back from the melee, spotting a familiar figure picking her way through the hard dirt ruts of the infield. Grandma. Wearing white cotton slacks, her best sandals, and that ever-present dignified posture, she looked out of place in the crowd.

"Hey, Grandma," I called as I jogged up to meet her. "Race is sure gonna be surprised to see you here."

"Not as much as you might think. He left a ticket for me at the front gate."

"Seriously?" I felt my mouth stretch into a grin. "So what did you think of the races?"

A pale glow from the track lights illuminated the grimace on my grandmother's face. "They scared me half to death."

"Yeah," I said, "but you gotta admit, Race really kicked some butt."

Grandma raised an eyebrow at my choice of words. "He does seem to have a knack for it," she admitted. "Though I'm not sure I'll ever really understand the appeal."

I took her arm and pulled her toward the Dart. "What's there to understand?" I said. "It's in his blood."

And in that moment I realized with absolute certainty that it was in mine, too.

About the Author

In addition to being a YA author, Lisa Nowak is a retired amateur stock car racer, an accomplished cat whisperer, and a professional smartass. She writes coming-of-age books about kids in hard luck situations who learn to appreciate their own value after finding mentors who love them for who they are. She enjoys dark chocolate and stout beer and constantly works toward employing *wei wu wei* in her life, all the while realizing that the struggle itself is an oxymoron.

Lisa has no spare time, but if she did she'd use it to tend to her expansive perennial garden, watch medical dramas, take long walks after dark, and teach her cats to play poker. For those of you who might be wondering, she is not, and has never been, a diaper-wearing astronaut. She lives in Milwaukie, Oregon, with her husband, four feline companions, and two giant sequoias.

Connect with Lisa online:

Twitter: http://twitter.com/Lisa_Nowak
Facebook: facebook.com/LisaNowakAuthor
Blog: http://lisanowak.wordpress.com/

Excerpt: Getting Sideways

(Available Summer 2011)

Chapter 1

The tired feeling that had been burning a hole through my brain since I woke up that morning disappeared as soon as I opened the school paper. My first published story, complete with byline, graced page four. *Foreign Exchange Students Bring Culture to South Eugene,* by Cody Everett. I'd looked at it about fifty times, but it still sent a shiver of pride through me. And Race was gonna love it.

I tucked the newspaper into my folder, opened my locker, and jammed some books into my backpack before heading outside. After a cool, foggy morning, the October sunshine was like discovering half a bag of M&Ms in an old jacket pocket. I decided to walk to the auto restoration shop where I worked three afternoons a week.

Exhaustion closed in halfway through the sixteen blocks, making me sorry I hadn't taken the bus. Were the damn nightmares ever gonna end? I trudged on until I reached 33rd then shut my eyes as I waited for the walk signal. Memories of the dream flashed through my mind. Race's Dart getting squirrelly as he hit a patch of water between turns one and two. Tom Carey's Camaro—stark white under the speedway lights—clipping the corner of his back bumper. The Dart rolling, underside exposed for one timeless second before it crashed back down on all four tires. And then the clincher: Jim Davis's car slamming into the driver's door.

The only time the dream was different was when it was about a funeral.

I opened my eyes, trying to chase away the images, but I'd seen them so many times in the past three months, two weeks, and three days, that they were permanently etched into my brain. At least they didn't come every night, like they had at first.

The light changed and I sprinted across Hilyard, jogging the last block to Eugene Custom Classics. The best way to banish the uneasiness would be to replace it with something else—like showing Race my story. After all the nagging he'd done to get me to sign up for journalism, he'd be jazzed to see my name in print.

My mood took a nosedive when I saw that my uncle's van wasn't parked out in front of the shop. If Race was running errands, he could be gone until closing.

I detoured through the office, tossed my backpack and leather jacket onto the scruffy couch, and went to hunt down Kasey. She owned the place and should've been my uncle's girlfriend, but. . .

"Hey, Kasey," I said when I found her lying under the midsection of a '63 Thunderbird. "When's Race gonna be back? He run to get parts or something?"

"No, he went home. He had a headache."

My stomach pinched in on itself. "He left with the quarterly payroll taxes still due?" Race had been working on straightening out Kasey's business records for months. One of his biggest gripes was how she always filed her taxes late and had to pay penalties. If he was letting that slide, he must be feeling pretty lousy.

"He finished up this morning and dropped the paperwork off with the accountant on his way to the house."

I stood staring down at the half of Kasey that wasn't under the T-bird.

"He's fine, Cody."

"I know that!" Instantly, I was annoyed with myself for letting my worries get away from me. Kasey had enough to deal with. She didn't need me giving her any crap.

As usual, she ignored the outburst. "Why don't you get started on those parts over by the solvent tank? There's at least a couple hours worth of work there—and wear the gloves this time." Kasey was always big on safety, even before the wreck.

"All right, all right." I hated how those big floppy things slid around on my hands, but I didn't much like the way the solvent made my skin go all tingly, either. I considered showing her my story—after all, Kasey had been reading my stuff as long as Race had, and she shared my passion for books—but I didn't want to interrupt her in the middle of a job.

I snagged a shop coat from the rack by the office and slipped it on over my *I'm marching to a different accordion* t-shirt. When I flipped the switch to start the flow of solvent, the acrid, chemical scent drifted up to wrinkle my nose. In spite of it, the act of washing parts always soothed me. Scrubbing the nooks and crannies, cleaning away grease, was a mindless sort of work, and it gave me time to think. There was something comforting about doing a job that produced dramatic results with so little skill or effort.

As I scoured black gunk from a small block Chevy intake manifold, I tried to figure out the details for a short story I was working on. But I was too tired to concentrate, and each time I focused my thoughts on the plot, they zipped off on their own, taking me back to the end of June. Why the hell couldn't I put that night behind me like everyone else had?

"Are you almost finished?"

Kasey's voice startled me. I jumped, sloshing solvent down the front of my shop coat and nearly dousing my new Converse high tops. As I turned away from the tank, her blue eyes met mine, full of sympathy. That look always made me feel like I should have done a better job of keeping my problems to myself.

"There's nothing to worry about," Kasey said, squeezing my arm above the top of the long rubber gloves. "Headaches are perfectly normal after a traumatic brain injury—you know that. Race is exactly where he should be in his recovery."

I stared down at the dusty concrete. "I wanted to show him my newspaper article, that's all."

Kasey seemed to think the headaches bothered me because I was worried Race might still keel over. It wasn't that. At least not too much. I just couldn't stand the way they took me back to that night.

Kasey's fingers tightened around my arm. "He'll appreciate your story just as much in the morning. Why don't you leave it on the kitchen table and I'll read it when I get home?"

I nodded, not looking up. "Sure."

"It's six o'clock," she added. "Jake's heading out. He says he'll drop you off. Unless you want to wait for me?"

I slid my foot back and forth against the smooth concrete. Wednesdays were one of the nights she worked late because Race and I were normally at his shop, messing around with my Galaxie.

"How long are you gonna be?" I asked.

"Another hour or two."

"I guess I'll go now."

Kasey dropped her hand and dug some money out of her pocket. She unfolded the bills—all faced the same direction, by denomination—to pull out a ten. "Stop and grab yourself something for dinner," she said, handing it to me. "There's no sense cooking just for yourself."

I jammed the money into my pocket.

"And no pizza," Kasey added. "Contrary to what you and Race might believe, it's really *not* the fifth food group."

* * *

I finished the oil pan I'd been working on, got my backpack from the office, and followed Jake out to his rust-and-primer '58 Chevy pickup. It sucked, having to rely on other people for transportation, but I wouldn't turn sixteen and get my license till the end of December.

Sinking back against the seat, I closed my eyes. Jake cranked the engine, firing up the country music—a taste he shared with Kasey. I'd developed an unwelcome familiarity with it in the last few months.

"How's the Galaxie coming?" he asked as we pulled out onto East Amazon. Jake was Kasey's painter—a quiet man in his forties with a crew cut and enough muscles to give Rambo an inferiority complex. He'd been with Kasey since she'd opened shop, fresh out of college, three years before.

"All we've got left is plug wires and stuff. We were supposed to fire her up tonight." The thought of my pale yellow '65 Galaxie brought an ache right along with the pride. All those hours spent rebuilding the engine, going through the brakes, replacing the hoses. . . . I still couldn't believe Race had bought it for me because he "just felt like it" when he couldn't afford the new helmet that would've kept him from damn near killing himself.

"It'll happen," Jake said, misinterpreting my comment to mean I was bummed about not finishing the car. Maybe I should have been, but the closer I got to driving the Galaxie, the more I realized I wasn't ready for the project to be over. Hanging out with Race was one thing. Having him teach me was a whole 'nother deal—a one-on-one kind of sharing I'd never had with anyone else. I mean, sure, Kasey showed me how to do things at work, but her head was full of so many projects I always worried I was distracting her from something more important.

"How's the karate going?" Jake asked, tapping the steering wheel to the beat of Reba McEntire's latest hit, *Walk On*.

"Good. I moved up a rank on Saturday."

"Race mentioned that." Jake shot a grin across the cab. "Twice, in fact. So what does that make you, a yellow belt?"

"White with one green stripe," I said, wondering why he was asking if he already knew. "We don't have yellow at my dojo, just white, green, brown, and black. For the kyus in between, they add stripes of the next color to our belts."

Jake nodded. "Makes sense."

I didn't want him to have to stop to let me get something to eat, so I didn't mention it. I could whip up a tuna sandwich and give Kasey back her ten bucks. Race wouldn't like me taking it, anyway.

After a five-minute drive, Jake dropped me off at Kasey's place on the butte above the University. It was a big improvement over our crappy trailer, where we would have wound up once Race got out of the hospital if Grandma hadn't sided with Kasey on us moving in here.

I grabbed the mail out of the box. Bills for Kasey, and a *Circle Track* magazine for Race. The cars on the cover, scrambling for the lead at some dirt track, put a little flutter in my gut. The season had ended just a few weeks after my uncle started racing again. I missed the hot, dusty nights at the speedway, the growl of engines, and that sweet, pungent scent of racing fuel. When Dad kicked me out last May after I got busted for graffiti, the last thing I'd wanted was to hang out with a bunch of redneck gearheads, but now I could hardly wait for April, when the new season would start. Maybe Race would even let me take the Dart out for a few laps at one of the practice sessions. I'd been itching to get behind the wheel.

I went back to flipping through the mail. Nothing for me. Not that it was any surprise. I hadn't heard from Mom since August, when she'd tried to guilt me into moving to Phoenix, and I'd refused, telling her to drop the head games or leave me alone. At the time I'd figured I was better off without her. Now

I half-wished I hadn't run her off. It wasn't that I expected her to be a real mom—and I sure as hell wasn't going back to getting smacked around and called names—but was it asking too much for her to send a card once in awhile? To step up and act like an adult, instead of being so spiteful?

A sudden rage ripped through me, and my hand clenched around the magazine. I wanted to level the mailbox with a roundhouse kick, but I squelched the impulse. I wasn't that kid anymore. I didn't have to give in to my temper. Forcing my hand to relax, I took a deep, centering breath and headed up the driveway.

Inside, the house was silent. Race's door was closed, and I knew he'd be in there until morning, his curtains drawn to create a dark, quiet cave. I slipped past his room, resisting the urge to knock on his door and ask if he was okay.

In my room, I dropped my backpack and jacket on the bed and sank down beside them. I wanted to take a nap, but with where my head was, I knew sleep wouldn't come.

The thing that bothered me the most, the thing I couldn't understand, was why everyone else seemed to have a handle on the situation, while for me it wouldn't go away. The night-mares, the prickling feeling of anxiousness—all that had made sense right after the wreck, but why now? And why me? Race was the one whose life had been trashed. The one whose career as an artist had been sidelined when the head injury screwed up his fine motor skills. Compared to that, what did I have to bitch about? I hadn't lost anything.

But it sure felt like I had. And it wasn't just the wreck. It was all the changes—moving in with Kasey, getting used to the subtle things that made Race different, knowing if I ever let my guard down, my world could get knocked out of orbit again. All I wanted was for life to go back to the way it had been last June, when it was just me and Race, and I felt like I was in control.

Well, feeling sorry for myself wasn't going to fix anything. What I needed now was a little karate to shake me out of this funk. I slipped into some sweats and went outside.

From low in the west the sun cast bronze rays over the trees on the hillside behind the house. The birches were beginning to turn gold, and the maple at the north end of the patio flamed scarlet.

Standing quietly, listening to the sounds of nature around me, I concentrated on my breathing. I drew a fresh breath deep into my chest, then exhaled from the belly, forcing out the old, stale air. A few minutes of that left me lightheaded from the surge of oxygen. My fingers and toes tingled, and I felt a rush of anticipation knowing this would be one of those times I entered that magic zone where my workout gave me a high.

I started slowly, with a series of kicks, warming up my body, getting it used to the motion. Front kick, roundhouse, side kick, back kick—the moves flowed together, and after a few repetitions I put more force behind them, adding some snap. The world fell away as I focused on the physical. There was no room for my feelings—my anxiety—as perfecting the execution of the moves became the only thing that mattered. For a few brief moments everything came together.

But ten minutes after I went back inside, as I sat in front of the TV with my lonely tuna sandwich, the worries came creeping back. The Galaxie was almost finished. Race wasn't going to wake up tomorrow magically restored to his old self. And as much as I wanted him and Kasey to be together—as hard as I'd worked to make that happen—I wasn't sure I could handle not having my uncle to myself.

CPSIA information can be obtained at www.ICGtesting.com
Printed in the USA
BVOW08s0621130116

432633BV00003B/17/P